# REBUILDING TOMORROW

## EDITED BY
## TSANA DOLICHVA

First published in Australia in 2020 by Twelfth Planet Press

www.twelfthplanetpress.com

Cover art by Geneva Bowers
Cover and text design by Beau Parsons
Typeset in Sabon

'I Will Lead My People' copyright © 2020 by Janet Edwards
'All the World in Seafoam Green' copyright © 2020 by Lauren Ring
'Merry Shitmas' copyright © 2020 by K L Evangelista
'Textbooks in the Attic' copyright © 2020 by S. B. Divya
'If This Was the Talon' copyright © 2020 by TJ Berry
'Kids These Days' copyright © 2020 by Tansy Rayner Roberts
'Ōmarino' copyright © 2020 by Andi C. Buchanan
'Rhizome, by Starlight' copyright © 2020 by Fran Wilde
'The Science of Pacific Apocalypse' copyright © 2020 by Octavia Cade
'The Rest Is' copyright © 2020 by Stephanie Gunn
'A Floating World of Iron Spines' copyright © 2020 by Tyan Priss
'Return of the Butterflies' copyright © 2020 by Emilia Crowe
'Leaving Dreamland' copyright © 2020 by E. H. Mann
'Nothing But Flowers' copyright © 2020 by Katharine Duckett
'The 1st Interspecies Solidarity Fair and Parade' copyright © 2020 by Bogi Takács

The moral rights of the creators have been asserted.

All rights reserved. Without limiting the rights under copyright above, no part of this publication may be reproduced, stored in or introduced into a retrieval system, or transmitted in any form, or by any means (electronic, mechanical, photocopying, recording or otherwise), without the prior written permission of both the copyright owner and the above publisher of this book.

A catalogue record for this book is available from the National Library of Australia.

Title: Rebuilding Tomorrow / Tsana Dolichva

ISBN: 978-1-922101-68-6 (hardcover); 978-1-922101-67-9 (paperback)

# TABLE OF CONTENTS

**I WILL LEAD MY PEOPLE** janet edwards............................ 1
**ALL THE WORLD IN SEAFOAM GREEN** lauren ring.......... 35
**MERRY SHITMAS** k l evangelista........................................ 45
**TEXTBOOKS IN THE ATTIC** s. b. divya................................ 85
**IF THIS WAS THE TALON** tj berry...................................... 109
**KIDS THESE DAYS** tansy rayner roberts............................ 119
**ŌMARINO** andi c. buchanan ............................................... 141
**RHIZOME, BY STARLIGHT** fran wilde................................ 151
**THE SCIENCE OF PACIFIC APOCALYPSE** octavia cade..... 165
**THE REST IS** stephanie gunn............................................. 181
**A FLOATING WORLD OF IRON SPINES** tyan priss............ 217
**RETURN OF THE BUTTERFLIES** emilia crowe.................... 239
**LEAVING DREAMLAND** e. h. mann..................................... 247
**NOTHING BUT FLOWERS** katharine duckett...................... 271
**THE 1ST INTERSPECIES SOLIDARITY FAIR AND PARADE** bogi takács..................................................... 299
**AFTERWORD**........................................................................ 333
**ABOUT THE CONTRIBUTORS**............................................ 335
**ACKNOWLEDGEMENTS**...................................................... 343
**ABOUT TWELFTH PLANET PRESS**..................................... 345

# I WILL LEAD MY PEOPLE
## JANET EDWARDS

I walked across Memorial Field, holding a bucket of water with my right hand, and carrying my bag of cleaning brushes and cloths hung over my left shoulder. We'd had sheep grazing here until yesterday, so the grass covering the thirteen long ridges that ran the width of the field had been nibbled tidily short. Once I'd cleaned the memorial stones, everything would be ready for the ceremony to commemorate the twentieth anniversary of the Culling.

I started with the stone at the end of the first ridge, which had two carved words: 'Day One'. I always felt guilty that the memorial stones didn't list the names of the people who'd been buried in each trench, but there were far too many to fit in the space. Besides, this minimal wording meant the stones didn't just commemorate all the people of this village who'd died on each day of the Culling, or even all the dead of England, but those of the rest of the world as well.

After I'd cleaned each stone, I said the same ritual words before moving on to the next. 'I will remember you.' There was the usual awkwardness when I'd finished cleaning the stone for Day Five. My parents' bodies lay somewhere about halfway along this fifth ridge. Whenever I came to Memorial Field, I felt compelled to say a few words to them, but it was hard to think of something suitable.

I'd only been sixteen when the alien ships came. Everyone changed a lot in the years between sixteen and thirty-six, but I'd had to cope with the end of the world as well. The schoolgirl who'd lived a sheltered life felt impossibly distant now, and I wasn't sure what my parents would think of the adult Megan.

As always, I solved the problem by talking about other people rather than myself. 'Harry and the children are all well. Little Violet is learning to write now. Everyone will be here next week for the Remembrance Ceremony.'

I hurried on to clean the other stones in turn, then settled down comfortably on the grass next to the one marked Day Thirteen, and started chatting to Barbara Corlforth about the crops we were growing this year.

I couldn't remember ever speaking to Barbara Corlforth before the Culling. She'd just been a distant authoritative figure who ran the village of Corlforth St Peter with intimidatingly brisk efficiency, but then the alien armada came, and systematically marked the left hands of the human race with the day of their death.

On Day Five of the Culling, my parents and I had come to lie down in the fifth trench in this field, along with everyone else in the village that had five blue dots on their left hand. I'd believed I would die with my parents and the rest of them at sunset, and the waiting bulldozer would shovel earth over us all. When everyone else stopped breathing, and I was still alive, I'd been a bewildered, broken thing that instinctively ran home to hide.

I'd never forget the sound of the volley of gunshots on Day Six that woke me from my stupor, or my first real conversation with Barbara Corlforth. She'd spoken to me with a chilling fervour, announcing I was one of the precious few who would survive the Culling, chosen to be the future of the human race. Then she'd casually told me she'd disposed of a few villagers who she thought might harm me out of jealousy.

From that moment on, I'd been utterly terrified of Barbara Corlforth, but she'd undoubtedly saved my life. During the remaining days of the Culling, she'd organised the whole village to protect me and pack all the houses with supplies to help me survive in future. Far more importantly, she'd found other survivors to join me.

All she'd demanded in return was my promise to remember her and the rest of the villagers. I'd kept that promise, and somehow the ritual of remembering Barbara Corlforth had led to her dead spirit becoming my main confidant. Given my fear of the woman while she was alive, it was strange that I found my chats with her so comforting now. Perhaps…

I was distracted by the sound of the church bell ringing in the distance. I didn't understand why it would be ringing so early in the day, but then I recognised a rhythm that I hadn't heard in eight or nine years. I scrambled to my feet.

'That's the gathering signal,' I said to the ghostly shade of Barbara Corlforth. 'I have to go.'

I abandoned my bucket and bag to be collected later, and hurried along the path that led to the village. As I arrived at the first houses, I saw James running towards me.

'Dad sent me to tell you that a deputation from Wales is here. Three men and one woman. Dad said that you'd remember their leader, Evan, from the third summer of Gather in Corlforth.'

I grimaced. 'Oh yes, I remember Evan. He's a hard man to forget.'

'Evan insisted on talking to Dad,' added James anxiously. 'We'd better get there before…'

I nodded, and the two of us hurried on towards the village green, where a crowd had gathered to stare at the four strangers. Evan's people had come on horseback, of course, with a couple of extra horses to carry their luggage. It was obvious at first glance that Evan's character hadn't changed a bit, though his face was even gaunter than the last time I'd seen him. The rest of his party had dismounted, but Evan was still sitting on horseback as he talked to Harry, looking down at him with the same arrogant air that I remembered from years ago.

# I WILL LEAD MY PEOPLE

I gestured to James to wait with the crowd, while I walked up to stand next to Harry. 'Have you come to Gather in Corlforth, or just to visit us?' I asked.

Evan continued speaking to Harry, not even bothering to glance in my direction. 'As we came down the road to the village, I saw you've some good flocks of sheep.'

Harry didn't reply. I could see his hands were starting to tremble from the pressure of the situation.

'Have you come to Gather in Corlforth, or just to visit us?' I repeated my words in a much louder voice.

Evan did look at me this time, but didn't seem to recognise me until he noticed the left sleeve of my jacket.

'The girl who was born with no left hand,' he said, in tones of disgust.

I was ridiculously startled. Before the Culling, I'd encountered this sort of thing almost every day, but everyone in the Corlforth Line knew me well. It was over a decade since I'd had anyone react to my missing hand rather than to me as a person.

'You were with Harry when he came to Wales,' added Evan. 'I'm surprised you've survived this long.'

I sighed heavily, and repeated my question for the third time.

'I'm discussing the situation with Harry,' Evan snapped impatiently, then frowned as he saw Harry turn and walk away. 'Where are you going? We need to talk.'

Harry glanced back at him and shrugged. 'You need to talk to my wife, not me. Megan is the one who leads the Corlforth Line.'

Evan gave me a stunned look, which was followed by a betraying expression of speculative smugness. He seemed to think for a moment before speaking again in an autocratic voice.

'We're interested in what Corlforth can offer us. If it seems promising, I'll go back to Wales and bring the rest of my people here.'

'Then you'd better dismount,' I said. 'I'm not standing here straining my neck looking up at you any longer.'

Evan finally slid off his horse.

'There's only one rule for those who wish to Gather in Corlforth,' I said briskly. 'You must be willing to help us build a new hope for humanity. If you want to see everything we have to offer, then I'll need to give you the full tour, which means you staying for at least two nights. I'll organise somewhere for you to sleep, and get someone to care for your horses.'

I wasn't surprised when Evan shook his head. 'We'd prefer to camp nearby and care for our horses ourselves.'

I looked at the other three members of the group. I'd met the woman before. There was also a man in his mid-twenties, and a boy of about sixteen.

'I remember meeting your wife, Olivia, back in Year Three,' I said pointedly.

Evan jerked his right thumb at the boy and the man in turn. 'That's my son, Noah. Aled is a stray that I took in after the Culling.'

I nodded and beckoned James across to join us. 'This is my eldest son, James. He'll…'

Evan interrupted me. 'He looks too old to be your son.'

I saw the pained expression on James's face, and had to force my voice to stay patient. 'I was the only one spared the Culling in Corlforth St Peter, but Barbara Corlforth searched for other survivors before she died.'

The name brought an automatic chanted response from the watching crowd. 'We remember Barbara Corlforth. She gave us the Corlforth Line.'

I gave the crowd a nod of approval before continuing my explanation. 'Barbara Corlforth discovered an unmarked six-month-old baby in the nearby village of Corlforth St Mary and brought him to me on Day Seven. She found out about Harry's existence too, but he was hiding in the outskirts of the nearest city, so it wasn't safe for him to travel to join us until Day Fourteen.'

'I hope James realises how much he owes you both,' said Evan. 'Any stray has a duty to be grateful, but especially one that was only a baby during the Culling. He could never have survived alone.'

I noticed James flinch, while Aled's face hardened. 'Harry and I have been greatly blessed to have James as our eldest son,' I said.

Evan grunted.

I turned to smile at James. 'Please show our guests the way to Crowe Meadow. You can take a couple of men to help them set up camp by the stream, and stable their horses in the barn. Once they've got everything organised, you can bring them back here to meet me outside the church. There should be time for me to show them a little of the village before they have their evening meal.'

'We've brought our own food with us,' said Evan.

'If you want to know what Corlforth has to offer,' I said, 'then you should surely try eating our food.'

Evan gave a grudging nod.

James beckoned his closest friends, the Makwala twins, over to join him, and the three of them led Evan's group off towards Crowe Meadow. I gazed after them, thinking through the first years of Gather in Corlforth. The Culling had happened during the spring, and I'd started my search for other survivors that summer.

The search had to be on a very small scale to begin with, because Barbara Corlforth had set up a farm to help us survive, and Harry and I had to care for the animals. Finding petrol hadn't been a problem back then, so twice a week, we'd taken baby James and driven a car along random main roads for a few hours, painting messages on the tarmac at junctions. Most of the messages had just said the three key words. 'Gather in Corlforth'. Sometimes we included the full village name, Corlforth St Peter, and some directions.

The first person to join us was Naomi Makwala, eight months pregnant and desperate to find help before her babies were born. More people trickled in by the autumn, so we spent the winter setting up a few nearby farms, and bringing in surviving farm animals from the area. Once spring came, Harry and I left the others to run things in Corlforth for us, while we took a camper van and went on some longer trips. We didn't make it into Wales until the third summer.

We discovered a group of people in Powys who were friendly, and then went on to a group in North Wales that was run by Evan. His reaction to our arrival was ... Well, there was clearly no hope of talking sense into Evan, so we'd left Wales and gone on to the Scottish borders. We'd found Scotland had its own well-organised gathering, and had a useful discussion with them about the possibilities of future cooperation, then turned around and went home.

That was the end of us searching for survivors, but there'd still been a scattering of new arrivals in Corlforth St Peter over the next few years, as isolated people finally discovered our messages. The Powys group had decided to come and join us in the autumn of Year Four, and we were still in contact with Scotland, but we hadn't heard anything from Evan's group until now. The thing that worried me most about their arrival was that...

'Megan,' a voice interrupted my thoughts.

I turned and saw Owen of Powys had come to talk to me.

'I came to see why the gathering bell was ringing, and saw Evan was among the group heading off with James,' said Owen urgently. 'You mustn't let Evan join us. Don't you remember me telling you about my disastrous attempt to merge my group with his in Year Two?'

'Of course I remember,' I said, in my best soothing voice.

'I hope you'll believe me when I say I did everything possible to make that merger work. All the problems came from Evan. We'd negotiated a list of compromises before I took my people to join his, and Evan claimed he was happy to work with those, but once we'd arrived…'

Owen shook his head. 'Well, Evan kept pushing for more and more concessions. The man's fanatical about his beliefs, and eventually I'd no choice but to give up and take my people back to Powys.'

'I'm sure that you did everything possible, Owen. We've worked together for sixteen years in perfect harmony. The only exception was the argument about the flooding in Corlbridge, and you turned out to be completely right about that being a bigger problem than a fallen tree blocking the stream.'

Owen only spared the briefest of smiles at our old joke, before becoming serious again. 'Evan's a dangerous man.'

'I know that,' I said grimly. 'After we first visited your people in Powys, we carried on to visit Evan's group. Within the first five minutes, it was clear what the man was like.'

'If you really knew what Evan was like, then you wouldn't allow him to set foot here, let alone invite him to set up camp in one of our fields. He'll try to take the leadership of the Corlforth Line from you, Megan.'

I patted Owen on the arm. 'I'm well aware of that. I saw the smug expression on Evan's face when he learned I was the leader here. He thinks it will be easy to overthrow me because of this.'

I lifted my left arm and laughed. 'Evan is underestimating me. He thinks he could easily win a physical fight with me, so he can easily win a mental fight too. He doesn't realise that I've met his type of obsessive fanatic before, so I know exactly how to deal with him.'

Owen gave the sigh of a man who wasn't convinced. 'You can't have met anyone as bad as Evan.'

I thought back to how Barbara Corlforth had ruled this village in the last days of the Culling. She'd shot the villagers she considered a threat to me. She'd considered killing James as well, because a six-month-old baby wouldn't remember anyone, and caring for him might be too much work for me. She'd stood in Memorial Field on the evening of Day Thirteen, gazed at me with a terrifying hunger to live on beyond her death, and ordered me to remember her before going to lie down in the trench.

'No, I haven't met anyone as bad as Evan,' I said. 'I've met someone worse.'

I gave Owen strict orders not to let Evan see him or anyone else from Powys, sent a dozen other people off to spread urgent messages about how to treat the new arrivals, and then went to Home Farm in search of Harry. He wasn't in the farmhouse, so I checked the fields, and eventually found him sitting by the stream, with a couple of our sheepdogs huddling protectively close by his side.

'I shouldn't have run away and left you to cope alone with Evan,' he said miserably.

I sat down next to him, and put my right hand on his arm in a gesture of comfort. 'You did exactly the right thing. If you'd stayed, then Evan would have kept talking to you instead of me.'

Harry kept staring gloomily at the water. 'When I came to Corlforth St Peter on Day Fourteen, I thought that I'd be the one taking care of you and baby James. Then the other people started arriving, and they assumed I'd be the one running Corlforth too.'

He groaned. 'I was so overconfident back then. I actually believed I'd be a successful leader, but then the winter came and I let everyone down, especially you.'

Evan had only been in Corlforth St Peter for a few minutes, and he'd already annoyed me and distressed both Harry and James.

I tried to keep my voice calm as I replied. 'You never let anyone down, Harry, and especially not me. We were all overconfident that first summer. We thought that we'd survived the Culling, could forget about everyone we'd lost, and create new lives. It was never going to be that easy surviving the end of the world though, and when it came to the long nights of winter…'

I grimaced as I remembered the people who hadn't made it through the winter, and how close I'd come to losing Harry as well. If I hadn't been lying awake myself that night. If I hadn't heard his bedroom door creaking open, and the sound of his footsteps going downstairs. If I hadn't followed him out to the barn…

My hand tightened on Harry's arm, and I forced away that nightmare thought. 'Well, we needed to rethink the situation,' I said briskly, 'and it ended up with me being the one running Corlforth. I couldn't manage it without you though.'

Harry sighed. 'I never know why you keep saying that. All I do is hide away from problems.'

'You do far more than that. You take care of the children and the animals, and you're always there for me.' I turned to hug Harry, and the dogs nestled closer to join in the embrace. 'Everyone needs a special person to be there for them.'

We sat in silence for a few minutes before I spoke again. 'My plan is to keep Evan perfectly happy today. I want him to spend the night dreaming of becoming leader of the Corlforth Line. The trouble shouldn't start until tomorrow, when I throw all the nasty surprises at him.'

I shrugged. 'It's possible that Evan will notice something suspicious before then though, so James and I will have to stay in the village tonight.'

Harry nodded.

'I'd like you to take the rest of the family back to Home Farm as soon as they've eaten,' I continued, 'and keep them safely out of the way there until after Evan's group have gone.'

Harry frowned. 'What about school?'

'I've already sent out word that the Corlforth St Peter school will be closed for the next two days. The other schools can open as usual.'

'And meals?'

'You can collect some food from the church hall kitchen to take to the farm, and there's always eggs from the hens. Violet would live on nothing but eggs if we let her.'

'That's true.' Harry gazed at me anxiously. 'Please be careful, Megan.'

I leaned to kiss him, and then stood up. 'It's Evan that needs to be careful.

# I WILL LEAD MY PEOPLE

The search for Harry had delayed me, so I arrived back at the village to find Evan's group were already waiting outside the church, with James and the Makwala twins standing nearby.

When Evan noticed me walking towards him, he gave me a disapproving look, but surprised me by not complaining about the delay. He was obviously on his best behaviour, which meant the situation in Wales was bad. I wished I could have a private word with Aled, but Evan would never allow his people out of his sight.

I pointed at the church, and launched into my old Gather in Corlforth speech from years ago. 'That's St Peter's Church, which is why this village is called Corlforth St Peter. Gather in Corlforth began here in the summer of Year One. At first, the goal was simply to gather more people together, but in the spring of Year Two we started following a proper long term plan for the future.'

'Who decided on this plan?' asked Evan.

I smiled at him. 'Me. We were blessed with a huge stockpile of supplies gathered by Barbara Corlforth and the local villagers, but the number of people was rapidly increasing. We needed to choose the buildings and farms we wanted for the future, begin a regular maintenance schedule to keep them in good condition, and start farming on a scale that would make us self-supporting.'

I paused. 'Even more urgently, we needed to think about genetic diversity. Not of human beings, because the survivors of the Culling were all random unrelated people, but our livestock and crops. Harry had started training as a vet before the Culling, and was worried that the modern breeds of sheep and cattle might not cope well with the changing conditions. We decided to track down some of the older British breeds of sheep and cows.'

I shrugged. 'So, Gather in Corlforth expanded its mission. We were searching for more people, but also bringing in more farm animals, plants, and seeds. We were blessed to find a survivor who was an expert in medicinal herbs, so we transported her whole garden back here in pots.'

'You use the word "blessed" a lot,' said Evan coldly.

'We need to remember what was lost, but also celebrate what we were blessed to keep.' I waved at a gate. 'The Gather in Corlforth Planning Centre is in the old vicarage. Please follow me.'

I led Evan's group through the gate, and up the vicarage path. I noticed James and the Makwala twins trailing after us, and frowned pointedly at them. They were too protective of me to go away entirely, but at least they waited in the vicarage garden rather than coming inside with us.

Andy was at his desk in the large front room, scowling at a piece of paper. I'd normally have asked him what the problem was, but I needed to focus on dealing with Evan.

'This is Andrew, our logistics officer,' I said. 'Andrew, this is Evan and some of his people from Wales.'

Andrew had spent a lot of time working with Owen of Powys over the years, so he'd heard all about Evan. Despite my instructions to be friendly to the man, he only gave an unenthusiastic grunt.

I sighed and gestured at the vast map that covered an entire wall of the room. 'The Gather in Corlforth plan was to have independent population centres in several of the local villages, each with its own surrounding farms, as a protection against disease, pests, fires, floods, and other kinds of disaster. We chose three other villages that were close to the same main road as Corlforth St Peter. That means the four villages are in a line running roughly north to south.'

Evan nodded. 'The Corlforth Line.'

'Exactly.' I pointed at the villages in turn. 'Corlforth St Peter to the north, then New Corlforth, Corlbridge, and Corlforth St Mary. By the end of Year Four, the population of the Corlforth Line was nineteen hundred people. There were only a handful of new arrivals after that, but we had a steadily increasing number of children being born, so we now have close to four thousand people here. About two thousand in Corlforth St Peter and the surrounding farms. Five hundred in New Corlforth. Fifteen hundred in the Corlforth St Mary area. We haven't expanded into Corlbridge yet.'

It was time to ask the key question. 'How many people would you be bringing here, Evan?'

'Two hundred.'

I was too shocked to speak. I was sure that Evan had had more than two hundred people in his group in Year Three. If their population hadn't increased since then, but decreased…

I'd been wrong about the situation being bad in Wales. The situation there must be dire. Had unyielding Evan increased his punishments for rule-breakers to include executions?

Andrew must have noticed my expression, and decided I needed his help, because he manoeuvred his wheelchair out from behind his desk and joined us in front of the map.

'The host of little coloured squares surrounding each village of the Corlforth Line are obviously the fields,' he said. 'Those coloured green are in active use for crops or livestock. Farms coloured yellow are in maintenance mode with most of the fields growing hay. Red areas have been abandoned.'

Evan was looking at Andrew rather than the map. 'How did he lose his legs?'

'I accidentally left them behind on a train to London,' said Andrew coldly.

Evan stared at him.

'That's a joke,' I explained hastily. 'Andrew once left a bag with his artificial legs on a train.'

Evan didn't seem to approve of jokes. 'What happened to his real legs?'

'I had an argument with a land mine and lost,' said Andrew bitterly. 'I was on a United Nations peacekeeping mission. I believed I was doing something important by saving lives, but it was a waste of time. The Culling happened less than three years later, so everyone died anyway.'

I could tell that Andrew was about to launch into one of his profanity-filled rants about past events, and would probably continue to aim some profanity at Evan for talking about him rather than to him. I heartily sympathised, but we needed to keep things peaceful for now.

'We'll go and talk to Rose,' I said firmly.

Evan's group shuffled aside to let me reach the doorway. I led them down the hallway, and tapped on the closed door of the back room before going inside. Rose was lying on her couch, making notes in one of her red exercise books, but she put the book down as we came in.

'Rose, this is Evan and three of his people from Wales,' I said. 'Evan is considering bringing two hundred people to Gather in Corlforth.'

Rose smiled at Evan. 'I apologise for not getting up to greet you. I have a condition that means I have to spend a lot of time resting, so I do my work lying down.'

Evan made a faint rumbling noise in his throat.

'Rose is in charge of work assignments and housing,' I said. 'If you decide to join us, then each of your people will need to have an individual chat with her about what skills they have to offer. Housing is usually much simpler to arrange. We give each family their own house, while a group of four single people share one.'

'You said that you hadn't expanded into Corlbridge yet,' said Evan pointedly. 'We could move there and organise our housing and work to suit ourselves.'

I could see Evan was already picturing Corlbridge becoming his own little kingdom, to be used as a power base to take control of the whole Corlforth Line. If Evan had been a reasonable man, I'd have told him why no one had moved into Corlbridge yet, and that we needed Andrew to organise crops centrally to avoid basic mistakes like all the farms growing wheat and nobody growing potatoes.

Evan wasn't a reasonable man though, and I wanted him to keep happily fantasising until tomorrow, so I just smiled. 'We'll now move on to look at…'

I was interrupted by a heavy thump on the door, which was immediately followed by Dipak bouncing into the room as if he was fifteen instead of thirty-five. 'Rose, I need to … Oh, new people!'

I tensed. Dipak must have been out working on one of his projects, and not received any of my warning messages.

'This is Evan and his party from Wales,' I said quickly. 'I'll introduce you to them properly tomorrow, Dipak. We need to go and eat now.'

Dipak could be painfully overenthusiastic at times, but he was also highly intelligent. He must have recognised Evan's name from conversations with Owen, because he gave me a single shrewd look, then stood in total silence as I ushered the visitors out of the door.

As we came out of the vicarage, James and the Makwala twins started trailing after us again. Fortunately, Evan didn't comment on their presence. He'd had guards watching us when we visited his group back in Year Three, so he probably thought it natural for me to have guards watching new arrivals in Corlforth.

'After we've eaten,' I said, 'you can go back to your campsite to rest for the evening. Tomorrow morning, I'll take you on a full tour of the Corlforth Line, and explain anything you want.'

'I'd like one thing explained right now,' said Evan. 'A lot of the people running your Corlforth Line seem to have … problems.'

I couldn't stop myself raising my left arm, and snapping at him. 'You mean problems like this?'

Evan nodded. 'I don't understand how this situation happened.'

I forced my voice back under control. 'It happened because people coped well during the summer sunshine after the Culling, but then winter came. The days were too short and cloudy. The nights were too long and haunted by too many memories.'

I grimaced. 'Some people found the burden of losing their old life and everyone they'd ever known was too much to bear, and didn't make it through the winter at all. Others suffered from traumatic memories of events during the Culling, or got lost in despair. Your people must have experienced the same thing.'

None of Olivia, Aled, or Noah had said a word until now, but Olivia finally spoke in a voice that was heavy with emotion. 'Yes, we did.'

'The easier someone's life had been before the Culling,' I said, 'the harder they found it afterwards. Those of us who'd had to struggle with obstacles on a daily basis managed better than the rest, so we had to keep things going for everyone else.'

I was relieved to hear the church bell start ringing. 'We'll go into the church hall and eat now. There's both hot and cold food available there for the whole of the morning and evening. Cooking at home is a lot of extra work, so most people either join in the communal meals or collect food to take home and reheat.'

I led the way into the large hall that was crammed with tables and chairs. 'I thought we'd get here ahead of the main rush, because it will be too noisy to have a proper conversation later.'

It had been a chilly day outside, with a hint of rain in the air, but this room was warm and fragrant with

# I WILL LEAD MY PEOPLE 23

cooking smells. I stripped off the jacket I was wearing, and hung it on the back of one of the chairs surrounding a nearby table. I watched Evan's people take off their coats too, saw how painfully thin they were, and turned away to grimace at the wall. Now I knew exactly what was wrong in Wales.

I bit my lip, led the way up to the pile of trays, picked up one side of a tray with my right hand, and supported the other with my left forearm. 'Take a tray and help yourselves to whatever food you want from the counter. There's never a shortage of anything, because we have a rule that we always grow twice as much food as we need.'

'That seems extremely wasteful,' said Evan, in a tightly controlled voice.

I shrugged. 'The rule dates from the first year of Gather in Corlforth, when the number of new arrivals meant our population was rapidly increasing. It may seem wasteful to keep following it now, but only growing the minimum amount of food we need would be dangerous. Now that the stores of tinned food are too old to eat, we'd be one bad harvest away from disaster.'

Olivia, Aled, and Noah were already moving across to stare in awe at the array of food. Evan gave me a single glare before following them. I felt a tap on my shoulder, turned, saw Dipak was standing behind me, and moved into the corner to speak to him.

'Andy and Rose explained what was happening,' he murmured. 'If Evan is as dangerous as Owen says, why are you hiding things to encourage him to stay? When Evan finds out the truth, there's going to be trouble, and he'll end up leaving anyway.'

'Evan's going to find out the truth tomorrow,' I said, 'and yes, there'll be trouble, and he'll end up leaving. The crucial point is that he won't leave until the people with him have seen what their lives could be like in the Corlforth Line. I can't imagine we'll be able to shake Evan's influence over his wife and son, but Aled has clearly been badly treated. I'm counting on him spreading the news about the Corlforth Line to the rest of the people in Wales.'

Dipak nodded. 'You aren't doing this to help Evan then.'

'No, I'm doing this to help two hundred people in Wales who are on the edge of starvation.' I grimaced. 'When our people were lost in despair after the Culling, they needed something to believe in, and I gave them Gather in Corlforth. Evan gave his people something to believe in too, and those beliefs are killing them.'

The rest of that evening and the night went by peacefully. The next morning, I took Evan's group into the church hall to have breakfast before beginning our tour of the Corlforth Line. When we came outside again, Evan frowned at the two horse-drawn carts waiting for us, with the Makwala twins holding the reins.

I spoke in what I hoped was a casually confident voice. 'I thought you'd like to get a good look at the fields as well as the villages. That means the tour will be too long to make on foot.'

'It would be better for us to ride horses,' said Evan. 'That way we wouldn't be forced to stay on the roads, but could follow paths across the fields.'

That was true, but I couldn't allow Evan's party to ride horses today. My plan depended on all of them completing the full tour. If they were on horseback, whether those horses were ours or theirs, it would be too easy for Evan to get annoyed at something, abandon the tour in the middle, and ride off with his people.

'I thought it would be easier for me to explain things to you if we're riding in a cart,' I said. 'We'll take the carts along the winding road through the fields to reach Corlforth St Mary, and then walk the shorter route back through the villages. We'll want to keep stopping in each village to look inside the more interesting buildings anyway.'

The suspicious expression on Evan's face worried me, but a second later he gave a sigh of annoyed resignation. 'You should just admit the real reason that you want us to ride in carts, because it's blindingly obvious.'

I gave him a wary look. 'It is?'

He sighed again. 'Of course. You can't ride a horse with only one hand.'

I blinked, and hastily faked an expression of depressed embarrassment. 'You're right,' I lied. 'It's impossible for me to ride a horse.'

I turned to beckon James and Dipak over to join us. 'James is coming with us to help answer your questions about crops and livestock, because he knows far more about farming than me. Dipak is in charge of our maintenance work, so can answer any questions about roads and buildings. There's room for four passengers in each cart, so I assume you'll want me, James, and Dipak to travel with you in the first cart.'

Evan nodded, we climbed aboard the carts, and the horses started moving. Evan was asking questions even before we reached the first fields, and didn't query the slow speed of our carts, or the fact we were taking a lot of side turnings. He was happy to spend a long day collecting detailed information about the people and resources of the Corlforth Line, because he was planning on running it himself.

As well as taking the most winding route possible, we made several stops to let Evan inspect the crops and livestock, and then had a leisurely meal from the baskets of food we'd brought along. That meant we didn't arrive at the outskirts of Corlforth St Mary until well into the afternoon.

As we left the carts behind with the Makwala twins and continued on foot, I gave a sigh of relief. We'd set

# I WILL LEAD MY PEOPLE 27

up the situation perfectly. Now it was just a question of timing the revelations correctly so Evan lost control at the right moment.

I pointed to a barn on my left. 'The Gather in Corlforth plan was for each village to be capable of functioning independently as a protection against all forms of disaster. As well as each village having its own surrounding farms, they also each have certain other basic facilities. For example, this barn has been converted to be used for carding and spinning wool.'

Evan didn't comment. His face showed that he regarded spinning wool as innocuous.

'The barn next to it has handlooms for weaving cloth,' I added. 'Would you like to see inside?'

Evan frowned. 'That's not necessary. Handlooms are dangerously close to the technology that led to the Culling.'

I walked on without comment until we reached the first houses. 'Several of these houses are part of the Corlforth St Mary Library. We've got both fiction and non-fiction books stored in each village.'

Evan's frown deepened. 'Books can lead people into dangerous ways. We don't need them.'

I ignored him and kept talking. 'The large building ahead of us is the village school.'

'You have a school here?' Olivia asked sharply.

'We have a school in each village,' I said. 'The old village schools were closed decades ago, and the buildings converted into houses, but we've converted them back. Most of the children leave school at twelve to start practical apprenticeships, but a few join the advanced classes in Corlforth St Peter, and continue studying until they're eighteen.'

'The classrooms are very overcrowded,' added Dipak. 'We're planning to add a new classroom to each school this summer.'

'Schools are a waste of resources,' said Evan. 'Children only need to learn enough to count livestock and tally crops.'

'Would you like to see one of the classrooms?' I asked.

'No,' said Evan.

Olivia threw a defiant look at him. 'Yes.'

I raised my eyebrows at Dipak. I'd assumed we wouldn't be able to say anything to shake Evan's influence over his wife. I'd been wrong.

'Given the overcrowding,' I said, 'we'll just take a look at whatever class is being held in the main school hall.'

I led the way into the school and through the double doors into the school hall. We only had time to glimpse the lines of children sitting at desks before they all stood up. They grabbed exercise books from their pockets, found the right page, and started chanting.

'Today we remember the Taylor family of Corlforth St Peter, and the Quin family of Corlforth St Mary.'

I nodded my head. 'Thank you, children.'

They all settled down into their seats again, and stared at Evan's party with open curiosity.

I turned to Evan. 'The children learn to write by making their own remembrance book. Would you like to ask them any questions?'

His stance was rigid with disapproval. 'No, I wouldn't.'

'I'd like to ask their teacher a question.' Olivia turned to the woman sitting at the front of the hall. 'Were you a teacher before the Culling?'

'Yes.'

'So was I.'

Olivia's face seemed to crumple as she said the words, and she turned and hurried out of the room. By the time we caught her up outside the school, she had herself under control again, but I knew we'd won an unexpected victory.

I led the way on through the village, making the odd detour down a side road to point out places like the herb garden and the shoemaker's house, then stopped when we reached the church.

'They'll soon start serving meals in the church hall,' I said. 'If anyone's hungry, then we can have something to eat before continuing to the next village.'

'We'll continue now,' said Evan grimly.

I smiled and walked on down the road. 'Ahead on our left is the blacksmith's forge.'

Evan glared at the man in the leather apron who was working next to the fire. 'Any working of metal crosses the forbidden line that could bring another Culling upon us.'

That statement surprised me enough that I forgot my plan and challenged him. 'Really? When Harry and I visited you in Year Three, you had a blacksmith.'

'That was an error,' said Evan. 'When the blacksmith died four years ago, I had a revelation and corrected my mistake.'

I shook my head in disbelief. 'But if you don't have a blacksmith, how do you make new horse-drawn ploughs, or mend those that get broken?'

'We make our ploughs from wood, with a stick attached to break up the soil.'

I grimaced at the idea of using a stick instead of a metal blade on a plough, and wondered what other things Evan had decided to forbid over the years. I was trying to lead the Corlforth Line forward, but Evan was taking his people further and further into the past. It was no wonder that they were short of food.

I marched on along the road, which turned sharply to follow the riverbank. 'You can see the watermill ahead of us where we grind our flour.'

'A mill?' Evan stared at me incredulously, and then spat out words in disgust. 'You've built a mill!'

'We were blessed to have the watermill already, so we just needed to learn to use it. This is an eighteenth-century mill that had been preserved in full working order, and regularly gave demonstrations of grinding flour before the Culling.'

I led the way on and stopped to point at the great wheel. 'The mill isn't working at the moment, but I can take you inside if you like.'

'No!' Evan strode on down the road. 'We'll go straight on to see Corlbridge. If I bring my people here, then we'll be living there according to our own rules.'

We continued in total silence until we reached the bridge that had given the next village its name. When Evan reached the middle of the bridge, he stopped, and stared across at the houses that stood window-deep in a wide lake of water.

'That's why we haven't expanded into Corlbridge yet,' I said. 'We have a slight flooding issue here. At first, we thought it was just because a fallen tree had blocked the stream, but it turned out to be much more complicated than that.'

Evan seemed completely speechless. His fantasy about having his own little kingdom in Corlbridge had just been drowned in cold floodwater.

'It's because of the reservoirs,' added Dipak sadly. 'There are two reservoirs up in the hills to our east. A small Victorian one, which we're using as our main water supply and is no trouble at all. The problem is coming from the newer and much bigger reservoir that was built to supply water for several nearby cities.'

He sighed. 'Since the Culling, nobody has been using the water from that reservoir, so it's all been running down the overflow channel. That leads into the stream that runs through Corlbridge and joins the river Corl. The stream can't handle the extra volume of water, so…'

'There must be a way to solve the problem,' Evan interrupted him.

'There *is* a way to solve the problem,' said Dipak eagerly. 'As I keep telling Megan, we just need to find some explosives and blow up the dam. Andrew knows all about explosives, so…'

'No, Dipak!' I said sternly. 'There are two reasons why we aren't going to blow up the dam. The first is that Andrew never wants to go near explosives again. The second is that if we did blow up the dam, then we don't know where all that water will go.'

'The water should all go further east to…'

'No, Dipak!' I repeated. 'We aren't risking flooding the whole of the Corlforth Line. We're blessed that the road here runs along the riverbank, and that's nice and high, so the flooding in Corlbridge isn't a major problem.'

'The height of the riverbank isn't entirely a blessing,' said Dipak gloomily. 'That's the reason the flooding is so bad. The water's only route through to the river is under that narrow bridge. Eventually, we'll have to divert the road and build a second, wider bridge.'

'Eventually.' I turned to smile at Evan. 'There's no need to worry about the flooding in Corlbridge. New Corlforth is set up for expansion, with lots of empty houses and farms. We won't have time to look around the houses today, because you'll want to get back to your campsite before it's fully dark, but we can come back tomorrow.'

Evan ignored me and marched off along the road. As the rest of us hurried after him, Olivia edged her way across to walk at my side.

'What are the empty houses in New Corlforth like?' she asked anxiously.

'New Corlforth is really just a sprawling new housing estate, so the houses aren't ideal,' I admitted. 'There was a community centre that we could use for the meals though, and we've converted some other buildings for things like the blacksmith's forge.'

Olivia shook her head. 'What I meant was ... have the houses been cleared of bodies since the Culling?'

'Oh, yes,' I hastily reassured her. 'We were worried about the disease risk, so we cleared the bodies from all our villages as soon as we could. It wasn't as bad a job as we feared. Barbara Corlforth had organised all the burials for Corlforth St Peter. The other villages were dependent on the death carts, and those stopped running on Day Eight, but most people went out into their gardens to watch the sunset on the day they were marked to die. There were just a few cases where people had chosen to die in their beds, which was obviously a bit ... messier to deal with.'

Olivia seemed reassured, so I risked adding an extra comment. 'We want to start running an extra class in each school this autumn, so a new teacher would be especially welcome here.'

The road was sloping steeply upwards to New Corlforth now. The situation was about to hit crisis point, so I had to leave Olivia to think about my remark, and chase after Evan. I caught up with him just as he reached the first few houses on the brow of the hill, and saw Owen standing in the middle of the road, with a crowd of his people behind him.

Evan stopped walking, and the two men stood staring at each other. It was Olivia's voice that finally broke the silence.

'Owen of Powys!'

'These are the Powys people?' The startled question came from Evan's son, Noah.

'Quiet,' snapped Evan.

Noah gave him a bewildered look. 'But you've been telling us that the Powys people were all dead. They chose to follow Owen, break the rules, and were visited by...'

'Quiet!' Evan thundered the word this time.

For a moment, I was shocked that Evan had claimed the Powys people were all dead. Foolish of me. I should have guessed that he'd lie and turn their disappearance into a dreadful example of what happened to those who disobeyed him.

Evan was focusing his attention on Owen again now. 'So after we threw you out, you came here and corrupted these people with your ways. That explains everything.'

Owen laughed. 'I didn't corrupt anyone here, Evan. They already had things like schools, the mill, and the hospital before I arrived.'

'Hospital?' Olivia tugged urgently at my arm. 'Megan, you have a hospital here?'

'Two doctors and some nurses survived the Culling,' I said. 'We turned Corlforth Manor into our hospital and medical school. The first six of our medical students have just completed their training as doctors, but two are continuing to study surgery.'

'Surgery,' repeated Olivia, in a numb voice.

'Yes,' I said. 'Now that we've come up with a fairly reliable anaesthetic, we can handle most simple operations.'

Owen gave Evan a triumphant smile. 'The Corlforth Line has a hospital, schools, libraries, even a printing press. All the things you denounce as evil and...'

I'd been aware of James sneaking off to light the bonfire by the side of the road. It was ironic that we'd fallen back on the old system of smoke signals to send the message we were ready. That smoke was heading up into the air now, and was clearly visible against the orange glow of the approaching sunset.

I knew exactly when the woman stationed by a crucial switch saw the smoke, because the evening gloom was suddenly dotted with increasing numbers of bright spots. The lights were coming on behind us in Corlforth St Mary, around us in New Corlforth, and further along the road in Corlforth St Peter.

Evan howled in outrage. 'You have electricity here!'

I nodded. 'We were blessed with wind turbines and a reservoir up in the hills, so we have electricity and a mains water supply in all three villages.'

Evan raised his arms, lifted his head, and bellowed out words to the darkening sky. 'Are you determined to bring destruction upon yourselves? Have you learnt nothing from the Culling? The alien ships came because of our technology. They slaughtered us because of our technology. We were arrogant, and they gave us a lesson in humility.'

He turned to glare at me. 'I was spared the Culling because I lived the simple life on my small farm. I was spared to spread the word of that life to others that they might follow my example. I was spared to...'

He ranted on, crying out the words with passionate fervour. This was the reason Evan was so dangerous. His striking looks, his commanding voice, and his intense beliefs combined to sway people into following him. I could feel the power of his words myself, tugging at me to listen and obey.

This was why I'd arranged for this confrontation to happen here, where I could make sure that the only Corlforth people hearing Evan would be those who I could trust to hold on to rational thought against his storm of emotion. Dipak loved engineering. James would defend me against anything and anyone. Owen and the people of Powys had made the mistake of following Evan before, and had had the good sense to walk away before he killed them.

Finally, Owen of Powys got bored listening to Evan, and tied a scarf round his mouth to gag him, so I had the chance to speak myself.

'The flaw in your argument is that we have no idea why the aliens chose to cull our species. They never communicated with us at all. They could have acted because of our overpopulation, our constant wars, the way we were polluting and damaging our planet, the number of other species we were driving to extinction, or a host of other reasons.'

I sighed. 'The only information we have is who was spared from the Culling. Rose is a mathematician, and she's interviewed every survivor who came to Gather in Corlforth. She's analysed every detail about them, looking for common factors. There's nothing at all. No hint of selection by lifestyle, religion, occupation, intelligence, or anything else. Survivors seem to have been chosen completely randomly, and sadly with no consideration of whether they were old enough to survive alone.'

Evan made a muffled sound of dissent through the scarf, but I ignored that and kept talking. 'We don't know the reason for the Culling. We may never know the reason for the Culling. We do know that some of us were spared to create a new future for the human race. It's possible we're supposed to create something better than the past, but I'd argue that doesn't matter, because we should surely try and create something better anyway. We certainly weren't spared so we could give up things like books, medicine, working in metal, or starve ourselves to death.'

I paused to look around at the lights of the Corlforth Line. 'We were chosen to live, Evan. We're going to do that here in the Corlforth Line. We're going to remember the past, but shine our lights to drive away the dark winter nights, so we can live for the future. Anyone who chooses to help us do that is welcome to Gather in Corlforth. Anyone who wants to stop us should leave.'

There was a long silence, then Owen warily removed the gag from Evan's mouth. He glared at me and spat out a single sentence.

'We'll go then.'

I nodded. 'Some of the people of Powys will escort you to your campsite. You can stay there for the rest of the night and leave at dawn.'

The crowd of people from Powys moved aside to let Evan through, and then a group of them followed him down the road. Olivia, Noah, and Aled exchanged some urgent whispers, and then Olivia nodded.

'Noah will stay here. Aled and I have to go back to Wales to get the others.'

'Just don't bring Evan back here with you,' said Owen.

'Evan won't make it back to Wales.' Olivia reached out her hand to give a fleeting caress to Owen's cheek.

# I WILL LEAD MY PEOPLE

'If I'd known you were alive, I'd have come to you before our son was born.'

I blinked, glanced rapidly from Owen to Noah, and finally saw the resemblance that should have been obvious from the start.

There was an impatient shout from Evan in the distance. 'Come on!'

Olivia and Aled hurried off, and I heard James's anxious murmur.

'Are we going to let Olivia kill Evan?'

'He's too dangerous to be left alive,' said Owen. 'He wants to take what we've built in the Corlforth Line and destroy it.'

I didn't say anything at all, just watched Evan, Olivia, and Aled walk off with their escort. I thought of how Barbara Corlforth had calmly ordered the deaths of some villagers to protect me. Now I was letting Olivia kill Evan to protect the people of the Corlforth Line.

I'd thought it strange that the spirit of Barbara Corlforth had become my confidant over the years, but now I understood the reason. I hadn't just remembered Barbara Corlforth. I had become her.

# ALL THE WORLD IN SEAFOAM GREEN
## LAUREN RING

A brushstroke here, a dab of pigment there. The slightest twitch of Kate's hand across her tiny painting could raise mountains or carve valleys. There were no mountains or valleys here in the sleepy town of Quarantine Cove, though. Just gentle sand dunes and the murmuring sea.

The sea itself had offered up Kate's latest canvas, a delicate cockle shell the size of her thumbnail. The intricacy of seashell painting allowed her to narrow her focus to a grain of sand, blocking out any noise or confusion. Life had become quieter after the pox roared through the world, but there was still nothing as quiet as when she was painting a nice landscape.

Always landscapes, now. Empty scenes of empty places. A creature here and there, sure, but ever since the pox, Kate had not painted a single person.

With the very tip of her brush and a hint of titanium white, Kate added a few seagulls to her tiny beach. Almost done. She just needed to mix up some seafoam green to cap off the crashing waves. A green base to start, then blue, but how much should she lighten it? Kate glanced outside to her best reference.

Lacy white foam rushed across the dark, wet sand, then bubbled away to nothing. A visitor, waiting to be greeted, knelt by a beached boat as the tide slowly receded. There were no crashing waves, but the few small crests Kate could see were a bold, minty teal. She mixed a little grey onto her palette.

When she checked her colours again, minutes later, both person and boat were still where they had landed. Everyone else must have been too busy with lunch preparations to welcome them. Kate's painting would have to wait a little longer. She set down her brush with a sigh.

When Kate cracked open her front door, the sea air greeted her like an old, familiar friend. After all, the ocean was the oldest friend she had left. She descended the few steps that separated her studio from the beach and padded across the dunes, leaving shoe prints in her wake. Inevitably, a few grains of sand made their way between her toes. Kate stopped to shake her feet until her skin no longer crawled. The day was warm and the sky was clear. The seagulls landed and hopped toward her, hoping for scraps. Some things never changed.

The boater stood as Kate approached. She appeared to be a young woman, about Kate's age, with sun-bleached hair and brown, pox-marked skin. Kate didn't recognize her face, but then, she never recognised anyone's face.

Perhaps this was a fisherwoman from a nearby quarantine town, someone whose hair and build and mannerisms Kate had not had time to learn. Perhaps this was a local trader just back from a long journey; so long that her hair had grown and her skin had tanned. Perhaps this was even an acquaintance from Kate's own town, who had just happened to style her hair and clothing differently that day.

The woman still hadn't spoken, depriving Kate of her most valuable clue. Kate, afraid of offending her guest, plucked nervously at the cuffs of her sleeves. When she spoke, it was in the casual tone she used for anyone that she might be expected to know.

'Hello,' Kate said. 'Welcome home.'

The woman began to cry.

'What's wrong?' Hoping that it wasn't her fault, Kate fumbled for the rag she used to wipe up stray drops of paint. 'Here, take this.'

With no regard for the smeared paint, the woman pressed the rag to her cheeks. Cadmium yellow dripped down and highlighted the pox scars on her jawline. Kate looked away but didn't leave. No one should have to cry alone. Not anymore.

The woman cried for a long while, then kept on with a sort of keening sob after her tears dried up. Finally, she spoke.

'Home?' she asked, and with the dry rasp of her voice, Kate knew for sure that she was a stranger.

'I'm sorry, I'm terrible with faces. I thought you were from around here. I didn't mean to offend you.'

'No, no.' The woman clung to Kate's rag as if it were a life preserver. 'You didn't offend me. You were kind, that's all.'

'Alright, well.' Puzzled and out of her depth, Kate pressed on with her welcoming script. 'Are you here to trade, then? Quarantine Cove mainly exports artisan goods. We have several shoemakers and bookbinders, and I'm a painter myself.'

'You paint?' The woman looked at the paint-stained rag as if seeing it for the first time.

'Seashells, mostly.'

'Well, seashell painter, I'm not here to trade either. I'm just passing through. I saw your town and thought I might try my luck for a hot meal, and maybe some help repairing my sails.' The woman handed back the rag, revealing extensive scarring on her forearms. The pox had hit her harder than most.

'I'm sure we can manage that. Wait here a moment, and I'll bring someone to screen you.'

The screening was mostly a formality at this point, since the pox had long since burned itself out, but it made everyone feel safer. Besides, Kate wanted a second opinion on the woman. Kate wasn't naïve by any means, but she knew her autistic self well enough to know that she often missed signs of danger.

'Thank you.' The woman sounded as if she might cry again.

'What should I tell them your name is?' Kate asked. 'And where are you from, if you don't mind? We keep a map of visitors.'

'My name is Shira. I came from Bay Quarantine Two, up north.'

'Welcome, Shira. I'll be right back.' Kate tried her best to sound comforting. Quarantine Cove had never had a visitor from that far north before. She didn't want to scare Shira off before everyone got a chance to meet her.

Kate trudged back to town, shaking sand out of her shoes between steps. She cast a wistful look at her studio, where the unfinished beach shell still lay on her desk, but forced herself to move along. There would be time to add the seafoam later.

Now, who to bring? Kate wasn't particularly close with anyone in town. Even before the pox, there were only a few people she had called friends, and none of them had survived. But Kate was fine. She had moved on. She just didn't want to go through that loss again, whatever the cause. So she kept to herself, and painted her empty paintings.

Ray, the gentlest of the town's elected leaders, would treat Shira kindly. Kate headed for their home. The scent of grilling fish guided her to Ray's backyard, where they stood tending charcoal and halibut. Their dark skin and close-cropped hair made them easy to recognise, as did their penchant for loose, flowy clothing.

'Well, if it isn't Kate Keller,' they said, surprised. 'What brings you here? Have you run low on paints?'

'There's a visitor on the beach.' She explained Shira's situation. Ray nodded along, then pulled their fish off the grill.

'I'll see to her,' they said, and that was that.

Freed of duty, Kate returned to her studio and bent over the cockle shell once more. She dipped her brush in the newly mixed green and blended it into the crests of the waves. When she glanced to the sea for reference, though, she expected to see Shira there waiting. But there was only her boat, and the empty shore.

Her brush hand shook, just a little, as she turned back to the shell. A tall splotch of seafoam green marred her perfect beach.

Kate groaned and set aside her brush. She would have to mix more sandy beige and cover up the error once it dried. Her hands continued to shake, and not in the joyful way she flapped when excitement overcame her. This was a venting of anxious energy. Something gnawed at the back of her mind, something that ground away at her focus like sand in the heel of her shoe.

She went outside to clear her head. Shira's boat was still on the beach, stranded there until high tide lifted it from the shore. Kate knelt beside it and carefully, methodically searched for shells suitable for painting. Many had shattered beneath the boat's hull, leaving shards that nicked Kate's questing fingers. Soon the sea would wash those shards dull again.

Kate felt dull herself. The sharp grief of years past had lost its edges with time. She had pushed it away,

# ALL THE WORLD IN SEAFOAM GREEN 47

time and time again, until it sank in her mind like a rock on its final skip. Kate ran her finger along the razor edge of a broken shell and tried to remember tears.

'I never got your name, seashell painter.'

Shira leaned against her boat and gazed down at Kate. She was smiling, but it didn't reach her eyes. Kate hadn't looked at Shira's eyes before. They were seafoam green.

'I'm Kate.' She selected a final shell and stood, facing Shira. 'Did you get your lunch?'

'Yes, and Ray is fetching someone to mend my sails.' Shira gestured above her to the worn fabric. There was no obvious damage, no gashes or holes, just the gradual wear of life at sea.

'Long journey?' Kate asked. She polished her shells with the corner of her shirt, removing any stubborn sand or bits of seaweed.

'It has been, yes.'

Kate continued polishing her shells. One had a nice spiral, suitable for a mountain peak or the twisting current of a river.

'I wanted to ask you a favour, while I wait for the tide,' said Shira.

'Go ahead,' said Kate, pocketing her shells. Quarantine Cove didn't get many visitors, and it was even rarer for Kate to actually speak to one. Besides, something drew her to Shira, some sense of kinship that drove her hands to shake and her mind to wander.

'Could you paint a portrait for me?'

'A portrait?' Even when Kate had painted people, portraiture had eluded her. She couldn't match a likeness that she couldn't recognise in the first place. 'I don't really paint people. I could paint your boat on a shell, maybe. Or the ocean, I'm good at the ocean.'

'I was wondering if you could paint my wife. She died of the pox, early on. I lost everything I had of her in the quarantine, between relocation and decontamination, and I'm afraid I'm forgetting her face too.' The last words came out in a rush, accompanied by a fresh wave of tears.

It was an earnest, heartfelt plea, and Kate was the worst person in the world to receive it. She bit her lip. She couldn't say yes, but she couldn't say no. After all, she herself had spent countless hours missing her departed friends, stoking their fading memories with letters and photos and any scrap of them she had left. To have nothing would have been unbearable.

'Come with me. I'll see what I can do.'

Kate took Shira back to her studio and found her a stool to watch from. Then she went to the back, where the studio's wealthy former inhabitants had stored everything from gold leaf to massive canvases. A portrait like this ought to be done properly.

'I thought you painted on shells,' said Shira when Kate returned with a mid-sized canvas. 'I can't carry that on my boat. I'd like a shell to wear on a necklace, to carry her by my heart.'

# ALL THE WORLD IN SEAFOAM GREEN

'Alright.' Kate's eyes stung with unshed tears, the first in a long time. No one carried her by their heart. She was left to carry the memories of all her friends, and that was a heavy burden to carry alone. 'A shell, then.'

She fetched a large egg cockle with a natural hole and brushed it with primer. A new, clean surface, ready for paint. Kate pushed aside her green-stained beach painting and turned to Shira, unsure of what to expect.

'Her favourite colour was seafoam green,' said Shira, staring at Kate's palette.

'Like your eyes?' Kate asked. She spread seafoam green across the primer, a mindless pattern, loose and free.

'Cass always said my eyes meant I was born to sail.' Soft tears traced their way down Shira's cheeks as she spoke. 'She was strong, stronger than me by far. She worked down at the docks while I just stayed at home.'

Kate painted the lines of a dock at the bottom of the shell.

'When the pox came, I got it first. She came to take care of me. She made me hot soup and put damp washcloths on my forehead. She was always there, no matter how much I protested. We didn't know how bad it would be, back then.'

A bowl of soup. A piece of cloth. A pair of hands. As the hands took shape in seafoam green, a tear fell from Kate's cheek and diluted her paint. She hadn't even noticed she was crying, but of course she was.

Of course. Kate's grief hadn't sunk like a rock. It had receded like an ocean, with Kate the unsuspecting beachgoer, picking shells as the tidal wave formed.

'Then Cass got sick. I didn't know what to do. I dragged myself out of bed every day, still feverish myself, to take her to appointments and to search for new remedies. Nothing worked. Nothing ever worked. You lived or you died, and she died, and it's as simple as that.'

A stethoscope. An ambulance. A gravestone.

'Can I see the portrait?' Shira asked, wiping her eyes.

Kate looked down at her work. Every inch of the shell was now seafoam green, with only brushstrokes and texture to indicate the objects Kate had painted. From a distance, it looked blank. It was not, by any definition, a portrait.

Shira leaned over Kate's shoulder and studied the shell painting for a long minute.

'If you just tell me what she looked like, I can try—' Kate began, but Shira cut her off.

'It's perfect like this,' she said. 'No painting or photo or video could compare to having her, anyway. When I see this shell, I'll remember Cass, and this day, and her story. It will keep her memory alive.'

It wasn't the portrait, Kate realised, it was the painting. The process. The memory was in the remembering, the story in the telling.

Kate strung the shell on a thick leather cord and helped Shira tie it around her neck. Outside, the tide rose and lapped at the edge of her boat, tugging it gently back to sea. Shira smiled, and this time, it reached her eyes.

'I'd better be going,' she said.

'When the paint fades, or chips away, come visit,' said Kate. 'We'll paint a new portrait together.'

'You're too kind, Kate. Cass would have liked you.' Shira stepped out onto the beach, backlit by the sinking sun. 'Another time, seashell painter.'

'Another time,' Kate echoed, watching Shira leave.

As the boat sailed away, Kate returned to her desk and picked up her beach painting. The seafoam green didn't look so much like a mistake anymore. Now it looked like a silhouette. The silhouette of a woman adrift in the sea of memory, finally coming to shore.

She dipped her brush in seafoam green and let herself cry as she began to paint Shira.

# MERRY SHITMAS
## K.L. EVANGELISTA

I don't want to brag or anything, but I've become a bit of an expert on dead bodies—I suppose it's an unavoidable side effect of living through a plague. I could go into great and disgusting detail about the different stages of decomposition, but I won't, because it's gross. So gross.

What I will say is this: thank fuck we are past the oozy maggoty stage.

Now that we are six months in, the bodies are all in dry decay. It's quite a civilised state of decomposition, really. And that is the only reason that I'm preparing to use the amenities of an unexplored house—I would never have attempted it in an earlier stage.

*Hurry*, my bowels murmur.

I'm on my way to visit Trav and the cows in Byron. Sam is driving us along a winding country road, still sticking strictly to the speed limit, even after all this time.

I'm the navigator, so I should probably know *which* road, exactly, but I'm hopeless without Google Maps.

Every bounce makes me wince.

'This one.' I point at an architecturally designed farmhouse with so many windows it may as well be made of plate glass.

*Hurry*, my bowels warn.

'You want me to come in with you, Jane?' Sam asks, turning into a gravel driveway. *Bounce—Jostle—Bump.*

'Nope!' I say tightly, and I pick up my trusty cricket bat. 'Carol will keep me company.'

I'm not worried about encountering another person—only one in a hundred thousand survived the plague, and all the ones we've met are fair dinkum sorts—but there *are* hordes of feral dogs. Plus, I'll need Carol to make an entrance.

'Carol is great,' Sam concedes, deadpan. 'But can she protect you against ghosts?'

'Do not even joke about that.' Sure, it's the middle of a hot sunny day—the first day of summer, in fact—but it will still be gloomy inside.

*Seriously, hurry!* my bowels insist loudly.

I jump out of the car before Sam has come to a complete stop. *RUN*, my bowels scream, *GO GO GO*. I run, swinging Carol wildly, and smash in the nearest windows—when you've got Crohn's disease and your bowels say run, you'd better run.

The people inside will be skin and bone. So long as no-one actually died *on* the toilet, I should be fine.

It's only when I'm sitting safely on the toilet that I realise the smell inside the house is wrong. And it's not coming from the toilet bowl.

'Are you okay?' Sam calls distantly.

'Yes!' I yell back, then, '… No. The smell.'

He follows my voice to the bathroom and stops just outside the closed door. 'Yeah,' he says, subdued.

'I'm going to be here a while.' Crohn's disease is like that—I spent my sister's wedding reception in the ladies. 'You don't have to wait in the house. I'm fine—I'll come out to the car when I'm done.' I try to make my voice sound confident, but it wavers slightly on the last note.

'No, it's okay.' I hear Sam settle outside the door, because he's the kind of guy who would never leave a girl sitting alone on a toilet in a house with a dead body.

'It's coming from behind that door,' Sam informs me, when I'm finally liberated from my tiled cell.

We look at each other for a long moment. Sam's grey eyes are serious behind his glasses, and his eyebrows are arched in a question.

I nod. I don't want to see, but at the same time, I can't *not* look. I have to know: why is there a freshly dead body? Now? Six months *after* the plague?

I take a deep breath, hold it, then turn the handle.

The first thing I see is a carved wooden chair, placed carefully in the centre of the room. A man is standing on top of it, but no, that's not right. He's not standing on the chair, he's *dangling*.

Sam makes a small choked noise and backs out.

I look up, trying to avoid taking in details of the man's face. He's hanging from the roof, which has exposed beams.

Like I said earlier, I'm a bit of an expert on dead bodies. If the smell alone wasn't enough, the waxy sheen on the bloated hands confirms my suspicions; this man has only been dead about a week. Ten days, tops.

I walk calmly towards the desk; my heart is starting to pound and I'm really struggling against the reflex to breathe. I rifle quickly through the drawer, looking for a note, a diary, but there's nothing like that. He must have thought he had no-one to write to.

With one last glance at the hanging man, I dash out of the room, slamming the door shut behind me. Every cell in my body is demanding oxygen, but I don't exhale yet.

I wait until I am out of the house before I let myself take a breath, gasping up the warm, fresh, clean air.

Air without bits of corpse in it.

I have so many questions. Who was this guy? Why didn't he reach out to the other survivors?

Why hang himself *now*, and not, say, immediately after the plague? Is there some kind of heightened risk six months after an apocalypse, once the new normal is established?

And the most important question: What's to stop *other* people from doing the same? The end of the world is pretty grim stuff. I think of all the people I've met since the end of the world … I'm not sure if I could cope if I lost any of them.

Sam is too upset to drive, so now I've got the wheel. 'Maybe he was depressed,' I say. 'Judith says there is a correlation between mental health issues and autoimmunes.'

'Wonderful.' Sam rubs his brows. 'Because the plethora of disease we all face was not bad enough.' So far, every survivor we've found has had some kind of autoimmune disease.

'I think we should keep this to ourselves,' I say. 'We don't want to upset people. And we don't want to trigger an outbreak of copycat suicides, Heathers style.'

'Heathers actually had murders, not suicides,' Sam points out as he studies the map. 'Left.'

'You know what I mean. They're contagious. You used to hear about suicide epidemics all the time on the news.' I've already suffered through one devastating epidemic this year; I'm not keen to go through another.

I tap on the steering wheel anxiously. 'Maybe we should think about something else for a while,' I suggest. 'Something happy.'

'You can help me figure out next steps for the Move,' he offers.

I sigh. The capital M Move is the plan to re-locate the entire community of Brisbane survivors—about two dozen—to a farming region. It involves a hundred moving parts and a great deal of effort. Trust Sam to think that was his happy place.

'No,' I say patiently. 'Something fun.'

'Left here,' Sam directs, and I obediently make another left turn. 'Well ... it's about three weeks till Christmas.'

Christmas! Now there's an idea. Mum and Dad used to go all out every year. Prawns on the barbie. Pavlova with lashings of cream and fresh fruit. Tinsel and Christmas lights everywhere you looked.

'We could do a big Christmas lunch.' I grin. 'You could dress up as Santa and get sunstroke when you try to play backyard cricket.'

'*You* could spend hours slaving over a hot oven and then get brutally honest after you have too much to drink.'

The more I think about it, the more excited I get.

'So, Christmas?' Sam asks.

# MERRY SHITMAS

'Christmas,' I agree, feeling better already.

It isn't until later that I remember that suicide rates peak over Christmas.

Trav lives on a dairy farm. He decided on day dot of the apocalypse that he was going to find some cows and save them from certain doom, and damned if he hasn't done exactly that.

Trav is part of the Brisbane community, but since he's based in Byron, he's an outlying member. We've been sending someone for a visit every week or so—they bring supplies, spend half a day shovelling muck or pressure-cleaning the milking sheds, and then drive back to Brisbane with a few vats of fresh milk—but Trav himself never travels to us.

I've always thought that it was cool that Trav is so independent. But after finding the hanging man, I wonder now if Trav's isolation makes him more at risk... and it makes me doubly glad that we've come to connect him to the rest of the group via HF radio.

I turn into a long driveway, and a bevy of dogs surround our truck, yipping in excitement. Trav has a habit of picking up strays.

I roll down the window and fill my lungs with a deep breath of dairy farm air—a mix of fresh-cut grass, cow pats and spilt milk.

The man himself is waiting for us outside of the house, dressed in big black gumboots and an apron. I look at his tanned face closely for any signs of impending suicide. I'm not sure if it's just me being paranoid, but he does seem kinda down.

'Is it just my imagination, or has your family doubled since we were here last?' Sam gently removes an inquiring muzzle from his crotch as he attempts to extricate himself from the van.

Trav blushes. 'I just can't turn 'em away.'

'Why should you?' I crouch down to distribute a few tummy rubs. 'They're good company.'

'It's better they stay here with you than turn feral,' Sam agrees, scratching a blue heeler behind the ear. 'They can help protect the farm.'

I wade through the sea of dogs to give Trav a kiss on the cheek.

It's *not* my imagination—something is wrong.

'Are you okay?' I ask.

Trav shrugs—but he's the taciturn type, so I just wait patiently. 'I lost two more heifers this week,' he says eventually, his voice gruff. 'There's only seventy-three left.'

Over lunch—tuna sandwiches, made on some freshly baked bread—Trav opens up a bit more.

'It wasn't long after the apocalypse when I got here—only a coupla days. The cows had access to the dam for drinking, but they hadn't been milked for all that time. You could tell a lot of them were in pain. I lost, I dunno, half the herd before I figured out they had mastitis and needed antibiotics. Then a few more died while I was figuring out how to use the milking machinery.'

Milking machinery. Yet another thing we'll have to figure out how to maintain.

'But why are you losing them now?' I ask.

'They've been dying during childbirth. A lot of them were pregnant when I got here.'

Sam nods in understanding. 'That's how dairy farmers keep up the milk supply, right? They keep them breeding.'

'Yeah,' says Trav. 'These guys imported bull spunk to keep them pregnant. I don't know how to do all that IVF stuff though.'

'You should ask Judith,' I mutter under my breath; Sam has sufficient tact not to comment.

'What's the fatality rate during childbirth?' Sam asks.

Trav swallows, and looks down at his hands. He washed up before lunch, but his fingernails are still grimy.

Sam places his hand on Trav's shoulder. 'It's okay,' he says. 'You're not an expert. We're all just doing the best we can at the moment.'

Travis nods. 'Sixty percent.'

*Sixty percent*. Sam and I share a shocked look. I can't help but wonder if Judith's percentages will compare.

I'm relieved when the discussion turns to our plans to connect Trav to Brisbane via HF.

'It'll be great to have you connected,' Sam enthuses. 'We can keep you involved in the Move, and you can let us know whenever you need new supplies.'

'Plus, you'll be able to tune into Alive@5,' I say.

Trav raises his eyebrows. 'You guys are still doing that?'

I grin at Sam. 'Every day we can.'

The first week of the apocalypse was rough. The survival rate was one in 100,000, and I think every survivor spent some time believing they were the last person left on earth. Sam and I were lucky enough to find each other within the first few days. We figured the easiest way to find other survivors was to put my amateur radio skills to good use by broadcasting our own show. That's how we found Trav, actually.

I thought we'd probably stop doing the show, once the community in Brisbane took off. But Sam insisted we keep it up—he says that communication is important.

I didn't need much convincing—spending that hour with Sam is the highlight of my day.

The apocalypse turned me into the world's foremost expert on radio. This is a very bad thing for the future of the world's communications, because I am basically just a hack.

Pretty much everything I've set up to date has been working on the principles of line of sight—if you see it, you can talk to it. That's why Sam and I set up our

## MERRY SHITMAS

Brisbane base at Mount Coot-tha; from up there, we can see almost everything. Height is might, as they say.

Long-range HF is trickier—you've got to bounce your signal off the ionosphere, kind of like trying to get bank shot in snooker. It's just a smidge of maths to get the angles right, and then we used our most sophisticated techniques to reduce the noise.

'Sophisticated?' Trav looks apprehensive—I've been explaining how it all works so he knows how to establish his side of the link.

'Basically, we just twiddle a bunch of knobs until the signal gets stronger,' I explain. 'See, if you look at the frequency spectrum, you can see a little bump here: That's Beth trying to get through. We just need to keep working at it together until that little bump gets bigger.'

I let him have a go.

'Trav, you should come up to Brisbane for a holiday.'

Trav frowns as he watches the signal fluctuate. 'You know I can't leave the cows.' Trav's schedule is pretty intense—he has to be up at the crack of dawn for the morning feed and milking. Then he labours over various other rural chores, before milking them again in late afternoon.

It is a disturbing preview of our future.

'What about Christmas?' I ask. 'What if you come up just for the day? I could drive you back in time for afternoon milking. No, even better, I'll *do* the afternoon milking. You can stay in Brissie and party on.'

'I dunno…'

'There'll be prawns…' I wheedle.

Trav's eyes light up. 'Well … if there's prawns…'

I smile. My mum always said prawns made great bait.

---

That night I hear the crackle of tearing pages and the soft hum of a laminator, and I know Sam isn't sleeping again.

Sam's had frequent bouts of insomnia for as long as I've known him. He doesn't like to lie uselessly awake in bed, though, so he uses the time to try to preserve human knowledge for future generations.

I pad out of Trav's guest bedroom and knock lightly on Sam's door. I'm not embarrassed for Sam to see me in my daggy old PJs; we share a Winnebago back in Brisbane, so he's very familiar with Dad's old Skyhooks shirt.

He invites me in; I push the door open gently to find him sitting at a small desk next to a single bed, methodically tearing pages out of a book. I jump onto the mattress and settle into a cross-legged position. 'How many have you done now?'

'Four hundred and twelve,' says Sam.

That is a lot of lost sleep.

Sam rests his head on a hand for a moment and looks at me closely. 'You're not usually up this late,' he observes quietly.

'Every time I close my eyes I see the hanging man,' I admit.

Sam nods, and lifts up his head to feed another page through the machine. 'Me too.' He feeds a sheet through the machine. 'I wish he'd left a note.'

I pick up a page and tuck it into a laminator sleeve. 'I wonder if it's our fault. Maybe we didn't make it easy enough for him to find the rest of us. Maybe if we'd just tried a little harder, he'd still be alive.'

Sam looks troubled.

'Do you think Trav's at risk, out here all on his lonesome?' I ask.

'I don't think so. Do you?'

'Maybe? Especially if things keep getting worse with the cows.'

Sam shakes his head. 'Jesus. Nothing's ever easy in the apocalypse.'

'I wish I knew what to look for,' I say. 'Like, what the signs of suicide are.'

'There's a few,' he says. 'Pass me my backpack—it's on the other side of the bed.'

I sling it over, and Sam pulls out a book, which he passes to me. *Mental Health First Aid*.

'How long have you had this?' I turn it over to read the blurb. The cover is worn and the pages are well thumbed through.

'A while.'

'And you've been carrying it around all this time?'

He nods.

It never occurred to me before now that post-apocalyptic suicide was something we might have to worry about. But of course, Sam had thought of it already. He thinks about everything.

'Thanks,' I say. 'Once I know what to look for, we'll be like a two-man Suicide Squad.'

'The Suicide Squad were a bunch of bad guys.'

'Okay, well, I'll be like Batman, then. Vigilant. Effortlessly cool. Always ready for action.'

Sam's dimple peeps out. 'I appear to have been cast in the role of Robin.'

'The Boy Wonder,' I agree. 'Supportive. Effortlessly dorky. Always ready for exposition.'

Sam grins, but then his brow furrows. 'Jane ... Even if you see the signs ... you might not be able to stop it.'

'Watch me,' I say, stubbornly.

'I know you'll try,' he says. 'Just ... be prepared for the possibility. We're all struggling still, every single one of us. And if it does happen, don't blame yourself, okay? Because it wouldn't be about anything you did or didn't do. It wouldn't be about you at all. It would be about them. About what they could and couldn't live with.'

'Sure, sure.' I say lightly. 'It's not personal. It's the apocalypse.'

## MERRY SHITMAS

Sam touches my cheek lightly, and I look back into his grey eyes. 'Seriously, Jane. Promise me that if something does happen ... to someone—to anyone ... Promise me you won't blame yourself.'

'I won't blame myself,' I promise, letting myself lean into his touch, just a little.

I won't *have* to blame myself, because I'm not gonna let anything happen.

I'm Batman.

---

We spend a few extra days with Trav. I watch him like a hawk, constantly analysing his behaviour for signs of suicide. I don't see anything but an increasing irritation with me, which is fair.

I'd like to stay longer but we have responsibilities back in Brisbane—Sam is the project manager for the Move, and I'm everyone's tech bi-atch. *Jane, connect me to solar, Jane, get me battery storage, Jane, fix the thing.*

I'm an electrical engineer, not a mechanic, so most of the time, no, I don't know how to fix the thing. But I'm not scared of tinkering, and I can usually figure something out.

This gives me plenty of reasons to check up on everyone I think might be at risk.

I start with Clare.

Clare is my yearbook pick for 'most likely to suicide'. She never comes to community meetings, and the only reason I've even met her is because I installed the generator at her house and showed her how to keep it running.

I knock on the door of a modern two-storey family house, and a few minutes later, a woman in her late forties peeks out. Her short blonde-grey hair is unwashed, and her thin dressing gown is grey and dingy.

*Neglect of appearance and personal hygiene?* I've memorised all the signs from Sam's book.

I hold up my tool kit. 'Hi Clare—I'm here to do some basic aircon maintenance.'

Clare stares at me blankly. *Feelings of hopelessness*, maybe? I wonder. Her eyes do look kind of glazed, though, so maybe *dependence on drugs*?

'Umm ... can I come in?' I ask.

Clare's gaze drops to the floor, and she shrugs, drifting away from the door but leaving it open. I get the impression that she's decided it's more effort to get rid of me than to let me in.

I hastily grab my tool bag, as well as the esky of fresh milk I brought from the farm. 'So,' I say, as I enter the house, 'how have you been?'

I just have time to address her slippers as they walk up the stairs.

'Uh ... Clare?' I call up, unsure if I should follow.

# MERRY SHITMAS

My only answer is the sound of a bedroom door being firmly closed.

That's fine, I think. I'll just use the opportunity to snoop. I mean, investigate.

Clare had two children; I can see their progress from toddlers to graduating students from the photos as I walk down the hallway and into the kitchen.

I put my bottle of milk in the fridge. Nothing is spoilt or rotten, so Clare must be doing a decent job of keeping the generator going—that's something at least. In fact, the whole kitchen is quite tidy. Tidier than my place.

I move my snooping to the lounge. The stereo has a few CD cases scattered around it. I pick them up—Amy Shark, REM, Joy Division … Sheesh.

The stereo radio is programmed to some pre-plague radio station. I tune it to 105.5, knowing Clare is unlikely to turn it on.

I've seen enough. Clare is definitely high risk.

The obvious next question is: what exactly do I do about that?

---

I find our doctor exactly where I expect to—the lab at the hospital.

'You're back.' Judith doesn't look up from her microscope. She refers to a textbook beside her—I'm not the only one having to expand my skill set. Not only is Judith our only doctor, she's our only pathologist, X-ray technician, and pharmacist.

'Whatcha looking at,' I ask.

'A blood sample. I want to keep an eye on Beth's inflammation marker—her Graves' disease may be in relapse.'

Have I mentioned that Every. Single. Survivor of the plague has some sort of autoimmune disease?

'How have you been feeling?' Judith asks when she's done. 'How is your Crohn's?'

'There've been some tummy rumbles,' I admit. 'But nothing too bad.'

'Take some prednisone.'

I wrinkle my nose. The side effects of most steroids are awful: puffy face, weight gain, acne. But the worst thing is that they change your mood. Specifically, they make you angry. *Really* angry. The last time I was on prednisone, I threw a tantrum at work because I couldn't find my pen. *Roid Rage*, they call it. 'I don't know…'

'Would you rather we leave this untreated and I remove your bowel?' Judith snaps. 'It's been at least fifteen years since I've performed any kind of surgery, but I'm sure it's like riding a bike.'

She stomps out of the lab and returns a minute later with a glass of water and two small tablets, which she slams on the bench in front of me.

'If you don't like the steroids, there is another option,' she reminds me. 'Pregnancy suppresses the immune system.'

I suppose, on the balance of things, a few tantrums aren't so bad. I toss back the tablets and hope they won't affect me too badly.

---

The first time I saw Judith, she was wild-eyed from lack of sleep, trying to keep a bunch of embryos alive in the face of mass electricity outage. Her eyes are less crazy now, but she's still got those embryos on ice, and I have no doubt that she remains committed to the survival of the human race.

But this is not *The Handmaid's Tale*. We're not going down the path of forced pregnancies. I attribute this in no small part to Sam, who has a lot of influence, and is the biggest feminist I know.

Recently, Judith has been taking a more passive aggressive approach, handing out pamphlets on IVF to every woman of childbearing age and even beyond. Judith seems to think drugs can do wonders.

I admire her drive, but I do think that when she looks at me, all she sees is a womb with clever hands.

'So, I need a favour,' I say, after I take my meds.

Now, Judith and I don't *really* have that kind of relationship. It's mostly Judith giving me orders: Jane, fix the thing; Jane, take your medication; Jane, have a baby. So I'm stepping outside my lane here.

Judith does not look excited at this development in our relationship. 'What favour?'

'Can you visit Clare for a check-up?'

'Is she having a relapse?'

'A mental check-up,' I elaborate. 'I'm worried she might be depressed.'

'Certainly. Right after I add 'psychologist' to my list of qualifications. It won't be that difficult. It's only a few additional initials after my name. Pass me that sharpie, I'll add them to my diploma now.'

I get where she's coming from, but Judith is still the most qualified person to help Clare. I rack my brain, trying to think of a way to convince her to help. 'You know how you said that there is an increase in rates of mental illness in autoimmune patients?'

'Yes.'

'Is it causal? I know when I'm stressed and upset, I'm more likely to have a Crohn's attack.'

'I believe there is some evidence to that effect,' Judith says cautiously.

'In that case, wouldn't it be better to try to be really proactive in how we deal with mental illness in the community? I mean, otherwise we're really shooting ourselves in the foot, health-wise.'

Judith sighs, and looks at her watch. 'I'll go visit Clare later this afternoon.'

I smile. Round two to Jane. 'Maybe you could also turn the radio on while you're there. It might help her to feel connected.'

'I've heard your show,' says Judith. 'It could also drive her to desperation.'

I glare at her. Usually I can take a bit of teasing, but this hits a nerve.

She matches my glare for a second, before rolling her eyes. 'Fine,' she says. 'I will turn on the radio while I'm there. Anything else before I travel across town for this unscheduled appointment?'

I think of Trav. 'You don't have any experience delivering calves, do you?'

Judith's eyes narrow, and she points at the door. 'Get out of my lab.'

---

There's not enough time for me to visit every single survivor for a suicide assessment slash pep talk. Luckily, I have a wide reach.

Sam's waiting for me at our Coot-tha studio. I say *studio*, but it is basically just a large van we've kitted out with our radio gear. He smiles when I walk in, and like always, I can't help but smile back.

Before we go live, I check the HF comms and see Trav's signal going strong.

'Hi Trav, this is Jane, do you read me?'

'Loud and clear. This works pretty well, huh?'

'That's human ingenuity for you. How are you? How're the cows? And the dogs?'

'We're all good, thanks Jane.' I am reassured by the cheerful tone in his voice.

'Still on for Chrissie?' I ask.

'Looking forward to it.'

'Stay on the line after we've finished,' says Sam. 'I want to ask you a question about bovine nutritional supplements.'

'Can't wait.'

'Enough chit-chat,' I tell them. 'It's only one minute till we're live.'

We always start each broadcast with a song. I'm the music producer, so I get to choose which one. Occasionally Sam makes a suggestion, but it rarely gets picked up by the music producer, who has more refined tastes.

Sam looks at today's song and raises his eyebrow. 'Amy Shark?' he asks, knowing full well I hate ballads.

I shrug.

Amy's plaintive vocals fade away; I give the song a second to settle properly, then lean towards my mike.

'Helloooooo Brisbane! This is Jane.'

'And this is Sam.'

'And we're Alive@5!' we say in unison. It took a lot of coaxing to get Sam to do that.

'As always, Sam is going to start out with some news. Try not to fall asleep, guys.'

Sam throws a matchbox at me. 'They're not going to fall asleep, Jane! Okay, Brisbane, it's the second of December, and day one-eight-two.'

Sam reminds everyone to enjoy those bottles of juice that are stacked in the pantry, because they've only got another month or so. He also puts out a call for more drivers, explaining that once the petrol goes bad, our diesel trucks will become very large paperweights. 'Electric cars will keep us moving, but there are some things that just won't fit in the trunk.'

Then it's my turn. I lean towards the microphone. 'I think we can all agree that a lot of heavy shit has gone down this year. That's why Sam and I think we should do something extra special to celebrate Christmas.

'Now, Trav reckons we need to throw some prawns on the barbie, and I'm of the firm opinion that it's not an Aussie Christmas without pavlova. But I'm putting this one out there for everyone—how do you want to celebrate this Christmas?'

On a regular day, we might get one or two people reaching out to share a story or some news. This segment drew in over a dozen callers.

One of them, I'm pleased to see, is Ruby, our oldest survivor. I know Ruby listens to our show without fail, but she's never called in before, because she's been too nervous to operate the radio.

'At my house,' Ruby says, in her quavery voice, 'we always have a roast chicken dinner.'

'Roast chicken is a classic,' I agree warmly. 'We're definitely putting it on the menu.'

Once the calls peter out, Sam gets back on the mic. 'We've had lots of great suggestions,' he says. 'But how are we actually going to manage this, Jane? Shall we do a pot luck, where we all bring something?'

'*Pot luck*?' I say with exaggerated scorn. 'You know that was invented in the depression, right? I think if we're going to host Christmas for everyone, we should do it right.'

'Meaning?'

'Alive@5 will put on the whole shebang,' I promise recklessly. 'We'll arrange the food, drinks, decorations, everything. All everyone else will have to do is turn up and celebrate. It will be our gift to Brisbane!'

※

After the show, Sam has a deep worry crease between his brows.

'I know you mean well, Jane,' he says as we switch off all the comms. 'But we're both already busy … I don't know if we *can* do Christmas on top of everything else. And the things that people are asking for … none of them are that easy. Have you ever been prawning? Or know anything about it?'

I open my mouth to defend my credentials.

'*Other* than from watching Forest Gump?'

# MERRY SHITMAS

I close my mouth. Sam knows me too well.

'I know it's a lot,' I say. 'But I want to take away as much of that stress for everyone as possible.' I hesitate. 'I get it, if you're too busy though,' I say, in the most neutral voice I can manage. I *do* want him involved—we make a great team and I have more fun with Sam than with anyone else. But I don't want to pressure him to do something he doesn't want to do.

I get enough of that from Judith.

'No,' says Sam, 'You're right. I'm in. Let's do this.'

---

So. Roast chicken. Prawns. Pavlova. We have our Christmas menu. Sam was right when he said that it is not going to be easy. Fresh food is still in short supply; we're not a thriving agricultural community *yet*. Sam found three chickens not long after arriving in Brisbane, but we didn't secure the Coot-tha Chicken Run, and they were attacked by a feral dog. RIP Chimichanga, Chuckycheese, and Chihuauha.

'If only we'd been better chicken farmers,' Sam says regretfully.

'Let's figure out the pav first,' I suggest. 'I think that will be the easiest. We can get Trav to bring up some fresh cream from the dairy. Ruby has passionfruit and strawbs, and there's mango trees all over backyard Brissie.'

'Sugar is easy,' says Sam. 'If we run out of our personal stock, I can go find the sugar truck.' He waves a binder at me, which I know contains an inventory of every packing box in every truck he's prepped for the move. 'If only we'd frozen some egg whites,' he laments.

'Yeah, we could have kept them near Judith's frozen embryos,' I say. 'Clearly marked, of course—you don't want to make *that* mistake … Wait, I've got it! We'll use those magic egg pavlova things.'

Sam scans through his inventory but can't find any mention of them. 'I mean, it probably is in one of the trucks,' he says. 'My crew wouldn't leave something like that behind if it had a long use-by date. But it could take us a lot of time to find it.'

'That's okay,' I say, 'We can go to a supermarket you didn't hit.'

---

Preparing for a grocery trip used to involve writing a list, checking your wallet for cards or cash, then hopping into a car. Immediately after the apocalypse, you ditched the wallet and picked up a peg for the stench, because, boy, the smell was *rank*. It wasn't long after that when the rodents moved in. Their sharp little rodent teeth tore apart packets of flour and sugar, bags of potato chips – pretty much anything that wasn't kept in glass, cans, or solid plastic. So now a 'trip to the shop' requires sturdy boots, heavy duty gloves and a thick jacket and pants. Even in summer.

The atmosphere inside the supermarket is oppressive; it's dark, and the air is stale and stinks like rat pee. I flap my jacket, trying to get more airflow.

The dessert aisle, traditionally home to packets of jelly and boxes of pudding mix, is now home to a large group of rats, crawling and scrabbling all over each other.

On any other day, I would take that as my cue to shriek and run away, but not today. Today, those rats are between me and my plans for Christmas. They are between me and the sanity of my people.

*What would Batman do?* I ask myself.

I glare at them and pick up a can of chickpeas. 'You dirty, no good stinkin' rats,' I say, and crook my arm, ready to throw.

'Hold up!' Sam crouches down and shines his torch over something on the ground.

It's the distinctive egg-shaped container. 'You found one!' I exclaim, but Sam shakes his head. I look closer and realise that the thick plastic has been gnawed through.

I lower the can. 'I didn't think they'd do that.'

'They must be getting desperate,' says Sam. 'Their population must've boomed right after the plague. All that food, nothing to keep them in check—the feral cats and dogs can't get in. I expect they'll attempt to migrate soon. We'd better check the protections around the food trucks.' He flashes his torch over the chickpeas, which are still in my hand. 'Do you mind if I look at that?'

I hand it over, confused.

'My old boss was allergic to eggs,' says Sam slowly. 'She told me once that she used chickpea liquid to make meringues. It contains a protein that whips up just like egg whites.'

Pavlova: check.

---

Next up: decorations. I'm guessing that most department stores keep their Christmas gear in a warehouse somewhere, but luckily, I don't have to Sherlock Holmes their supply chains because there is a Christmas specialty store near Chisholm listed in the phone book.

It's getting hot in the middle of the day, so I get up with the sun. Normally, this would be an issue for me, but the steroids are giving me lots of pep.

By the time I get back, Sam has only just gotten out of bed.

'Wanna help me set these up?'

'Can't,' he says, a little tersely. 'It's only two weeks till the Move. I've got to go open some shipping containers, then later I'm going to research prawning.'

## MERRY SHITMAS

Shipping containers are basically a giant lucky dip. They might have industrial batteries—or they might be filled with a million ping pong balls. 'Want some help?'

'Yes,' he says, 'But you can't. Judith called—she wants to see you. Also, we still haven't found a chicken we can roast.'

So back I get into my ute, drive all the way back down the mountain and back to the hospital. I take a long winding route through suburbia, driving slowly in case I can spot a chicken coop in someone's yard.

Judith, as is her wont, starts to give me jobs to do. First, I am to check on the generator, as well as the backup. She's worried about the embryos during the heat.

'The longer we wait to implant them, the higher the risk that something will happen,' Judith warns, as she checks on my work.

Once I'm finished, she instructs me to install air-conditioning in Ruby's house.

I mentally review my to-do list. 'Aren't we leaving in a few weeks, though?'

Judith looks at me like I am an imbecile. 'Yes—and those will be the hottest weeks of the year. Do you know the consequences of heat stroke for the elderly?'

I immediately feel terrible. 'Of course,' I say, and pick up my gear. I pause at the door to ask about her visit with Clare.

Judith sighs. She does that a lot in our conversations, I've noticed. 'It would not be appropriate to discuss this with you, Jane. But I can see that you are concerned, so let me reassure you that Clare is managing her health effectively.'

'Did she listen to the show?'

'The song, yes. But then she got quite upset and turned the radio off. Is it true that you stole one of her CDs when you were in the house?'

I bite my lip. 'Not *stole* ... but ... borrowed without permission, maybe.'

'Well, Clare was very upset by the theft. She seemed to feel that we were not the kind of community she wanted any part of. And she certainly doesn't want to see *you* again.'

I leave the hospital feeling generally shitty about myself. Part of me is annoyed, as well, that Clare would react so pettily to a minor transgression meant to make her feel more included.

Ruby's house is a breath of fresh air, both literally and figuratively. She takes one look at my face and pats my hand. 'You look like you need a chat, dearie. Let me get my hearing aid and we'll have some lemonade in the garden.'

Her garden is stuffed with several veggie patches, and hundreds of flowers. The sun is very high now, and the air thick with humidity, but it is pleasant to sip lemonade in the shade of the massive fig tree and listen to the bees buzz around.

# MERRY SHITMAS

I pour out my story in a rush. Ruby listens with one hand pressed to her aid, and when I'm done, assures me that an apology can always put everything to rights.

I don't exactly know how I'll apologise to someone who doesn't want to see me, but the prednisone is giving me a lot of self-confidence.

I'm sure I'll figure something out.

❦

By the time I arrive at Clare's, it's mid-afternoon and the thermometer in my truck says it's forty-one degrees outside. Humanity may have stopped emitting carbon, but global warming is a relentless sonofabitch once it gets started.

Clare doesn't answer my knocking. I can tell she's home, though, because I can see her Sedan in the garage.

Now I know, logically, that she's sleeping, or avoiding me, but my head can't stop seeing the hanging man's bloated purple face.

I equivocate for a few minutes, before I return to the truck, which is an oven. I turn the engine on, then open all the windows and wait for the heat to escape.

Then I radio Judith for help. 'I'm worried about Clare,' I say. 'She's not answering the door.'

'I think that's her way of saying she doesn't want to see you.'

'But what if something's happened? Like she's ... fallen, or something? Should I break her door?'

'I wouldn't recommend it.'

'Well, could *you* come, and just check that she's okay?'

'Jane, I have more important things to do. And frankly, so do you.'

I wipe some sweat away from my eyes. Judith's right, of course. And even if the worst *has* happened, what can I achieve, really, by bursting in right now?

Nothing. Just like there's nothing I could have done for the hanging man. There were signs all over—he could have found us if he'd wanted to. And Clare could tune into the show if *she* wanted to.

But ... If only she *knew* what she was missing out on. I might rag on Sam for his 'boring' news segment, but it was actually really useful. And my segment was all about helping people solve their problems together.

As I sit there, hot and uncomfortable, and waiting for the aircon to *work already*, I start to get angry. What is wrong with her? Why *won't* she just listen to the radio show, just once?

Couldn't we *make* her listen?

I switch to Sam's frequency and press the talk button. 'Sam, this is Jane, are you there? I've been thinking—let's produce today's radio show on location...'

If Clare can't—or won't—come and be part of the community, the community will just have to come to her.

# MERRY SHITMAS

It takes me the rest of the day to figure out how to route everything through Coot-tha, and down to Clare's house.

The radio set-up is old-school Sam and Jane, using the same equipment from our first shows. This includes an absolutely enormous loudspeaker—we didn't know how many people would find our frequency, so we aimed to make as much noise as possible.

The loudspeaker, which used to be directed out into the empty evening, is now pointed defiantly at Clare's bedroom window. Occasionally I see her curtains twitch, so she knows I'm here.

*Good*, says the prednisone.

The sound of a car approaching makes me perk up, hoping it's Sam—it's almost showtime—but it turns out to be Judith in her Mercedes.

Almost everyone drives fancy cars, now, but I suspect Judith's was pre-plague.

*You can tell she comes from privilege,* mutters the prednisone. *That's why she feels so comfortable telling you what to do.*

I narrow my eyes. 'I thought you weren't coming.'

'I didn't want to.' Judith eyes the loudspeaker in disgust. 'But you mentioned breaking down a door. I see you decided on harassment instead.'

'It's not harassment…'

'Before the apocalypse, if someone blasted loud music on your front lawn, you'd call the police.'

'Not if I thought I was in an eighties teen romcom.'

Judith glares at me. 'You can't bully someone into being part of a community,' she says flatly.

I meet her stare for stare. 'Watch me.'

---

At five o'clock, I am ready to go. There's only one thing missing: Sam. He's not responding to his radio, which means it's off, or—more likely—out of range. It's not like him to be late, but I guess I did move the venue at very short notice.

Luckily, I picked up Sam's notes while I was at Coot-tha, so I decide to just go ahead without him.

I push up the volume on 'Our House', by Madness, just to make sure Clare can hear.

I read out Sam's updates, in what I feel is a very credible caricature of his radio persona, before reassuming Jane-voice.

'So, peeps—open mic time. Do any of you have any problems you need help with?'

No-one replies. Sometimes this happens, but please not today—not when I need to convince Clare of our general awesomeness.

Then Trav's voice crackles over the HF.

'Trav!' I exclaim in relief. 'How's everything going? How are the cows?'

'I lost another one. She was calving. It got stuck, and ... I just couldn't help her.'

Oh no. 'I'm sure you did everything you could...'

'Yeah,' he says bitterly. 'I did everything *I* could. But that's the problem—I don't *know* what I'm doing. I thought, with a bit of hard work, I'll figure it out. But I don't know if I can. The family who ran this place before me had *generations* of experience. They wouldn't keep losing their stock like this. I need help delivering these calves.'

'Okay, Brisvegans, Trav needs you,' I say. 'Who can help him out?'

*This is perfect*, I think. *Now Clare will see how this community pulls together.*

The silence drags on into discomfort.

*C'mon Judith, I know you've delivered babies. Sure, you're mad at me, but how can you refuse the call?*

'Maybe we need to think about that one,' I say at last, and glance up at Clare's window, disappointed.

A strange thing happens then. I imagine myself crouched beside a bed with a pillow around my head, terrified by the woman on my front lawn, and wondering what crazy thing she'll do next.

It's a good question: what crazy thing will I do next?

I pick up the mic.

'So, Judith put me on prednisone recently. Steroids are a first line of defence for most autoimmunes—I assume you all know what that's like. Anyway, long story short, I've just realised I'm being a massive dick. So … I'm really sorry, Clare.'

I pause—still no movement from the house. Not that I expect there to be.

I suppress my disappointment and continue with the show. 'I'd love to hear that I'm not alone, so next question—what have you done under the influence of steroids?'

Sometimes a question will generate so much interest that I have to moderate the line. Given everything, I was expecting this to be one of those questions—but it's not. For the second time tonight, I receive nothing but silence.

I look over at the antenna. Hmmm.

'Trav,' I say, 'I think I've stuffed up the comms. I don't think anyone else can hear us.' I can't tell for sure that's what happened, but it seems likely. 'Don't worry about the cows—we'll ask again tomorrow afternoon. And if we can't find someone better qualified, I'll come down myself, okay?'

'Okay. Thanks.'

I'm glad that I can do this right, at least. 'You're still coming for Christmas, though, yeah?'

'Nah, not any more, I've got another couple of calves due around then. I don't want to leave even for a few hours. Sorry mate.'

---

It's dark when I finally get back up the mountain. I tap gently on the Winnebago door. 'Hey,' I say softly. Something about the quality of the silence tells me Sam is not inside. I push the door gently open to find his bed tousled and empty.

*He's probably laminating,* I think, but no, there is his laminator on the floor. Next to it is his dog-eared copy of *Mental Health First Aid*. At some point he must have taken it back from my ute.

A sliver of fear crawls up my spine. Why *does* he carry it with him everywhere?

And that's when I hear it—the slight scrape of a wooden chair being moved into the foyer of the main Coot-tha building.

The foyer. Which has exposed beams.

---

I want to run towards the foyer. I want to scream for Sam to stop. But I can't. My legs have turned to concrete blocks, and my voice seems to have caught in my throat.

I was so worried that the contagion of the hanging man would spread, just like the plague had spread—but of course the only person to have been exposed to this particular virus was Sam. Sam, who is prone to anxiety, and has been putting himself under so much pressure with the Move—pressure which I've added do.

I force my legs to move. Where I'm standing is dimly lit, but I can see the foyer is ablaze with harsh, artificial light.

I know—*I know*—that if I lose Sam to this epidemic, it will take me too.

I can see the chair, yes, and a figure. Both seem still. I freeze, unable to breathe now, but then I see Sam move slightly, and I can draw in a ragged breath of relief.

Then he throws a loop over one of the beams and secures it tightly.

'No,' I croak, but even I can barely hear the word. 'Please, no.'

Sam teeters on the edge of the chair, and he looks at me. I can't see his eyes behind his glasses—the lenses simply reflect the cold white light. But I do see him step off the chair.

The world narrows to a single point of light, then disappears completely.

I wake up in the recovery position. And I start to cry, because I know who must have put me there, and I know whose gentle fingers are stroking my hair back from my face.

'You didn't do it,' I whisper.

'Didn't do what?' Sam murmurs, tucking a strand of hair gently behind my ear.

'I saw the chair ... and the rope.'

'Oh Jane.' He moves—just for a moment—and suddenly the harsh white light is gone and the room is aglow with the soft flickering fairy lights and glittering tinsel.

'It wasn't rope. It was Christmas lights. I wanted to apologise for missing the show and being such a stress-head.'

I push myself up to sitting position. 'But ... why did you take back *Mental Health First Aid*? Why is it so well read?'

'Ah.' He clasps his hands around his knees. 'You remember my autoimmune?'

'Yeah,' I say. 'You had it when you were a teenager. It affected your testicles.'

'I was so ashamed, in so much pain, so miserable. I really considered taking my own life. My brother saw what was going on, and he made sure I got help before I did anything. Once I was better, I got myself the book so that I could identify any warning signs early and seek help. And yeah, I've struggled with anxiety off and on over the years, but I was never troubled like that again ... until the plague. When everyone died. I promised myself one month. One month of trying hard to find another survivor, and if I couldn't...'

'But you found me after only a few days,' I remembered. 'You were so clever, to send up those flares.' I blanch, when I remember how I first ran away from him in terror ... What if I hadn't come back, and a month had gone before he'd found anyone else...

Just thinking about it makes my chest hurt.

'You've been worrying about Clare and Trav as well, haven't you?' Sam asks, and I nod. 'You know, the best thing to do, if you think someone might be suicidal, is to ask them.'

'It is?' I ask in surprise. That ... would have saved a lot of effort. And drama.

Sam gives me quizzical look. 'It was in the last chapter of the book. Didn't you read all the way to the end?'

'I've been busy. It takes a lot of effort to mess things up as much as I have.' I take a nervous breath and pick up both of his hands in mine. '*Do you* have thoughts of suicide?'

'I do not,' Sam says gravely, and I close my eyes for a moment, overcome by a surge of relief. 'Do you?'

My eyes pop open in surprise. 'Me?' I ask, incredulously.

'Well,' says Sam, 'you have been talking about it obsessively ever since Byron.'

'Hell no,' I assure him. 'But,' I acknowledge, 'I'm not sure my thinking has been particularly healthy, either.'

❦

The next day, Judith storms into the main building at Coot-tha and accosts us at the dining table.

'You,' she says to me with so much cold anger that I flinch and drop the butter knife. 'I went to visit Clare today, to check on her after your—your stunt. Do you know what I found?'

*Clare in a bathtub? Clare with her head in the oven?*

Sam puts a supportive hand on my shoulder 'What?' he asks.

'An empty house! Her car gone.'

Gone, not dead. I sag in relief. 'I'm sorry,' I say, 'I haven't been making the best choices lately.'

Sam stands, and offers her a chair at the table.

Judith deflates at last, her anger leaving in a sudden rush. 'I suppose we should have known that the cracks would show eventually.' She sits in the proffered chair. 'Almost a third of us are on steroids.' She lets herself slump into her seat, possibly for the first time in her life.

My eyes widen, shocked that there are so many.

'It is a shame to lose Clare from the group.' Sam pours Judith a coffee. 'But is it really that terrible? She's free to make her own choices after all. And most of us barely know her.'

'You don't understand,' Judith says wearily. 'Clare is a *midwife*.'

My chin drops almost all the way to the table.

Then I start to laugh. A midwife. That's just perfect.

'Don't worry Judith,' I say. 'Clare's not gone for good.'

'Where is she then?'

I grin from ear to ear. 'She answered the call. She's gone to Byron to help Trav.'

---

We switch back to Sam's original idea of pot luck. I tell myself that if everyone brings just one dish, it shouldn't add *too* much additional stress to their Christmas.

Coot-tha looks fantastic, at least, and the tree has so much bling that it is hard to look at directly. My dad would have been proud.

On Christmas eve, the hanging man feels close. I tell Sam, and then we drag our mattresses out and place them under the tree, like two kids at a sleepover.

The morning disappears in a flurry of cooking. Trav and Clare arrive early, surrounded by several yapping dogs. Trav is ecstatic, because they've had three successful births.

'Clare's a marvel, Jane. Thanks for sending her.'

I wince. 'Well ... I didn't send her so much as drive her away with my crazy...'

Clare smiles, but she doesn't meet my eye and her voice remains distant. 'I do get it. I'm still adjusting to my antidepressants.' Antidepressants! That explains her fatigue, and Judith's insistence that Clare *was* managing her health.

'I guess we're going to all have to make a lot of allowances for each other,' I say, and this time Clare does look me in the eye when she smiles.

Everyone else arrives in a rush, filling the house with the comfortable chaos of fresh food and chatter.

As soon as every dish is placed, and we're all seated at the table, I stand. Sam sees what I'm doing and *tinks* a fork against his glass to get everyone's attention. Forty-eight eyes immediately shift towards me, and I feel my face go red. I don't mind spouting off on the radio, but addressing a group directly like this is different.

I clear my throat. 'This was always going to be a pretty shit Christmas. All of our friends and family are dead and the world as we know it is gone. I wanted to throw the kind of Christmas feast that you all deserved—the kind of Christmas that my Mum and Dad always made for me.' My voice cracks a little.

'But as you all know, I failed spectacularly. We can't expect our small group to take on every role in society.

We can't all be prawn fisherman *and* chicken farmers *and* air conditioner repairwomen. We have to accept that we'll just have to do less with less.

'Anyway, this Christmas I've decided to lean into the shit-ness of it all. That's why contributions reflect the kind of Christmas that this year deserves. So please, do try the prawns. They are fresh from a tin, and we've fried them into a kind of mush. It has a strong fish taste that I think you will find distinctive. Ruby, I thought about trapping a bin chicken, but in the end, decided against it. So I mixed some canned chicken with gravy in the hope that it might fill your roast chicken cravings.'

I raise my glass into the air. 'Merry Shitmas everyone! And a crappy New Year!'

I sit down, then realise I've forgotten something important, and stand back up.

'Seriously, though, the pavlova might be made from chickpea juice, but it is legit. We made five, so … yeah. Go nuts on the pav.'

※

'I must ask,' says Judith, as she tucks into her lunch. 'Why *have* you been so obsessed with Christmas?'

'It was just me being paranoid. What with Christmas having the highest rates of suicide and all…'

'Actually,' says Judith, 'that's a common misconception. There is actually a significant drop in the suicide rate over Christmas.'

I almost fall off the chair.

'Yes.' She takes a sip of Shiraz, obviously enjoying my reaction. 'The holidays might be more stressful, but people also feel more connected at Christmas. And social connection is a protective factor.'

I look around. Clare is sitting with one of Trav's dogs on her lap. Ruby is waving a Christmas cracker at her; it is unclear whether she is planning to offer it or use it as a weapon (Clare doesn't look too sure either). On the other side of the table Sam is talking animatedly at poor Trav, who has just taken a large mouthful of prawn and is now trying to unobtrusively spit it out into his napkin—he grins sheepishly at me when I catch him at it. Further down the table survivors are talking, laughing, and even weeping together.

Judith nods towards Clare. 'You were right to try so hard to bring her further into the group.'

'Even if I went the wrong way about it?'

'Was it wrong, if it achieved the right outcome?'

Interesting that we both took away a completely different lesson from the same experience. And since this is Judith, who has a well-documented obsession with IVF, when I say interesting, I mean terrifying.

Trav's already gotten stuck into the beer, so I keep my promise and leave the party early to do the afternoon milking. Sam, ever the gentleman, asks if I would like company—under the proviso that I drive. I happily accept. Ten minutes into the trip Sam connects his phone to the car USB, and my happiness turns to alarm.

'Ummm ... what's this?' Sam should know by now that *I'm* in charge of the music.

'Oh, that's right, you don't know yet.' Sam's grin has a touch of the devil in it. 'It's your Christmas present to me. A three-hour car ride, where I get to choose the songs.'

I gaze at him for a second longer than a driver really should. 'I do love you,' I say, without thinking.

Sam, who had been looking through his playlist, looks up quizzically. 'What was that?'

'Christmas.' I correct myself quickly. 'I was saying how much I love Christmas.'

He smiles, and my heart does a little flip flop. 'I love Christmas, too.'

Then he presses play and Wham's *Last Christmas* assaults my ears. I shriek, and move to cover them with my hands, but I can't, because I'm driving.

Suddenly I love Christmas a little less.

# TEXTBOOKS IN THE ATTIC
S.B. DIVYA

The first flood of the season arrived last week. It takes a while for the waters to rise, but the ground floor is mostly submerged already. I warned Rishi not to play near the water, but he is five years old and, much like his father, insists on learning by experience.

When I hear him shriek, I know from the tone that he's gotten hurt. Jin and I exchange a glance across the kitchen. I put down the carrot I'm peeling and head toward the sound.

Rishi sits at the top of the staircase, tears spilling down his round cheeks, his left palm a bloodied mess.

'Jin,' I call, trying to keep my voice steady. 'Some help, please.'

I lift my sobbing and sopping wet boy and carry him to the bathroom. Jin arrives and, without a word, he grabs a washcloth and presses it into the wound. Rishi clutches me with his other hand.

'Shh, it's just a cut,' I say.

As Jin blots the blood away, I can see that it's deep. I hug Rishi's body tight as Jin douses a clean cloth with alcohol. We ran out of ointment two months back, when Rishi took a nasty spill off his bike. Though I'm expecting the howl of pain, it still makes me wince. I hold the wriggling little body tighter, always surprised at his strength as he tries to squirm away.

Jin is efficient and has the cut wrapped and tied in less than a minute. He follows us to the kitchen where I fish out a peppermint from the good-behaviour jar. Rishi gasps for air as he sucks on it, and my shoulders relax.

If it weren't flood season, I'd take him to the hospital to get stitches, but transporting him in the rain carries as much risk as a wound. He's young, I think. He should heal fast.

---

The next two sunrises bring barely more light than the nights that precede them. I always kiss my sleeping child after I get up. This morning, his forehead feels warm under my lips, more than usual. I sniff at his wounded hand and almost gag. Angry red streaks radiate away from the bandage.

Jin stirs as I pull on my raincoat.

'Where are you going?' he murmurs.

'Rishi's cut is infected,' I say softly. 'I'm going Uphill to see if I can get some antibiotics before I go to work.'

I step onto the balcony and uncover our small boat. We removed the railing when the rain started, turning it into a dock for the wet season. I push off into the turbulent water flowing through the street and start the motor. The boat putters upstream. Four houses down, the Millers are on the roof in slickers, checking their garden. They wave as I pass by, and I slow down enough to ask if they have any antibiotics, but they shake their heads, No.

'Good luck!' Jeanie Miller calls after me, her brow furrowed in concern.

Their youngest died last year, just six months old, from a nasty case of bronchitis.

Above, tendrils of moisture-laden clouds reach toward me from the sky. Heavy drops pelt my head and shoulders. My fingernail beds are blue from the chill in the air, and I flex my hands to keep the blood going. The water around me runs muddy brown, the opacity increasing as I approach Uphill. I navigate by memory. The neighbourhood looks different during the wet season, the buildings like peaceful islands, the destruction of the last few decades hidden away.

We live upstairs all year long now. I barely remember when the first chain-storm happened. I was six, and today all I have are impressions of being wet, cold, and hungry. Of my father in tears. Of sitting at the top of the stairs watching the inexorable rise of water.

I round a corner. The street rises from its submerged state like a concrete scar. Uphill begins a hundred yards from the water, walled off from the rest of us. Beyond the locked gates stand two-storey shops, and further up, stately brick houses with verdant lawns. The neighbourhood looks much like the memories from my childhood, but a little worn at the edges.

I cut the motor and paddle the last few boat lengths to the dock house, an old church with columns repurposed for tying up boats. I slosh through the calf-deep water then up, to the guardhouse.

Jack is on duty, his greying head bent over a piece of wood as he whittles. I rap on the window. He squints at me through the rain-blurred glass, then deigns to crack it an inch.

'Everything's closed,' he growls.

'I need some antibiotics for my son. Can you radio to the hospital?'

He slides the window shut, then picks up the walkie-talkie. I can't hear what he says, but he's shaking his head in the negative as he cracks it open again.

'Supply flight didn't make it last week, what with the early storm. Emma says the Downhill allotments have run out, plus there's a flu going round at school. They're saving up for the pneumonia and such that comes with it.'

I open my mouth to protest and then close it. What good would it do? I have nothing special to offer in trade, nothing they'd want. The Uphill areas weathered the early storms better so they quickly became prime real estate, and after the initial riots, they turned into secured enclaves. They have the only airstrip, and it might be weeks before a flight can land.

Jack's expression softens by a hair's breadth. 'It's nothing personal, okay? Your dad was a good man, but we gotta look after our own first.'

I manage a curt nod before walking away. Back in the boat, I don't bother with the motor. I grab the oars and secure the strap of my adapted oar above my left elbow. I wasn't much older than Rishi when they took most of my left hand off. I'd mangled it in the propeller of our old boat, but my father was a doctor at the Uphill hospital, and they treated me well.

'The greatest threat to our lives is once again bacteria,' he said more than once. 'Wash every cut or puncture, no matter how small. Keep it clean and dry until it heals. With so much moisture, who knows what new germs we'll have to fight.'

That was before the supply shortages gave his words greater truth. At one point, he and my mother considered returning to India, but every part of the world faced climatological problems. They stayed here in Iowa with the hope of giving me a better chance at an education, going so far as to send me to California for college.

That's where I met Jin, and also where I discovered a new program in distributed horticulture, part of a push from the US government to move away from mass agriculture. It boiled down to, 'Don't put all your eggs in one basket,' or in this case, all your seeds in one field. California kept getting incinerated and learned its lesson early.

As one of the program's first students, I got a full-ride scholarship. I chose to return home and settle outside of our gated enclave. The people Downhill needed my help more, but my father's former colleagues didn't appreciate my 'defection.' This isn't the first time I wonder if I made a mistake.

At home, Rishi sits at the kitchen table and munches on bread with jam. Jin hands me a slice with cheese and fresh tomato slices from our roof garden. My stomach growls in anticipation.

'May outdid herself with this loaf,' I say, savouring the crunch of grain as I lick tomato seeds from my wrist.

'She had a shipment of whole wheat last week from her cousin, harvested just before the rains started,' Jin says. 'Bread won't be this good again for months. Where are the antibiotics? Rishi should have one with breakfast.'

'They didn't have any,' I say.

'At all?' Jin's dark eyes widen in alarm.

'For us.'

He locks eyes with me. I can see the anger build.

'I'll go after lunch and have a *word*,' he says.

Rishi picks up on the tension in his father's voice and looks up from the table. He has Jin's eyes and my unruly hair, which frames his face in thick, dark curls. I've nearly given up on trying to comb out the tangles.

'What word?' our boy asks innocently. Dark brown stains the bandage around his palm.

'A bad one. Very, very bad,' Jin says.

I swallow the last bite of my toast. 'Give me some time to ask around first.'

He glances at Rishi and presses his lips together. A nod, a shrug, and he moves back to the dishes.

Jin had a hard time adjusting to the Midwest when he moved here with me. He's happy now in our community, which welcomed him as a new neighbour, but he's never made peace with how we're treated by Uphill. San Diego has its fair share of problems, but they aren't the same as ours.

As I shower and get dressed for work, I savour the lingering taste of May's bread in my teeth. My dad lectured me on the importance of antibiotics from an early age, telling me about Alexander Fleming's famous experiment gone awry and his accidental discovery of penicillin on mouldy bread. My work involves stopping the spread of mould in rooftop gardens, but perhaps I can flip the script.

I climb the ladder into the attic and find the box of textbooks from my dad's time in medical school. *Microbiology. Biochemistry. Organic Chemistry.* I grab them all and stuff them in my dry bag along with another slice of bread from the kitchen.

I kiss the top of Rishi's head on my way out. 'Be good and keep your hand clean and dry. Stay out of the water!'

He waves at me nonchalantly as I leave for the lab. Jin does most of the work of raising our child and maintaining the house. Someone has to, and he's better at carpentry and a more patient teacher than I am. Outside, the street water swirls with oil slicks and debris as our world washes itself clean.

---

Paul, my labmate, peers over my shoulder. 'What are you reading?'

'I'm trying to figure out how to make penicillin,' I say.

'What on Earth for?'

'Rishi cut his hand playing a few days ago. I want to make an antibiotic. Any ideas?'

'Um ... something about mouldy bread?'

'Yes, the blue-green mould in particular, but you have to extract and purify the antibiotic part.'

'Couldn't you get any Uphill?'

I shake my head. 'Their supply is low.'

Paul picks up the radio. 'You're going to need more than textbooks to figure this out. Let me see if the internet is up and running at the comm-house.'

# TEXTBOOKS IN THE ATTIC

While he does that, I tear myself away from the books and check on my other fungal work. A particularly nasty strain of leaf mould hit the region during last year's flood season, and we lost half of our legume crops. We can't afford that for a second year or we'll run low on essential proteins.

'You're in luck,' Paul says.

I look up from the microscope. 'Oh?'

'They're running about five megabits right now. Go!'

'Thanks, Paul!'

I take the elevated walkways that connect the buildings of what used to be a university campus. The older stone structures have held up better than the later wood or concrete ones. The mechanical engineering department built the drawbridges that we use every wet season out of reclaimed steel. Their surfaces clatter under my steps as I run to the comm-house. It used to be the alumni house, but it has the best line-of-sight to the communication satellites that provide internet so, like most other buildings, it's been repurposed. The parking structure beside it is now the town's transportation hub, and its roof our primary source of solar panels.

The rain thins as I approach the house, and I race up the steps without opening my umbrella. A break in the clouds allows a beam of sunlight through, enveloping the five meter dish atop the house in brilliance. I take it as a sign of hope.

'Hi, Menaka,' greets Jonette, shoving the sign-in clipboard at me. 'Paul radioed that you're coming and why. Doctor Branson gave up fifteen minutes for you. Work fast!'

'Thanks,' I say, breathless.

The history professor nods at me from the waiting area. As a faculty member, he's allowed priority over nonprofit community projects like my horticulture lab. The university campus has diminished, like everything else, but they do their best to maintain academic standards. I give him a grateful smile as I slide into the empty workstation chair. A stack of notepads and pencils sits next to the keyboard. Bamboo loves the new climate and it makes good paper, too.

I do a quick search for how to make penicillin and come up with plenty of archived information as well as more recent instructions. *There's no such thing as an original idea.* The same sites warn me that pencillin isn't effective against all bacterial strains. I dig deeper and learn that the reduced supply of antibiotics worked in our favor. In an ironic twist, the drug-resistant germs from the turn of the century had been replaced by newer, more vulnerable strains. Penicillin might actually work against whatever Rishi contracted.

I write down the ingredients needed for the nutrient solution, the best way to filter the drug, and methods to test the results. Then I review the risks. The two biggest are impurities in the solution and failing to isolate penicillin. Another type of mould, Aspergillus, has a similar appearance and colour, but under a microscope, they look different. My biggest problem, however, is time. It typically takes a week to grow a decent-sized batch of penicillin, enough for one person with a minor infection. If their blood is septic, forget it.

By the time I get all of that written down, my time is up. The rain must have resumed because the bandwidth drops. I apologise to Doctor Branson on my way out.

'No need,' he says. 'History has no sense of urgency. I hope you found what you were looking for.'

'Yes, thank you.'

The tornado sirens start to wail halfway through my return. I get to the building that houses my lab and head to the shelter room, a windowless space in the centre of the building. Paul is crammed in there with another dozen people. I squeeze my way to him with apologies to the rest.

'Good news and bad news,' I say.

He cocks an eyebrow.

'I can make the penicillin,' I whisper, 'possibly even a safe version, but it'll take more than a week.'

'That's a problem?'

I lift my shoulders in a tiny shrug. 'Rishi's cut is already infected. He might recover without intervention, but he was in the floodwaters.'

Paul frowns. 'If it gets bad enough, the Uphill hospital will have to admit him.'

We both glance at my left hand. I know what he's thinking: that unless it's a life-threatening emergency, they won't take Rishi. *By then he could have sepsis*, I think. *That might be too late, especially if they already have a supply shortage.*

※

After the all-clear sounds, we return to the lab. I place a small piece of May's bread, moistened, in a sealed bag and then head home for lunch. Rishi is napping when I arrive, his cheek warm under my lips.

'Well? What did you find?' Jin demands as soon as I'm away from the bedroom.

'No one nearby has antibiotics, but I found a recipe to make penicillin. We have the equipment and I think I can find the ingredients to extract it from mould, but...' I trail off.

'But what?'

'It'll be a week before it's ready, and it might not work against the bacteria in our water,' I say reluctantly.

Jin's face resembles the thunderclouds outside. 'That's too long. Remember the Arken girl?'

'Lily,' I reply.

Eight years old. Her family didn't recognise the signs of infection until it was too late. I recall her mother sobbing at the funeral, 'It was just a scratch. A scratch!'

Jin walks away without another word, heading for the attic. I follow him. I need to find a medical textbook this time, one that lists the signs of sepsis. I find what

I need and turn to see Jin slipping a gun into his jacket pocket.

'What are you doing?' I ask, trying to keep my voice steady.

'What someone needs to do. I'm going to round up the militia and take them with me. We're not going to let another child—my child—die because Uphill refuses to help us!'

'And what about the next person? And the one after that? How many of you will die along the way from injuries? Do you remember what war used to be like?'

'This isn't the eighteenth century,' Jin says. He stabs a finger in the general direction of Uphill. 'They have everything we need, and if they won't share willingly, then we'll take it by force.'

'Even if that works this time, what happens in a month or next year? They're low on supply because the storm delayed the latest drop. We're fighting for scraps from them. How much longer can we go on like this? We need to take charge of our own destiny. We've already done it in a hundred ways—we grow most of our own food, we repair our houses, we teach our children, we make our own electricity. Now we'll treat our own illnesses.'

I head for the ladder.

'Where are you going?' he calls after me. His tone indicates he isn't done arguing.

'Back to work,' I say. 'Your armed incursion can wait.'

I drop down from the attic before he can form a retort. Maybe I'm overreacting, but I'm too angry to care. *Reckless. Stupid. Selfish.* My mind flashes through all the ways Jin could get injured or killed trying to force his way into Uphill. They have guns, too, and they won't hesitate to use them. The law is on their side.

---

Paul spins on the lab stool like a child. 'We need to create a shadow hospital.'

'What?'

'A hospital of our own, independent from the one Uphill.'

'And how do we get the nurses and doctors to work there? Uphill has them all because they can pay. We can't.'

Paul shrugs. 'We trade, like we do for everything else. Money is a social construct built on value, right? If we provide what they need—food, water, shelter, utilities—then they don't need "money".' He puts air-quotes around the last word.

As he speaks, I start sterilising a flask. I want to start a second mould culture using a rotting cantaloupe I got from the Ayala's hothouse. According to my notes, the mould on its rind should include Penicillium chrysogenum, a more potent form than the one on bread.

'It's a good idea,' I say, 'if we can make it work.'

'We can,' he says firmly. 'After emancipation, we had Black hospitals run by Black doctors and nurses. If my people could do it back then, no reason Downhill can't do something similar today.'

I nod, trying to be supportive. Paul turns back to his work, and I start looking at the ingredients for the nutrient broth. Cornstarch and Epsom salts are easy enough. I grab a handbook of common chemical compounds to look up the rest. Lactose monohydrate comes from milk sugars. Crystalline glucose—more sugar to feed the mould. I have a bag of sodium nitrate for when we need extra nitrogen in our soil. Potassium dihydrogen phosphate brings down the pH—I'll probably need to visit the chemistry lab for that. Magnesium and zinc or ferrous sulphates—more items from the chem lab—or a combination of the metals with sulphuric acid, which might be easier to get my hands on. Hydrochloric acid to fine-tune the pH. And after a week of growth, acetic acid—the primary component of vinegar—for the purification process.

I can work with this list. Even if I can't get the exact chemicals, I can substitute. I've grown enough fungi to know that the basics of nutrient broths are the same: sugars for energy, acids for pH. The details have to do with optimisation, but I'm not going for industrial production. The hard part will be waiting for the mould to grow.

By the work day's end, I've cultured my broth with cantaloupe mould and set it in the incubator. Low-voltage lights glow from wet rooftops as I row home. Street lights became impractical along with pavement. Exposed wiring could fall into the flood-season riverways, and anything buried underground needed repair too often. Thanks to the leftover solar panels from the boom years, we could light our own way.

I try to drink in the beauty as stars twinkle from the breaks in the cloud cover. Wind blows over my exposed skin, carrying scents of wet wood and mouldy leaves. A lone, brave bird calls from a nearby roof garden. Ripples shatter the street lights into a thousand tiny fragments all around me.

I try to focus on my surroundings and avoid thinking about the confrontation waiting at home. Or the state of Rishi's wound. Or whether penicillin will be an effective antibiotic. Or any of the other problems that I can't solve. Starting the Penicillium culture left me feeling powerful, the same way I felt after the first year that our neighbourhood grew its own crops. The militia started in those early days, to protect the gardens from opportunistic thieves, especially in the dry season.

I step onto our balcony and haul the boat up after me. Warm air blows from the electric room heater inside. Rishi lies on the sofa, eyes bright—fever bright?—and watches a show on his tablet. I avoid Jin's gaze as I hang up my wet clothes to dry.

'Hi Mommy,' Rishi says as I stoop to kiss him.

'Hello, love,' I say. His skin feels less hot. 'Let me see your hand.'

He shakes his head and grimaces as he tries to hide it from me.

'He hasn't let me clean it all day,' Jin says quietly from behind me. 'Temperature was at one hundred when I last checked.'

I dread what's coming, but it's unavoidable. Dealing with a kicking, howling five-year-old is a two-adult process. Jin holds him while I get a good look at the wound. I try to remember what I read in the medical textbook. The swelling and redness have increased. The smell is worse, and the pus might be greenish—I can't tell for sure in the dim light. Rishi's screams are heart-wrenching as I pour diluted alcohol over the wound.

After it's all over, we give him two pieces of hard candy and ourselves a glass of whiskey each. At least children have the luxury of forgetting. I hardly remember my amputation anymore. My parents probably had a worse time of it.

Once Rishi is asleep, we finally have time to talk.

'I think it's going to work,' I begin. 'My penicillin extraction. A few more days, and it'll be ready. I don't have to wait for the full growth to complete.'

'I radioed Loqueisha earlier. She agrees with me.'

Loqueisha started the militia and became its de facto leader as a result. She has a sensible nature, and I usually trust her judgment.

'What did you tell her about our situation?' I ask.

'The truth. This goes beyond the three of us or your lab experiment. This is about Uphill monopolising health care and not taking our problems seriously enough.'

'So you're going to confront them no matter what?'

'Yes. Tonight. I was just waiting for you to get home.'

'Give me a few more days, please.' I reach for his hand, and he pulls me into a hug. The hard lump of a gun in his pocket presses against me.

'I won't risk Rishi's life,' he whispers into my ear. 'You keep doing what you're doing. It's important no matter what happens tonight. I love you both.'

And with that, he's out the door.

'Goddammit,' I mutter.

I remember the images of gunshot wounds from my father's textbooks. I sit at the kitchen table and vow not to sleep until Jin comes home.

My head jerks up from the table. My heart thuds. A flash of lightning blinds me, and seconds later, thunder rumbles overhead.

'Mommy?'

I hear Rishi calling from the bedroom and glance at the clock. Four in the morning and no sign of Jin.

I pad over to the bedroom and squeeze in next to my boy.

'Where were you? Where's Dad?'

'Hush,' I say, pulling him closer. 'It's okay. Go back to sleep.'

He whimpers and snuggles into me as thunder cracks directly above. I listen for the sirens, but they remain silent. Heat radiates from his little body. I don't need a thermometer to know that he's feverish. It must be disturbing his sleep because storms don't usually wake him.

As the front passes, the steady sound of rain begins, and Rishi relaxes into my arms. He sleeps. I worry. Where are Jin and the rest of the militia? If they'd succeeded, he'd be home by now.

My thoughts go around and around until dawn fades in. I lie still as long as I can, not wanting to disturb Rishi's slumber. At some point, I must doze off because the doorbell startles me awake.

I ease myself from the bed without waking my boy. I open the door to a familiar face, round and lined with soggy grey curls framing it. It takes my sleep-addled brain a few seconds to remember the name.

'Doctor Mitchell?'

She nods and steps inside. 'How are you, Menaka?'

'Worried,' I say before I can stop myself. What a ridiculous thing to confess to the surgeon who treated my injured hand decades ago. 'Not to be rude, but what brings you here?'

She reaches into an interior pocket of her raincoat and pulls out a small bottle. 'I heard you were in need.'

Before I look at the label, I know what must be inside. 'Thank you.'

Anger deepens the furrows around her eyes. 'We learned about the demand from your husband and the others over the network last night. Some of my idiot colleagues thought they shouldn't be rewarded for coming at us, but we took an oath when we became doctors, and I for one intend to uphold that. Stockpiling life-saving drugs for the eventuality of greater need? What phenomenally arrogant bullshit!' She examines me from head to toe with a professional eye, then nods in satisfaction. 'I'm glad you're well at least. They have your militia people in our little jail. I'm sorry. I don't know how long they'll be held or what the charges are.'

I curse Jin's folly in my thoughts and try to keep my expression neutral.

I must have failed because Doctor Mitchell says, 'Don't be too angry with him. If he hadn't acted last night, I wouldn't be here.'

I blow out the breath I'd started to hold, then say, 'Is there anything I can give you in return?'

'Of course not,' she says. She opens the door.

# TEXTBOOKS IN THE ATTIC 119

'Wait,' I say. 'I'm working on something—on making penicillin. I heard the hospital is short, and I thought it might be better than nothing. If it works, I'll bring you some.'

Her grey brows rise in surprise. 'Good for you! Take a culture from your child's wound and test that it's effective. With all the turn-of-the-century overuse, you can't be sure what's growing in the floodwaters these days.'

'Thank you,' I say again, at a loss for words in the face of her kindness.

With that, she's out the door and motoring back upstream.

❦

Later that day, after dosing Rishi and settling him in the capable hands of May and her baking, I check on my lab culture. The liquid has turned murky brown. No sign of the layer of green-grey-blue mould that should have formed on the surface.

I growl at it in frustration.

Paul turns from his bench. 'Problem?'

'Yes, but I'm not sure what.'

He shrugs. 'You don't need it anyway.'

'Yes I do!' I snap. Then, taking a breath, 'Sorry. I know Rishi will be fine—this time—but I was hoping to start another small industry. We're going to need essential drugs, and the supply drops are less reliable each year.'

He holds up a placating hand. 'Okay, chill. You have more of everything, right? Even that half-rotten cantaloupe. I know 'cause I smelled it when I opened the fridge. Be a good scientist and start over.'

'Fine. Yes, you're right. I've only lost a day.'

'What's the rush?'

I wave my hands vaguely at the outside. 'Whoever next gets sick or injured and doesn't have a friend Uphill.'

'I'll say it again: we need a shadow hospital. Then someone with better lab hygiene could do this instead of you.' He grinned.

'Thanks, buddy,' I say drily. 'Your confidence is inspiring.' Then, more seriously, 'It's a good idea. You should bring it up at the next community council meeting.'

Paul taps his temple with his index finger and turns back to his work. I dump the flask into the organic waste and begin again, this time wearing a mask in addition to gloves and working under an improvised tent of plastic sheeting. With the overseas trade routes disrupted by storms, any kind of plastic is precious, but so are the nutrient broth chemicals. The only thing we have in abundance is rainwater.

A week later, the new Penicillium culture reaches the disgustingly black stage that means it's almost ready for decanting. I'm bumping around our small kitchen, riding high on my lab success and trying to find the ingredients I need for a casserole. Rishi sits at the kitchen table, swinging his legs and constructing something with bamboo sticks and glue. His cut isn't fully healed, but the wound has closed, and the swelling and fever are gone. I have to bribe him with apple juice to get the antibiotics down, but it's a trivial cost. Our attic is well-stocked with cider from last Fall's harvest.

'Is Daddy coming home tonight?' Rishi asks.

The question has become part of our nightly ritual. So has my answer: 'No, but maybe tomorrow.'

We've heard that Uphill is going to charge Jin and the others with aggravated assault. I'm fairly certain the charge is bullshit, but that doesn't mean I get my husband back any time soon. The community lawyer lives two streets over and will do his best to defend the group. At least I won't have to worry about legal fees.

A boat clatters against the balcony, the sound followed shortly by a sharp rap at the door. I open it to find Doctor Mitchell at our doorstep. I don't like the look on her face.

She comes in and, upon seeing Rishi, puts a smile on. 'How are you, little one? Looking well, I think.'

'I made a boat,' Rishi beams, holding up a bundle of sticks and glue.

'That's wonderful,' the doctor says, sounding genuine. 'I need to borrow your mom for a few minutes. Is that okay?'

My son nods. In the next room, Doctor Mitchell leans close to me. Her raincoat drips on my arm.

'Jin tried to stop a fight at the jail,' she says in a low voice. 'He's been stabbed.'

I try to process this as everything fades but her voice.

'It didn't hit anything vital. He's out of surgery and stable, but we're still waiting on our supply drop,' she says. 'We're out of antibiotics. A bout of bronchitis swept through our middle school last week, and we dispensed the last of it two days ago. The city council is debating whether to pay for an expedited shipment, but even if they do, I'm not sure how incentivised they'll be to help a potential Downhill criminal.'

'He's not—'

'I know,' she says, her voice gentle. 'But that's how they'll frame it. Your penicillin—is it ready?'

'The culture's growth is good,' I say. 'I haven't decanted or purified it yet. Or tested it.'

'How long will that take?'

'I don't know. I've never done this before. Hours, maybe?'

My heart starts racing at the thought. I have to do it carefully, without contamination or waste. I know the quantity won't be much, not compared to a pharmaceutical grade, but it has to be better than nothing.

'Can you wait here while I make the extract?' I ask.

'I'll do one better—I'll come and help you.'

I stuff a sleeping bag and pillow into a dry bag, then bundle Rishi into his rain clothes. Thankfully, he's excited about the night-time journey and the prospect of staying up late. We take Doctor Mitchell's boat, which is better than ours. I direct her to Paul's house.

He takes one look at my face and asks, 'What's going on?'

'I need your help in the lab.'

I can see him put the equation together: Lab plus emergency equals penicillin.

'Gary, I gotta run out for a bit,' he calls to his husband. 'Don't wait up!'

***

It takes us four hours to correctly decant and purify the penicillin from the growth medium. Rishi is fast asleep under a desk, and Doctor Mitchell dozes in the chair we have for visitors.

With a trembling hand, I place a few drops of the antibiotic on a petri dish. Next to me, Paul takes a sterile swab and collects some bacteria from the test culture. After he inoculates my dish, I close the lid and set a two hour timer. We roll up our lab coats and use them as pillows on the floor.

The buzzer wakes me from a deep sleep. A dream about deadly amoebas fades as I remember where I am and why. Paul snores nearby, and Doctor Mitchell has moved to the floor as well.

I tiptoe to the lab bench and prepare two slides, one from the healthy bacteria and another from our penicillin test. It takes me extra time to get the microscope's focus right with my sleep-blurred eyes, but once I do, I can see the broken cell walls.

'It works,' I whisper.

Tears well and take me by surprise. I bite my knuckle to keep from sobbing and waking everyone. I hadn't admitted to myself how scared I was that all of this would fail. That Jin wouldn't make it ... he still might not, but at least now we'd have a fighting chance.

After I compose myself, I gently shake Doctor Mitchell's shoulder. As her eyes focus on my face rather than her dreams, her mouth widens in a smile.

'You did it,' she whispers.

As she rouses from her seat, Paul wakes. He gets the doctor the vial with all of our precious penicillin extract. I scoop Rishi off the floor and heft him, still asleep, onto my shoulder. Pre-dawn lightens the eastern skies, heavy with clouds, and a gentle breeze ruffles my hair.

Doctor Mitchell leaves us at home with a promise to get word on Jin's status in a couple of days. 'I won't give you false assurances,' she says, 'But this is far better than nothing.'

---

I examine the new hundred gallon tank installed in the corner of what used to be a classroom in the humanities department. Doctor Branson was generous with more than his internet time. 'Making history is at least as important as studying it,' he said. 'I'll teach from the town square or my own home if I have to.'

We've taken the first step to larger production, and I have a plan for making other antibiotics once we're successful. At the other end of the room, behind a partition, Paul hunches over the extraction and purification equipment. He wears a sterile jumpsuit, face mask, and gloves, and his brow furrows in concentration.

I slip a glass container filled with crystalline penicillin into my pocket and head downstairs. The week before, I'd mailed a sample to a pharmaceutical plant in Oregon for testing, and the result had just come in: a solid yes.

On the floor below, a series of offices is now filled with cots. Two of them have patients, and I find Jin and Doctor Mitchell in one of them. Jin meets me in the hallway. He walks with a limp from a tendon that got cut during the fight. The stab wound in his side had been the greater danger, but the assailant had nicked his leg as well.

'Is that the good stuff?' he says, taking the bottle from me with a smile.

'Certified Grade A Penicillin,' I reply. 'I'm off to pick Rishi up from school.'

'See you tonight.' Jin kisses me and heads back to work as Doctor Mitchell's assistant.

I row my way to the Millers' house, which doubles as our newly minted elementary school. Rain dribbles down my hood. I'll need to oil the cloth again soon to keep it waterproofed.

Ahead of me, a handful of solar panels glisten on top of our community hospital. Each one comes from someone's home. We'll have to live with fewer lights at night, but that's a small sacrifice to take charge of our own health.

I pull the boat against the Millers' balcony. Rishi steps in, a wide grin on his face, and hugs me before sitting down, making the boat rock. He laughs at my alarmed expression, then pats the water like an old friend as I row us home.

# IF THIS WAS THE TALON
## TJ BERRY

I no longer like the smell of cooking meat. The alien bodies smell like steak when they burn. Along with a hint of nail polish remover. We don't eat steak anymore. Not just because of the alien smell, but because cows are extinct.

They're not really extinct, but I crossed them off my list anyway. Someone from Minnesota made it all the way out here and said there are no more cows, buffalo, horses, elk, deer, or moose in the western half of the country. They weren't sure about the eastern side.

The cows might not be completely gone, but I also leave them crossed off because it feels good to check something off a list, even if it's a bad something.

There aren't many things to check off these days. All the tasks are recurring. You pull a weed and in two days there will be another one. You hunt a rabbit and, in a few hours, you will need to find another three. You lose your parents and five more show up to take their place.

You can't check things off because they never end. They just keep going. Not like television programs or novels, which always end. There are no more shows to binge. No more movies to see. No more books to read.

That last part is not true because there are books, but they're more valuable for heat than for reading. I tried to sneak one off the burn pile and I got a talking to that lasted one thousand and fifty-nine seconds. That's a lot of time to be looked at. It felt like the heat of the sun aimed at my face. I had to squint against the glare.

For a long time at the start, no one noticed that I'm pretending to be human. We were all so consumed with trying to stay alive that no one heard the noises I made when bad thoughts came into my head. Or the numbers I said out loud when I made a mistake. I don't mind the noises or the numbers. They keep more bad things from happening. It's the other people who mind.

My little voice blended in with the sounds of clearing rubble and finding survivors. But when that task metamorphosed into collecting bodies and burying friends, people became quiet and then they heard.

I think grief is probably a feeling like when you drink too much coffee and you feel sick with it, and you have to wait for it to wear off. I'm waiting for that feeling to come. I'll know when it gets here because I'll cry like everyone else.

My job is building ramps. I like this task because every nail takes the same number of hits. One to bite into the wood and six more to sink it all the way in. I could do each one in six, but seven is a better number.

All of our new buildings need ramps. I'm in charge of that. The aliens crawled around at the height of our thighs, eating everything made of meat. An alien bite—even a graze—was the catalyst for a fast-moving necrosis that spread three inches in every direction, leaving a gaping hole where the flesh used to be. Their iridescent lonsdaleite talons glowed amber in the moonlight in front of our car. There were four of them and only one of her.

I keep a talon in my pocket. I wish I could say it came from the alien that killed my parents, because that would make it meaningful, but if anyone ever discovers I have it, I'll tell them I found it outside of camp and it means nothing to me.

If this was the talon that killed my parents, its translucent surface would have a gouge in it where my mother's diamond ring scratched down the side as she raised her hands in self-defence. Deep in my coat pocket, where no one could see, I would worry my fingernail along that line, remembering how her breath cut off mid-scream when the talon punctured her lungs and she hissed out air like a deflating balloon.

It's good there are no balloons anymore.

There are birthdays, though. My birthday was three weeks ago. I didn't tell anyone. When it's your birthday, the whole camp gathers around you and sings. I don't want that much glare on me. I'd rather never have a birthday again.

Everyone smiles during the song—even the people who sing badly. I can't tell if they don't know they're singing badly or if they just don't care. Either way, it makes me want to hide whenever people start to gather.

I stand in the back and pretend to sing. It's the easiest way to trick people into believing you're a human. Just mouth the words.

When we moved from nylon tents into long sheds made of wood, we graduated semantically from a camp to a settlement. It's kind of a big deal. You're warmer. Safer at night. Other settlements want to trade with you. I help with that. Making ramps. And I'm learning how to build other items that we can swap for useful things.

Sleeping sheds can't be built level with the ground because then the rain gets in when the valley floods. But going up steps is hard when there's a chunk bitten out of your calf. My ramps are strong and safe. I have more ideas for things to build because I'm good at seeing what people need. In exchange for my building, I get a spot in a shed and two meals a day. It's a good thing I don't need much more, because there's not much else to be had.

People in cities might have access to buildings with canned food and libraries, but we're too far away from a town to scavenge resources. It's our fault for going on a family camping trip right before an alien invasion.

When the ships arrived, Mom and Dad stuffed me into our car and drove back toward the city. But we ran out of gas and had to walk back here. Or, at least, I had to walk back here.

The aliens were fast and hungry, but their skins were thin and easily punctured with sharp things. I am also fast and hungry, and my skin is thin and easily punctured.

Mom told me to wait in the car while she went after Dad who said he'd find us some more gas at a nearby ranch. But I didn't have to wait. She'd hardly walked five feet from the front bumper when the aliens surrounded her.

If this was the talon that killed my parents, one of the grooves on the underside would be filled with a crust of dried blood that belonged to my mother as the aliens dug through her body for the choicest cuts of meat. I would run my thumb across the groove until two or three flecks of dried blood stuck to it like little russet freckles.

I'm not supposed to be carrying around the talon. The scent of it will draw the few remaining aliens toward the settlement. At least that's what everyone says. I don't think that's true. I've had this talon with me for months and months and no alien has visited us in all that time.

The things that people need most in the settlement are ways to get around. I don't mean cars. There are lots of those sitting around with empty tanks. I mean crutches, and legs made of wood, and wheelchairs—except that I made someone a leg made of wood and he said it pinched, so I don't yet know how to do it right.

I think he was mad, because he made a lot of sighing sounds. Remembering those sounds makes me not want to try making a leg again. But we don't need that many ramps anymore. Every building in our settlement has one—plus the settlements to the north and east. So I have to come up with something useful to make and trade if I want to keep my spot in the shed. Otherwise I have to move back to a tent. It's not a fair system, and I want to say so, but to complain you have to stand up in front of the whole group and say a speech for people to vote on. I don't want to do that part, so I'll figure out something useful to make. Or I'll become a radish farmer.

We grow a lot of radishes here. They grow fast. We had our first crop in less than a month. Not like those settlements who started with potatoes. They took over a hundred days. We helped as much as we could, but a lot of them died. I made coffins instead of ramps for a while.

There's talk of saving up a lot of radishes and heading east to see how that side of the country made out. Maybe everything's normal out there and they're just not telling us. Maybe they're laughing at us behind our backs.

The aliens ate the cows first. I think that's why they smelled like steak. The ships only dipped into our atmosphere long enough to drop off millions of taloned creatures. We thought it was an invasion. We tried to negotiate with half a billion voracious mouths. By week two, we realised that these creatures had no ability to reason. They were not intelligent spacefarers.

They were livestock and we were eight billion morsels of food.

The real intelligent life was still up in the ships, watching. Our leaders and scientists made a valiant effort to get their attention, but we were not even worth answering. Maybe they were laughing at us behind our backs too.

People in the settlement are starting to notice that I'm not human. It isn't the noises I make or the little rituals I do to keep everyone safe that tipped them off. It was my coat.

All of this started in winter, when having a coat on was sensible and not at all out of place. Even in the spring, there were enough cool and windy days that no one seemed to notice. But when the long days got hot, and we spent hours working under the crackling sun, people started asking questions.

I'll admit, the coat was really hot. And the collar scratched my neck where the inside had worn down. Also, a bit of detached lining hung out of one of the sleeves. I couldn't stop stroking it with my fingers, even though it was so filthy the cream fabric had turned dark grey.

'Aren't you hot?' asked a boy near me in the building area.

'No.'

I had to say a lot of excellent numbers under my breath to make up for that blatant lie. I moved away from that boy so that I wouldn't have to answer him again. There are only so many excellent numbers in the world and you can't use them all up in one day.

I was sweltering. But taking off this coat would be like peeling off my own skin. How could I stand among everyone, skinless and bare, and expect their eyes not to burn me to the ground?

The pocket of this coat is where I keep the talon.

If this was the talon that killed my parents, I would collect those flecks of dried blood on my thumb and then touch my thumb to my tongue until I tasted something metallic that used to be my mother.

I keep the coat on, even when I feel dizzy and sick. The boy brings me extra water when my breaths get fast and loud enough for everyone to hear. He sets the water on the bench next to me and doesn't say anything about it at all, which is the nicest thing anyone has ever done for me in this place.

I think if people found out that I was just pretending to be human, they would hunt me down like they did with the aliens. They can't be sure that I'm not dangerous. So I hide in my coat and pretend to sing along.

My second try at a wooden leg was better and the man didn't sigh at all. The shape wasn't right, but the height was spot on. We didn't have any bandages left, so I told him to stuff the concave end with the dried moss that we used in our beds. Or ask that little girl for the stuffing out of her panda. He should probably just put the whole panda in there, fur and all. He laughed at me, but I was being serious. That fur is soft.

If this was the talon that killed my parents, on bad days, I would press my tongue directly onto the lonsdaleite, where I would taste not only blood, but something exotic that didn't come from Earth, like the burnt tip of a graphite pencil. I would nearly lose my balance from the wonder and awe that rose in my body as I felt the alienness of that body. And then I would feel shame for wishing the aliens would return and let me come away with them this time.

I'm so afraid the others will find out that I'm pretending to be human that I spend all of my non-working hours alone in my bed. People try to coax me out with games of checkers or titbits of extra food, but I'm so afraid to give myself away that I shake my head, even though I'd very much like to play and eat.

When they find out, they'll ask me to leave the settlement. It's too much of a risk, having an alien like me here. Look what the last ones did.

I can't make it to the city on my own. Two adults couldn't even manage it, and they were the smartest people I knew.

I need to have a talk with that boy who brings the water. He should know what he's getting into by associating with me. But I'm not sure how to start regular conversations, let alone approach a confession of this magnitude.

'I have to warn you,' I say, one day in the shop.

His eyes get big and I think I've started off wrong. This is not about aliens or food shortages or extinction level events.

'It's about me,' I clarify.

Now he's looking right at my face for so long that the temperature inside my coat surges.

'I'm not human.'

He nods sombrely. Purses his lips at me in a flat little smile that doesn't glare too brightly.

'I know. We love you just the same.'

If this was the talon that killed my parents, I would bury it far outside of the settlement in a hole I dug out with the back of my hammer—which has exactly the same curve as a lonsdaleite claw. I would cover the talon with dirt. Sprinkles of it at first, then two-handed piles as big as I could hold. I would sit and watch that spot, saying all of the excellent numbers I could think of until the sun got low and the sky went red.

Then I would go back to camp and sit in my dinner spot. And when it was time to sing to someone else, I would stand in the back and mouth the words.

# KIDS THESE DAYS
## TANSY RAYNER ROBERTS

One year after the world ended, a bunch of raggedy teenagers gathered in State Stadium to learn the truth: we had been tricked. Left behind. The Pulse that took out our city's power grid wasn't an accident: it was a parting gift from the scientists who saw us as failed lab rats.

We were all between the ages of twelve and eighteen.

It was a miracle that we survived that year alone on this abandoned colony planet with nothing but the husks of our robot foster mothers, streets and streets of abandoned suburban houses, and what little tech and medicine we could scavenge. It was more than a miracle that, in the years that followed, we kept surviving.

The trick to miracles is, you have to make your own.

The trick to rebuilding the world is, you have to start somewhere and keep going.

See? It's easy to sound wise if you state the obvious in a serious tone of voice.

That's the trick to me. I sound like I know what I'm doing. I set that precedent long ago. Somehow, I forgot to turn it off.

I'm forty years old. It's been twenty-five years since the world ended.

Kids these days ... well, kids these days think I have all the answers. Isn't that the funniest thing you've ever heard?

I'm not a leader.

I'm not a mother.

I'm not the saviour of the world. (That's my brother.)

I dig veggies. I know herbs. I make medicines when I can. I provide contraceptive teas, wound poultices, and a cannabis oil that's the closest we have to a mood stabiliser. I dry seeds so other people can plant crops too.

The kids call me the Witch Doctor, and they look at me like I'm some kind of hero. No matter how often I tell them to leave me the hell alone, they keep coming back.

---

'Aisha? Aisha. Wake up.'

I don't want to wake up. I just had a bad night on top of a week of bad nights. That means today is a Bad Day. I need to stay under the covers until the voice is gone, and I can dope myself back into something resembling sleep...

'Auntie,' she says, hitting below the belt.

My eyes are open now. 'Don't call me that.'

'I made tea.'

Yasmin moves through my house like she belongs here, her long braid flicking behind her from one room to the next. I can hear her in my kitchen, making deliberate noises.

I'm awake. I can do this. I can manage a conversation with a person I've known since she was a squalling baby on a literal garbage heap. That's what people do.

The kitchen is tidier than it was when I crawled into bed last night. I can't think about that, can't think about what state it was in when Yasmin found it. She must have cleaned week-old food off plates before waking me up. Difficult thoughts get stored in a deep cupboard somewhere inside my mind. I close the door on them.

She puts a cup of lemon verbena in front of me with all the confidence of an adult. I suppose she is an adult now. Sixteen, seventeen? I lose track. No one expects you to remember birthdays when you refuse to even let them call you Auntie.

[Key] I sign at her. Sign language is second nature to our family, though she and I are both hearing people. I love sign language for its directness. I once spent nearly a year without talking out loud because the world was too hard. There's nothing like silence for helping you process the bad stuff.

Yasmin rolls her eyes at me and signs [Dad] twice. 'I'm not giving the key back. No point. They have copies.'

'Your Dads are interfering old bludgers.'

[Love you] she signs at me with a sweet smile.

I breathe in the fumes of my tea. 'What's the crisis?'

'Emmy was arrested last night.'

'Shit.'

Yasmin looks away, and I see it, the first hint that she's barely keeping it all together.

I'm selfish. I'm despicable. Because my reaction is not, *how can I help?* It's, w*hat will they want from me?*

Yasmin keeps talking, knuckles white around her own cup of freshly brewed herbal tea. 'The Freewaves hit the Hub last night, stealing some communications gear. I don't think Emmy was with them—Della was on duty, she'd have told us—but Emmy was picked up on her way home, not long after. Everyone knows she's been hanging around that crew.'

The Freewaves are a movement of young people, protesting the decisions of our Rising Council. It seemed innocent enough, when Emmy first got caught up in that lot. Protesting the government is what young people do. But the Freewaves are getting louder and more popular, demanding that the communications blackout on our city be lifted. They want to make contact with homeworld.

They want to rejoin the galaxy, or whatever is out there beyond our world—a home planet, an empire, a conglomerate of other worlds that were terraformed and seeded and abandoned just like ours?

We don't know what's out there for a reason. And the reason is, we don't want any of them out there to know we're still here. But apparently 'we' is no longer universal. The kids have their own ideas, damn it.

'I thought she agreed to concentrate on her music,' I say now, fighting a headache. The herbal tea isn't making a dent in my stress levels. 'She promised to keep her activism on the down low because of your Dads…'

My brother Billy and his husband Jin are members of the Rising Council. They've both put their time in as leader of the city. It's not going to look great for either of them if their youngest daughter is exposed for her role in a cult that is endangering our colony's safety.

Last I knew, Emmy was all about becoming a pop star, a bold choice in a post-apocalyptic society where power is rationed more tightly than sugar. She records her songs on an old vid device and shares them with her friends. There's no network in our city, which makes it hard for her to break a wider audience.

Maybe now she's found her answer.

'Seff's trying to get her out on bail,' says Yasmin. 'The Dads are going spare. Can you come to the house? We all need to talk through what to do next.'

I love my family, but I've done a damned good job at convincing them I'm okay. Yasmin has no idea how impossible her suggestion is.

'I wouldn't be any use,' I say, feeling sick.

Yasmin stares at me. 'But you always know what to do. We need you.'

'Yas,' I say, meeting her gaze so she knows I'm serious. 'I'm not good for anything right now. And I'm staying here.'

---

When I'm not digging potatoes or distilling the cannabis oil that helps to keep my anxiety manageable (on Good Days, at least), I've become something of a career counsellor for the local teenagers. It's not an easy task in a world where resources are scarce, and we haven't nailed down a currency.

But everyone needs to find their place in our new world. I have a knack for pointing kids in a realistic direction.

There's farming, of course. Always, farming. Most of us put in our hours to making the vegetables grow. But not everyone has the temperament to do that all day, every day. What's the point of being a society if we can't pool our skills?

I knew that Dani from down the road could use her writing skills as a teacher, but I also knew that Micks and Jedda had a mind to start a newspaper on the side, and the three of them should talk about that.

I figured out that Yuri would do better in the security force than trying to enlist at the Hub.

I've had two boys and a girl come to me for health checks before starting sex work, stocking up on the supplies they needed to stay as safe as possible.

Teddy, Dani's brother, is doing a good job running the local market while his mother recovers, but he's going to need a bigger challenge soon.

All five of my nieces have come to me over the years. I like to think I've helped them.

When Yasmin was eating her heart out about wanting to contribute more to the family, I found a connection for her with a gang that needed a reliable courier. She's too smart for a gig like that, but the pay is generous, and she has muscle at her back if she ever gets into trouble. (It's very important my brother never finds out I had anything to do with this one.)

After Seff got into one fight too many, standing up for injustice on every street corner, I found her the books to train up as a legal advocate.

When Marnie and Della were frustrated that their Dads thought they were too young to work at the Hub, I may have helped them start their own under-the-table business, repairing private generators and solar chargers around the neighbourhood.

Then there's Emmy, our starlet. Emmy, who wanted to be famous before she even knew what that meant.

Emmy, now up to her neck in trouble because I got annoyed at her complaining one day and told her if she wanted something badly enough, she should *get creative*.

Not every piece of advice is worthy of a gold star. Before today, I figured I was achieving more good than harm overall. Now, I'm not so sure.

※

I head out to weed the garden. This gives me something to do with my hands, and if I think too much about the look on Yasmin's face when I told her I wouldn't go with her, I'll break into a hundred pieces.

It wasn't disappointment, but it looked a hell of a lot like pity.

That's what they get, these kids, for building me up into some kind of legend. Their Dads don't help, always giving me credit for the old days, when we began the hard yards that turned our damaged city of broken children into a halfway functional society.

I was a leader then, alongside the boys, for a while. I was good at it, too. Decisions came easily. I pointed everyone in the right direction, and they jumped to it. I had confidence, and competence, and a solid stash of prescription drugs to keep me on an even keel.

It's harder now. Everything's harder now.

※

Della turns up not long past midday, to update me on the Emmy situation. I don't know what Yasmin told her, but she doesn't act like it's weird I need to be here, inside the solid weatherboard walls of my house and my high-fenced garden.

She's still in her uniform, grey and red. It's only two months since she scored herself an interview at the Hub at age fifteen, with several years of unofficial work as a Fixer as her resume. Her Dads were shocked she applied without consulting them. Marnie was furious that her sister was willing to ditch their thriving business to work for 'the man.'

Even I was wounded that Della made this particular career change without consulting her friendly neighbourhood Witch Doctor. Seems laughable now.

'I was on duty last night,' Della says, pacing the length of my garden and back again, gesturing with a stalk of fennel. 'So I'm under investigation now, because my own sister is a *selfish cow*.'

I breathe, looking at my hands. That's easier to deal with than Della's anger. She was always a vocal kid. Marnie was the quiet one. The two of them were inseparable from the moment that their too-young mothers abandoned them together as babies, side-by-side in an old produce carton left on Billy & Jin's doorstep. Everyone knew by then that my brother and his husband were suckers for adopting kids no one else wanted.

Della was a loud, squalling, red-faced child, while Marnie was silent and accusing. There was nothing sweet or cute about either of them, but their love for each other was tight.

When a dozen or more kids were orphaned, years later, thanks to the worst flu season our city has ever known, Billy and Jin brought home Emmy, a toddler with a malformed leg who needed a cane to walk. She was the only one they couldn't house elsewhere, because she looked like too much work.

(Too many orphans in our world; we've all lost people quickly from infections or complications of childbirth, or anaphylaxis. It's hard, remembering a time when they might have been saved with easier access to pharmaceuticals, but you can't keep hating the world for getting harder, not if you want to live in it.)

Marnie and Della closed in on that kid like she was their own baby bird, shaking off all attempts the older sisters made to be involved. Emmy was *theirs*, and they would die for her.

'She didn't do this to hurt you,' I tell Della now, passing her another stalk of fennel because she's already ground the first one into slush. She'll have greenish stains on her fingers for days.

'I know that,' Della bites. 'She wasn't even thinking about me. That would require actual *thought* about someone other than herself.'

I get to my feet, because this requires tea. Besides, the kitchen feels like a safer space for me right now than the garden, with the sky blazing bright overhead.

'They got a broadcast out,' Della whispers, as I put on the kettle. 'Last night. Twelve of us on duty at the Hub, and they didn't just make away with stolen equipment, they got a broadcast out.' She looks at me, terrified. 'I shouldn't have told you that. But this is bad, Auntie. Really bad.'

I don't even correct her for calling me Auntie.

Jin comes to collect Della not long after that. What she didn't tell me is that she's practically under house arrest. The only reason that she hasn't been held for further questioning is because her Dads used their considerable social currency as members of the Rising Council to have her released into their custody.

It never occurred to me that we'd ever have an administration or a security force that was organised enough to be this scary. But I'm scared for Della now, falling under suspicion like this. I'm scared for Emmy.

Jin looks like he's been through hell. I start to apologise for not coming to the family meeting—he cuts me off with a hug.

[Look after yourself] he signs as he pulls back, eyes warm and caring. He doesn't look surprised that I've let my anxiety get this bad. Maybe he's been paying more attention to me lately than I have. Jin and I have been friends and in-laws for more than two decades; he's better than most at reading people in crisis.

If he ever needs a career change away from politics, he can take over from me as unofficial post-apocalyptic suburban jobs advisor.

[I want to help] I try.

Jin shakes his head, and turns away from me, classic power move from the non-hearing member of the family. If he's not looking at me, I can't talk to him.

---

Rebuilding our world was mostly about potatoes, for the first few years. Potatoes and cabbage and power generators. Once we accepted that no one was coming back to rescue us, and that we could only survive so long as scavengers eking out the meds and canned food and batteries left behind in old houses, our focus was on feeding ourselves. Feeding each other.

Seeds, garden plots in every empty house, more seeds. We found a bank of supplies in the secret base early on, enough to get things started, but they wouldn't last forever. We shared tips for growing good spuds and beans and how many vitamins you could get from a freshly grown lemon.

The gangs 'kept the peace', when they weren't trying to kill each other.

But they dug in the ground too. Dirt under everyone's fingernails.

Leadership, in those early days, was about sharing ideas and keeping everyone going. Billy and Jin pushed to get the tech working again, to light up the city. The Hub formed around the lab left behind by the scientists who abandoned us here.

There was a joy in thwarting them, our creators. They wanted our world to end and we would not let it. We tended our sick and fed our hungry. We lived.

As our post-apocalyptic leadership team began to transform into something else—what would become the Rising Council—there was one policy that Jin and Billy and I always insisted upon. Those who picked up the work we started held to the same line. I've never met one of the Left Behind who disagreed.

The ones who abandoned us must never know that we survived.

But everything gets forgotten, eventually—and a sensible pronouncement can easily become reinvented as a terrible injustice. Every month we hear about more young people joining the Freewaves, demanding that we reconnect to the rest of the galaxy. That we proclaim our identity as a thriving colony, loud and proud.

I assumed they were crackpots at first. I'm sure most of the Rising Council and the security force and the Hub administration all felt the same. And yet...

Well, these kids are our future. It's easy to dismiss their ideas as simple, or not-properly-thought-through.

It's easy to think, they don't know. They weren't there. They didn't live through this.

But a lot of those kids are older now than we were then, when the world ended and we began to rebuild. Who are we to say we're better at this than them?

Anyway, it's too late.

The broadcast has been sent.

The cat's out of the bag.

And my family is right in the middle of it all.

---

Seff drops by next, later in the afternoon. It's useful to have a lawyer in the family, but I always figured the most likely of us to end up under arrest was Yasmin for her connection to the gangs, or Marnie for her illicit Fixer business. Seff sits at my kitchen table and drinks three cups of scalding hot chai like she's holding a grudge against the recipe.

'They're not letting anyone see her,' she says grimly. 'Not family, or friends. Same goes for the rest of the crew they picked up. But Emmy— because of who she is, they don't want to be seen to go easy on her.'

This conversation I can handle. I'm the one who set up the security regs for the city, back when our administration was new. 'They can't hold her for long. Some kind of public trial, perhaps. But you know how it works.' Redemption and repentance are the order of the day. We've never had enough bodies on the ground to justify any kind of prison system. What are we going to do with our convicts, punish them by making them dig potatoes for the rest of us?

'They used the word treason,' Seff says bleakly. 'There are no regs for this, Aisha. This is new. I think they want to make an example of the Freewave cult. Like it or not, Emmy is their voice.'

'But she wasn't even there when they stole the gear from the Hub, was she?' I ask impatiently. It's so hard, getting the story in long distance fragments. Every member of the family forgets what I already know, and what I don't.

'Her voice is on the broadcast,' Seff says heavily. 'They must have recorded it days or weeks ago, ready for this. She's one of four named speakers, telling the story of our colony, our survival and rebuilding. Spilling our secrets to the homeworld. She sings a fucking song at the end.'

'Shit,' I say, after a minute.

'Yeah,' Seff agrees. 'Shit.'

---

I try to leave the house three times before night. I know I can't help. What can I offer Jin and Billy? There are no strings I can pull more effectively than either of them. If they're out of resources, we're all screwed.

But. I could be there. I could hold their hands. I could hug the girls. I could be a real member of this family instead of another liability they have to check in on.

Did I mention? This is a Bad Day.

A week ago, perhaps I could have made it. I was doing pretty well last week. I managed to get as far as the local market, traded some new seeds. The sunshine made me feel like everything was okay. I slept through the night, several days in a row.

The Aisha of last week could deal with a day of crisis and family drama without falling apart.

But I'm standing at my garden gate, breathing too hard, counting the slats in the fence because counting calms the pulse. I can do counting.

What I can't do, today, is step out of my goddamn garden.

So I make soup, and I wait.

Somewhere past nine pm, there's a creak on my back steps. I go out to find my brother Billy sitting there, wide-shouldered and heavy. I sit beside him and lean my head on his arm, remembering when we were teens together and the world wasn't ending yet.

It didn't end. That's important to remember.

It didn't end.

It didn't

'She's home,' he says.

I blow out a breath, so relieved that it's staggering. I could plant out half my garden with the lightness that bleeds into my muscles. 'What happened?'

'They let her go.' He sounds numb, dazed. Like he's the one who has been using far more cannabis oil than is medically recommended.

'How? Why?' My hands clench and unclench. I need to count my fingers, or I need to go back inside.

He watches quietly as I do it, my fingers twitching with every count. I count them through, three times, then six. Ten is a round number. I can stop after ten.

'Soup smells good,' he says.

'What did it cost you?' I ask.

Billy stands up. [Soup] he signs. [Hungry]

So, we go inside and I feed him. Finally, he's ready to make eye contact and explain a little. 'I'm not a member of the Rising Council anymore.'

Damn.

[Jin]? I ask, using the name-sign.

'He's on probation. Know any reliable citizens with leadership potential who might be looking for a new career?'

He's mostly kidding, but I think about it. 'Teddy from down the road has been managing the market, after his mother hurt her hip. He turned nineteen recently. I know he has a lot of strong ideas about governance. It might not hurt to have a few of the younger generation stepping up to the Rising Council. The ones who were born after … well. After. It makes a difference.'

Billy looks amused. 'Jin told me you were mothering half the kids in this city, and I didn't believe him. It didn't sound like you at all.'

'I'm not mothering them,' I say sharply. That's not what this is. 'They need guidance, that's all. Not everyone is born knowing what they're good at, or how they can contribute to society.'

'Yeah,' my brother sighs. 'Remember when all I wanted to do was make art?'

I scoff at him. 'Make art and save the world, as I remember.'

'It might need saving again,' he adds. 'If that broadcast made it through, if they come looking for us. We're sitting ducks here.'

'That,' I tell him solemnly. 'Sounds like a problem for members of the Rising Council.'

He laughs, a sharp bark. 'Wow. You haven't lost your edge. You know I'd recommend you take my place, if I thought you…'

'No.' I shake my head quickly. 'That's not what I'm good at now.'

'You mean it wouldn't be good for you.'

'That too. Let the kids save the world. I have veggies to grow.'

It's not that easy. Of course, it's not that easy. But we learned something, long ago, when our lives were ripped away from us overnight. When the robot foster mothers went blank-faced and useless. When our world stopped being a maze of endless suburban houses full of families and became something new and terrifying.

We learned that this planet was made for us, by some messed up terraforming program, and we were an experiment doomed to fail. Abandoned. Our world stopped making sense, and we devoted our lives to creating one that did.

When the world changes, you can't hold to the old rules. You have to adapt fast or die. You have to save what you can from the wreckage and move the fuck on.

You have to keep making your own miracles.

The Rising Council are still debating how to deal with the rebellious Freewave Cult when the game changes.

Della isn't on duty that night, but she hears about it from her colleagues. She sits on it for two days, never saying a word.

It's Jin who tells us: the last member of our family with an official foot in the Rising Council. He and Billy bring the girls around for family dinner, acting like it's completely normal to turn up on my doorstep with boxes of food and shove themselves around my tiny dining table.

[The Hub, a broadcast] he signs and the rest of us stare at him. Sign language doesn't always provide enough context, especially the butchered version of Auslan that our family have adapted over the years. We already knew that there was a broadcast from the Hub. Emmy and Della are right here, still not speaking to each other about it…

But I see it in Della's face. She understands something different from his signs. 'Received, not sent,' she says aloud, signing along. 'Are we allowed to talk about it now?'

[Probably not] signs Jin and then makes another sign, an old family favourite usually translated as 'who cares' when the girls were little and 'fuck it' as they grew older.

Emmy's eyes are round and bright as she limps across the kitchen, and hugs her Dad. 'They answered us?' she breathes, so happy that the rest of us can't even look at her for a minute or two.

She is the only one at the table unafraid of what's coming.

Two days after that, a spaceship lands in the middle of State Stadium. I'm not there. It might be the biggest thing to happen to our colony since the Pulse, but that doesn't mean I'm functional enough to witness it in person.

Emmy and I stay at my place, watching on the grainy vid screen that is only used city-wide for Council announcements, the annual holiday speech, and the few sporting events that are considered worthy of broadcast.

'Do you wish you were there?' she asks in a whisper, knuckles gripping hard against the handle of her cane. Her Dads refused to let her go, worried that her identity as the voice of the Freewaves would make her a target of the crowd.

'We can watch it from here,' I say firmly.

'But why can't you just … you can't *want* to be stuck here.'

I sigh. 'I think of it like a big cloud of bees.'

'I like bees.'

'One or two bees at a time are fine. Very useful for pollinating. My garden wouldn't be nearly as healthy without them. But a big mass of them—that's what it feels like, when my anxiety gets bad. Like a cloud of bees, buzzing in my ears, pressing against my skin. I can't function like I used to. It takes over everything. Imagine trying to make a sandwich with a giant cloud of bees surrounding you, threatening to sting you at any minute. Imagine trying to walk down the street or have a conversation.'

Today is a Good Day. I wouldn't be able to talk about this at all, otherwise.

'It's different for other people,' I tell her. 'But for me, visualising the bees is helpful. Sometimes I count them. Sometimes I talk to them. But mostly thinking about bees reminds me that it's real. It's something I have to deal with every day. I'm not imagining it.'

Emmy's looking at me like she's never seen me before. 'How do you even get out of bed?'

I laugh at her. 'Some days I don't. Anyway.' An awkward shrug. 'It's been not great lately. I can't do a lot of the stuff I used to.'

Her eyes are fixed to the crowded stadium, to the spaceship sitting there, on the grass. Just when I think she's too distracted for this conversation she says. 'You still help people. Kids like me. All the time. Does it make it harder for you, the way we land on your doorstep and ask for advice all the time?'

'Not harder,' I say, after a moment. 'I don't mind random teenagers dropping in, most days. As long as you help with the weeding, and don't ask me to talk about myself. *These* visitors, I'm not so sure about.'

On the screen, we see the door of the spaceship detach and fall slowly to the ground. Several figures step out, and I know them. Those are the same faces as the foster-mothers who cared for us when we were children. Different, but the same. 'Robots,' I tell Emmy.

'Duh. I guess they thought we were going to shoot them a bunch.'

'Still might.'

After six robot women, three human-looking figures step out. Two men and a woman. Grey hair, thoughtful expressions.

The representatives of the Rising Council step forward to greet them. One of them is Jin. If today turns to shit and he gets himself killed, I'll never forgive him.

'What do you think they're going to say?' Emmy whispers, eyes glued to the screen. 'Do you think they'll apologise for leaving us?'

I snort. 'Not on your life.'

Are these the same scientists who left us, twenty-five years ago? Were they the ones controlling the robot bodies? Did one of those grey-haired old dears hit the pretty button that wiped out our electronics as they sped away? Did they vote to leave us behind? Or are they all complete strangers, here out of curiosity, entitlement, guilt? What do they want from us?

I wonder if they've brought fresh supplies. If they have given any thought at all to what we have needed. Is that spaceship filled with condoms and antibiotics and irrigation hose and chocolate? Can they fill a prescription for me?

'What do *you* think they want?' I ask Emmy. She must have had a specific goal when she recorded that message. For the life of me I can't understand what she was trying for, unless she really did just want to be famous.

My niece shrugs her shoulders. 'I think *they* think they're here to save us,' she says. 'But it's too late, isn't it? We saved ourselves.'

# ŌMARINO
## ANDI C. BUCHANAN

The road to Wellington, cracked and near empty, stretches out before us. The fields beside us are overgrown and wild, bush returning to land once taken for maize, rye-grass, canola. Cars along the side of the motorway have rusted to shells; windows smashed, contents looted. We don't look too closely at them; even here, and even fourteen years later, there are still skeletons left unburied.

We're just going for the night. To pick up medical supplies and a few other orders, and drive them back to Ōmarino, the home we've built for ourselves, the home that gave us life after years surrounded by death. It is usually others who make this trip. We're going to the city that was once our home, to decide if we want to stay.

It's been years since I've driven, and the car shudders uncomfortably beneath us. In our little pockets of land, the places where we've survived or congregated, we've been comfortable, and almost allowed to believe the sickness never happened. But once you leave, it's all like this; a population a fraction of what it was, and decay everywhere.

In the back seat Ollie is huddled with his tablet, his sun-browned legs, hovering on the edge of a growth spurt, still curled up beneath him. There's no signal out here but we have plenty of power banks and solar-charge cells taped against the hot windows. He's never been this far before; doesn't know what it used to be like. Doesn't have anyone from before to miss.

Next to me, Mikkie looks young again, like from before the sickness. When we didn't know each other, really, but our circles overlapped, because Wellington is like that, and queer Wellington circles even more so. Back when we lived for the late nights and lazy brunches, in between study and low paid jobs.

I've seen her happy since then, but not like this, all nervous smiling and excitement. She tracks the road against an old map on her phone. A map filled with landmarks that are no more.

⁂

After the sickness burned itself out, taking most of the world's population with it, I travelled because I couldn't bear to do anything else. Everywhere reeked of death and stolen possibilities if I stayed there too long, even places that had been cleaned and repainted. I took cars without bodies inside; switching batteries and bartering for vegetable oil when the petrol went off. Three years before, I'd been head girl, now my most useful skill

# ŌMARINO

was hotwiring. I hitch-hiked. I walked until my feet calloused right over and I barely needed shoes.

I slept under canvas most nights. Heaping all the blankets I could find on top of me, I listened to the birds; a ruru, far away, and the chorus of tūī at dawn. In the winter, I broke into abandoned houses. I sat on forgotten sofas, spinning my fidget toys endlessly until I was calm enough to sleep. When I was lucky, I was given shelter in marae, offered a comfy mattress, clean water, and kai that felt like the best I'd ever tasted. I gave what I'd been able to loot as koha: packs of ibuprofen, small children's toys, batteries. It never felt like enough.

It was nights like those that I met others like me. It was on one of those nights I met Mikkie.

❦

We drive mostly in silence for the first part of the journey. I keep my eyes focused, my hands gripping the wheel. I don't know what to say. But then Mikkie starts signing to me and I struggle to take it all in, to process: her hands, her movements, her facial expression, while also keeping an eye on the crumbling road. It's too much. I laugh and pull over, throwing my hands up with an exasperated smile. We get out, swap places, and Mikkie begins to drive.

Her ability to sign while driving terrified me when we first met. Even now I'm uneasy as she talks fast, her elbows on the wheel or not at all.

[Do you think they still have cafés? Waffles with chicken? Halloumi?]

Ollie waves to get our attention, then asks what halloumi is. I'm taken back to worlds far away, the salty taste, the squeak on your back teeth. For Ollie, cheese means home-made ricotta from our goat. I can tell him halloumi is a type of cheese, but I can't convey late, hungover brunches with friends, those perfect years of young adulthood.

[There'll be some sort of café, I'm sure,] I say.

When I first met Mikkie, my sign was clunky and I had to resort to fingerspelling every few words, but it was still better than that of anyone she'd met since she left Wellington. I speak it better now—every child at Ōmarino is brought up speaking NZSL as well as English and te reo Māori. They roll their eyes at less proficient adults, which is better motivation than any— but I'll never have Mikkie's fluency. Nor Ollie's.

We stop at Paekakariki where there's a community we're in touch with—neighbours who make this trip have told us it's a good place to stop for bathrooms and a rest. In the community hall there's filter coffee and wifi and clusters of people who want to know how we are, all talking at once. I get overwhelmed quickly, wishing I could just pull my headphones on, but I know what's normal in Ōmarino would not be polite here.

I don't know how I'll cope in the city.

---

When I left Wellington, the first thing I packed was my headphones. The good ones that I'd saved up for when I worked a summer job. They sat comfortably, even if I had to wear them for hours, and had both active and passive noise cancelling.

When I first started travelling with Mikkie, she told me her hearing aids weren't working properly. We drove up to Hamilton and looted an audiologist's; got spare parts, and the equipment she needed to adjust them. And then, somehow, in the middle of an abandoned clinic with a smashed window, I'd started to laugh, and couldn't stop.

There'd been a time when my life plans involved a policy analyst job and postgrad at an overseas university. Looting audiologists was not on the list. But now I wasn't at all the same person, and I could never ever explain this to a younger me. I thought of my father, if he were still alive, writing his Christmas update to the family (if any of them were still alive) and including the line: *we are proud that Laura has successfully looted her first audiology clinic.* And I suddenly missed everyone so much it hurt, and it seemed so surreal that everyone was just *gone* that I couldn't stop laughing.

And then Mikkie had hugged me and made it clear that I didn't have to explain any of it.

Mikkie doesn't wear her hearing aids much anymore; I don't think I've seen her with them for years, except to Bluetooth music through. But she's wearing them now, on this long drive.

The road reaches the coast. The waves dance excitedly before us, speckled with sunlight. The train track is still there, hidden under weeds and grass. It could almost be as if none of this had ever happened. As if at any moment the road could fill up with cars, a train glide past, as if there could be little boats out on the water.

When we reach Porirua, the abandonment becomes more eerie. Empty houses over the hillsides, cars rusted in place. Climbing plants making their way over the mall and the supermarkets with weather-faded signs. Ollie presses his face to the glass, at once scared to look and unable to look away. Mikkie speeds up for the last part of the journey, down through the hills and to the harbour, and then makes a sharp turn into the central city.

It wasn't as easy for people who stayed in Wellington as it was for us. It wasn't an exciting renovation project, a chance to build a new settlement. We've heard the stories about how they couldn't bury all the bodies, or even burn them. Eventually they filled trucks with them and drove them into the bus and bypass tunnels and sealed them in with bricks and concrete.

The biggest community is out in Newtown now. It's easier to maintain single storey weatherboard houses than crumbling city blocks. It's a hub for the region, and even the country, with a community in Marlborough sending supply runs across the strait almost every month.

It's the Newtown community that manufactures insulin, which we can collect in battery-powered cool packs, and that has managed to import other medication since a proper factory started up in Sydney. They have the largest servers, which together with those in a few other locations mean we have a rudimentary internet connecting most of the settlements in the North Island—though no further, not yet. They also have a wider supply of clothes than anywhere else we're in touch with.

I suck in a breath as we drive through. To Ollie, this is just a new place. To me, this is both home and unrecognisable, a jarring reminder that things now are not just different but destroyed. That so much is lost.

But in Newtown there are open shops and market stalls by the side of the road, with families stopping to talk. There are cafés that smell of bacon and warm bread.

After the virus burned itself out, we built Ōmarino. The idea came in dribs and drabs, snatches of conversation at first, and then like a torrent, like everything we'd been holding back all our lives. I talked of constant overload and exhaustion around sound. She talked of how much harder background noise made her hearing. We said, almost in unison: *what if things were different?*

I felt properly myself for the first time since the plague. My mind was racing all over the place. I sketched Gantt charts on pieces of paper—I love Gantt charts; even doodle them for imaginary projects. I started thinking about teams and projects and delegations.

Mikkie was into the big picture stuff, the philosophical stuff. 'It's not about making people be quiet,' she'd said one winter night curled up with me in my tent, both our minds too buzzing to sleep. 'It's not about rules and restrictions. You know, like old-fashioned libraries that frown on babies crying or people who can't hear how loud they're being. It's about a space that manages that background noise.'

Mikkie liked saying, 'it's a structural issue, not an individual one' a lot, and I liked saying 'we need actionable specifics'. We made one hell of a team.

We made one hell of a couple.

We asked representatives of the local Iwi for a place for our community. Not to own: a place to farm and to build. To live.

The way government was organised in those days was … complicated. It still is. But it was their permission that counted. The settlement they offered us was tiny; a few houses and a pub along a road, not far from Levin. It was perfect for us.

It had been named after a long-dead surveyor. We took the sign down and put up a new one. We called it Ōmarino. The place of peace.

---

Mikkie and I eat poached eggs on toast while Ollie explores. I was nervous letting him, but he's a sensible kid. We looked at a map together and delineated his limits.

There's no halloumi but there's feta and bacon, spinach sautéed with garlic, hollandaise sauce. There's no smell of death or decay, just of breakfast. Someone is painting a building across the road. A radio blares in the café, and there's bustle outside, but I slept surprisingly well overnight, and I can handle it for now.

These past months, Mikkie has been tense and unsettled; I've been frustrated by my inability to make everything perfect for her. But now she's relaxed, at home in the café more than she is at home with me. And I'm unsure how to handle this either.

[The toast is good,] I sign, not sure how to start conversation.

[It should be,] the café owner signs, slowly but clearly, as he walks past. [That starter is from before.] He leaves the rest unsaid, the fact that it survived when little else did.

❦

We researched. We raided university libraries and professional offices, stepping round bodies on the floors. How to make an acoustically smart civilisation designed to meet the needs of people who require minimal background sound?

And then we built it. We built curves in the walls of public spaces, and insulated rooms. We looted warehouses until we found stocks of the best headphones—comfortable, noise-insulating—to listen to music without disturbing others, or to protect ourselves from the remaining ambient noise. We found ways to dampen the sound of power tools. We replanted lawns with native grass and left them unmown.

Others joined us. Some were autistic, like me, or Deaf, like Mikkie. Some just felt more comfortable in Ōmarino.

❦

I know—I knew all along—that Mikkie would want to stay in Wellington. She's balanced everything—what she's gained and what she's missed. Decided which sacrifices are worth making. The only question, really, was if Ollie and I would stay with her. But this isn't our home.

She tells me through tears that she's sorry. That she'll be back every month, to see Ollie, that she hopes she can take him with her for a bit, once she's settled, but she understands if I'm not comfortable with it. I say it's up to Ollie.

We all drive back to Ōmarino, and the years come rushing back as we turn the corner and see the houses we designed: the curved fences growing with crawling plants to muffle the background noise, the rubber-cushioned pathways.

She loads the car and drives south, alone.

I stay, alone.

Except I'm not alone. There's Ollie, and there's a lodger living in the sleepout, and there's everyone who lives here, more than three hundred of us now and growing every month as more people find us.

Part of life being normal again—or at least a kind of normal—is that people grow apart. People have choices—about who they're with, where they live, what kind of life they want. I tell myself that, when I feel cheated of the future Mikkie and I were going to have, when I feel raw and empty and end up crying as I sand down a doorframe because I miss her so much. What was once not much more than an hour's drive is a long way in this empty country.

I look out the window and across to the central area where Mikkie and I planted trees, dug weeds, grew vegetables, laid bark, built seating. Ollie and three of his friends have headphones on, all synched to the same music, and they're dancing on the wooden path through the community garden.

And I know exactly where I'm meant to be.

# RHIZOME, BY STARLIGHT
## FRAN WILDE

*A Propagation Manual for The Glass Islands Year Two, Day 120.*

*Remember: Removing kudzu is different than splitting a rhizome.*

*Remember also: Keep the vines away from the greenhouse. Keep yourself within.*

*With kudzu, you must reach in, rip it all out, then throw it into the sea. Don't think. It's the only way. There can be deviation when splitting. Preservation is your goal. Either for yourself or for the plant. Learn to discern the difference.*

*So much has been lost to the sea, the heat, but we will continue to tend.*

*Edward Greene, Senior Conservationist, Longitude Seed Bank and Laboratory*

My great-grandfather's words form a grid, each letter a seed, planted neat and black on the yellowing page. My mother's notes, scrawled below her mother's, come after, and before the kudzu took her.

I can't quite read them, but I understand: *Year 42, day 87. I am turned to salt and gnarl. Genes and seeds. I must go before I crush you.*

The wind calls through the vines for me to follow her, but I'd promised them all that I'd tend the greenhouse. As the last of us, I can't leave. Longitude Laboratory trusted us with a duty: keep the seeds safe. The greenhouse will fall without me, and the seeds will disappear. Birds might have dropped the kudzu, we (my great-grandfather's colleagues' experiments, that is) may have made it worse.

With the rest of his laboratory atop the sea-surrounded glass-and-metal island, grandfather had tried to help us withstand the heat, to be resilient, despite everything, to the pain of being left behind. The kudzu, when it took the island over, was the most determined thing he knew, but he swore to never try that. His colleagues did. And were lost to it.

Later, my grandmother and then my mother decided to let the vines have the daylight. To tend our rhizomes at night. To not divide too much. To keep to the greenhouse and defend it.

And our promise? I fulfil it each day. The original seeds are carefully preserved by my family. The last of the Longitude team. We stayed and tended the past. We protect the new growth as well. We last.

My joints creak as I work. I cannot quit our promise. Before she'd left, before the small bones in her fingers finished hardening together as her skin turned to bark, my mother had said the same. She'd wrapped around me, one last time and told me to be strong. To not give up. I could feel her fighting against herself, wanting to hold tight. She tried to protect me as much as the seeds.

But I have no one to worry about crushing, I've made sure.

When I reach fingers deep and sharp into the dirt and pull the young vines away from the greenhouse, I do it only on my own account. When I fling the kudzu over the dawn-bright cliff where the greenhouse is perched, its runners spread like fingers grasping for purchase, then drop.

Once, a gardener would make clippings, or split rhizomes as a scientist might split genes. Now, I am the last gardener and what I do is weed. Kudzu moved fast before. *Year Three, Day 47: They called it mile-a-minute once. Now it is smarter, and faster.* Those words, in less-neat letters. An aging hand, with trembling ascenders and descenders. The manual evolved as we, those who stayed behind, who evolved into our roles, learned not just to tend, but how to survive.

My grandmother wrote happily about her palms sprouting. My mother braided the flowers in my hair into a crown.

There are clippings in the manual. How to care for the seeds. How to call for help. (Not that this does any good: the vines got the radio tower a long time ago). There's a water-logged photo of great-grandfather as a young man with a cane, standing with the others in neat white coats as they prepared to isolate this small corner of earth on top of the world. All somewhat less than those who made the ships. But still determined to save as much as they could. There are pages torn out of the manual, a whole decade's worth. One section is burned. There are drawings, much later, of leaves bigger than a man. Of vines that double in size and grasp in a single night. I do not know who made those, but the ink is rust coloured.

My mother, after everything, read the manual aloud to me by starlight, as my great-grandfather had read it to her. She'd found herself alone, read the manuals on propagation. My grandmother's investigations, her grandfather's experiments. By then, the others had been lost—some to science. Some to the sea.

She did it so that we could keep our promise: to tend the seeds and keep them safe for those who would return. That was the promise. She divided, grew, and taught me from the manual, she said. That's how I'd learned my words. How I'd understood that we were born to preserve, to weed, to count the days, until we could no longer do so. I was small then, a breeze could turn my head, but she taught me to focus. To range the island, as I do now, digging deep into the dirt, stopping the vines. Looking for green shoots.

It was left to us to tend the seeds because something in grandfather's genes wasn't right. That's what he wrote in the manual. He, and others like him, stayed with the greenhouse, while others, much stronger and better, found safety on the ships. At least that's what the neat seed-letters say. His young daughter, her genes like his, remained too. She, and we became the promise he made: to stay, to be gardeners. Each day that my great-grandfather and, eventually, my grandmother marked in the manual was a promise: to keep the seeds away from the vines, and ourselves away too.

Now, as the stars shine above, and reflect on the ocean below, I make the same promise, in my own ways.

Today, the island smells of bark and dirt. The kudzu—some of it as thick as my own limbs, and stronger—is winning. But there's a small scent on the wind. Something not kudzu. I sniff it out, a tendril rising from where I'd worked the day before. *A gardener is never finished, until they give in.*

Sometimes, when the sun tries to beat its way through those panes, I trace my great-grandfather's seed-script—all that I know of him—with a fingertip, in the bright when there's only the one star and it's way too close. The glass island reflects off the sea and the day heats up. The thick reaching vines that wrap our island love this. I do not.

*Day 167—a small apocalypse, in a larger one. The plants I salvaged have escaped the greenhouse. The trees around us are changing. I've brought what I can back inside. I've set a boundary. I'm training to protect what we can, but the kudzu has already taken several of my best colleagues.*

I trace the scent. Find a ginger stem. Pluck it and take it with me to keep it safe from the vines.

On my own pages, I make notes about the latest rain-driven encroachments. The vines this time were fat and fast-moving, and just enough had shoots that I could grab onto and pull myself over until I found their rootball. I'd used my knife.

In the propagation manual, I make my own notes. My spelling is almost non-existent. Mostly, I draw what I find, and mark how-tos in with stick-figures, as well as the words I know. *Propagation, structure, rhizome, weed.* I make kudzu ink. It's bright green but fades fast to a sour grey.

My mother read the old pages to me by starlight, the ones with blue ink like sky and sea, or purple ink. She read as she plucked small leaves from my skin and hair. She used to save those, for the archives.

*Day 1.* I'd written the first day after she'd gone. *The vines are invasive. But the greenhouse is too.* I drew both, twined together. The greenhouse glittered: a spoiled frame, three plexiglass panes, in the clearing I'd maintained all these years. The greenhouse held a seed archive once, and the kudzu is still after it. The only way to save the archive is to beat back the vines. *Day 1*, I write each day. Each day, I pull up more rhizomes, and put them in the archive.

I didn't write: *How I miss you. How I remember you on my very skin.*

Instead, I changed the calendar. Stopped the count.

Her mistake, I'd reasoned, was she counted too much, and on too few things. On my drive for survival, on others coming to get the seeds, if we waited long enough. On us beating the roots back. On finding a way around the twisting-in of our own genetics. She stuck to the book's way: dates and memories. I keep my own time.

There's no one here to tell me different. I'm all alone in the greenhouse, a splitting knife in one hand, and a bucket in the other, ready for what comes next. It's raining outside, so I figure that next will be soon.

In the morning, I wake to a bucket full of cuttings. A new bottle of ink. And the roots grown again: this time into a wall all around the greenhouse that nearly cuts off the light. The kudzu mutes the sound of ocean against the island. The vines rise so high and so thick, they dim my view of everything but the stars. I realise, paging back through the manual, that I've made a mistake. I can count the days even when I refuse to number them.

A hundred since she'd gone. And thousands since the world had. But they'd all been wrong. Isolating the seeds, and us, meant the vines would win, all around us. All of them, somewhere out there, got caught by vines or sea, one by one. I won't get caught. I go out with my splitting knife to pare a path.

After it's all over again and I've got the roots divided and pushed back from the greenhouse, I make a new entry in the book. The pages are thick—the early ones from the damp, the later ones because I've sewn in sheets of bark and homemade leaf-vellum—and my writing is worse than everyone's. *It's time*, I write. *To go.*

*Day 1: This is a picture of the greenhouse, the sole structure still standing on the research base that used to be on top of a city.*

*This is a picture of a shovel.*

*This is a rhizome—not a root, by any means, but a stem that's evolved to survive.*

*This is me, with a cane that I carved myself from a kudzu root. And my root knife. And this is my mother with hers. She made the cane, still in the corner, beneath the big plexiglass pane — when her grandfather was training her. Made it easier to walk and bend, or … at least for me, makes it harder to fall. I made mine when the vines tried coming in the house.*

# RHIZOME, BY STARLIGHT

*Day 1, again. This is a picture of me scouring the greenhouse for any last seeds and rhizomes.* I enter them in the book, recording what will come with me as I travel. I've found some hostas, ginger. Irises. Bamboo of course, but bamboo's almost as bad as the root-plants. I sketch a bit of it on the page, anyway.

*Day, before 1: This is a picture of the last person who came to the island. He shouted as he climbed the glass cliffs that he'd heard of my great-grandfather, using the name from the clippings. That he'd come for our seeds. My mother had hidden us from him but forgot the manual. He'd poked through the greenhouse, seen our cots, our kettle. Shouted for us to come out.*

He said he was a scientist. Invited the air to go with him, said he had a boat. We refused to listen.

Before he gave up, he searched the greenhouse once more. Found the book. Paged through it. 'Seeds are like stories,' he'd said. 'They change depending on where they're planted.' But he didn't stay. The kudzu frightened him, the way it moved so fast. He'd lowered his small boat back down the cliff and sailed away. I'd watched him go.

Before he stepped from our island, he'd put a small rhizome on the ground. Turmeric. 'A gift then,' he'd said.

That's how I knew what I needed to do. And where I would have to go, when I had a boat. But I didn't go then.

My mother had waited until the vines drove the scientist away, then took the rhizome into the greenhouse, to protect it. 'We stay,' she said. 'Until we can't anymore. We keep what's wrong here from getting out into the world.' She often said that. She meant the kudzu, I think, but she might have meant more.

But she's gone now, and it's just me, and my seeds and plants, and I've decided.

*Day 1: It's not enough to keep our promise: Hers, to tend the seeds; mine, to stay safe. It's not enough to stay anymore. I think she saw the danger in us, but not in the world beyond.*

I work until my hands ache for days, and the bones stiffen into each other. Soon I won't be able to use the knife either. But I'll still be able to paddle.

*Day 1: I've pieced together a boat out of the greenhouse and a tree fall that nearly took me too.*

*Day 1: I've filled my bag with seeds and rhizomes. Kept my mind from wondering what happens when we all go out into the world.*

The greenhouse was a nursery, not just a seed bank. I know, because I was born in the greenhouse. Like mother was.

I say it in past tense, because I am the last to grow here.

*Day 1: This is a picture of me, climbing into my boat, which used to be a greenhouse.*

*This is the sail I've woven out of hemp and reeds, and bamboo. That took a long time. This is a picture of the sound of the boat creaking, in the wind.*

The boat groans when I let it down the cliff, hand over hand. It thuds when I lower myself to it, wave-slapped and crackling pitch seal on the plant parts, a ghostly chime on the metal, a bit of a sour sound on the plexiglass.

But I'm light, and I'm learning to speak the boat's language as it drops to the sea and I fall after it.

The promise was not to leave the greenhouse, and I haven't, not really. The clearing's already filling in, I bet. I have the manual and both canes and my knife. Let the vines have their way.

I put up the sail like the scientist did. It fills and the wind and currents take me where they want, straight out from the island. When I look back, the island seems made of roots wrapped around and through pieces of glass and metal like the greenhouse grew from, all the way down to where the sea catches it.

*Day 1: This is a picture of me wind-blown.*

I can see more in the clear water below the boat, metal and glass, window and frame. The wide roots twisting around everything, holding on, binding it all together. Our small home on top was a last enclave—a forgotten garden—an attempt to cling to a memory of ourselves. It grows smaller in the distance as I let the sea take me out, towards the rising stars and the gleam of another glass island far ahead.

*Day 1: It's a start, and that's what all of these are—starting points. This bright light out there is mine, the ocean heads me straight for it, and my past splits away from my present.*

But the gleam isn't glass. I've never seen a light that sharp before. If I had time and my hands weren't bent in and clutched at the tiller, I'd draw what it looked like. It deserves to go in the manual, even if no one's here to read it.

In my pack are all the roots and rhizomes I've ever found, plus the turmeric and the book—the one with my great-grandfather's writing, which I can just barely read, and my grandmother's, my mother's, and mine. The turmeric's gone grey and soft over time, despite my tending.

Soon enough, and with some paddling, the island shines right ahead of me. Except that it's moving, the spray blowing from each side of it. It is an enormous ship, sleek and fast, unlike my boat.

And when ropes are lowered, I am lifted. Uprooted from the sea. And from the concerned looks and the motions, I can see they think they're rescuing me.

They tut over my hands. Try to get them to unclench my paddle. Until I show them how to slide the tool from my grip. Until I show them my plants. And until they wrap me in concern and isolate me.

Then I must wait while they spray me down and try to feed me something awful and gelatinous. And the sun comes out and all I want to do is sleep. But that seems to be the noisiest time on the ship. They take me below. Away.

And in a bright room, where my boat and my plants wait, they pinch me hard with something sharp, and I see pale fluid well into a tube. It looks like ink. I want to write in the manual, but I will not.

Soon, but not soon enough, it is dark again, and this night, they've found someone to come speak to me.

He is much older, but I recognise him. He knows the same words I do, but they're ordered differently. 'How long' and 'how far' repeat and repeat until I frown at him. How can he not remember? *A story is like a seed.* I was a child, though, and child-memories grow deep and hold fast. Perhaps he visited many islands.

So then I pull the manual from my pocket and begin to show him his story. His eyes light up. The scientist remembers. 'You *were* there.'

A companion arrives, smelling of sharp chemicals and very white, clean clothing. She gestures to my arms and legs, says something unintelligible.

He frowns. 'She says you're lying, that you cannot possibly be your great-grandfather's child. There was no-one left, when we found the seed-bank. And you're too frail to have come all that way, on purpose, on a rusted boat.'

The woman tries to take my book away. The turmeric falls from the pages, and the scientist puts a careful shoe over it, to hide it. Tend it.

When I yell this time, he leaves with the rest of them—tall and long-limbed—taking my plants, and my book too. I expected the ocean to steal me, like my mother said it stole most people from before, but I didn't expect it to be like this. My island past and my boat past and this present divide again. I am many stories now.

⁂

They want to know where the others are. I ask them the same question. They will not answer. So I don't answer. I stopped counting beyond myself a long time ago.

I draw on their walls: *Day 1: This is a picture of my mother with her cane and her knife. This is a picture of my great-grandfather with his instruments and machines. This is us, dividing and splitting. This is gene and rhizome. These are our pathways forwards, and how we survived, one and then the next, when no one knew we were there.*

They—the smooth, sharp-smelling woman, and the scientist, who's also wearing white— squint at the drawings. *Impossible.* That is the sense of their words, the set of their shoulders. And yet, so much of what I say is possible. I am possible. I pull some leaves from my hair and hide them in my bag.

They are scientists, I begin to understand, but nothing like my great-grandfather. They've forgotten so much: dirt and starlight; the ways nature finds. They keep me confined to the shadows of my room for far too long. I begin to fade to grey. My hair no longer flowers, my skin begins to split.

I'm starting to go, to crave starlight, then sunlight, sea air, and dirt. Even kudzu. I desire growing things, not poking things.

They will let me have none.

So I wait, and wilt. And then, finally, the scientist comes back. He greets me again, but with more respect. 'You are what you say.'

'Take me outside. To the deck. I need starlight.'

He starts to shake his head, but I hold out my hand. A thin leaf curls there. He stares. Touches it. Then takes it, hungrily.

He opens the door.

And in the light and sea air, I begin what I promised I'd never do. I let myself go wild. My arms and legs itch with it. A tendril of vine curls beneath my ear. 'I cannot stay here. They'll take me apart.'

He looks a long time at me, then at the leaf in his hand, then shows me where my boat is kept. The bag of seeds and rhizomes is lost. I cannot stay where they've taken so much already. So I go, over the metal edge, away from the sharp smells.

The wind helps me leave the ship behind, once I set my sail again. The scientist grows smaller, where he stands by the stern.

I scratch behind my ear, carefully. Look at my arm, then my leg, beneath the sack dress I wear.

New rhizomes. Each their own beginning. I will plant these parts of me somewhere new. Everywhere, maybe. Someday, they'll make their own canes and knives, they'll help hold back the weeds on different islands. And someday, perhaps, they'll add pages to the book. The manual for propagation, made from a different island's plants. This time, we'll give what we have of ourselves, growing beyond where we began. *Day 1, of many.*

# THE SCIENCE OF PACIFIC APOCALYPSE
OCTAVIA CADE

## ABSTRACT

It had been ten years since Anna founded the journal. Eleven since apocalypse, and looking back she laughed—not at the loss, but at the sheer silliness of thought that had decided, so soon after Armageddon, that academic publishing was a fundamental part of revival.

'It didn't seem so silly at the time,' she said. It was the tenth anniversary, and this was their retrospective issue. Scientists all over the country, listening in. The radio and their fieldwork were the tethers that held them together.

'Yeah it did,' said Mo, who was spending the summer at the Portobello Marine lab with Anna. 'But you were all of fifteen and we felt sorry for you.'

'You did not!'

'Would you like to take a poll?' said Mo. 'There you were, fifteen and *blind*, and we felt sorry for you. For about ten seconds, and then we started to get interested.'

There were so many old journals in the lab, and in the university library across the harbour. There weren't enough scientists left to read them all; there certainly weren't enough scientists left to *fill* them all—even in a country that was mostly scientists now, two hundred of them that had been doing remote field work, in the ocean and Antarctica, when the plague hit. For people trained to publish data, the absence of opportunity to do so had been one more loss piled on the rest.

'I heard you all sulking and moping,' said Anna. 'I heard it *distinctly*.' There'd been nothing she could do about everything else they'd lost. Nothing she could do about what she'd lost, the last of her family left alive, and abandoned in a university research lab out on the peninsula. For a while she'd thought she was the only one left in the world, and even though she hadn't been very interested in science herself, sheer boredom and the availability of equipment had led her to start conducting her own experiments, out on the sea shore, recording the re-colonisation rates of shellfish.

'I was this close to hurling cockles at you,' she said, and there was an aggrieved sound from the radio.

'You *did* hurl cockles at me,' came a voice out of the Karori sanctuary in Wellington, half a country away. 'One of them drew blood too, you little brat.' Despite the words, there was laughter in his voice.

'Is that any way to speak to your esteemed editor?' Anna replied. 'Besides, you deserved it.' And for all his grumbling, her target had been the first one to support

# THE SCIENCE OF PACIFIC APOCALYPSE 191

her when she had presented the idea of a journal to the rest of them.

'Anyway,' she continued. 'It's been ten years. Those of you who weren't scientists then are scientists now. Even if it's part-time science, it still counts. Those of you who weren't bird scientists then are bird scientists now.'

'I stayed with reptiles!' came a rejoinder from Southland, where the resident tuatara expert was tearing her hair out, trying to get the disinterested creatures to breed.

'Still a botanist,' a third voice pointed out, one that Anna knew was out at the Chatham Islands, shooting any feral creature that came near to stomping his precious forget-me-nots.

'And I'm still surveying those bloody shellfish,' said Anna. 'You know what I mean!'

'Yeah, yeah. There's an albatross chick sitting in her lap right now,' said Mo. 'Give it a poke, An, make the thing squawk.'

'Pay no attention to her, poppet,' said Anna, cuddling the chick close. It was an orphan, brought back from the colony at Taiaroa Heads, just down the road from the lab. The chick squawked anyway, and snapped its little beak. It was such an improvement from the sad, shivering sack of feathers it had been when Mo had given it into her care not two weeks back.

Then it vomited partially digested fish all over her.

'This was supposed to be a dignified event,' she said, sighing, trying not to make gagging noises herself. 'This was supposed to be our retrospective, so we could look back on how far we've come!'

'Not a lot of dignity in publishing these days,' Mo replied. 'Give us a minute, guys, I'm going for a cloth.'

And for ten minutes the dignified retrospective was put on hold as scientists up and down the country argued as to whether albatross vomit was more or less pungent than seal breath.

(The general consensus was less.)

## INTRODUCTION

If academic publishing was less dignified these days, it was also more interactive.

'I think for many of us it was a way of going on,' said Mel. She'd come out of Australia, from a small research station on the Reef, leaving behind a daughter on the mainland who'd died of the plague and a husband who'd been on the research station with her, and distant enough to avoid it. A husband who'd curled in on himself and wanted to work out his own grief in continued isolation. 'You invest so much of yourself in your kids. And then they're gone, and there's nothing to do but go on, as if the future suddenly hasn't become this bare and hopeless thing, and there's no part of you left to live in it. It just seemed so *pointless*.

'I don't want to say that this filled a hole, because it didn't. Science will never be to me what Sarah was. But it was something I loved, even if the love was different, and it was a comfort, somehow. To know that something I could do, that I could contribute, would survive. Even if it's only words in a file somewhere. I know it sounds like ego. Perhaps it is. I can live with that. But it's also, I think ... I used the word 'contribute'. I think that's it. I want to know that I can give something of value to the future, still. Because there's going to be one. I believe that now.'

The apocalypse had come with death, that was a given, but it had cut them all to bone to realise that the deaths weren't only human. There weren't enough people left to even attempt to bury all the dead, and the rats and starving pets had eaten and hunted to survive. It was a vulnerable ecosystem, Aotearoa; always had been once it had been breached. All the small endemic creatures ... the birds especially, dying in the egg and the nest. So many species huddled on ecological islands, their numbers whittled down to nothing, with no one to protect them any longer.

When it came down to it, there was only one science that mattered any longer, and it was a science built on hope and love. Hope for the future, love for the present.

'It was fucking spite, too, and don't you forget it,' said Mo. She and her sister Minnie had been marine biologists in their former lives although much of their time now was spent in ecological salvage, like the rest of them. 'I remember stomping along Taiaroa Heads, resenting the hell out of those bloody albatross just for existing. How dare they, when so much hadn't? And I remember seeing the broken eggs, and the empty nests. I let myself into the station there and had a look around, saw an article pinned up to one of the notice boards. I hadn't known that albatross could be eaten alive by mice while they sat on their nests, because they didn't want to leave their eggs. I remember just *bawling*. On and on, like a little kid, as though albatross actually meant something to me, like I'd given them more than a minute's thought in my life.'

She'd gone back the next day with traps, with tools taken from the lab to cobble together the stretches of fence that were falling down. Gone back the day after, and the day after that, furious with the world and snapping at the other survivors for not being willing to go with her.

'Then one did,' she recalled.

'And you didn't want me,' Anna said. 'Were none too polite about it, either. Said I'd be useless, that I'd just be one more thing needed looking after. Then you took me anyway, out of guilt.'

'She'd rustled up a number of sacks,' said Mo, telling a story they'd all heard many times before, but finding satisfaction in the retelling. '*You check the traps, I'll collect the bodies*, she said. So I led her up and down that bloody hillside. She stuffed sacks with rats, with dead possums, the odd moggie. And all she said was

*If we can set up rope lines, I can do the traps too and we'll work faster.'*

It had shamed the rest of them, to see the future going out to find itself, and not being part of it. So they had chosen to be part of it, and given themselves futures thereby.

## METHOD

'Explaining what we were doing to the rest of you, that was when I first thought of it,' said Anna. 'The journal. It was something to go on with.'

She had introduced the first paper of the first issue with a song. *Whaling*, which everyone knew, and which made them smile and sing along. It wasn't really about whales; the lyrics spoke of going on, of bravery and finding love. All of them, up and down the country, linked through networks cobbled together by the two surviving engineers, could hear each other. They needed the connection as much as anything else, Anna thought, and she knew better than any of them what the sound of another voice could mean. For all of them, she believed, the future of academic work was going to be aural. There was too much history of loss, too much need for the immediacy of contact, for the written word to suffice.

When the song was over she'd introduced Minnie, who talked about tracking the migration routes of great whites. 'Her sister's doing the follow-up paper sometime soon,' Anna had said, 'so tune in then!'

The first paper was memoir as well as method. An explanation for intelligent people, albeit most of whom knew nothing about sharks. There were simple words and humour.

Minnie had read Anna a draft beforehand, something suited to old-world journals, and saw the scepticism on her face, and the boredom. 'You kind of sound like a dick,' Anna had said. 'Really pretentious. I mean *really* pretentious. Can't you pretend you're at the pub or something?'

There'd been a small silence, and then she'd heard the smile in Minnie's voice. 'Ernest Rutherford used to say if you couldn't explain your experiment to a barmaid you needed to build a better experiment,' she'd said.

That night they were all barmaids.

Afterwards there were questions. From geologists, from astronomers. From people who'd spent their lives on leopard seals and starfish. From people on islands and behind fences, from people who'd never seen a shark in their lives. The conversation went off topic. It branched and turned back in on itself. People argued amongst themselves, offered up suggestions that were sometimes stupid and sometimes not, but they were engaged, Anna thought. They sounded happy in their arguments, as if they were having *fun*. They brainstormed ways to do further work, without taking anything away from the needs of the birds that had increasingly become the primary focus of the rebuilding efforts. She recorded it all. There'd be a transcript, of course, and room to add tables and charts if needed, but the recording, the interaction and excitement, the singing and the jokes and the sadness together ... *that* was the paper.

There was already a list of people volunteering for the next issues.

'You're next,' Minnie had said, under her breath. 'And maybe your second paper will be on raising chicks, but the first one's going to be those cockles.'

'It's what I imagined an academic journal should be, post-apocalypse,' Anna said, ten years later. Reaching out, and reaching forward. Something to bring wonder back into the world.

'That's what it should always have been,' said Mo.

## RESULTS

Martin was in Fiordland, on Resolution Island with the kākāpō. His voice was slow, deliberate. There were lots of pauses, but apocalypse had taught them all a respect for silence. 'I was never much of a writer,' he said. 'Dyslexic as a kid, you know? Got through uni with hard graft and good practical work. I never thought I'd be a researcher, get stuff in a journal. And I remember thinking, when Anna started talking this up: it's never gonna work. But I thought I'd give it a listen anyway. Not so much because of the content—sorry. I know you're all having a chuckle right now. All the stuff we do, it's good, but I remember thinking, when I was at school, how what those scientists were doing must have been good too, before the journals got hold of it. Then all the life got sucked out.

'It's funny—all I could picture, in my head, was that it'd be no different. That we'd all start writing papers and it would be just like before, and I'd listen like someone was reading aloud, reading all the old papers aloud. And I'd have listened, I really would, but mostly I'd have listened because for so long there was no-one else to listen to. It was just me on Resolution, during. Me and the dog, and he was a good mate but I'd have given my left eye-tooth to have heard someone. Anyone. Just to know I wasn't alone. So I would have listened anyway, but it turned out what I ended up listening to was different than what I thought, and pretty bloody quickly different too. And I just wanted to say: I'm not glad for why it happened, but I'm glad that it did.'

Martin hadn't contributed anything for the first four years, but there'd been five articles from him since. 'And I'm working on a sixth,' he said.

Martin hadn't been the only one who had been slow to sign up for presenting. Keith hadn't contributed anything for the first few years either. He'd barely managed to listen. 'I broke the radio,' he said. 'You know. Before.' It was an old confession, but one that still made them wince; a reminder, to survivors, of the loneliness that had at one point come close to crippling them all. 'I was so certain I was the only one left, out on the ocean alone with the kelp.' He'd made that his name for a while: Kelp. The identification had allowed him to distance himself from what he was—human, and hurting. 'I'd spent so long listening for responses that never came. It was driving me mad. So I broke the thing, so there'd be no more reason to sit in front of it and hope.' It had been difficult for him to come back to society. 'I was always expecting it to be taken away again,' he said. 'Even when the radio was fixed. I could hardly bear to hear you all. It made me feel sick. When Anna started talking about a journal I threw up over the side of the boat. I had all this research, see. Even when I thought there was no-one left, I kept at it, this automatic carrying-on, because I was afraid to have nothing to do. And I knew I'd have to do a paper eventually, because what good was all the knowledge I'd collected if it didn't get shared? But the journal, when it came, was so *different*, and it was just one more difference, and I kept waking up in the night and wondering if, when I presented it, there'd be any response. If I'd wake up in the middle of it and realise I was reading to no-one. That I'd gone mad and imagined you all.'

He'd never thought he could do it. Had confessed to them all his weakness, the way the papers shook in his hands when he tried to read them, the way his throat closed up when he tried to speak. In the end they'd read it for him, scientists up and down the country. They'd taken a paragraph each, read his work back to him in a long compassionate chain, and he'd sat on his boat and wept at the sound of their voices.

'It took me three years after that to be able to get through one myself,' he said. 'I never said how grateful I was to you all. But I was. So grateful.'

## DISCUSSION

'I wanted you to have something you loved,' said Anna, describing how the journal had come into being. 'And I wanted to be part of what you loved.' Because she hadn't been, not really. Not at first. 'I was just this kid,' she said. 'Playing at science to pass the time. I'd been so pleased with myself for cobbling together this little experiment, but you all started trickling in, *real* scientists, with training and vocation and there I was, messing about, and if apocalypse hadn't swept down on us I'd never have dreamed that science was something I could make of my life. You made me feel stupid. This stupid kid, dreaming.'

'We never thought you were stupid,' Mo interrupted, and Anna waved her off.

'I know,' she said. 'You didn't think it and you didn't mean to make me think it. I'm not blaming anyone. It was just overwhelming, you know? One more thing amongst the rest. You just all seemed so capable. It wasn't because I was blind. I'd worked around that, kept myself alive, started doing science on my own. I was capable too. It was that I was young. I didn't know as much as the rest of you. I hadn't been to uni like you had. And it was such a ridiculous idea, this journal. I didn't know how to put one together or anything. But we had a small library at the lab, so I started going through the back issues. And that was when it hit me.

'It's different for all of you. You *read* science. I *listened* to it. I took random issues off the shelves and scanned them into my laptop and listened. And there was no rhythm to it. The words were all so ugly. The sentences were all so awkward. And I couldn't understand half of it anyway.' She'd trailed around after the surviving scientists, begging for definitions. 'I remember thinking it seemed like it was created to keep people out. You tried to explain, some of you, why those fancy words were needed. Jargon. I know. It's for clarity and shit. But those papers I listened to ... they weren't *clear*.

'It was just all so closed-in. I remember,' she said, 'lying in my bed one night and thinking that all that clumsy, horrible phrasing might actually be the future of literature in this country. It was a horrible thought, I can tell you, but we were all a little morbid back then. It's just there you were, and nearly all of you were scientists, and I thought *If I make this journal, this is how they're going to write. And there's going to be no incentive to change, or to write differently, because this is all they know and there's no one else around, no one not like them, to write differently for.*

'Well,' she added. 'Except for me.'

'So you thought you'd just change a tradition,' said Mo, laughing, half in pleasure and half in old disbelief. 'Change a whole professional code. It wasn't enough that you were going to start publishing, you were going to make us all publish differently on top of it.'

'You couldn't see it, that there was another way, all stuck in ruts as you were,' said Anna. 'But no way was I going to listen to that ugly, boring shit for the rest of my life.

'I said they weren't clear, those journals. But they'd also stopped being something that was a pleasure to listen to—if they ever were. And I wondered, well, why *should* something clever and useful not be appealing as well? Why did it all have to be so distant, why wasn't there any feeling in it—why were the words picked so as to get rid of feeling? You loved what you did, all of you. I know you did, I heard you talking.' About the science that they'd done, about how they didn't know how to carry on after the apocalypse, if there wasn't something else they should be doing. 'And you know, none of you *ever* said you liked writing those papers. Or that you liked reading them. It was just something that had to be done.'

'It was the only way to get grants, to get employed. Just this constant, desperate push to keep producing,' Mo remembered. 'Publish or perish.'

'Well I'd had a gutful of perish,' said Anna. 'We didn't need a scientific language that would kill off community. We needed one that would bring it together. And I knew that if I started a journal, what with us all so spread out, it would have to be aural. For the connection, like Keith said, and Martin. And I knew that if you had to listen to it like I did, if you had to experience it like I did, then you'd hear the problems as well.'

It was discussing those problems, and finding ways around them, that had created a blueprint for greater access.

'We're going to need to focus on access even more soon,' said Anna. 'I'm going to hand you over to Dara now. She's in the Orokonui sanctuary, if you recall.'

'Cheers,' said Dara. 'I appreciate the time. I know this is meant to be a celebration, but I've got a bit of a problem, and it's kind of on-theme, so Anna said to go right ahead. There's no easy way to say this, but the fact is, I'm losing my hearing. I wish I could say it's a surprise, but my family's got a history of hearing loss when we get on a bit, and ever since my sixtieth I've been waiting for this. I've managed to source some hearing aids from the hospital, but they're not very comfortable and there's the issue of batteries to contend with. I'll make do as much as I can, but one day it may not be enough. So what I'm wondering is how we can maybe adjust things with the journal, so I'm not left out.'

'Now obviously we keep transcripts of all our issues,' said Anna, breaking in. 'And with things like tables, for instance, or maps, that's been really helpful. And we've got programmes that'll turn speech into text so that Dara can read issues as they're happening. But I thought maybe we could crowd-source some other ideas, see what might work.'

'Hey Dara. This is Mike, out at Tekapo.' There were a couple of astronomers that had been picked up from Antarctica, and afterwards they'd made their way to the observatory in central Otago, combining atmospheric data with ecological work. 'Those speech-to-text programmes will work for the spoken word, no problem, but they won't work for things like music.' Which had become an increasingly important part of the journal. Each issue tended to have songs that people could sing along with, and every so often the more talented musicians amongst the survivors would introduce instrumental pieces inspired by their own work. 'We can use fractal imagery, though, to translate music to images on your screen. You should be able to experience rhythm and beat that way. Hell, you'll even get colour.'

'I wouldn't mind seeing that myself!' said Mo.

'And this is probably going to sound stupid,' broke in Jenna, who was up at Karori, working alongside the scientist Anna had once thrown shellfish at. 'But I've kind of been wondering about murals. There's all this fence space, all these empty buildings, and if papers can be turned to music I don't see why they couldn't be turned to art as well. God knows I'd love to go down to the Beehive, to the old Parliament Buildings, and start turning all that dead space to something useful. It's not like we have a government anymore, but symbols are important. Why not scrawl experiments over the inside of the debating chamber? I know you wouldn't be able to see them, Anna, but art doesn't have to be two-dimensional.'

'You want to do a collage of kiwi breeding records?'

'Well, why not? Why not make science something pretty? And *tangible*. Something that people can touch.'

'You know,' said Mike, 'I had a cousin who was a sculptor, before. He'd make these things, and they were pretty big some of them, and a couple of times I'd scan them for him, do 3D prints in miniature. That's something we could do. Especially if part of the texture of that mural or sculpture was Braille. I'm not saying this to replace the ways we do things now, mind. But as a supplement …

'As a supplement,' said Anna, slowly, 'we could turn science into a *gallery* as well as a song.'

'You should see her *face*, guys,' said Mo. 'You've done it now.'

## CONCLUSION

'No, don't laugh,' said Anna. 'Or, bugger it. I don't know. Go ahead and laugh if you want to. I'm laughing myself. It's ridiculous, but then so was this when we started. Reading science to each other, up and down the country, as a *fuck you* to apocalypse. But it worked, and in this new world it worked better than before. We adapted. There's nothing to say we can't keep adapting.

'I mean, imagine it. What if our science libraries aren't poky little rooms in the back of laboratories anymore? What if they're great big spaces filled with gramophones and sculptures and sound?'

'Filled with colour, and texture,' said Dara. 'Somewhere people can go to play.'

'It's not replacement,' said Anna. 'It's evolution. Taking the most successful, the most *adaptable* parts of each medium and making it serve.

'I know this was about survival,' she said. 'At first, anyway. And I'm not talking about physical survival here ... it was emotional, psychological. Something to put our backs up against, to claw back something we valued. But it's been over ten years now. We need to start thinking of survival in terms of culture as well. There aren't enough of us to recreate an entire society. Not yet. Our focus still needs to be ecology; we simply don't have the population base to support, I don't know, ballerinas and bakers and candlestick makers.'

'Mixing a metaphor there, An,' said Mo.

'Ah, you know what I mean. Science was a crutch for me at first; you lot made me love it. But it's not enough. And if there are ways we can use science to bring back other things as well, museums and art and music, then I say we've got the responsibility—and the opportunity—to do that as well.'

'In service to the future, to something other than ourselves,' said Mel, her voice quiet over airwaves, and they all of them knew she was thinking of the future that had been taken away.

'Yes,' said Anna. 'And that's why I think ... oh, fuck it!' she said, over sounds of gagging. 'This bloody bird has puked again. Where's that cloth gone?'

# THE REST IS
## STEPHANIE GUNN

Every morning my grandmother tells me how long it will be until I die.

I stand naked in front of the stove, Grandmother facing me. She is ready for the day in her long-sleeved dress, apron strings and boot laces tight, chatelaine at her waist. Mother's wheeled chair stands empty at the table, Mother still asleep in bed. It's been days now since we've been able to wake her.

Grandmother used to predict Mother's death, too. Eighteen months ago, she gave Mother a year to live. After that prediction, she used the small gold key on her chatelaine to unlock the high cupboard where she keeps the poppy syrup. From behind the bottles of poppy, she fetched out a small black bottle. Kindness, she called it. Ten drops on the tongue and never feel pain again.

Mother's speech had long ago stopped then, but she still had enough muscle control to be able to shake her head, her eyes on me. Grandmother made no more predictions for Mother, and never offered her the kindness again.

The moon has set, the room illuminated by the lantern I brought in from my night's work in the garden.

The candle is burning low, giving off curls of black smoke. Porridge bubbles on the stove, and the water in the kettle hovers on the edge of boiling. I breathe in, smell lavender and rosemary soap on my skin, and the ever-present darkness of earth beneath.

The candlelight flickers in Grandmother's eyes as she performs her examination. She peels back my eyelids, presses her ear to my chest. Her fingers are cold as she palpates my stomach and throat, pinches the skin over my hips and ribs. She taps her nails against my teeth, rubs her thumbs over my gums. Her skin leaves the taste of sour apples in my mouth.

'Pain?' she asks.

I take inventory. There are deep gravelly aches in my hips, a clenching between my shoulder blades. Smaller pains in my fingers and toes, permanent tight bands in my wrists and neck.

'About normal,' I say.

'Clumsiness? Shakes, tremors? Visual disturbances?'

'Nothing unusual.'

Grandmother steps back. She places her heels square, folds her hands. The candle flame lengthens as it consumes the last of the wax.

'A year,' says Grandmother. 'Maybe less.'

The flame sputters and goes out.

Grandmother keeps talking as she lights a fresh candle, words flowing around me like a river, only the occasional one dropping like a stone.

Headaches. Weight loss. Seizures. Loss of speech. Incontinence. Paralysis. Coma.

Grandmother says that this is how my grandfather died.

This is how my mother is dying.

This is how I will die, too.

Only Grandmother is untouched by this illness. My father, too, for all that he lies buried in our garden. Sometimes I envy him his simple, painless death, his heart simply giving out one day. Though I was too young to remember, Grandmother tells me that he was like a puppet cut from its strings.

Grandmother turns to the porridge, the candlelight glinting on her chatelaine. Two silver keys there for the bedrooms in the cottage, and the gold key for the poppy cupboard. The large black key opens the gate in the wall around our property, the only way in or out. I have never walked through that gate. Have never touched any of those keys. Have never wanted to.

'Mother had been having seizures for months before you gave her a year. She'd started to lose control of her bladder,' I say. 'I don't have any of those symptoms.'

'You will,' Grandmother says, stirring the porridge. 'I'm a doctor, remember. I know what I see. Do you want the kindness?'

I do another mental assessment of my pain as I get dressed and braid my hair. Truly, none of the aches seem worse than usual. When I look down the hallway that leads to the bedrooms, I can see Mother in the bed we share. She refused the kindness to stay here for me, I know. I owe her the same. 'No.'

People shouldn't know how they'll die. Mother said that to me once, back when she could speak. Better a swift, unexpected accident than a slow, known decline. She wept for days after Grandmother gave her a year. My eyes are stubbornly dry.

We eat breakfast and clean up, then Grandmother doses Mother with poppy syrup. I lie down next to Mother, listen to the wet tide of her breath in her chest.

'Are you sure?' I ask. 'About the year?'

'Maybe less,' Grandmother says. 'Once the seizures start.'

She picks up the lantern, closes the door and locks it, leaving us in darkness. Even once the sun has risen, this room will be dark. The window is boarded up and covered over with layers of thick blankets nailed to the wall. More blankets serve as curtains on the other side of the door. These things keep us safe.

A year. Maybe less.

I still don't feel anything. I should feel something, shouldn't I?

Mother's breath hitches, then stops. I count seven beats of my heart before she starts again. Mother has fallen into deep sleeps before, and always she's woken. She'll wake from this one. All I have to do is wait.

# THE REST IS

This is a world of walls, Grandmother says. A world where it is necessary to keep things *out*.

The world before didn't need walls. Grandmother and Grandfather grew up in that world, and Mother was born into it. When Mother was six months old, a flu pandemic came, followed by a war. The old world was shattered.

Grandfather died early in the war, and Grandmother left the city, taking refuge in our cottage on the hill, behind the wall that keeps us safe from the broken, savage world outside.

Our routines keep us as safe as the wall. The light of the sun sickens Mother and me, so we sleep during the day and work at night. Grandmother's work with herbal medicines requires good light, and so she lives a life opposite to ours.

Our property is bountiful, but it doesn't produce enough to feed us, and so once a month on the day after full moon, Grandmother goes out to trade with the village beneath our hill. She always goes out with one of her kitchen knives thrust into her belt, and often returns with the blade stained with blood. She will never speak of what it was that bloodied the blade, but her trembling hands and pale face tell me enough.

The evening after Grandmother gives me a year (maybe less), I wake to the sound of Mother choking. I roll her onto her side and thump her back until she coughs up the mucus that's blocking her throat. I'm wiping her face when Grandmother unlocks the door. In the light of the lantern Grandmother carries, I see that Mother's pillow is slimed with a tremendous amount of mucus, all of it streaked with blood.

Grandmother sighs. 'We'll need to change the sheets.' She fetches Mother's wheeled chair from the kitchen and sets it in the hallway. The doorway here is too narrow to bring it into the room. 'Help me lift her.'

We work together to get Mother out of bed and into the chair. In truth, I could easily have lifted her myself, Mother weighs so little now. She remains unresponsive as we settle her in the chair. If not for her breath bubbling faintly in her chest, it would be easy to think her dead already.

We don't talk as we strip the bed and remove the padding beneath where Mother sleeps. Those linens are almost dry, but the small amount of liquid Mother has passed is acrid and stinking.

Grandmother picks up the sodden pillow, wrinkling her nose. 'Everything will need to be boiled with lye soap overnight. The pillow will take a day or two of sun to dry. We don't have any spares.'

'Mother can have my pillow,' I say quickly. 'I'll go without.'

We remake the bed, then sponge Mother down and change her into a fresh nightdress before tucking her back into bed. Grandmother gives Mother poppy syrup, then goes out to finish dinner. I braid Mother's hair and tie a yellow ribbon around the end, arrange it so she can see the bright colour when she wakes.

In the kitchen, Grandmother is slicing the vegetable tart I baked earlier and preparing tea for us both. I go out to fill the copper from the tank, submerge the dirty linens, add lye soap and set it on the stove. The water clouds immediately, a thick, greasy scum rising to the surface. The smell of it is vile.

The light of the full moon spills onto the long bench, filled now with Grandmother's medicines for the village, everything labelled with a picture to represent the contents. Easier for the villagers, Grandmother says, most of them unable to read. There are a lot of packets of willow bark and valerian, with space left for the bottles of poppy Grandmother will fetch down from the locked cupboard in the morning. This month, all of the other herbs are almost outnumbered by purple pennyroyal flowers.

'Why so much pennyroyal this month?' I ask.

'Two moons past spring equinox,' Grandmother says. 'Time enough for the girls with bellies to know about it, and still early enough for the pennyroyal tea to fix it without endangering the girls' lives.'

'Do none of the girls want to keep their babies?'

Grandmother brings the food and tea to the table. 'They're not babies, Helena. What grows in those girls' wombs are monsters, and no doubt about it. Most of the girls would die trying to birth them, and any of the offspring unlucky enough to survive birth would know a lifetime of pain. The world isn't kind to monsters.'

Her eyes linger on me, weighing and measuring the way she does during her morning examination.

Not wanting to meet her piercing gaze, I busy myself with my food. The yams in the tart have been in storage and are woody, with a bitter tang, but the eggs and spinach are fresh. We've eaten worse.

Grandmother pours the tea. She mixes herbs every day for the both of us, varying the blends according to our needs. Today mine is mostly mint, with a pinch of willow bark. The scent of the steam rising from her cup tells me that she's added willow bark with a heavy hand to a base of chamomile and valerian.

'Are you in pain, Grandmother?' I ask.

'Rheumatism,' she says, her voice sharp. 'Something you'll be lucky never to be old enough to know.' She takes a mouthful of her own tart, makes a face and spits it back out. 'The yams have turned, I think.' She gets up and empties her plate into the scraps bucket.

My own plate is empty. Apart from that tang, mine tasted fine. 'Do you want me to make you something else? There are more eggs.'

'Tea will do me,' she says, sitting back down. 'The taste of that has turned my stomach.'

'I could go and do the trading,' I say.

'At night?' Grandmother asks. 'Normal people are asleep at night.'

'There's at least—' I bite off that sentence as Grandmother's eyes narrow. 'Someone might be awake?'

Grandmother makes a dismissive sound. 'And would you know what a fair trade is for the pennyroyal? Could you tell someone with a sick babe what kind of poultice to make up to draw out the fever? It's more than just handing over bundles of tea, girl. No, it's my burden to carry, and carry it I will.'

From outside comes the call of a raven, long and low. A mourning call. Quiet for a moment, as though it's waiting for a reply, but none comes. It calls a second time, then falls silent for good.

'I still can't get used to that,' Grandmother says. 'The silence. There was always noise before, even in the dead of night.'

It's not often that Grandmother talks about her old life. 'What was it like? The world before the war?'

Grandmother stares at the steam rising from her tea. 'It was cold,' she says, her voice far away. 'It was painful. It was lonely.'

'But you had Grandfather. And Mother.'

'It doesn't matter what anyone had. That world is dead and gone and good riddance to it all. The rest is just this. Silence, and waiting to die.' She picks up her mug and heads for her bedroom.

The sound of Grandmother's door being locked echoes through the house. I drink my tea and clean up from dinner, sniffing tentatively at the remains of the vegetable tart. It smells fine. All of the rotten yams must have been in Grandmother's portion. I wrap up the remains and take them down to the root cellar.

I go back to the bedroom to check on Mother. She hasn't moved and doesn't react when I hold her hand. This is the longest and deepest sleep she has ever been in.

I lie down next to Mother, arrange my body in imitation of hers. How would it feel to lie immobile for days on end? After only a few minutes, my back is aching and my legs crawling with the need to stretch. Mother must be in so much pain.

I wonder if she regrets not taking the kindness when Grandmother offered it. Ten drops and all of this would be over.

There are more than just ten drops in that bottle. More than enough for both of us.

I don't want to live the way Mother is living. I don't want to die in pain.

Mother's eyes flicker beneath her closed lids, and she makes a soft sound in the back of her throat. It sounds like the mourning call of that raven.

Ten drops twice over, and no more suffering for Mother and me. Even Grandmother would be free. Our garden could produce enough for her alone, if she was frugal, no need for her to leave the safety of the wall.

'It's going to be okay, Mother.' I curl up at Mother's side, the way I used to do as a child. 'In the morning when Grandmother wakes, I'll ask her for the kindness for us both. We don't need to wait to die.'

Silence is my only reply.

The night is warm, a soft breeze moving through the garden. I walk the perimeter of the property, checking for any signs that rabbits have tried to burrow under the wall. Though I can hear the rustling of animals outside, there's no sign that anything has tried digging tonight.

There are a few snails in the cabbages, which I drop into a lidded bucket, and several new anthills, easily treated with boiling water. Some of the tomatoes have been chewed by a rat, and I set out traps. I leave the ruined tomatoes; Grandmother forbids me from touching the plants, not trusting me to see the difference between healthy and diseased leaves at night.

I move on to the herb garden, breathing in the mingled scents. The lavender is flourishing, as is the yarrow. Grandmother says that the flowers are only worth their seeds and medicinal effects, that the scents are useless, but I think the scent is part of their beauty.

In the farthest corner of the garden stands a ghost gum. Beneath, a small flat stone marks the place where my father is buried. Rosemary grows in a low, clipped hedge around the grave, the plant thick with fading flowers. I pause to breathe in its scent before I turn my attention to the tree.

It takes almost no effort to pull myself up into the ghost gum's branches, the sun-banked warmth of the bark beneath my hands almost as familiar as my own skin. Every night I've been able, I've pulled myself up into the ghost gum, shimmying out along the branches until I can see over the wall. Not even Mother knows that I climb. She's been in her wheeled chair since my birth, and the stairs leading from the house make it impossible for her to come out into the garden.

Going outside the wall is forbidden to me. Grandmother has never said anything about looking over it.

Most of the valley below us is filled with tangled scrub, the remnants of walls and chimneys poking out here and there, the remains of the city that used to fill the valley. Farther out, there are clearings in the bushland. They're completely black, and don't reflect the moonlight. Those are marks from some of the weapons used in the war. Places where nothing will ever grow green again.

Directly below our hill is the only portion of the valley that's been cleared. There lies the village.

The first time I dared climb, I expected the village to look chaotic, but it's neat and ordered. There are rows of cottages and larger buildings, with wide paved walkways and gardens in between. The far side of the village contains no buildings, the space holding a large garden of some kind. From where I sit, I can't see which plants grow there, but I assume they're all food-bearing.

At night, most of the windows in the village are dark. There's a cottage bordering that large garden which has a kind of tower set to one side; every night I've climbed, there's been a lantern burning in that tower window. I can see the shadow of someone inside that room, sometimes standing still for a long time, sometimes pacing to and fro as though worrying at a problem.

Tonight, for the first time, that window is unlit. I feel an odd kind of disappointment at that. I've grown used to seeing that light, to wondering what kind of work the occupant does that needs the night. On very rare occasions I've even allowed myself to think that they might be like me, unable to walk beneath the sun without growing ill.

Maybe it's a sign, that the tower window is dark tonight. A sign that my choice to ask Grandmother for the kindness is the right one.

The soft breeze that's been twining through the leaves grows suddenly stronger, the branch I'm sitting on swaying. I start to slip, realising as I do that I've moved far enough from the trunk that I can't easily reach back to steady myself. There's nothing else to do but lunge for the top of the wall. My fingers scrape across the rough stones then grasp at the edge, the pain making me gasp.

From below, someone echoes the sound.

From below, and from *outside* the wall.

I peer over the wall and forget all about the pain in my hands. Because standing there looking up at me is a girl.

She has dark skin, her black hair twisted into a knot on top of her head. There's some kind of heavy pack on her back and a pocketed apron around her waist. Her fingers are curled around a handful of leaves that she's just stripped from a plant.

She stares up at me, eyes wide, then turns to glance behind her. I get a good look at the pack she wears, and shock loosens my grip on the wall. I fall, landing hard in a patch of mint, the wind going from me.

For a long time, all I can do is lie there gasping for breath. When I can finally get up, I move tentatively, but nothing seems to be broken.

By the time I manage to climb back up into the ghost gum, the girl is gone. I wait as long as I can, but she doesn't return. Finally, I climb back down and go inside.

The medicines are still arrayed along the bench, waiting for Grandmother to take them to the village tomorrow. I pick up a bundle marked with the pennyroyal flower, weigh it in my hands.

None of the girls in the village want their babies. Grandmother's pennyroyal tea makes certain that none of the girls have them.

And if that's true, how could I see what I saw?

It wasn't a pack the girl was wearing, but a long length of fabric wrapped around her torso. Snugged into a pouch of that fabric on her back was a baby, its skin gleaming as pale as mine in the moonlight.

There's no answer when I knock on Grandmother's door.

Usually Grandmother is already awake and dressed before I knock, my waking only a formality. Sometimes she's still pinning her hair or lacing her boots, and it takes her a few minutes to emerge.

A few minutes pass. A few minutes more.

I knock again. 'Grandmother?'

No answer.

'Are you awake? Grandmother? Are you okay?'

There are other ways to die than the known course of a disease. Father dropped dead when he was much younger than Grandmother. Grandmother might be lying on the floor of her room even now, growing cold.

I pound on the door, so hard that my hand stings. 'Grandmother!'

Silence.

I try the door, find it locked. The key is inside, hooked on Grandmother's belt as always. I've never thought about what would happen if Grandmother died before me. It's never seemed possible.

I'm searching around for something to smash the door with when I finally hear the creaking of Grandmother's bedsprings. Her footsteps drag across the floor, agonisingly slow, until she finally reaches the door. The scrape of metal on metal as she misses the keyhole once, then twice. On the third try, key meets lock.

The door doesn't open. Assuming it's jammed, I set my weight against the door and push. At the same time, Grandmother pulls, and we both tumble into the room. The air goes from me, bruised muscles contracting painfully. I lie there dazed, only half aware of Grandmother struggling to her feet.

The air in the room is musty and heavy. There's a lantern on the table, the candle burning low. Curtains which I'd always thought to be simply drawn closed have been stitched together in the centre and nailed to the wall around the edges, rust bleeding in long streaks down the fabric. Grandmother's bed is rumpled, sheets and blankets sliding onto the floor. And most odd, the far wall of the room has been stacked high with faded cardboard boxes. One near the bottom looks to have gotten wet at some point and is soft and wrinkled, one corner torn away to reveal a jumble of small jars, boxes and books inside.

Grandmother grasps my wrist and hauls me out of the room, dumping me on the hallway floor while she relocks the door.

'What's in those boxes?' I ask. 'They look old. Are they from before?'

'None of your business is what they are,' Grandmother says. She's dressed, though her apron strings are hanging loose. She ties them, wincing as she pulls them tight, the expression quickly smoothed away. 'That room is my private space, Helena, as well you know.'

'I'm sorry,' I say. 'I was worried. Are you okay?'

'Of course I am,' she snaps. 'It's just my rheumatism, nothing else.'

She walks to the kitchen with one hand on the wall. In the kitchen, she seems her normal self as she prepares tea and stirs the porridge. I strip off my clothes and stand naked before the stove. Grandmother flicks me a sideways glance.

'No need for any more assessments,' she says, then pauses, turning fully to me. 'You're bruised.'

'I fell.'

'You fell? From where?'

My throat is dry. 'I ... tripped, I think.'

Her eyes narrow. 'Over what?'

She's looking at me too closely now. Can she tell how far I fell from the bruises? 'Maybe it was a seizure,' I say quickly. 'I felt dizzy, I think. Confused a bit.'

A small smile curves her lips. 'I told you, didn't I? I'll add extra willow bark to your tea and we can use some arnica salve before you go to bed. Some astringent wash for those hands, too. We don't want infection to set in. Poor thing, you must have tried to catch yourself during the seizure. I remember Cordelia doing the same more than once.'

I hadn't even noticed that my hands were scraped, but both palms bear deep grazes from where I'd caught myself on the wall.

We sit down to breakfast. There's porridge and tea for me, but Grandmother only serves herself tea. From the scent, it's mostly willow bark.

'Rheumatism,' she says, seeing me looking at her cup. 'They'll feed me in the village, besides.'

My gaze goes to those bundles and jars on the bench. 'Do none of the girls have their babies? None at all?'

'None.'

'But without babies, won't the village die out?'

'Of course. They're all waiting to die, same as us.'

I sip my tea. It's bitter enough to curl my tongue. 'Why … why did Mother not take the pennyroyal?'

Grandmother stares out of the window for a long time before she answers. 'It was too late when she came back.'

I blink. 'When she came back? Came back from where?'

Grandmother's eyes turn back to me. I wish she'd look back at the window again. 'She never told you? What, did you think your father flew over the wall? No, that foolish girl took it upon herself to steal the gate key and run away. Came back with you on the way and fear in her eyes. The birthing was hard on her, as well you know. She was so weak, and it took little for her illness to sink its claws into her.' Grandmother stares at Mother's wheeled chair sitting in the corner of the kitchen. 'You're a good girl, aren't you, Helena? Not foolish like Cordelia? If I handed you the gate key right now, you wouldn't take it?'

'No,' I say, even as I have to curl my hands into fists to stop from imagining the weight of the key in my fingers.

It's only later, lying beside Mother in the darkness of my room that I realise I'd forgotten completely about my promise to ask for the kindness for Mother and me.

'I'm sorry, Mother,' I whisper. 'I can't do it, not yet. I need to know. You understand, don't you?'

The sound of Mother's ragged breathing is the only answer I get.

---

The next evening, Grandmother is drawn and white when she wakes me. She's silent as we change the padding beneath Mother and sponge her down. Her hands are shaking, and when she gives Mother poppy syrup she spills several drops before getting any into Mother's mouth.

'Was it bad at the village today?' I ask.

Grandmother gestures to the knife thrust into her belt. The blade is bright with fresh blood. 'There's food in the kitchen. I'm going to bed.' She leans heavily against the wall as she makes her way to her room, the door closing with a hollow thud.

The stove is cold. I scrape out the ashes and build a new fire, set the kettle to boil, blend mint and willow bark into a passable tea. The long bench is fairly groaning under the weight of food from the village. I saw off a hunk of bread, spread it with butter, chew mechanically, tasting nothing.

Grandmother's wagon stands in the corner of the kitchen, black dirt still clinging to the wheels. There are only a few bundles of mint tea remaining inside. Grandmother was right about one thing: all of the pennyroyal is gone.

None of the girls in the village keep their babies. Grandmother's pennyroyal tea makes certain of that.

And yet I saw the girl with the baby.

Both of these things can't be true.

Outside, the night is still. The moon is just beginning to wane, the barest hint of shadow veiling its light. The ghost gum stands tall and proud and pale.

I climb.

And I find the girl there again.

She's sitting right beneath me, back to the wall. Her eyes are closed, mouth slightly open. Her chest rises and falls in a slow, even rhythm. It's strange to be close to someone breathing normally. I find myself counting her breaths, waiting for a silence that doesn't come.

There's a rustle in the bushes, and then a boy appears. He's tall and thin, his fair hair hacked off just above his shoulders. He's wearing that length of fabric wrapped around his torso, the baby tucked in against his chest. The baby is awake, blinking peacefully. The boy yawns, jaw cracking loudly, and stretches out his arms. His shoulder joints move loosely in their sockets, as though they're about to pop loose.

'I know Brigid said she wanted to take tonight, but she's utterly exhausted,' he says. His hands move as he speaks, inscribing almost dance-like gestures. 'I got Meg to make her some valerian tea, see if she can get her to sleep. I don't think Brigid slept at all last night, even with all of us taking turns with Carol.' His hands come up to cradle the baby briefly. 'At least the little rat is calm now. Got her own way. You know, I think—' He breaks off as he looks up and sees me. 'Greta!'

The girl below me stirs, opening her eyes a crack before letting them close again.

'Greta!' the boy says again. 'Wake up!'

'Not sleeping,' she mumbles, eyes still closed. Her hands move as she talks, too. There's a strange beauty to it. 'Need me to sling Carol up and walk around with her?'

'Greta, you're already out on a walk. Sans baby,' the boy says. 'And you were sleeping. And I already have Carol in the sling. And you're not alone.' He points up at me.

I shrink back instinctively, ducking down below the wall.

'It's okay,' Greta calls out. 'We're not going to hurt you. We can't even reach you up there. The wall is too high.'

My heart is hammering. I wrap my arms around the tree branch, press my cheek against the cool bark. I want to run back inside, lie down next to Mother and wait and be safe.

But I also want to know the truth.

I look back over the wall. Greta and the boy have both backed away. They're holding their hands by their sides, palms out. The baby is looking up at me. Her eyes are dark, almost startlingly so against her pale skin.

'We're not going to hurt you,' Greta says again, her hands dancing. 'I'm Greta, and this is Karl. What's your name?'

'Helena.' My voice comes out as a shaking whisper, barely audible. The urge to run wells in me again. I dig my nails into the tree branch, clear my throat and try again. 'I'm Helena.'

'Do you live here?' Greta asks. 'With the w—' Karl sets a hand on her shoulder and she stops. 'With the old woman?'

'Yes.' I look past them. There's a light burning in one of the smaller cottages in the village. The tower window is dark. 'Do you live there? The village?'

'Arcadia,' Karl says. 'It's called Arcadia.'

Greta rolls her eyes. 'It's not called anything, because no one can decide on what we want to call it. Karl thinks it should be called Arcadia, though, in case you didn't notice.'

'It's a better name than Xanadu. Or Rivendell, or El Dorado, or whatever other idea Lee has this week,' Karl says. 'Arcadia. It rolls off the tongue.'

'It's pretty,' I say.

'See?' Karl puffs out his chest. 'Helena likes it.'

Greta thumps him in the ribs. His breath expels with a soft *oof*, his hands coming up to cradle the baby, who takes the opportunity to snuggle in closer to him.

'Where did you come from?' Greta asks. 'We thought our pilgrimages had found every enclave around here.'

'What do you mean, where did I come from?' I ask, frowning. 'I've always lived here.'

Greta stills. 'Always?' Her voice is low, words deliberate. Even the dancing of her hands is slower. 'How long is always?'

'I was born here, of course. It's safe here behind the wall.' I realise something else. They're both outside of the village wall, and don't carry any weapons that I can see. 'You shouldn't be outside of the walls. It's not safe.'

Karl frowns. 'The biggest things out here are a couple of feral pigs that have escaped being captured. I don't think the foxes, rabbits or cats are really going to have a go at anyone.'

'But Grandmother always takes a knife with her. Uses it sometimes.'

Both of them stop and stare at me.

'*Grandmother?*' Greta asks. 'Do you mean the old witch is your grandmother?'

'It's hardly a secret,' I say, starting to get irritated with them both. 'Yes, she's my grandmother. And she's not a witch. She's a doctor, as you both know.'

'Helena, this is very important,' Greta says. 'I need to know. Was your mother's name Cordelia?'

I nod. 'Yes. Why?'

'Oh Gods.' Greta clutches at Karl's arm. 'Oliver always said that he didn't trust the old witch. But I don't think even he thought she'd lie about something like that.' She looks up at me, eyes shimmering with tears. 'I'm so sorry.'

'Sorry about what? And who's Oliver?'

'Oliver is...' Greta shakes her head. 'We shouldn't be the ones to tell you any of this.'

'You're the ones who are here,' I say. 'Who is he?'

'Oliver is your father,' Greta says.

I stare at her. Something feels funny in my head, and I wonder for a moment if I'm about to have a real seizure. I press my nails harder into the tree branch. The sharp scent of eucalyptus steadies me. 'My father is dead. He's buried in the garden beneath me.'

'*Oh.*' Greta's tears spill over. 'So she lied to you, too? No, Helena, your father is alive. If he knew ... this is going to change everything for him.'

A crash and a scream shatter the stillness of the night. I jump, half slipping from the branch. 'Mother!'

'Wait, what?' Greta asks. 'Is Cordelia still alive?'

Another crash. 'Not if I don't go and help her. She'll be weak after sleeping so long, and she's likely to hurt herself badly without help. I'll come back tomorrow night. Will you be here?'

'We'll be here,' Greta says. 'Go and help her.'

I slide down the tree and run back inside. I feel as though the moonlight has seeped into my skin and is bouncing around inside of me. Mother is awake. Father is alive. Everything is going to be okay.

It wasn't Mother who screamed, but Grandmother.

She's lying unconscious on the kitchen floor, a dark bruise blooming on her temple. In one hand is her chatelaine, the keys splayed like petals about to fall from a flower. In the other hand is a bottle of poppy syrup. The cupboard stands open. It's almost empty. There are only four bottles of poppy remaining, and the bottle of kindness shoved into a back corner, the black glass thick with dust.

'Grandmother?' I ask.

There's no response. I gingerly probe her skull but can't find anything obviously broken. Grandmother would know some kind of poultice to use, but I have no idea what would be helpful or harmful. I settle for a damp cloth pressed against the bruise.

There's nothing else I can do but take her to bed and hope she sleeps it off. I lift her up, surprised to find that she's even lighter than Mother, seemingly no flesh at all between her skin and bones. Her chatelaine slides from her hand, and I leave it where it falls. It takes no effort at all to carry her into her room and lay her down in bed.

In her bedroom, I find the source of the first crash. The boxes that had been stacked against the walls have fallen down, several splitting open. Dozens of small boxes and jars have spilled onto the floor, several of the jars shattered, spewing small white objects everywhere. When I step back from Grandmother's bed, my boot heel comes down on one. It crushes to a bitter-smelling powder. There's a heavy book lying nearby, pages open to a drawing of the human arm, skin flayed open to reveal the muscle and bone inside. The margins are filled with Grandmother's handwriting.

Grandmother makes a soft sound, drawing my attention from the mess. She's shifted on the bed, her nightgown bunching up around her thin legs. I go to pull it down again but stop with my hand on the hem. There's a long cut curving around the outside of her thigh. I move the fabric up and uncover another, and another.

There are wounds climbing up both of her thighs, some of the higher ones deep and black, the lips of the cuts sewn together with thread. They're too neat and numerous to be accidental injuries. Is it some kind of disease? Has she been hiding her own illness from me?

I pull Grandmother's nightgown down and tuck a blanket over her. Against the white pillow, her skin is yellowish and dull. Her hair has come loose from its braid, and it's so thin in places that I can see bare scalp shining through. She looks old. She looks ill. She looks as though she's the one who is dying.

'I hate you,' I whisper. 'Why did you lie to me? To everyone?'

There's no answer.

I go back out into the kitchen, fetch down the black bottle of kindness, uncork it. The liquid inside is thicker than I expected. It smells just like honey. Odd, to be so sweet, when most of Grandmother's other medicines are bitter.

I could pour this whole bottle between Grandmother's lips right now. Make her pay for her lies.

But then I'd never know the truth.

I lock the bottle of kindness back in the cupboard, sit down next to Grandmother's bed and wait.

The next evening, Grandmother is still unconscious. The bruise on her temple is darker, sliding down into her eye socket. I sponge her down, trying not to touch the strange wounds on her legs, change her nightgown, braid her hair. Go and do the same for Mother.

Grandmother's chatelaine still lies on the kitchen floor. I pick it up, loop it around my waist, and go outside.

Something scurries through the vegetable beds as I pass. A rat, I think, probably the one that's been chewing on the tomatoes. The trap that I set has closed, but caught nothing. Normally I'd reset it, but tonight I leave it be. The rat's just trying to stay alive, after all.

The keys chime softly together as I walk to the gate. The black key slides soundlessly into the lock, the lock turning as easily as though it's been freshly oiled. It only takes the smallest of pushes to open the gate.

I expected a path here, but there's only ragged scrub right up to the gate. Everything is still, not the barest breath of air stirring the leaves. There's a scent like old smoke hanging over everything.

Greta and Karl aren't here, but they will be expecting to see me in the ghost gum, around on the other side of the property. I close the gate and lock it, then follow the wall around.

The scrub thins out as I walk, and when I turn onto the side of the wall the ghost gum overhangs, the plants change altogether. My focus was on Greta and Karl before, and I hadn't noticed then, but here the scrub has been cleared away. The area is filled with plants I recognise. Rosemary and pennyroyal, lavender and mint, valerian and yarrow. All neatly pruned and recently watered. There are even dry remains of plants which I recognise as poppies died down in summer. Have the seeds blown over the wall and taken root here, our garden spilled out into the greater world?

I pluck a sprig of lavender and rub it between my fingers. The scent is much stronger than anything we grow within the wall. It feels as though this is the first time I've ever smelled lavender. Every other flower has been a ghost, a dusty memory of scent.

There's a path here, too, winding away through the scrub towards the village. As I see it, I also hear footsteps. Greta and Karl appear a moment later, a ladder balanced between them. When they see me, they set the ladder down.

'Helena,' Greta says. 'We were expecting you to descend from above.'

I jingle the keys at my waist. 'Easier to just unlock the gate.'

'The old witch gave you the keys?' she asks. 'I didn't think she ever let them out of her sight. Even when we come to trade, she usually keeps one hand on them the whole time.'

I frown. 'When you come to trade? You mean when Grandmother comes to the village.'

Greta turns her head to one side. 'She never comes to the village. She never even sets foot outside of the gate.'

'But she takes her knife. She—' I break off, thinking of the bloodied knife, those too-even cuts on her thighs. 'She really never leaves?'

'She really never leaves. Even when Cordelia ran away, she was too afraid to leave. That's why Cordelia knew she was safe with Oliver. She knew her mother could never follow her. She wouldn't have gone back at all, Oliver always said, but she was afraid of losing you.

Instead, thanks to the old witch and her lies, Oliver lost you both.'

'Is he here? My father?'

'We didn't get a chance to tell you,' Karl says. 'He's off on pilgrimage right now. Gone to raid the libraries of the old world. Those of us who can, take turns going out into the world, either to look for anyone who needs us, or to find lost knowledge. The current project is to try to get some kind of real power working again. Mostly so we can have power wheelchairs for the people who need them, and breathing assistance and things like that.'

His words rush past me, most of them almost without meaning. I latch onto the one thing I do understand, the thing that's squeezing my chest tight. 'So my father isn't even here?'

'If he'd known you and Cordelia were alive, he wouldn't be anywhere else,' Greta says. 'He would have torn the wall down with his bare hands.' She stops, looking around. 'Where is Cordelia, anyway?'

'I didn't get to tell you that, either, did I?' I ask. 'She's sick. Sleeping, for days and days now. Grandmother gave her a year to live eighteen months ago. I put a yellow ribbon in her hair for her to see when she wakes up, but I think that maybe she isn't going to wake up again.' The words spill out of me, and tears prick at my eyes. 'I'm sorry. I just … I don't want her to die.' The last words are tiny, barely there at all.

Greta holds out her hands. 'Can I hug you?'

I just nod, and her arms close around me. She's warm, and her heartbeat is steady, her breathing deep and clear. There's a scent clinging to her skin, a flower that I've never smelled before.

'First thing,' Greta says, releasing me from the hug but keeping her hands on my arms. 'The old witch doesn't know everything. Or much of anything, really. Oliver found out that she was never even a doctor before the world ended. She wanted to be, but there was something different about her brain, with the way she reads and writes. She can manage both, with an effort, but even with all the help they gave her at university, she fell further and further behind, and eventually gave up altogether. She's learned a lot from books, but she doesn't know everything. Whatever she's said about Cordelia, or about you, might not be right.'

I just stare at Greta. It's never occurred to me that Grandmother might be wrong. 'You mean Mother might actually wake up? She might be okay? That I might not die?'

'Well, I think we can guarantee that you're going to die one day,' Greta says with a smile. 'We have a few people in Arcadia who are studying medicine using old university texts and guides, and it would be worth having them look at both you and Cordelia.'

'But what if … what if I do only have a year?' I ask. 'No one's going to want to waste time on me then. There's no point.'

'That is pure bollocks,' Karl says. 'A boulder might fall on my head tomorrow. That doesn't stop me from doing something useful today. No one knows how much time they get. You just get to decide what you do with it.'

'Oh gods, you and those old self-help books.' Greta rolls her eyes, then winks at me. 'You'll get used to him in time. Learn to listen to only about half of what he says. But he is right about this. It doesn't matter how much time you have.'

Karl pokes her in the ribs and she laughs. I feel faintly dizzy as I listen to them, and I have to step away, breathing deeply of the herbs that are growing here outside the wall. I stare at the plants and something else occurs to me.

'You were gathering herbs here when I first saw you,' I say. 'Weren't you?'

'Valerian,' Greta says. 'Our partner Brigid needed to sleep. You saw Carol, our daughter? She's not fond of sleeping at night unless she's glued to someone, mostly Brigid. I figured I'd see if I could get Carol to sleep in the sling and collect some valerian for Brigid in one fell swoop.'

'If you can gather herbs here, then why were you trading with Grandmother? Almost everything you trade for is growing here.'

'The truth is that we don't need a lot of it,' Greta says. 'But we know that your grandmother needs some of what we produce. We would have happily given her food, but could you see her accepting anything as a gift?'

'Well, no.'

'Exactly.' Greta smiles again, her teeth white against her dark skin. 'Anyway, we didn't come here to talk about herbs and grandmothers. We came here to take you to Arcadia.'

We walk together down the track to the village. Halfway there, Karl leans over to me and whispers: 'You'll notice that Greta's calling it Arcadia now? I think that means I win.'

'I heard that,' Greta throws over her shoulder. 'And no, it doesn't.'

The wall surrounding the village is pale, gleaming in the moonlight. There's a gate, more ornate than ours, made of black metal curled and twisted, somehow, to look like growing vines. It's so beautiful that I stop in my tracks, and Greta has to take me by the elbow and guide me in.

'Wait,' I say as she pulls the gate closed again. 'If there's nothing out there that'll hurt us, then why do you have the wall? Are you keeping someone locked in?'

'Firstly, we're not the only people left in the world, and we need to have some means of keeping safe if required,' Greta says. 'Mostly it's here to provide a boundary for people who need it. Some need it to feel safe. Others can't see well, and it stops them from wandering away until they learn the bounds of Arcadia.'

'See, she said it again,' Karl whispers.

Greta pokes him again. As they both laugh, a man with greying hair approaches us. He smiles at me but says nothing. His hands perform the same kind of dance that Greta and Karl do every time they speak, though his lips stay sealed. He nods at me, then walks away again.

'What was that?' I ask. 'Does he have some kind of sickness? Do you…?'

Greta looks at me for a moment. 'Oh. I don't even think about it most of the time. It's sign language. Darin is deaf, and he uses it to communicate.'

'But you were doing it when he wasn't even around,' I say.

'It's easy to make it a habit for everyone all the time. And it's not that hard to learn. Makes sure that Darin doesn't get left out of anything accidentally,' Greta says. 'We want Arcadia to be different, Helena. The old world treated a lot of people badly, and we want the new one to be different. One where everyone is valued, where everyone is equal.'

We keep walking through the village. The road beneath us is wide and even, and the houses all open off one level, no stairs. Mother wouldn't have an issue going anywhere in her wheeled chair here. I think of Darin and sign language, and know that the village's design isn't accidental. There are probably other people who use wheeled chairs here. Mother wouldn't have to be alone.

Each of the houses have their own gardens. Some grow vegetables, others herbs. At one, I stop. There are no vegetables or herbs here, only flowers of a kind I don't recognise. The blooms are large and velvety, and they carry the scent Greta wears on her skin.

'What kind of flowers are they?' I ask. 'I've never seen anything like them.'

'They're roses,' Greta says. 'Pick one if you want—Keiko doesn't mind sharing—but be careful of the thorns.'

I brush my fingers across the petals of a rose, though I can't bring myself to take one. 'They're beautiful.'

'Roses were important to the family who founded Arcadia,' Greta says. 'Keiko makes perfume from them, too. She'd be very happy to give you a bottle if you want. Or show you how to make it if you're interested.'

'Perfume? What's that?' I ask.

'Scent?' Greta waves her wrist under my nose, and I get a waft of that beautiful heady scent again. 'So you smell good? Not gross like Karl.'

Karl pokes out his tongue. 'I'll have you know that I bathed only last September. With soap.' He winks at me.

'But what else does it do?' I ask. 'Do roses help you sleep, or stop you feeling sick?'

'They smell good,' Greta says. 'Maybe they have some other use, but that's not why Keiko grows them. Maybe you can do some experiments. But we didn't bring you here for the roses. We brought you here to show you where your father lives.'

I know where we're going even before I see the cottage with the tower. Greta lights a lantern and hands it to me before pushing the door open. It isn't locked.

'Go upstairs. I know that Oliver would want you to see what's up there,' she says.

Inside the house it smells warm and good, like the scent of the fresh bread Grandmother brings from trading. The flickering light shows me that the lower level of the cottage is one large space. There are shelves holding what must be dozens of books, a kitchen with shelves crammed with canned and preserved foods. All of the windows have heavy blinds pulled down over them. In the corner, a large bed with a cradle set beside it. Does my father have another child? Another family?

My eyes sting, and I turn to the staircase in the corner and walk slowly up. There are other scents here, sharp and bright, making my eyes smart in a different way.

There's the large window I've watched so many times. From here, I can see our cottage, our wall. The limbs of the ghost gum are swaying in the wind. They look as though they're dancing, trying to tell me something in Darin's language.

I hold the lantern up and I see at last what my father has been doing all these nights. The walls are covered with sketches and paintings. In every one of them I see a woman. She looks like the reflection I see in water, only her hair is darker, her body fuller.

She's dancing, and she's climbing in a tree, and she's baking bread and she's laughing. Her belly is swelling, and she's sleeping on the large bed I saw downstairs and she's sitting next to that cradle, her hand on her stomach, smiling softly as she looks down. She's happy, and she's my mother and she's free.

'Keiko told us that Cordelia had started to cramp and bleed,' Greta says. She's come up the stairs and she stands behind me. 'Oliver had gone on a short pilgrimage, and she was scared and did the only thing she could think of. She ran home and she didn't come back. Oliver pounded on the gate when he returned and found her gone, but no one answered. The next full moon, your grandmother was there waiting as usual, and she told us that both of you had died.'

There's a small window on the opposite side of the room. It looks out over the expanse of gardens at the rear of the village. In the moonlight, I can see that there are roses growing there, as well as a group of young ghost gums.

'That's the memorial grove,' Greta says, pointing to the trees. 'We plant a tree over everyone who dies in Arcadia. The oldest ones are for the family who founded the village. Annalee and Eliza were twins, both of them with cystic fibrosis, a disease that could be treated before the world ended, but was deadly without that treatment. They died soon after they arrived here, but it was their initial idea to make this a haven for everyone who needed it, especially those rejected by the outside world. Their older sister was Georgie. She was Karl's grandmother, and she's the one who started the pilgrimages to rescue people who needed to find home here. The oldest tree of all is for Mari, a friend of the sisters' who died before Arcadia was founded. Her daughter was Keiko's aunt.'

'Are there ... did my father plant a tree for my mother? And me?'

Greta nods. 'He said it never felt real, because we didn't have your bodies to lay to ground, but he planted the trees all the same.'

I turn away from the window, find the painting of my mother standing over the cradle. 'Did he ... does he have another family? He still has the cradle downstairs.'

'No. There have been plenty of people interested, but he never did. And he still has the cradle only because he could never bear to have another child sleep in it, when you never did.'

It's all so much to take in. I feel hot, and my breath comes fast and shallow. My knees tremble, and then I'm sinking down onto the floor, Greta beside me immediately, holding my hand. I breathe deeply of the scent of roses and feel some of the panic fade.

'It's a lot, isn't it?' she asks. 'It's normal to feel overwhelmed, and you have all of this on top of the normal adjustment. When they found me, I was so scared that I shut myself in the bathroom for a week.'

'But how did you eat?' I ask. 'And sleep?'

'Even a tiled floor is pretty comfortable after you've spent your life being locked in a basement,' Greta says. 'And they passed me food through the window. We look after one another here. Someone helps me now, and I help them later on. Someone gives and someone takes. It all balances out.'

'But I'm useless. I can't even be awake during daylight. The sun makes me sick.'

'So you work at night instead. We have beehives, so we have plenty of candles. And you could stay here—tonight, if you wanted—since there are blinds on every window.' Greta reaches up and touches the rolled-up blind on the tower window. I hadn't noticed that both of these windows had blinds, too. 'Oliver installed them for Cordelia, and they kept her safe enough from the sun. And even if that's not enough for you, we'll work something out. It's what we do.' She smiles. 'A year is a long time, Helena. Time to make something, to be something. To find out who you are.'

❦

When I return to the cottage, the first thing I notice is how musty the air is. Everything smells dusty, heavy with mould and rot.

This place is dying.

Grandmother and Mother are both still sleeping. I remove the black gate key from Grandmother's chatelaine and tuck it in my pocket, then lay the chatelaine beside her in bed.

I don't hate her anymore. She's a frail, frightened woman, and I feel both pity and sympathy for her. How would her life had been if the world had shown her more real kindness? How will it be if I show her some now?

I go into my room and lie down next to Mother. The scent of roses lingers on my skin. I breathe it in and let it lull me to sleep.

---

The next night, I am woken as usual by Grandmother knocking on the door.

The bruise on her temple is covered by a clumsy bandage, the skin around it shiny with arnica salve. She says nothing as we tend to Mother, but I notice that she has to stop to catch her breath more than once, leaning heavily on the edge of the bed as she gasps for air.

There's tea blended for us both, but the fire hasn't been stoked nor water boiled. I take care of both, Grandmother sitting and watching me from the table. For breakfast, I scavenge up some stale bread to toast and slice an apple that's only a little mealy. Grandmother's tea is pure willow bark, so bitter that it must curl her tongue, but Grandmother drinks it down steaming, along with the second cup I make her.

Grandmother says nothing about the injury, or the key I took, though her hand goes to her chatelaine more than once. When she finishes her tea, she goes straight to her room, leaning heavily on the wall as she walks. For the first time, I don't hear her door lock.

There's work to be done in the garden tonight, and once I'm done, I'll go down to Arcadia again. I'll ask Greta if I can have some honey for Grandmother's tea, and maybe this time I'll be brave enough to pluck a rose from Keiko's garden, to ask her to show me how to make perfume.

And I will ask Greta and Karl to help me carry Mother down to the village. Maybe they'll be able to help her. She'll live in a place where her wheeled chair will never be stopped by steps and narrow doorways, a place where flowers are grown simply because they smell nice. And even if she can't be helped, she'll die free with her family and Father and I can plant a tree over her in memory.

And I will come back to Grandmother, and I will bring her honey and roses and I will find a way to ask her why she hurts herself, why she hides behind her walls. Maybe, with the help of people in Arcadia, we can find a way around her fears. Even if we can't, there will be kindness. Real kindness.

And I will live. Even if only for a minute or an hour or a day or a lifetime.

The rest will be what I make it.

# A FLOATING WORLD OF IRON SPINES
TYAN PRISS

The world ended a hundred years ago. Funny, how it hasn't stopped turning. Some things meant to drown just learn how to swim.

Or float, Lou contemplates, on her back with her legs and arms spread out, basking in the heat of summer nights and the warmth of urbanscape waters. Like that—weightless, strainless—the pain in her back eases, lifts itself from her s-shaped spine and her trapezoids. She'd close her eyes and fall asleep if she didn't risk being swept away by the soft current that slithers here. You never know where it can take you, onto whose territory. Some communities don't want you on their ruins unless you're planning on joining, especially those that are just starting out and are in dire need of more members; but Lou didn't leave hers, four years ago, just to find another one. She lends communities her talent as a mechanic only temporarily.

Lou takes a deep breath before curling under the surface. She sinks down in the underwater landscape: abandoned building debris, water vines crawling among crackled submerged walls, peaks of tower tops and electric poles and rooftop decorations. A city under a city. When the Great Flood started, people built their buildings higher and higher to outrace the rising waters; but even those have aged and crumbled and turned into the ruins of the urbanscapes. Buildings drowned. People swam.

Lou watches it all, endlessly fascinated. She feels no sting at keeping her eyes half-open: it's freshwater, kept unsalted by the Semryan aliens ever since their arrival during the Great Flood. For the longest time, she had no idea why—it's only after she met Evan that she's learnt about Semryans' allergy to salt water.

Her ignorance wasn't surprising. People from communities know next to nothing about the aliens. Semryans don't come often to urbanscapes and interact with humans living there even less, preferring to live in their round silver ships or in their own towns, where aliens and humans live side by side. Outside their cities, though, most humans remain wary of them. There are even rumours that Semryans caused the Great Flood. There's much more water now than Earth ever contained, after all—and who else could do that but aliens?

But the truth is, nobody knows. Even Lou has never gotten a clear answer out of Evan about that.

Something breaks the surface above her: a robotic hand, bursting towards her through the water, tied to a cable. She grabs it with both hands. The cable pulls her up in one swift motion.

# A FLOATING WORLD OF IRON SPINES

Lou flies out of the water like a shooting star. She emerges into the urbanscape, soars between the plant-devoured building ruins and the makeshift bridges and platforms made out of the fallen debris—the remnants of a last human attempt at a pre-Flood city, lost within the fresh water that stretches all around, infinite, up to the ends of the Earth. Lou lets go of the hand—

—and finishes her course down against Evan's metallic chest, banging against him with a swearing mixed with pained laughter, air knocked out of her lungs. The cable retracts into Evan's arm, hand snapping back in place.

'Ow,' Lou says as he puts her down, sheepish. Evan catapulting her against him is nothing new, but it never ceases to embarrass him. 'What's going on?'

Evan looks like most Semryans, at first glance—tall and humanoid, wrapped in a scarf and a long-hooded cloak with a parka and cargo pants underneath, and combat boots to complete the outfit. He has the Semryans' smooth, pitch black skin; and across his featureless face, the two glowing horizontal stripes that allow them to see. An almost exact copy of his peers for anyone who doesn't know better.

But the lower part of Evan's face is a BIBS mask—a Built-In-Breathing-System—and that's just the tip of the ruin. There is much more beneath his layers of clothing: alien silver metal parts over his torso and his limbs, plates and nails and more, clasped and clipped and screwed to keep his body together. His left arm is entirely robotic, with a cable launcher integrated inside to replicate the Semryans' expandable tendrils. He is the peak of Lou's crafting skills—perfect-suited prostheses, smooth fitting replacements, adapted aid components, foolproof ligatures. A patchwork of alien and machine, half-cyborg, built with the silver remnants of his crashed solo ship.

'There's a minipod.' Evan's arm whirrs when he points to a lone ruin, about a hundred metres away. 'An egg-shaped one, with a tinted top glass, the size of a large backpack. It floated up to here and got caught in the debris.'

Lou frowns. That sounds like the evacuation pods used by communities when they're endangered, to send away precious goods or things they don't want falling into the wrong hands. Finding a minipod doesn't mean good things, usually—bandits or gangs, at worst. People who want to claim control of resources and territory while civilisation is still being rebuilt. Not all communities wish to live alongside each other peacefully.

'Let's go see,' Lou decides.

They hike along the debris—Lou first, Evan clanking and buzzing right behind her. It's a lot of trudging around on uneven ground, and the pain in Lou's back flares up again. She has to stretch up and roll her shoulders backwards for a minute once they reach the minipod. She's definitely going back into the water after this. Staying hunched forward, even to climb over debris, is not something her back appreciates.

Evan fetches the minipod from the water, and hands it to Lou. It's still warm and about the maximum weight Lou is allowed to carry—somewhere around ten kilograms—which is surprisingly heavy, for precious goods and whatnot. Lou rests the pod against her hip under one arm and brushes a hand over the glass to unlock it.

When she sees what's inside, her eyes widen. Evan's metallic breath hitches.

It's a sleeping baby.

---

'A human baby?' Evan asks. He doesn't sound at ease, as ever around fragile things. With his accident, Evan has lost the delicateness and precision of touch of Semryans, and no amount of robotics or cyborgery will ever replace it. 'What is it doing here?'

Lou pulls out a small piece of paper tucked into the bundle of blankets the baby is cocooned in. Her back is starting to strain from holding the pod. She flicks the paper open.

'*To whoever finds Marlin: please bring him to the Turning Barrows in Arpetia*,' Lou reads. '*With luck, that's where we'll be.*' She turns to Evan. 'Arpetia? Isn't that the big Semryan town in the South?'

'It is.' Evan isn't very expressive, both because of the BIBS mask and because Semryans lack facial features; but Lou knows when he does the equivalent of frowning. 'It looks like this baby's community had to flee fast. They probably got attacked.'

'There must be a gang around,' Lou mutters. 'We better hurry to leave the area.' She dumps the paper back next to the baby, takes the pod into both arms. Her back is screaming now. Pods, even mini, are heavy. 'And we have to take this kid back to his family as soon as we can.'

'Neither of us knows how to take care of a baby,' Evan reminds her, unconvinced.

'Yeah.' Lou used to have little siblings, back at the community, but it's her mother who did most things. Now, Lou regrets not having helped her more. 'But if we don't at least try, he'll die.'

Evan emits a long wheezing sigh. He closes the top glass and takes the pod from her, hesitantly. But as rough as his touch has become, Evan's cyborg hands are still far more secure than a human's. The hesitation fades in a second. 'Let's go.'

They go back to their camp, on the topmost floor of a high ruin, and Lou makes a list of everything they will need to take care of the baby. Plenty of baby stuff: baby food, baby bottle, baby diapers, baby clothes. At least. Babies this size usually don't do much besides eating, sleeping, and crying; but who knows what else it might need? She asks Evan if he thinks they should also get toys, and Evan somehow manages to fix her a pointed look even with his eye-stripes.

Well. If there are toys needed, Lou has plenty of bolts too thick to be swallowed. Hopefully this baby—Marlin—will have the same taste as she did when she was his age.

'We'll need a boat, though,' Evan notes.

He's right: Lou and Evan usually travel by foot, but that won't do if they have to hurry. Lou can't stand or walk for too long—she needs regular breaks to sit and stretch, or to bathe in the water. Evan is the one carrying their equipment, and that, along with the amount of metal on his body, limits his movement and weighs him down. They're slow in their daily travels, and that's without counting the number of times they have to stop somewhere for at least a day.

Evan needs regular checking from Lou to make sure everything is functioning correctly and to do some maintenance. They also need to clean his BIBS mask and change the filter every five days: Evan is allergic to some particles in Earth's air and has to stay underwater until he can put the mask on again, which only further slows their progress.

Lou, for her part, occasionally has awful days during which the pain leaves her crying and unable to move. She tires easily and has to get a lot of sleep—which would be manageable, if it weren't so easy for her to end up hyperfocusing on something until late at night, or to be struck by a bad memory right as she's trying to sleep. Lou's mind can be as unkind as her spine. When dark thoughts keep her awake sobbing on her bunk or send her curling up against Evan, she never wants to spend the next day on the roads, with a back full of pain.

So if they want to hurry, they definitely need a boat. But first: the baby stuff.

Lou allows herself half an hour of bathing next to their ruin before she goes scouting around, waterproof satchel under her arm. She'd have sent Evan in her stead, but he wouldn't know what to grab for Marlin, and if there's a gang around, the baby will be safer with him. Luckily, Lou already knows where to go. With her goggles and her oxygen mask on, she uses her underwater seascooter to swim back up the current that brought the minipod here, going back to the surface regularly to check her surroundings.

It doesn't take her long to find the place she was looking for: a high ruin covered in moss and vines, with the remnant of wooden gates that look like they've just been burnt down. Lou makes sure the ruin is empty before sneaking inside.

The storey she enters through is one huge room, half of the floor and end wall broken, giving out onto the water. The rest of the room contains damaged furniture, scattered food, overturned planters, and other obvious proof that there were people living there until recently. As she thought, it belonged to a community.

Well. Had.

# A FLOATING WORLD OF IRON SPINES

From how mismatched everything looks, it was a brand new community. They're the easiest targets for gangs: just settling, not fully united, no defence system in place yet. Lou doesn't find blood or traces of a fight; but most things are still there, albeit destroyed, which means the community left in a complete rush.

There must be a reason why Marlin's parents had to send him away in an evacuation pod; but there's no way to guess what. Lou climbs the stairs up to the next floor with a wince, finds the baby supplies in a ripped open cupboard, and stuffs as much as she can into her satchel. She has no idea how much she'll need. Better safe than sorry.

Baby stuff acquired—now, the boat. All communities have several: boats are essential for communities, whether to scavenge or find more space to grow things. People who don't actually need them and travel exclusively by foot, like Lou and Evan, are an exception.

The community left in a rush and the gang that attacked them destroyed what they could find; but on the rooftop—her back on fire from crouching and from the stairs—Lou manages to find a functional inflatable boat stuck in a corner, behind two broken canoes. It's not one bit dusty, the tank still full. It must have been brought recently by a newcomer, but never used by the community. Lou pretends nothing hurts and pushes the boat up the edge of the rooftop, then down onto the water.

Her back is one sharp scream of agony, and it's even worse once she's climbed down, out of the ruin. She has to float in the water until it lessens before she can get into the boat and sail back home.

She is still dreaming of staying underwater for hours when she reaches their ruin and hides the boat inside. Unfortunately, the baby is crying and Evan won't know how to stop it. The noise rings in her brain, knocking at her eardrums. Lou drags herself to the hole that passes through all the floors up to the ruin's rooftop and claps her hands to signal her presence. Talking seems too tiring.

Eventually, Evan's cable comes down, and she wraps it around her waist. He pulls her up to the floor where they've made camp. Up there, the baby's cries are so loud she has to put her hands over her ears.

'He's hungry, I think,' Evan says, looking uncomfortable.

'I just remembered that I hate crying babies,' Lou says. 'So I really hope you don't.'

If Evan had human eyes, he would roll them. 'I should be fine.'

Lou tries to remember how her mother prepared baby formula and gets to doing that, while Evan covers her ears for her. She doesn't fare too badly for her first time feeding a baby then changing his diapers—it just reaffirms her decision never to have children of her own. To hell with any duty to repopulate the Earth. At least, when she's finished, Marlin is calm, sucking his thumb in the minipod, wide brown eyes analysing the world around him. Lou gives him a large bolt to play with. He seems very interested.

Lou, on the other hand, feels like she's going to faint. She's sitting cross-legged, in a position that is slightly easier on her back, head swimming with tiredness. Pushing through the pain is, more often than not, unavoidable; but she's really outdone herself this time.

'We have a boat,' she manages to tell Evan, who is checking his prosthetics. He occasionally has to take them off to air out his actual body. He's learnt to do it himself, over time, although he still relies on her and her skilled hands for his maintenance. All his limbs whirr softly when he turns to her. 'I scavenged it in Marlin's old community. They seem to have all fled, but the place was wrecked. There's definitely a gang around. We should leave as soon as—*ow*.'

She's just moved slightly, but her entire body has flared up in pain. Her sentence turns into a stream of curses. Evan sighs with a wheezing breath, gets up. He grabs her oxygen mask and hands it to her before picking her up with one arm.

'He'll be fine without supervision for five minutes,' he declares, glancing at Marlin, who has fallen asleep in his pod with his tiny hands wrapped around the bolt.

Then he leaps over the window, robotic grappling hand on its edge. With his cable, he lowers them down to the water. Lou would like to thank him; but she's given up on words at this point, and it's lucky Evan doesn't need them to understand her.

She just puts her oxygen mask on—and then, blessedly, soothingly, the water closes around them.

---

Marlin has been fed and his diaper changed; but that doesn't prevent him from crying his heart out as soon as they start the boat, as dawn breaks. Lou knows that babies cry because they have no other way to communicate: it seems that Marlin hates the boat and relays the message loud and clear. Evan said that maybe Marlin just misses his mother and his usual environment. It must be a mix of everything.

But there's no other way to get him back to his community—or at least to somewhere safer than in the care of two disabled travellers with zero parenting experience. The boat is the fastest way to Arpetia, and they can't give him the time to adapt to it. Until Marlin gets used to the rough change, Lou and Evan can only bear his cries and hurry.

'I'd take a break,' Evan says, features still but a grimace in his voice. 'But we don't know where the gang is, exactly. We better get away as far as we can. At least for today, we have to keep going.'

Lou nods, cross-legged in the boat, pressing the minipod against her to keep it from rolling around.

# A FLOATING WORLD OF IRON SPINES

She's given up on trying to calm down Marlin. His cries drill into her ears, hammer into her brain—heart-wrenching, gut-tearing, like the shrill hiss of a kettle after a funeral. She begs for silence in her mind, over and over. Part of her feels like throwing up and another part feels like throwing herself overboard; but neither is an option, so Lou can only grit her teeth and focus on the solidness of the pod under her fingertips until her ordeal is over.

Then finally, after what felt like an eternity, Evan stops the boat.

Hold Marlin, Lou wants to tell him. Fails to tell him. Her ears are ringing and her voice is missing, and tears have welled at the corners of her eyes. Once Evan has fastened the boat's mooring to some concrete debris stuck against the wall of a ruin, she hands him the minipod with Marlin still crying in it, and, with fumbling fingers, rifles through her satchel for her oxygen mask. She throws it on, takes Evan's metal hand. Dives into the water.

Sinks. Deep, deep, deep down. As down as Evan's cable allows it.

And she remains there, curled onto herself in the underwater ruins, a four-limbed fish with a mind like a raging storm, until the quiet of the abyss swallows her like it swallowed the world.

The following days go better. Lou is getting the hang of this whole taking-care-of-a-baby thing, Evan is getting better at steering the boat smoothly, Marlin is getting used to his new lifestyle. They take breaks as often as they can. Lou has one terrible day and stays underwater until she feels better, then decides to clean the filter of Evan's BIBS mask, so they're back on the boat only the next morning. While Evan and Lou are busy, Marlin plays with his collection of bolts in his minipod. He seems to really like them.

Eventually, they cross a ruralscape. Unlike urbanscapes, there is nothing but water on the surface: one has to dive to see the pre-Flood remains of fields and roads and villages that lay at the bottom and stretch between the now-submerged cities. Because there's barely anything to scavenge there and no one to trade with, their supplies deplete fast; but once they reach the next urbanscape, they get lucky and stumble upon a community almost immediately.

Lou usually visits communities alone, as Evan shys away from humans. But this time, she takes Marlin with her, strapped against her chest with Evan's scarf—she has no idea what the community will be like, but humans almost always take pity on people with babies.

Good call: it turns out to be a community that doesn't accept passing travellers. A common thing, unfortunately. Communities aim to expand and prefer to share only with those who can give back, in these times of rebuilding. It's wariness, too: only people eager to join can be deemed fully safe, and not bandits or thieves willing to trick them and stab them in the back.

Maybe it's also the difference in mentality. A community is unity, society. It all started with families and neighbourhoods that stuck together through the Great Flood and its aftermath; communities were born with the purpose of finding others to join. Gathering numbers, being many. Someone choosing to be alone is inconceivable.

But thanks to Marlin's presence, Lou is invited into the community regardless. While some mothers in the community take care of Marlin, she dines with the leader: an old man with a severe face, who has refused any payment for the supplies he's given her.

'Why won't you stay?' he asks. His community is full and well-organised, like a perfectly oiled machine, which impresses Lou and intimidates her at the same time. It's nothing like the community she grew up in; yet, those memories nag at the back of her mind. She misses Evan's presence by her side. 'You'd have a home, here, you and your baby.'

'It's not my baby.' Lou fiddles with her fingers. Her mother used to hate her constant fidgeting, she remembers distractedly. It's only when she met Evan that she allowed herself to do it again. 'We—I found him in a minipod in some ruins. I think his community was attacked. There was a note with him saying to take him to Arpetia.'

At that, the leader softens. 'I understand. But you could come back here, afterwards.'

She could never; but how to tell him that?

How to tell him that although it doesn't show, her back is a tense nest of pain, which means there are a lot of things she can't do, or can't do as she'd be expected to? How to tell him how terribly she failed to fit into her old community? That she could never do things right, that she was a disappointment, with her peculiar pace, her weird way of tackling things, her forgetfulness and messiness, her overreactions? It doesn't matter that she's a good mechanic: communities favour the constantly functional in the hope of rebuilding some semblance of society, and Lou is the opposite of that.

But worst of all, the memories of her old community plague her, here. There's more bad than good in them, and maybe that's why she never wishes to stay, even when a community is nice and would welcome her as she is.

It's the similarities. The parallels. The fact that the dark thoughts are eager to jump out when Lou is reminded of why they appeared in the first place. Living in her community felt like sinking deeper and deeper into the abyss with no hope of swimming up for oxygen, cracking up and splitting open on the way down like a crumbling ruin, suffocating and losing pieces of herself. She could never bear to constantly remember that, to constantly fear being put through the same thing all over again.

But, 'I don't really belong with others,' Lou just says.

Which is a lie, to be fair. She belongs with Evan—with someone who knows about her pain, who's seen all her flaws and failings and bad sides and has accepted her anyway. He rescued her too, in a way. Pulled her out of the abyss, breathed air back into her drowned lungs, patched her up as much as she did him. Evan always says he did nothing special, but it doesn't matter.

To Lou, his kindness will always be surer than any cyborgery.

After the dinner, the community returns Marlin with bags of supplies and tanks of fuel for the boat, and bids her goodbye. As soon as she's out of their sight, Evan steps out of the shadows to help her carry everything, no words needed. They walk back to their camp in a silence broken only by Marlin's soft giggles.

Lou has never felt more like she was coming home.

A summer storm strikes them less than a week later, deep in the urbanscape, starting with a downpour. They have to take refuge in the nearest ruin. Lou closes Marlin's minipod, and Evan takes it with him up the ruin, looking for a floor sheltered from the rain. There's no time to wait for him to come back and drag the boat inside: Lou has to moor it herself as best as she can.

A few seconds later, the storm hits. Lou screams. She runs to Evan as soon as he comes down, both hands against her ears, her mind convinced that the hammering of the rain and the rumbles of thunder and the blow of the wind are going to cleave her in two. Evan lifts her in his arms, climbs up to the floor where he's set down their bags and Marlin's pod. He curls up with her and closes his cloak around them both.

Like that, pressed against him, Lou can feel the metallic parts of his chest through the fabric of his parka. She traces the outline with her fingers. Evan's BIBS mask nuzzles her hair gently. Lou closes her eyes and forgets about everything else.

The storm reduces to a trickling rain two hours later, just in time for Lou to feed Marlin and change his diaper before he starts crying. She plays with him to ease her mind. For once, Evan joins her in entertaining the baby. He lets Marlin poke at the nails and screws and metal bands that keep his flesh hand in place, tickles him with the edge of his scarf until Marlin laughs. Lou finds herself smiling, watching them together.

She stops smiling, however, when Evan goes down scouting and reports that their boat got blown away.

Lou starts panicking. 'What do we do, now?'

'Let's stay here until the storm has fully passed,' Evan says, practical as ever. He's good at preventing her brain from making the situation seem bigger than it actually is. 'We'll go looking for it later. Let's rest, for now.'

She takes care of his maintenance while Marlin watches eagerly, giggling whenever she shows him a new tool. Evan gives her feedback on each adjustment she makes. She hyperfocuses and doesn't move the whole time, and her back takes revenge afterwards; but floating is off-limits as long as it rains, so she settles for lying down on her stomach instead, both legs tucked to the side to stretch her spine. It doesn't take the pain away, but it's better than nothing.

'You should sleep,' Evan says, moving around to test his prosthetics. Semryans can block out pain—lucky them—but it doesn't mean Evan can't feel discomfort. He sits down next to her, satisfied. 'You've worked hard, Lou.'

'You too.' She tugs his cloak until he lies next to her. Marlin has dozed off in his pod. 'You should sleep too.'

Evan lets out a soft wheezing exhale. His metallic fingers brush her cheek. They stare at each other for long seconds before Lou closes her eyes, and they both fall asleep to the sound of the rain.

Lou awakens first. Swearing when her back cracks as she gets up, she crawls to the window, and tears the blinds open.

Night is falling, but the storm is over. The sky is clear and an incredible shade of blue, golden fractal lines appearing between the stars, the moon casting its pearly light over the infinite expanse of water. Lou wonders if that's what the first post-Flood humans saw, when the rain finally stopped for good and the waters stopped rising, and the Semryans had finished setting up lanes for their spaceships around Earth.

Then she spots something in the horizon: a glimmer of silver, approaching at great speed. Her body moves before it can seem like a bad idea. She sits on the windowsill, waves her arms as wide as she can.

'OVER HEEEEERE!'

Behind her, Marlin starts screaming along happily. Evan gets up in a cacophony of whirring and clanking and swearing, then joins her.

Before he can ask her what she's doing, the Semryan ship lowers itself in front of them.

A couple of minutes later, they've explained their situation and been invited to come aboard. Lou holds Evan's hand as they step onto the ship, the Semryan crew loading their stuff and taking care of Marlin. Evan might act casual, but she knows he's just pretending. Between his appearance and the fact that he's lost some of his Semryan characteristics, his accident has made him terribly self-conscious around his own kind.

But after they talk to the captain, who agrees to take them to Arpetia, Evan fully relaxes. While he talks with the crewmembers, Lou sits cross-legged on a guest chair to observe him—it's the first time she sees him so animated around other Semryans. When they started traveling together, Evan used to refuse categorically to see any of them again.

Still too hurt. Too ashamed. With time, he stopped being so adamant about avoiding his peers; but even then, his awkwardness remained. Truth is, Lou feared it always would.

But now, seeing him so at ease and happy, she thinks that maybe they could start visiting Semryans more often.

The Semryan captain sits down in front of her, taking her attention. His outfit is similar to Evan's; but his clothes are cleaner and fancier, and instead of a BIBS mask, a hooded scarf hides the lower part of his face. Lou thinks he's smiling as he watches her, in a fond way.

'If I may ask,' he starts, 'what happened to Evan?'

While Lou feels uncomfortable being asked about her disability if she's never mentioned it before, Evan told her she didn't have to keep his a secret from others. 'His solo ship crashed down,' she replies. 'I found him underwater. He was alive, but his body was falling apart.'

The captain nods at Evan. 'Did you do this?'

This—the metal parts, the prosthetics, the cyborgery. 'No,' Lou says.

When she found Evan, she stayed in one place for the first time since leaving her childhood community. She decided she wouldn't move until she'd given him all the aid she could, because there wouldn't be anyone else to do that for him—or for her, or for any disabled person in need. She made a home with him in a ruin near a nice community, and spent a whole year working with him to patch him up: scavenging his ship for materials, designing replacement parts, adjusting them the right way. She constantly checked with him if this was what he wanted, what he needed. Constantly listened to his feedback and tweaked things until they fit, until finally, Evan told her everything was good as it was.

It was a year of Lou learning to be around people again, of learning not to fear being herself—with her quirks and her needs and her pace—with someone else; of Evan adapting to his new body, of mourning what he'd lost, of getting used to his new normal. A year of swimming after drowning, of rebuilding and moving on.

And after that year, Evan started travelling with her. 'We did this together.'

True to his word, the captain takes them to Arpetia and directs them to the Turning Barrows. Like all Semryan towns, Arpetia floats in the middle of a ruralscape: an alien-human hybrid town, built on a layer of buoyant Semryan concrete, its scavenged buildings and materials giving it the look of old pre-Flood cities. It couldn't be more different from their usual landscape. A new sort of place for all of them, especially Marlin. It hits them as soon as they step inside the city.

Here, ruins and debris and abyss have been replaced by streets lined with brick houses on low stilts and tram tracks that spread through the main avenues under a zigzag of cables. Streetlights on thin metal poles stand dormant, waiting for the night. Lou had never seen one whole and intact before: in the urbanscape, they are all underwater, damaged and covered in water moss.

But it's the people that are most different: in stark contrast to the emptiness and the calm of the urbanscape, they flow along the streets, trickling down one and dripping out another, their clamour and chatter rising in the air that swirls with unknown smells and fresh perfumes. It soon gets overwhelming, and both Evan and Lou hurry towards their destination.

The Turning Barrows is, they discover, an inn in the centre of the city, a small square building surrounded by humans and Semryans. A woman leans against a wall by the door, and someone near Lou and Evan, catching them staring, whispers that she has come here every day ever since she's arrived. It does seem like it: her face is tainted with a dark shade of gloom, a rich nuance of despair, as if at that point, waiting here was the only thing keeping her upright. Still, she raises her head at their approach.

And as soon as she spots the minipod, it's like her entire world has been turned over.

'Marlin!'

She doesn't even look at them when Evan hands her the minipod. All that matters is the baby. Her baby. She collapses to her knees and takes Marlin out of the pod, presses him against her heart. A curious crowd has gathered, watching her, drawn in by the noise.

Evan and Lou exchange a glance.

And when Marlin's mother tries to thank those who have brought her baby to her, she finds they are long gone.

―

They've left Arpetia on a ferry that goes back to the nearest urbanscape. Arpetia is nice; but there's too many people, and it's definitely not for Lou. Not for Evan either. They're both better on the roads, just the two of them—and maybe Marlin, if he behaves.

Lou threw out the idea of coming back, every once in a while, to see how he's doing. Evan argued that they wouldn't even know where to find him, but that's beside the point.

'Where to, now?' she asks.

'Wherever we want.' Evan gives a whirring shrug. 'There's no rush to decide. The world isn't going to end again anytime soon.'

Lou laughs. She's slid her hand in his, twined their fingers together. The metal parts of Evan's hand are cool and bumpy against her skin. She doesn't want to know anything else.

'You're right,' Lou says. Like the rebuilding civilisation around them, they've left their own abysses to float at the surface of the world's waters. Meant to drown; learnt to swim. Now, the future is an open sky. 'We can go anywhere.'

# RETURN OF THE BUTTERFLIES
## EMILIA CROWE

When the sky begins to grow light, I dress Luka in long pants and his fur-lined coat.

He fusses as I push his arms through the sleeves. 'I know, I know,' I hush him, conscious of my sister and her husband still asleep in the next room. 'I don't like the sleeves either, but it's still too cold. You'll get sick without them.' He whines, face crumpled up as he bats at my hands, but I am quick to fasten the buttons before he can pull his arms back out.

This will be harder someday, my sister warns me often. You can barely take care of yourself now, let alone your son. He is only seven, what will this be like when he is as strong, stronger even than you?

'*Luka*,' I sign, my own distress at his upset cutting off my voice. He turns his head away from me, scowling at a point somewhere off on the wall as he rocks himself. '*Luka, Luka*,' I sign, over and over, and the repetition of the familiar motions soothes us both. Slowly, he stops rocking, looking now at his sleeves, which he twists angrily in his hands.

I reach up and pull my own coat down off the rack. I put my own hands through the sleeves, cringing at the texture of the wool lining. 'I hate it too,' I sign to him, allowing my face to scrunch up in distaste, trying to let him know we're in the same boat. 'But outside is cold. Warm is better than sick.'

He accepts this reluctantly, letting go of the hand-stitched cloth bunched in his hands. He lets me pick him up, coat and all, and we slip out into the chilly morning air, our breath puffing in front of us as I carry him through the village.

The first few people are out, tending to the morning chores. My neighbour waves at me. I can hear the near-silent hum of the detoxifier as she pours water from the river into it, the clean water running out the other end into the goats' trough. I wave back, and so does Luka, burbling in my arms.

'Mornin', Melody!' she calls out. 'Maggie not coming with you?'

'Good morning,' I respond politely, covering my impatience as I approach the fence. 'She's still asleep, it's just me and Luka. I'm taking him to the woods.'

'Ah,' she says, grinning at my son. She wiggles her fingers at him, but he ignores her, turning away and gnawing on his own fist. There's always a softness to her weathered face when she looks at Luka. She had a son of her own once. Maybe that's why.

'That means he likes you,' I tell her. It doesn't, but that's what my sister always says when people try to interact with him like that, and it makes them laugh instead of getting upset.

Sure enough, my neighbour smiles and chuckles in response. She reaches over to switch off the detoxifier, and I relax in relief. I hate the hum it makes, the way it makes my very skull vibrate. I always make Maggie or her husband run ours. 'You two be careful out there,' she tells us, turning to head back inside. 'Stay close to the border.'

'We will,' I assure her, already edging back towards the path, relieved that she doesn't seem to be in the mood for small talk. I'm too eager to get out to the field. And besides, Maggie is the one who's good at that. She's the one who tied us into the community in the first place. My job, as she tells me, is just to not screw it up.

None of the few other people we hurry past try to talk to me, to my delight. I think some of them can tell I don't want to talk to them. Other people seem to know that sometimes; Maggie always tells me I'm terribly rude not acting like I'm happy to see them. I've never known how to fix this, but right now I am grateful for it.

Finally, we reach the steel fence that marks the border between the colony and the rest of what's left of the world. Barbed wire lines the top, rusted black against the navy sky. I worry that the gate may be locked, that we'll have to find the watchmen for his key, even though the metal panels are beginning to peel back where the edges are rusted away, and I'm sure I can find a spot to slip out if I have to. But although the gate is pushed shut, as it always is at night, no one has bothered to lock it. We leave the colony unimpeded. The fence is a relic at this point anyway. There hasn't been an attack in well over a year now. I've heard that most of the raiders are either dead or absorbed into the slowly-forming colonies and regrown cities.

The trees start only about fifteen feet past the fence, ashen branches crowding in as though ready to swallow our little town whole. I tread carefully along the dim and barren path, the light that seeps past the scraggly, radiation-twisted trees stained blue with night. It takes ten minutes, a small eternity, before I finally spot the tree I'd marked, and my heart leaps in my chest. I step off the main path, and the road behind me is swallowed by shadows within moments.

This area survived the bombs, though not unscarred. The dead trees tower above us, skeletal hints of the forest they once were. Nothing has rotted the way it should. But here below, where we walk, some of the saplings are as tall as I am, and my footsteps fall softly on the green undergrowth that peaks from the carpet of fallen leaves. These trees too are twisted, and I know it will be a long time yet to come before any grow straight again, but their few spring leaves are green and fresh all the same.

I move faster the closer we go, uncaring of the heavy weight of Luka in my arms, striding along on the balls of my feet. Miraculously, I don't trip or stumble even once.

In the light that turns everything the same pale grey, the boundary between the trees and the clearing is almost invisible until we cross it. But suddenly, the trees around us part, and there is nothing but the grass against my knees.

I prod Luka gently to get his attention from where he dozes against my shoulder. 'We're here,' I mouth to him, unwilling to force the words from myself and break the delicate silence.

I kneel at the edge of the field, and Luka wiggles, impatient to get out of my arms. I let him down, and he takes off to explore without a backwards glance. I arrange myself to sit cross-legged and wait, keeping half an eye on him as he scampers about. The sun is nearly up by now, the field growing steadily brighter.

Luka has found a stick, which he's using to prod at clumps of grass and bushes, searching for small animals and treasures. I whistle softly to him, and he looks up, eyes fixed on a point somewhere on my forehead. 'Quiet,' I sign against my lips, and he bobs his head in understanding, returning to his exploration with slightly less rustling and jabbing. The chilly wind whispers through the meadow and I shiver, huddling down into my jacket a little more.

My eyes scan the grass, the colours of the wildflowers growing increasingly vibrant and visible in the swelling dawn. Luka finds a sparkly rock, which he lays beside me before going to intently scan the ground for more. I resign myself to heavy pockets when we return home.

The tips of the grey trees begin to turn gold, the first rays of sun slowly creeping down their trunks.

We've come into the field from the north, far enough towards the west for the sunlight to touch us. I welcome the warmth against my skin. Off in the distance, I hear the sound of the church bell ringing, rousing the town to full consciousness.

Finally, at long last, I see something flit between the grasses, towards our end of the field. A sparkle, like a little butter-yellow star at the edge of my vision. My hands mimic it, fluttering wildly, somewhere between a joyful flap and a wave to get my son's attention. He comes over as my joy bubbles up, blooming warm and sunny in my chest and throat until I can't even speak, just open my arms so he can sit in my lap. I point, and Luka looks with wide eyes.

'Orange sulphur,' I whisper at last. 'Colias eurytheme.'

These butterflies were common when I was a girl, easy to find in every meadow and vacant lot I explored. But this is the first of its kind I have seen in fifteen years, the first I've seen since before the war.

It is the first butterfly my son has ever seen.

'The caterpillars eat at night,' I tell him in a hushed voice, and for once the words aren't a struggle, they flow from my tongue as easy as breathing and just as hard to stop. 'They're called orange sulphurs, but they used to come in all sorts of colours, that's why this one's yellow. They were pale and dark and orange and white and so many shades in between, and they lived all over the place. So many that some people saw them as pests because they'd eat the grass the farmers planted for their animals. They don't have wings yet, when they're babies, so they crawl around on leaves and grass and eat it all up, until they're fat and strong enough to turn into a butterfly, just like that one right there. Then they go into their chrysalis, where they grow during the winter. This one is probably a new butterfly, this early in the spring. He's got brand new wings to fly around on.'

'Bah?' Luka says inquisitively, and I reluctantly tear my eyes away from the precious creature to look at him, following his finger to where it points to the other edge of the field.

I hadn't even noticed the large brown butterfly as it emerged, fluttering lazily near the ground by the trees. I laugh softly, delight beating within me like little wings.

'Mourning cloak, nymphalis antiopa. They don't drink from flowers much, not like orange sulphurs,' I murmur. 'They drink from tree sap and rotting leaves, mostly. You don't usually see them this time of year. Or at least you didn't used to. I guess the seasons are so strange now that they're as confused by them as we are. There must be willow trees in this forest somewhere, still. That's a baby mourning cloaks' favourite food, before they get their wings.'

'Morn'?' he questions, chubby fingers fiddling with a rock he picked up while I spoke.

'Mourning,' I confirm, nodding. 'Not like when the sun comes up, but like when people are really sad because someone they love is gone.'

He frowns, forehead wrinkling. 'Sad?'

'Mhm.' I let out a breath against his hair, the brown of the mourning cloak vanishing back into the dark background of the trees. 'Like Mummy was sad, because I didn't think I'd ever see a butterfly again.'

He is quiet for a long moment after that. The breeze blows softly through the flowers, stirring the orange sulphur from its temporary perch. It takes to the air again, drifting along until another flower catches its fancy. Somewhere, a bird begins to sing.

Eventually, he tugs at my arm, getting my attention once more. 'Happy?' he asks, tongue clumsy on the two-syllable word, outside of his usual comfort zone.

I smile, resting my chin on his head for a brief second before scooting back to give him space. 'Yeah, baby, I'm very happy.'

He makes a satisfied chirp and returns to his rock.

A flicker of motion makes me turn my head, and a tiny grey-brown mote comes into view, landing on a flower mere feet away. My breath stutters.

'Look,' I say, so softly it's barely a whisper. Delicate, lacy wings open and close slowly, catching the light with the faintest coppery gleam. 'Frosted elfin,' I tell him, the Latin name rising up from some deep and buried recollection of a book undoubtedly burned long before my son was even born. 'Callophrys irus.'

Warmed by the sun, the butterfly takes off again, vanishing within the blades of grass, my heart aching to follow it. 'I've never seen one before,' I breathe. 'Not in real life, just pictures. They didn't live where I grew up, before we had to—' I stop, swallowing hard, my mind skirting around—

*Maggie and I in bunkers where we huddled together for warmth and everything was too loud and when it wasn't it was too quiet and there was no food but what the soldiers could spare—*

—that part of my life, between Before and Now. I swallow again, licking my lips before trying to speak. 'They used to be classified as endangered. That meant there weren't enough of them, that people needed to try and protect them. They probably still are, or should be, but no one's counting anymore...' My voice trails off.

We sit in silence, the trees creaking faintly in the morning wind.

Luka pats my cheek gently, and I look down at him. My eyes are damp, but I'm not ashamed for him to see.

He holds up one little finger.

*One.*

The smile grows on my face, as easy as my breathing and my words of butterflies. 'Yeah,' I whisper. 'One.'

In the gilded morning, the grey trees stand over us as we watch the butterflies flit between the shining blossoms.

# LEAVING DREAMLAND
## E. H. MANN

Looking back from the top of Hillcrest Road, Dreamland sits among the lifeless streets and storefronts like a young Frankenstein's monster blinking in the late-afternoon sun.

Gone are the neat lines of suburban separatism. Their dividing fences amputated, each block of houses has become a single organism contained within its own skin of repurposed brick, wood, and wrought iron. Food gardens sprout from the decayed remains of sports fields; rainwater tanks open like pores beside every building. The whole creation is stitched together with gleaming thread: portable solar panels laid out on balconies, windowsills, anywhere there's a bit of space open to the northern sky.

And in the middle of it all, the monster's heart, secure behind the wooden ribcage of the scenic roller coaster: the fun park.

When Rina and I moved into the fun park, that was the first time I started to think we might actually survive the end of the world. High walls, shelter, food—even if our diet those first weeks would have made a dentist weep. And the best part: it was open to the sky.

Solar power was where Dreamland really began. Once we had lights, we became a beacon in the night. People started turning up at the gates. Suddenly we weren't just a couple of survivors; we were a community.

I turn around. Dreamland disappears behind the curve of the hill as I walk away.

---

Fiction failed to prepare us for how quickly the real zombie apocalypse would fall apart.

The virus, whatever it was, went through the human race like a bad kebab. Half the victims just straight up died. Maybe ten percent pulled through okay—like me, sweating it out for two weeks on a street not far from here, in the friend's spare bedroom I used to call home.

The rest became *infected*. Higher consciousness erased, strength dialled up to eleven, and a single-minded hunger for meat. For people like me, the virus was only the start of the fight for survival.

But the infected were still human, and natural predators we aren't. They were tool-users who'd forgotten how to use tools.

The first few months were a nightmare, but those of us who survived the nightmare did it by finding boltholes like the fun park—places the infected either couldn't find or couldn't reach. Wild animals were too fast for them, and the remaining house pets had figured out to stay the hell away. That only left one prey slow and stupid enough for the zombies to reliably catch: other zombies.

Between that and the rigours of their first Australian summer, it only took eighteen months to slash the ranks of the infected down to a few solitary holdouts.

I'm not saying it was easy. No one got through the end of the world unscathed. But in less than two years the zombie apocalypse had literally consumed itself.

And that's a good thing ... right?

*Jesus, Jacks, are you playing games on that phone again? You know it's a waste of solar! You said you were going to get up today.*
*I'm trying to.*
*That doesn't look like trying to me.*

The houses I'm passing sit in various states of silent wreckage. The worst are reduced to shells: every window smashed, doors ripped like cardboard straight off their hinges. Somehow these are less shocking than the ones that look outwardly untouched, a mere step away from the lives we all thought of as normal.

The only visible difference, besides the jungles that used to be gardens, is the numbers neatly spray-painted onto each front door. Some sport padlocks too; others will have been locked with their own keys, where the salvage teams could find them. Everything useful from the surrounding homes has been carefully catalogued and stored in the most intact houses, secured for future use. That was one of my ideas: now that things are quiet, why waste time and manpower bringing back supplies we don't yet need?

*I don't understand—what happened to all that energy, all those ideas? You used to be so capable.*

Echoes of my mother, my teachers: *You used to be so gifted. What happened?*

*Rina, I keep telling you, I can't just ... I can't. It's too much.*

*What is?*

*All of it!*

My mind is channel-surfing, as it does when I don't have a good distraction. It's worst when there's quiet. When I can't fill up my head with music or other people's voices, that's when my brain starts trying to fill in the space. Only my brain can't hold the thread of any single topic; it flits between them like a bumblebee sampling a field of flowers. Thoughts connect to memories connect to ideas connect to snatches of songs I just can't get out of my head, around and around and back again.

*We don't have to fix everything at once, love. Let's just focus on one thing at a time.*

*Rina, I've told you: that's not how ADHD works.*

*For pity's sake, will you stop using your condition as an excuse for everything? We all get overwhelmed sometimes. If you'd just stop wallowing in it, it wouldn't be so bad.*

The trees lining the street scream at me in passing, the standard evening cacophony of lorikeets, mynahs and starlings. I consider screaming back.

There's a solid ache building in my shoulders. I shift the weight of the hiking pack, obtained from one of the camping stores that have furnished so many of our needs. The pack obligingly resettles, relieving the worst pains and immediately birthing new ones.

I miss my own pack, but that's still living with my parents out in the wilds of Yarragon. Or rather—

No. Don't go there.

This one's a perfectly good pack—it just weighs a tonne. All those years of family hikes, I never learned how not to pack far too much and half of it unnecessary. Overpacking: just one of the habits I've acquired to compensate for the inevitability of forgetting things.

*We built Dreamland together, remember? It's like you don't even care about it anymore.*

*Of course I care! I just don't know how to fix any of this. I don't know how to make myself have solutions.*

This afternoon, of course, my bumblebee brain keeps circling back to the argument.

*You could start by getting out of bed, putting on some fucking clothes, and actually coming to a council meeting!*

*Stop saying that like it's easy!*

*It* is *easy!*

Picking it apart. What she said and why she was wrong and *what if she was right?*

Justifying my anger. Blaming myself for my anger.

*Stop treating me like I can do these things! I can't! I'm not like you!*

Trying to rewrite the script to reach an ending where I don't walk away.

And what a genius idea that was, walking out two hours before sundown with a bag packed even more haphazardly than usual.

I'll have to start looking for food tomorrow; the muesli bars and packet noodles I grabbed will barely last me two days. And right now I should really be looking for shelter, even though Dreamland's only just disappeared behind me. Shame I can't use one of the better houses. Whose bright idea was it to have those doors locked?

Hey, I used to love that cafe!

Something shoots out from under the postbox I'm passing: low and fast, straight at me.

I spin away from it, but I haven't allowed for the weight of my pack. It pulls me off-balance and I go down, tailbone slamming into the concrete.

The cat runs across my feet and disappears into a garden opposite, hissing as it passes.

I sit on my arse on the footpath, heart hammering on my ribs to get out. The throbbing in my butt keeps time with the blood thumping in my ears.

Oh yeah, then there's the part where I'm completely distracted while *walking through possible zombie country*. Just because I haven't seen an infected in over a year doesn't mean there isn't still the odd one around, waiting for some idiot to wander past with her head in the clouds.

This is stupid. I should go back.

Then I realise the pounding in my ears isn't coming from inside my head anymore.

Is that…?

Yes, right on the edge of my hearing: a dull clanging. Metallic?

Slowly, silently, I slide to my feet.

As I track the sound, my mind is diamond-sharp. The old instincts have kicked right back in. I stick to fence lines and shadows, bent low to keep from presenting a recognisable silhouette, ears sharp, eyes taking in everything: the road ahead, the houses and jungle gardens around me, every slightest movement of a leaf in the breeze.

For the first time in over a year, I feel *alive*.

※

The noise is coming from a couple of streets over, an area the salvage teams haven't reached yet; it's easy to tell by the lack of spray paint, and by the bones. I guess it's lucky I've gotten used to bones.

I'm crouched opposite a house that must have been in poor shape even before the world ended. Its roof is shedding shingles like dandruff, timber frame sagging into the jungle of thistles growing up to claim it. And right there among the weeds, beneath a spreading oak tree: a cage. With a distinctly humanoid figure huddled inside.

The sound pauses—my breathing follows suit—and then the figure groans, raises whatever it's using for a club, and starts banging on the bars again.

Adrenaline buzzes up my spine. Silently I lower my pack to the ground and reach for the handle sticking out between zippers. My old friend the fire poker.

My preferred survival strategy against the infected was always running away, but it never hurt to have a backup option. Right now, I only want to confirm what I'm seeing—but there's no way I'm going in there without protection.

I creep across the street, poker held low and ready. Tiptoe through the open gate...

And try to swallow my disappointment.

The guy in the cage is wiry, maybe a little younger than me—and entirely human. As for the object he's wielding ... Is that—?

Just then he twists around with a startled yelp and throws it at me. The matte brown pillar smacks solidly into my shins and I nearly go down for the second time today.

After an awkward pause, he says, 'Sorry about that. May I have my leg back please?'

❦

'What are you doing out here?' I ask as I look around for something to help lift the cage.

His voice is soft, with what I still think of as a city accent. 'I ... grew up in the house next door. It's my parents' place. Was my parents' place.'

There are questions I could ask. I don't ask them. In a world full of survivors, there are unspoken rules about this kind of thing.

'This block is on the salvage roster for next week. I wanted to come by first, see what was still there.'

His face is familiar—one of the newer residents of Dreamland, I think. David, maybe, or Devin? He's dressed in basic apocalypse practical—a T-shirt and cargo shorts—and is currently hunched over in the small space, reattaching his prosthesis.

A thin satchel is slung over his shoulders. I wonder what he chose to keep and what to leave. How would I make that kind of choice, if I ever make it all the way to Yarragon again?

'Our neighbour was Mr Angelo, a real hoarder. I was always trying to sneak into his house. I thought while I'm out here I might as well seize the opportunity.' He pulls a face. 'I suppose Mr Angelo wins again.'

I pause to stare at him. 'What, did he always rig booby traps around his place?'

'No,' he admits. 'This is new. He used to just come out and yell at me in Greek.'

The cage is solid iron, heavier than the two of us together can lift. A thick rope runs from it to a pulley in the tree above and back down to the tripwire rigged across the cracked remains of the front path.

I wedge my fire poker between two of the bars and lean my full weight on it, to see if I can widen the gap between them. To its credit, the poker doesn't bend. Neither do the bars.

'Don't you know the rules?' I grumble. 'You're not meant to go out alone.'

There's a pause before he answers. 'I thought it would be safe enough just to nip over here and back.'

I'm looking around the garden again, and it takes me a second to connect the dots. When I do, I sidle hastily behind the tree so he won't see me go red. He's not the only person out alone today.

From this side, I have a better view of the pulley up in the branches—or rather, the pulleys. Four of them in two pairs, with the rope looped around and around them in a way that triggers something in me—an old memory from a high-school physics book…

I grab the other end of the rope and tug, and the cage lifts like it hardly weighs a thing. I wonder what became of Mr Angelo—Dreamland could use more people with his kind of skills.

'Wow,' says Devin, sounding impressed. 'Thank you.'

He shuffles out from underneath and goes to stand but sways hard left. I drop the cage just in time to catch him.

'...uh. Sorry about that.' I help him to sit, and he massages his flesh-and-blood leg. 'It's just gone to sleep. Give me a minute.'

'Take your time.' Looking down, I realise his dark hair is darker on one side, and matted. 'Hey, did you hit your head?'

'*I* didn't. *That* did.' He nods towards the cage and winces. 'Got a shocker of a headache.'

I crouch and inspect his head. The bleeding has stopped. It looks like it was heavy, though I don't think that's unusual for head wounds. I try to recall my first aid training.

'Any nausea? Dizziness?'

He frowns. 'Not that I noticed. Should I be worried?'

'I don't think so, but I'm not a doctor.' I give him a hand up. 'Better get it checked out at the med centre just in case.'

'Thanks, I will.' He stands, shaking out his limbs. 'I'm Danny Khan, by the way.'

Oops. Well, I was close.

'Jacqueline Keeley. Everyone calls me Jacks.'

'That's right, you're Rina Paczkowski's partner, aren't you? On the council? I saw you at a town hall meeting.'

I'm not sure how Danny interprets my facial expression, but he doesn't push the question.

'Well, I'm very grateful you came past.' He glances at the sky. 'We should get moving while we still have some daylight.'

Ah, crap. He thinks I'm going back to Dreamland with him. Of course he does—where else would I be going?

If I walk away now, he'll want to know why. More importantly, if I walk away now, I'm abandoning a guy with a possible concussion to get himself home through an apocalyptic wasteland—even if it's not much of a wasteland anymore. That's a level of shitty I like to think I wouldn't stoop to.

But if I go back with him, I can't exactly turn around and walk out again into the night. I'll have to go home. To Rina. I don't even know if she's figured out yet that I've left, which adds a delightful level of awkward on top of the whole unknown of how *that* conversation will go.

My brain flails between equally awful options and chooses plan C: think about something else.

Danny's already heading for the gate. 'Hey,' I call after him. 'Why don't we have a quick look around while we're here?'

'Pardon?' He looks back in surprise.

'You said this guy's a hoarder, right? There could be all kinds of good stuff inside.'

'Sure—or all kinds of booby traps like the one I already ran into.'

I wave off his concern, riding high on a fresh wave of enthusiasm.

'It'll be fine if we're careful. Forewarned is forearmed, right? Come on, we've got time. Don't you want to know what he thought was so important to protect?'

He shoots an intrigued look towards the front door, which is all the affirmation I need. I head for the house, then wheel around. 'One sec.'

A quick dash to my pack, trying to decide which items are most likely to come in handy just in case of … anything. Multi-tool, torch, first aid kit? In the end I just grab the whole pack and heave it back on. Better safe than sorry.

I still don't charge straight into the house—I'm not an idiot. The fire poker takes the lead, prodding every loose stone on the front steps for a possible trigger. When I reach the door unscathed, I poke the handle gingerly, half-expecting it to be electrified—as unlikely as that is these days. Nothing zaps me, so I turn the handle as quickly as humanly possible. The door unlatches, and I step back and use the poker to push it ever so gently open.

Nothing continues to happen.

I step slowly through the doorway. The floor creaks ominously underfoot, but no paint cans fall on my head.

Danny's right behind me by now. I look back to grin at him, but he's staring past me.

'Wow.'

My first impression of Mr Angelo's house is: *junk*. Piles of it. The front room would hold a family of five if it wasn't stuffed full. Walls are lined with shelves that are lined with every item imaginable: books, magazines, kitchenware, candles, mysterious glass jars, the works. Even the couch and the coffee table are stacked with stuff.

'Oh,' says Danny, stepping in past me. There's a strange catch in his voice.

I look where he's looking, and that's when I realise the pile of rags on the couch is a dead man.

He was easy to miss among the chaos—desiccation hasn't been kind. There's a wooden stake buried in the remains of his chest; my eyes track a line back from there to a set of wires and springs installed at ceiling-level.

Still trying to figure out exactly what I'm looking at, I step forward—and the floor gives way beneath us.

So, okay, maybe I am a bit of an idiot.

Here's what we figure out later, with the luxury of too much time: this wasn't even a booby trap. Just a combination of rotten old floorboards, two people plus my twenty kilos of pack, and a big hole in the ground where the house supports should have been.

I barely have time to register that I'm falling, leaving my stomach in the room above, and then I'm punched in the back by my own overstuffed pack.

Time passes while I try to remember how to breathe. My chest feels stretched taut. The world has been reduced to a jagged square of orange light in the centre of my vision, a television set in a dark room.

Damn, I miss television.

Eventually, I realise I'm splayed out on top of my pack, spine bent achingly around its mass with its straps dragging down on my shoulders. I really *am* in a dark room; the jagged square isn't a visual artefact, but the edges of broken floorboards surrounding a view of the ceiling of the room above, lit by the setting sun.

Sunset. Oh no.

I wrestle free of the pack's embrace. Danny is already sitting up. He's hunched over, face lost in shadow. I'm about to ask if he's hurt when I realise he's got his satchel open in his lap. As he sifts around inside it I hear the tinkle of fragile things that have not been treated kindly.

'Ah, shit. Is it...?'

He doesn't look up. 'Some things will be all right, I think. The photos. It was lucky I found anything at all, really. Anything could have happened to that house since ... Don't worry about it.'

So of course, I worry about it. 'Danny, I'm so sorry. If I hadn't—I should have—'

'I said don't worry about it.' His voice is flat. He still hasn't moved. 'We need to get out of here. Did you bring a torch?'

'Yes!' *Yes!* Thank you, Lord, something I can fix.

Torchlight makes our situation clearer but weirder. We've fallen maybe three metres. Most of the space is floor-boarded with wooden planks, which would have hurt, but at this end the floor is dirt—as is the closest wall, lumpy and half-finished, complete with a shovel and wheelbarrow standing beside it.

We're in a space maybe five metres by six, although it's hard to judge because the clutter down here makes upstairs look spacious. I can see tools, camping gear, canned food—so much canned food—clothing, folding chairs and tables, a stack of mattresses…

Mr Angelo was a full-blown survivalist. For what good it did him.

'Damn—the salvage team's going to love this.'

Danny's voice is strained. 'Can we focus on getting out of here, please?'

Oh yeah.

'Okay.' I shine the torch around. 'No sweat. There has to be a way out of here, or how was your mate getting in? Ah-hah!'

Through a maze of shelving, the torchlight picks out a wooden staircase at the other end of the bunker. I clamber over to it, dodging tangles of hose, a gutted lawnmower, and other hazards. The stairs lead up to a pair of flat metal doors. Jackpot.

I put down the torch to mount the stairs, brace my hands against the cool metal, and shove. For a blessed moment, the doors lift—and then they stop dead, accompanied by the rattle and clank of chains on the other side.

'Jacks,' says Danny from behind me.

'It's okay, we can figure this out,' I mutter, peering up through the gap I've made. It there a padlock, or just a chain? There's got to be a solution, there *has* to be a way out, because if there isn't then I've gone and messed up completely—

'Jacks.'

'*It's fine*,' I snap, turning to face him. And then I forget whatever I was going to say next, because his face is a sickly, fading orange. Behind him, the accumulated detritus of the late Mr Angelo has turned insubstantial in the growing gloom.

'Did you bring any spare batteries?'

Of course I didn't.

It's all very well to say *we might as well get some sleep, it'll be easier to find a way out in the morning*. Danny did, in fact, say that three times before I finally gave up on knocking things over in the pitch black of the bunker. Now I'm lying down on a dubious-smelling mattress.

If only lying down was the same as sleeping.

I squeeze my eyes shut, willing my body to get the hint. How long has it been—two hours? Ten minutes? I have no sense of time at the best of times.

My bumblebee brain is in overdrive. If only I'd this. If only I hadn't that. Who the hell brings a torch but doesn't think to bring batteries?

I guess Rina knows I'm gone now. Is she feeling guilty? Angry? Worried? What if she thinks something's happened to me and sends a search party? Leaving aside that something *has* happened to me, if I have to get rescued, she'll have one more reason to think I'm completely useless.

Maybe I am completely useless.

'Jacks?'

'Hmm?'

'You're muttering.'

'Sorry. Didn't realise.'

'It's okay.' He doesn't sound any sleepier than I am. I wonder what it's like inside his head tonight.

'Danny? I really am sorry about this.'

'I know.'

After a minute or an hour, his voice emerges from the darkness again. 'Can I ask you something?'

'Mmm?'

'Do you think it's going to work out?'

'What?' How the hell does he know about the fight? Did Rina send him? No, that makes no sense.

'Dreamland. Do you think it will work out?'

'...oh.'

*Oh.* I wish that one was any easier to answer.

Funny thing about living in a city. People get so used to having everything they need at their fingertips, they never think about how little of it that city actually produces.

So far, we're eking out the supermarket cans and packets, rationing them carefully and supplementing them with tomatoes, potatoes, carrots, anything you can find in a hardware store seed packet. But urban stores don't sell seeds for rice or wheat. To say nothing of protein or dairy—I would cry genuine tears if I saw an edible block of cheese.

Then there's clothes, tools, fuel for our work vehicles... None of them are in danger of running out yet, not with three hundred of us scrounging from suburbs with a pre-zombie population of maybe twenty thousand. But more survivors show up every week, and none of that pre-made stuff is going to last forever. We have so many wheels to reinvent.

And that's just the start of the problems.

In all those zombie shows, the survivors were always turning on each other; in reality, it's when people feel safe that cooperation breaks down. The bigger Dreamland grows, the bigger the questions we have to answer: how do we ensure fair distribution of labour without punishing people for what they can't do? How do we keep crime down without marginalising the perpetrators? What do we do about old prejudices resurfacing?

And on and on and on.

'...sure. It'll work out,' I tell the darkness.

'It's just that you're on the council, so I figure you should know. And, well ... that's an awfully big backpack if you were only out for the day.'

*Shit.* I don't answer. But I guess that's answer enough.

'Can I ask why you're leaving?'

'Look, it's not about Dreamland, okay? It's not anything going wrong.' Which is at least halfway true, and I owe it to Rina not to start some mass exodus.

'Okay.' I can tell he's waiting for more.

Maybe it's the way he says it: quiet, non-judgemental. Maybe it's the dark, like a confessional.

'It's just ... it's me, all right?' I close my eyes, which make no difference at all, and take a deep breath. 'I was good at the apocalypse. Running, hiding, finding what we needed, keeping us safe. Staying on the ball, never knowing where the next attack might come from. It was ... look, I know exactly how awful this sounds, but it was exciting.'

See, there's an exception to the rule of the bumblebee brain. Usually all the flowers look equally enticing—but when one of the flowers feels like a genuine last-chance, do-or-die scenario, the bee-brain gets real focused real fast.

It's what got me through the first year of university, before my breakdown. Before my diagnosis. I churned out five-thousand-word essays the day before they were due; stayed up panic-cramming the night before exams. I passed everything with flying colours, because failing felt like the end of the world. And then I dropped out, went home to my parents, and didn't leave the house for three months.

And seven years later, when the world did end? When every decision really was life or death, my brain was an absolute hero.

It wasn't exactly healthy, but I had Rina to look after me when I crashed. When the adrenaline ran out and I couldn't even find the energy to get up and feed myself, she took good care of me. I really thought she understood.

'But then things got better...'

The world began to be about more than life or death. And somehow Rina expected me to start functioning like a normal person.

My mouth's still moving. 'Know what I did before the end of the world? Gardener. Before that, childcare. Before that, *yikes*, telemarketer. Four roles in five years, all of them entry-level. I'm a college drop-out who can't hold down a job. What part of that makes me qualified to run a brand-new town?'

'You feel overwhelmed.'

'Yes!' My laugh is too loud, brittle in the crushing dark. 'I survived the zombie apocalypse, and apparently that was the easy part!'

'That makes sense.'

'Very funny.'

'No, really. When the world was in chaos, you *had* to be on the ball all the time. Now that things have settled down, you're struggling to engage in the same way. Building a fully-functioning society is a very different challenge, and I'm guessing it doesn't feel that important by comparison.'

'But it *is* important. If we can't make this work, we're still going to die out—we'll just do it slower.' That's not my line. How did I become the Rina in this conversation?

'I know that. And so do you, clearly. But knowing it isn't the same as feeling it. That's not something you can control. You can't just force yourself to engage with something that doesn't interest you, no matter how important it is.'

*I don't get to decide what I can do, Rina! I can't just turn this on like a switch!*

I smother my face in my arms so Danny won't hear me sobbing.

Rina's the one who's good at this. She's got a picture in her head of the future she wants us to build, and somehow she can hold on to that in all its complexity while she figures out the paths to get us there.

I love that she can do that. I want to help her find those paths, I really do. But whenever I try to see the picture it's like trying to see through fog. I don't have the tools to navigate through it, and I don't know how to make myself have them.

The tears are starting to soak through my sleeves. Intense, confusing-as-hell emotions are another quirk of my brain. Fortunately, it's just as easily distracted from them as it is from anything else. Danny's words keep replaying, and the tears evaporate as I latch onto something else about them.

'Y'know... you sound just like my last counsellor.'

'Um.' He sounds embarrassed. 'Actually, I studied psychology.'

'You were a psych?'

'I never actually practised. I was three months out from the end of my Master's when everything started.'

'You, um.' I sniff. 'You should set up shop. A lot of people around here could use a good counsellor. And... it seems like you're pretty good at it.'

He laughs softly. 'Thank you. But a counsellor isn't the first thing Dreamland needs right now.'

'Hah! So what is?'

I mean the question rhetorically, and the silence that follows is long enough that I half-assume Danny's gone to sleep. I've finally started to drift off myself when he murmurs, 'I think … trade.'

'Huh?' I stifle a yawn. 'Trade what with who?'

His own voice is thick with sleep. 'Well, *who* is the part we have to figure out. But there must be other groups out there. Even if we lost, I dunno, ninety-nine percent of humanity, that still leaves tens of thousands of people. We can't be the only ones banding together.

'As for what ... Solar panels, hardware, candy, all the things you get tonnes of in a big city full of shops. People living out in the country won't have as much of things like that, but they'll have what we don't—meat, natural fibres, grain ... Imagine eating bread again...'

I push myself up on one elbow, staring fruitlessly in his direction. I'm nowhere near drifting off now. 'So you're saying we need to find them, start setting up trade routes. But—wait, hang on. What do we do when the candy and solar panels run out? It's not like we can just make more.'

''S not hard to make candy with a good thermometer,' he mumbles drowsily. 'But eventually we're gonna have to learn to make all of it. Hammers and shovels... decent prosthetics ... maybe even solar panels ... Learn to make 'em or learn how to live without them. The more people we know, the more skills they have, the more...' He yawns. '...the more raw materials we can access, the more options we have for making a life that'll survive even after the pre-made stuff runs out.

'Trade's where it all starts ... Filling needs, building connections ... If we don't wanna end up fighting each other over what we've got, we need t'have connections. Like what Australia used to be before the Europeans showed up. Interconnected communities sharing goods, news, people…'

His voice is fading into the night. 'Trade … thass where it starts.'

The gaps between his sentences have been growing longer, so it takes me a while to realise he's done.

'Danny?' I whisper. The only answer is a soft snore.

I settle back into my sleeping bag, but my eyes are wide open now.

---

I must have fallen asleep at some point, because the next thing I know, Danny's touching my shoulder and there's morning light streaming in through the hole in our ceiling.

Now that we can see, it's the work of a minute to find the actual frigging ladder stashed in the corner. Well, okay, more like fifteen minutes of sifting through the mess, but still.

It doesn't quite reach the hole, but it gets us close enough for Danny to boost me out and then pass up our bags. After that I grab his arms, and there's an awkward scramble and a precarious moment when I think we're both about to end up back down the hole headfirst, but finally we're both sitting in Mr Angelo's doorway, panting and grinning triumphantly at each other.

When we reach the front gate, Danny says, 'So ... I guess this is goodbye?' But he says it like a question, not an answer.

'Nah. I'm coming with you.' He raises his eyebrows and I shrug. 'If I'm going to mount an expedition to find us some trading partners, I need to be better packed than this.'

I've been working on the idea most of the night. Yarragon may not be as easy to reach as it used to be, but I'll drive when I can find car keys and fuel, and walk when I can't, and there are other places along the way where survivors might gather. The council can put together a list of what we need and what we can offer, and what kind of exchange rate we think our goods are worth, and I can take a few samples to show to any interested customers.

The thought of getting out there with a purpose is lighting up my brain like a million solar panels.

I know it won't be as easy as it feels right now, in that first adrenaline rush of a new idea. There are some tough conversations ahead. I hope Rina will forgive me for leaving the council. If it helps, I already have an ideal candidate in mind to replace me.

And as for us...

Yesterday's anger hasn't so much faded as settled into today's conviction. I still love Rina, but I can't be the person she wants me to be in this new world we're building. The more I try, the more it's making us both miserable. But I think—I hope—this is a chance to figure out who and what I *can* be. And if Rina can accept that person, bumblebee brain and all, then maybe we can still make this work. I guess we'll see what happens when I get back from my first expedition.

The sun hits my face as I step out onto the street. I don't know what this new day will bring—but for the first time in a long time I can't wait to find out.

# NOTHING BUT FLOWERS
## KATHARINE DUCKETT

When hard rain falls on the Bowery, the apple trees all shake. The birds stop their singing and the kids run inside, shrieking as they sprint past me to get dry. I make myself a mug of tea, pull up a chair on the porch, and watch the fat grey drops plop down across the avenue become orchard. Watch Sylvan's machines gather up the moisture, watch the overflow run down the gutters as I let the sound wash over me, the pattering on the tin roof over my head bringing a calm to the Garden that I relish more and more as my body ages. No one can do too much work when it rains like this. Everyone's got to stop and rest for a minute, let the thunder pass and the lightning fade before they start their labouring again.

Used to be—fifteen years ago, twenty—that there would still be people kneeling there, over those gutters running along the bottom of the tree trunks, swallowing whatever they could. Desperate people, dying of thirst. Always too many, and not enough clean water for all those mouths, those long-parched throats. More acid rain, back then. Blighted enough to make you ill for days. But people still drank. People will drink a cup of cold poison in the desert if it's hot enough, if only for that last fatal draught of relief.

'R—Radisha?'

I turn my eyes from the sight of the storm and find Sylvan standing beside me. He's holding a clipboard and looking grim, though whenever I call him out on his dour expression he says that's just what his face looks like. A young face, not suited to the ravages of this world. Not that any of us are. But we make do, as we all must.

'It says they're coming in one week.' He's looking down at the letter that's laid out on his old office relic, the letter that found us from a state away even though nothing like a state or a mail system really exists anymore. We found it taped to the front door of the compound, in an envelope that looked like a missive from another world, pristine and expensive, a navy-blue square stamped with the official insignia of the family corporation that used to own this place, back in an era that seems two or three lifetimes ago. 'What day does that mean?'

I close my eyes, ancient calendars flashing through my head. Squares laid out on a grid, given the arbitrary names of useless gods, with no meaning to what work's meant to get done that day, to what part of the natural world needs honouring. 'Beesday.'

'Beesday,' he echoes, and jots down a note. We make up our own days now. No more of the tyranny of artificial time, of the system that strove to mould us to its killing rhythms. Our little family of four meets to decide on about twenty days' worth of plans, basing our intentions on the growing seasons of the Garden, on how everyone's feeling, on who needs to heal and rest and who wants to dive into new projects or wrap up old ones.

Sylvan stills his pen, looking past me, past the sheet of water dripping from the slanted porch roof, to the painstakingly planted orchard beyond, the leafy arbour that marks the edge of the Garden. Our neighbours, with whom we've shared the bounty of our harvest and the best of our building methods, respect that boundary, letting us know with a whistle or a wave if they're coming to visit. We've had others, though, who haven't been so gracious. All who come in peace are welcome here, but we've had to protect ourselves, too, and there have been bad nights and days, times that Sylvan and the others remember too vividly.

I can see he's frightened, try as he does to not show it. It's a skill all the children his age learned, though they're still children, after all. Sylvan may be twenty-one now, but he'll always be a child to me, always the little one who turned up on my doorstep, half-dead and mute for more than a year. He gave himself his name when he finally spoke; I don't know if he knew his old one, or if it meant anything to him. Most of the young ones have claimed their own names, rechristening this world in words of their own tongue. 'And what will we do then?' he asks, eyes still on the tempest. 'What will we do when they try to make us leave?'

I watch the raindrops roll down the curves of our apples, almost prime for plucking. On the roof up behind us, Abril was tending to the hives, though I'll bet she's gone inside now, where she and Lale are likely boiling honey and jam for the kids. We've got new arrivals coming from Brooklyn soon, if the waters are calm, and rumours that there might be more from Queens not long after that. Forty-eight of us living here now, scattered throughout the restored ruins of what used to be The Eastrow, a luxury housing development built with all the features of the future, back when people believed in such a thing.

I'm the only original resident left, the winner of a lottery required by the city to open up a few of those top-of-the-line units to disabled people and people without a million dollars to their name. There used to be more of us, and we restored these ruins ourselves, every inch of them. We made ourselves a home in the wreckage after the rest of the city left us behind, after the blast shook down the walls, after the flames burst through the windows, after the deaths of too many friends and loved ones and strangers whose names I never learned to count. We replaced the sterile white interiors with high hanging shelves of verdant plants, stretching up to the sky, protected by tarps, giving us food and fresh air and the joy of coaxing life out of a necrotic world. We built modular homes that could be reshaped and recombined around the central atrium, and sent out teams to rescue those who were struggling, those who needed shelter most, who needed a place that fit them.

Sylvan designed the sense-rooms in our family's modular home: the seery, where our resident artist, Lale, hangs our illustrated calendar; the gustatorium, which mostly ended up being a fancy word for kitchen; the auditory dome where we've set up steelpans and flutes; and the tranquil, dim olfactory, where I sometimes sit in silence and sniff the bundles of herbs and flowers Sylvan's collected to evoke the scents of places he's heard about, places it's unlikely he'll ever visit, like California and the Caribbean Sea. He has a talent for reimagining the strictures of old societies; maybe he's so good at it because he was never part of one. I was skeptical when he wanted to engineer our whole mode of living based on ideas he found in some old book, but I'm willing to try almost anything as long as it's new. Moving forward, never back: that's the philosophy I live by.

We called our community the Garden, and I promised we wouldn't lose it this time. I promised myself, and I promised my children. This Garden is ours, no matter what some writing on ancient stationary might say.

'Don't fret, mon chou.' I raise my tea to my lips, the luxury of water that can be transformed from anything other than itself not lost on me. 'Let your mother do the worrying. Leave it all to me.'

I was born in New York City, on Lenape lands. Long before colonisers named the wide swath of trees-turned-concrete-turned-trees again outside my door 'the Bowery' (after 'bouwerij,' an archaic Dutch word for 'farm'), the Lenape people used it as a footpath to travel from the bottom of the island of Mannahatta to the top. It's the oldest thoroughfare in this place, lasting through centuries, through generations, the scores of people who have travelled upon it impossible to count or imagine.

I took my first laboured breaths in a hospital not very far from this old road, going on seven decades ago, though I've lost track of the precise span of years. Before the worst of the floods, anyway, and the hungriest of the fires, and the first plague, or the fifth one. Before most of Lower Manhattan sank below the waves and the north disappeared into dust. Before milestones I can't even remember now, or may have missed altogether, holed up hiding or sick as a dog or scared out of my mind, the only blessing that memories wouldn't form, wouldn't hold together in my conscious hours and would only come back to haunt me in my nightmares. The city I was born into was crumbling, but it was still a city then, still pretending to function, still full of people playacting their way through quotidian existences even as the trains failed and the bridges broke and the buildings tumbled, as the fault lines appeared in everything, as the earth they thought they knew gave way beneath their feet.

My pa, he was a builder. Had his own construction company, and made plenty of money that way until my mother convinced him his hands could be put to better use than making empty identical boxes for billionaires to park their money in, and he went into partnership with her. My mom, she was a farmer. She studied agricultural science, and she helped design farms for city living, vertical farms for growing food indoors, in the limited spaces offered by urban life. People thought things like that might save the world, back then.

Maybe they did. After all, I used a lot of her research to help design the Garden, and the world is still here. I didn't think it would be. I didn't think it would be when my parents died, or when I took in Sylvan, or at almost any other moment through these terrible years.

But I kept fighting anyway.

It is, after all, what I've been doing my whole life through.

The man they send on the day I've forgotten to call Monday or Wednesday or whatever it may be is young. Almost everyone is young these days. There aren't many people my age who made it through everything, the brutal blows and long aftershocks. But the young ones in the city are sharp, always on their guard, ever heedful of the lessons of the heaps of rubble all around them. They're the ones who have had to learn to exist side by side, to show kindness when your body aches to do violence, to hurt the world back in all the ways it's hurt you. I've tried to teach them how to exhibit that. Kindness. Patience. Virtues lacking in the old world, and infinitely more precious in the new one.

This young man—his name is Maxwell—he's soft. No edges to him at all. Round and pale as a potato, which makes some sense, as he's spent most of his life underground. His people are entombed in what used to be Connecticut, in the labyrinthine bunkers some of the richest rich fled to when reality started to go to hell. He's producing papers, old ones, though I can only tell their age by the dates in the signature lines. Those old bastards—his great-grandparents, most likely—must have stored them somewhere climate-controlled, sucking up resources just to stage this gotcha moment they'd never live to witness.

'You'll find it's very clear.' He's pointing to some fine print, but my eyes are too shot to make it out. 'We still own the property. Always have, even in absentia.'

'Property.' I spread out my hands, encompassing the space all around me. The roof with its ramps and lifts. The back bedrooms where Sylvan sleeps with soundproofing and calming wave-coloured walls and Abril and Lale share a bed that's the right height with the right grips for Abril to get in and out of her wheelchair on her own. My own room, which I've lived in now in one form or another for decades, and all the common rooms we share, as well as all the other homes of the chosen families that move in and out of the Garden.

We're still on the porch, and I have no intention of letting Maxwell cross our threshold. Let him try. I'm just as good with my cane as I've ever been. It's got all the protection Sylvan could pack into it, from a spike in the base to a hidden knife in the handle. But at the end of the day, what's always mattered most is that it's a big goddamn stick.

At the moment said stick is crossed in front of Maxwell's ankles, blocking his path. He clears his throat, taking a tiny step back on the stairs. 'You've certainly done a—remarkable job with the place.' His dimpled hand comes up to shade his eyes. 'Although— didn't it used to be taller?'

I laugh. I can't help it. 'Oh, baby, everything used to be taller.' I hoist my cane up, towards the roof of the porch. 'Buildings high as the eye could see. They made them so high we couldn't get up them. Couldn't climb or pay our way to the top. When the power went out, all those years, do you know how many people were stuck up there?' I bring my cane down with a thump. 'But most of them fell. First the storm, then the bombs. Well, mostly *the* bomb. The one that did most of the damage. Might even have hit y'all up there, all the way up in Connecticut, if that's still what you're calling it.'

Maxwell's face is screwed up tight, like I've just said whole slew of words in a language he doesn't understand, which I'm betting for him includes any language other than English. He wouldn't do well in this neighbourhood, where everyone speaks at least a smattering of Spanish and Polish and Arabic, where most of the intact streets go by their Mandarin and Cantonese names, where new ways of speaking spring up on every block, new methods of communication for bridging gaps in understanding, new ways of signing and scribbling and sending signals across the patchwork grid of communities that's beginning to revive itself into something like a city.

I sigh. 'But you wouldn't know about all that, would you? Your folks probably just showed you some photographs of the Empire State Building in its heyday. The Chrysler, maybe, and the Statue of Liberty.'

He's nodding. 'Yes, the Statue, I've heard of that one—'

Gone. Sunk, from what I hear. And the other two—well, you can just look north, and see they're both gone too.'

We remain in silence for a time. Behind me I can hear the farm working, the whir of Abril's wheelchair as she moves through the wide paths of the Garden. When I've dispensed with this pest, I may go join her. Tend to the radishes that are my namesake. My mother named me for the NICU nurse who cared for me when I was born, and for the way she hoped I'd be: 'Spicy and hardy, with just the right amount of bite.'

Maxwell clears his throat again. The air quality is terrible, sure, but there's no call for all this phlegm. 'We appreciate everything you've done. Keeping the property in—' His gaze scans the place again. 'Acceptable condition. But I will have to ask you to leave, Ms Persaud. And if you and your collective won't go willingly, my lawyers and I will resort to other means.'

It's remarkable. Go through what the world has gone through, live your way through hell, and you get pretty sure you'll never hear a phrase like 'my lawyers' ever again. I'd counted it as one of the few good points of the apocalypse. But here's this young white boy before me like Encino Man in a suit his family's been saving beneath the dirt for an occasion just like this one. Waiting for the dust to settle on our bones.

Bet they're mad as hell to find we're still here.

❦

When I was born, the doctors predicted I wouldn't make it a month.

I came out of the womb at thirty weeks, and once upon a time, I would have been almost sure to survive. But I was born into troubled times, when things were getting bad, or were already bad, or were well and truly fucked, depending on who you asked and when. At the hospital where they had me on oxygen, the power flickered on and off as a hurricane raged. The water was already of a questionable quality, the pipes corroded and leaking. Anyone who could afford it was having home births, because of what you could catch just by walking through the hospital doors. But my mother went into labour working on her rows of cabbages and lettuces long before I was due, and they rushed her there to save her as much as to save me.

The odds were against us both. The toxins of white America seeped so deep into the soil in those days that they even poisoned healing hands, sanctuaries of care. The mortality rates for Black women giving birth were higher by far than any other group, regardless of factors like education, which my mother had plenty of. She was in danger just going through those doors.

Somehow we made it, though not without our scars. My vision was never right, and my hypothyroidism opened me up to a whole host of other autoimmune issues I've been battling my whole life. And the spastic cerebral palsy—that's what has my muscles strung tight, my balance off. The old world wasn't built for me, but at least back then there were treatments. Options. Surgeries. For years I had none of that: no guidance, no doctors. None of us did. We pieced together what we could from what we remembered, from the training of an EMT who came to stay with us for a while, from soggy and scorched medical books we scavenged from libraries and university buildings.

When things calmed enough outside of our doors, I sent out teams to teach clinics, sharing the knowledge we'd gleaned, the best makeshift methods for treating wounds and diseases. I didn't want for us to lock ourselves up, to wither from terror, even though there was plenty to be had. I wanted the Garden to grow, to spread its seeds. And so it has. The people in the neighbourhood know they can find friends and allies and resources here, and word has travelled far enough to bring us news of those who need a home with us, for us to prepare new modular units for their arrival. Sylvan's designed those parts to be replicable and easily transportable from a building yard nearby, and we can always modify and tweak the simple building blocks he's made into versatile templates. Space is made to serve our needs, structures to support our bodies: not the other way around.

We have a natural division of labour here, by and large, as we prepare for new residents and families, as we maintain the compound. Those whose feet can support them scout for what we need and collect what they're able, and those with arms to lift hammer and saw offer helping hands. And those with vision to see draw the plans and charts, and those who can hear and give voice tell tales and sing songs. And those who can do none of this, on one day or all, are loved and listened to, whether they speak or sign. These are the rules we live by. Compassion. Empathy. Understanding. With the world a mess, we don't have much else.

---

When Maxwell returns a few days later, he does indeed have lawyers by his side.

It looks like he dug them up from under the dirt too. They're fresh out of the package, clean as one can be when spending more than a minute in this city, where grime and detritus cling to every surface. 'Your resistance is unwise,' one of them says, his flesh as thick and shiny as an eggplant's. 'Don't think we'll hesitate to take this matter to the courts.'

I crack up. I laugh so hard, and so long, that eventually Sylvan and Abril come out onto the porch. Sylvan's got his hands protecting his ears, and I know I've been too loud. 'Courts.' I finally manage to spit the word out through my teeth, dry as they are with laughter. 'There are *courts*?'

The three men look at one another. Sylvan bends beside me, speaking low. 'If you want me to get rid of them—'

I hiss at him, nearly pushing him back, but stop myself just in time. 'I told you not to worry, all right? I'm handling this.'

The quieter lawyer, the one with a head like a tomato, pipes up. I guess he's playing good cop, but one lesson I remember from way back on my mother's knee is that there's no such thing. 'We'll relocate you. Upstate. It's a beautiful place. Really springing back after the, uh—' His flapping fingers are vague. Does he mean the haze that still hangs over the sun? The water that's encroached all the way to Avenue A? The dead, the countless dead, animals and humans alike, and the way no one's keeping a tally? 'Lots of wildlife returning. You'll love it up there.'

'Upstate.' The term leaves a sour taste in my mouth. 'To fend for ourselves.'

Maxwell, still tuber-bland in manner and appearance, tries to intervene. 'Ms Persaud, please consider it. It's a very generous offer—'

'No.' I hold up a finger. 'Do you know what this is, ma pomme de terre? Do you have any idea? This is the home we made when you left us all to die. Built to our own needs and specifications exactly. Does your holding pen upstate have a way for Abril to get to the hives? Does it have the rooms we've created for ourselves? Does it have paths for feet and wheels and canes, to go and visit friends, to leave the house, to get what we need?' I sweep my hand, taking in all of the painstakingly installed features of the Garden, of the whole neighbourhood. 'If we were going to be left with rubble, I decided a long time ago we were going to rebuild it our own way. You can't take that from us. There's no other place like this one we made.'

'Well, actually,' says the first lawyer, sliding his glasses—unscratched, only slightly speckled—up his aubergine nose, 'We can. Take it from you, I mean. The catastrophe clauses are very clear on that.'

I ignore him. I get to my feet, though the movement pains me, and I glare at Maxwell, fixing him with my stare. 'You don't have to do this, you know. Whatever stories your folks told you, whatever picture they painted of the old world, I promise it wasn't half-true.' I tilt my head northwards, towards the absence where shiny towers used to rise. 'It was a brutal country. People like you ripped people like me out by the roots. Ask your people if they know the name Seneca Village. Ask them if they know about all the people who disappeared from the middle of the city so they could have a lawn. Central Park, it was built on the bones of those people, and that's just one story out of a million. From the beginning of its history, this whole city's built on bones of people who were pushed aside, pushed out. You don't have to repeat those sins, young man. You don't have to listen to whoever's telling you to do this. They didn't leave the bunker. You did. You've seen the world. Now let us live in it.'

Maxwell's face is scrunched up tight, and for a moment I think I've reached him. But his eyes shift to the suits that flank him, and he takes a stiff step back. 'We'll be back in a week, Ms Persaud. With enforcement.' He looks up at Garden. 'I'd hate to see anything happen to your—people. I really would.'

There is a scar on Maxwell's temple. I wonder how he got it. I wonder who sewed it up.

I feel Sylvan on my right, Abril on my left. Tense. Ready to strike. 'Get off my porch,' I say, and Maxwell raises his hands in the kind of mock surrender that means *I'll be back, you know I will.*

---

The minute you get yourself something good, these men always come. Now that land they'd written off as lost is practically waterfront property. Now that people aren't as terrified, as skittish, they might be able to make a buck off them again someday. They've been biding their time like toxic mushrooms, waiting underneath our feet, ready to burst up from below. I'd gotten too secure, too sure of the ground beneath me. I should have remembered that there's no rubble, no fallout, no pile of bones deep enough to bury men like these.

---

My mother was from Trinidad. My father, Jamaica (one of his mothers) and Haiti (the other), by way of Flatbush. I don't know what happened to any of those places, which I never got to see. I wish I had, but we island people can make even the coldest places feel like a warm summer street, carrying our music and our stories and our recipes along with us wherever we go.

It was my mother who taught me how to make buss up shut roti, back when you could pull things from the shelves in grocery stores and put them together however you chose. We don't have that luxury now, but Lale's been keeping chickens for those who want meat, and we have curry channa and aloo for the vegetarians like me. Lale and Abril work diligently away, side by side, following the recipe I've given them to the letter. It's true that nothing tastes like it did when I was young, but maybe that's nostalgia for you. Nostalgia, or the long-tainted soil, or the crucial, transformative spices we can longer find to season the food.

I'm making callaloo, chopping an onion and trying to calm my mind as I inhale the scent of paratha and listen to the others in the kitchen around me, but the arthritis makes my fingers freeze up like pincers that won't close. I manage to peel the thin skin off the bulb and then the room dims as I feel ghosts that aren't there crowding in around me—

*Skin peeling off skin peeling off skin peeling off skin—*

My fingers dig into the onion. I breathe; three counts in, three counts out. Without any summoning, Sylvan is there, at my elbow. He doesn't always pick up on all the convoluted social signs that were so important in the old world, but of all my children, all the ones I've taken in, he's the most observant. The most attuned to the patterns of this little home we've built, the most likely to notice a disruption in its flow.

I release my death grip on the onion, my knuckles swelling. 'I'm fine.' I'm lying, but I can't for the life of me think of a way to explain. How my body aches, and how beyond the pain it's exhaustion that's killing me, the strain of holding this together all these years, of building something out of nothing, out of worse than nothing, out of poisoned ground and blasted ruins. I don't know how to explain that, despite what a triumph this is, this meal we're making will never taste like it did under my mother's hands, that certain flavours and smells have left the world forever, that I'm not sure I even remember them except that sometimes I wake from dreams with their spices tingling on my tongue.

'I'm fine,' I say again, this time to convince myself. 'Just about ready to burn Babylon down. But what's new about that?' I look sideways at Sylvan, who picks up the onion from the counter and takes over the dicing. 'And I'm sorry. For snapping at you when they were here. I was tired, I was—anyway. It's no excuse. I know you were only trying to help. I know that wasn't fair to you.'

I want to reach out and lay my hand on his shoulder, but while touch is a balm to me, it's the opposite to Sylvan. Touch feels like hurt, like pain, like ants crawling on skin, he's told me. He nods at my apology, once, and that's enough for both of us. 'So what are we going to do?' he asks, his voice quiet.

'I don't know, baby.' I sigh. 'I really don't know.'

We have dinner on the tomato terrace, my little family and a few other members of the collective: Anzu, who's studying bodywork and lends her nimble fingers and expertise to those whose muscles are aching, and Mallory, who's a whiz with succulents and temperamental flowers, and funny, thoughtful Kal, who Sylvan considers his closest friend other than Abril.

It's a nice evening, not too muggy, with only the faintest miasma of steam rising off the East River. We're inside draped layers of mosquito netting, and butterflies flit around outside, using their tiny feet to cling to the threads. Nearby, flitting over the bursting red blossoms of the trumpet vine and the pink of the bee's balm, I catch sight of an electric green hummingbird, drawn by the syrup I've mixed to lure it and its kin in.

These are things I thought I might never see again. Butterflies. Hummingbirds. The sun. For a long time there, as the black dust fell: the sun.

Around us, the land is a combination of chaos and craters. You could almost imagine this is a city again, if you don't look west and remind yourself of what became of Chelsea. The flooding has made the Lower East Side more or less an island, and lately anyone with able hands has been working together to shore up the bulwarks for when the storms come. There are skeleton staffs in the hospitals again, people teaching themselves from textbooks, a few old-timers, who actually remember when surgery was done with adequate lighting and antiseptic, giving lectures when they can. I've had to avail myself of their makeshift services more than once, and I decided on the last visit that I wouldn't be going back. Not to that darkness, to that fear. If I have to wither and break down, I vowed to do it here— in this garden, with my family. All I needed to do it gracefully was to look to the plants, the trees. They lose limbs, their flowers fall, and they draw strength from the roots beneath them, from the way they tangle with all the living lives around them.

Every bud in this garden, no matter how small, how spotted, is a victory. The memorial we've made along the azalea path reminds me of that, filled as it is with little mementos from people we've lost, with a mishmash of the figures and symbols that guide us—gold Buddhas collected from abandoned shops in Chinatown, evil eyes hanging from trees and scraps of cloth tied around branches, a Virgin Mary statue rescued from a fallen church. We'd lost the habit of graveyards in the times where bodies had to be left where they fell, when there was no safe or sanitary way to honour the dead. This collection of remnants, like my mother's beaded bracelet, my father's cap—they had to stand in for everything that vanished. For the ghosts of those who were struck down, vaporised, starved and drowned and torn apart.

We've fought so hard for this place, for every inch of it, for every bit that grows. But the plants don't only show a body how to die with grace. They tell us how to live again when we've been transplanted, how to find our feet in new soil. I love this place more than I can explain, but I love the people sitting around me much more. I can't lose any one of them, not now, not when we've made it this far. They are the Garden: its vitality, its resilience, its wonder and its future. I need to protect them, like my mother and father always tried to protect me, until the day they weren't able to any longer.

I drain my glass of strawberry kompot and tap it thrice, waiting for everyone to quiet down. Their faces turn to me, and I stand with some difficulty, letting the pause play out, the weight of what I'm about to say settle over the space. 'I've decided we should take their deal.'

The outcry is immediate, and Abril's voice, as ever, is loudest and first. 'What are you talking about?' Abril, who installed spikes on the side of her wheelchair so people would think twice before fucking with her on the streets. I wish none of my children had ever had to know violence. But I've been around too long to believe that's going to happen today.

'I don't want any of you getting hurt.' More muttering, though a touch subtler. 'They won't hesitate. I know men like this.' I'd hoped they'd been blasted off the face of the Earth, is what I don't say. But then, roaches always survive the longest.

'But the preppers are coming out of the ground,' signs Lale.

'And the bears,' Abril adds. 'They say bears are back, and wolves, and deer—'

'Are deer the ones with the big teeth?' Anzu asks.

Mallory shakes her head. 'No, you've seen deer, it was deer that ate our roses—'

I close my eyes, holding up my palm. 'It's done.' I get to my feet, the cane under my hand steadying me as much as it can. 'Get packed, and get ready. Tell the others, Sylvan, and make sure they're ready to leave. We're going north.'

Their questions and cries of protest follow me as I limp away to my room, but I trust my children to listen, to start preparing once they've calmed themselves down. I'm the one who's kept them safe this long. I thought I'd protected them from some of the worst of the world, but I can't even protect our own home now.

Sylvan's the one who comes to me after dinner's long done, after the composting bins have been loaded up, after the dishes have been sopped and rinsed in their buckets. I can hear the chirping of crickets outside, their songs carried by the evening breeze through the screened window into my small room. I don't spend much time here: I prefer to be out with my family, out in the Garden, talking and laughing and tending to the oasis we've made. Sylvan barely fits at the foot of my narrow bed, but he sits down anyway, carefully avoiding my feet, knowing the closeness comforts me.

'We can find another way.' His voice is quiet. 'We don't have to give it to them. They're men like—the ones from before. The ones you told us about. The people who made this world.'

I nod. 'They are. But I meant what I said, Sylvan. I know these men—I've known many men like them—and they're dangerous. We can't stay. They'll raze this place to the ground out of spite, with all of us in it, and salt the earth before they build whatever they want atop the ash of us.'

He doesn't speak for a long minute. I'm sorry to scare him like this, but I need him to understand. Whatever the hardships to be endured up north, they're worth the risk to preserve our family, our brave band of survivors, against certain death.

'But they could change.' His fingers are kneading the cloth of my light blanket. 'They've seen what happened to the world, the same as we have. And if they won't acknowledge it—if they want to start the same cycle again—Abril thinks she may be able to build some mines, some kind of weapon for the perimeter—'

I'm shaking my head, sitting up in bed to stop him. 'No. No violence, you hear me? No bloodshed.' I resist the urge to smack the wall to drive my point home. 'That's what got us here, and anyway they'd win the fight.' Sylvan's still looking at the blanket clutched in his fist. 'Do you hear me, Sylvan? We're not going to war over this.'

He doesn't say anything; only inclines his head, after a silent moment. And then, after murmuring 'I'll let you sleep,' he's gone, and I'm alone. Sylvan will do what needs to be done. I've laid it out for him, as plainly as I can. There's not much time, nor any other way. We have to take this escape route while they're still willing to offer it to us.

❦

In the last days of the Garden, I can't get myself out of bed.

The fight's gone out of me. All these years, running on instinct. All these decades, battling fierce because there was no other way to survive. But now there's a choice, and I'm giving my kids the one that grants them the best chance at life. If we stay, those men will never stop coming. They'll always return. It's a story as old as the world.

Sylvan brings me food, and Abril puts flowers in my vase. I rest. I keep the blinds pulled low, in my little cave, and I sleep.

❦

The shouting is what wakes me.

I told Sylvan yesterday to have everyone ready by the morning. We can take clothes and some equipment and medicine with us, depending on what method of transport Maxwell has in mind for our exodus, not that he's been courteous enough to send ahead the details.

But the most important things—the rooms we've built for ourselves, the ramps, the very architecture, the bones of our home—we can't. So I don't know what's been decided, what we're bringing and what we're leaving behind.

When I step into the gustatorium though, blinking my eyes against the light, it looks like: not much of the former. The place is untouched. Bowls and utensils and cracked mugs where they always are, the cushion still on the sliding stool that we installed for anyone who needs to sit to cook. I rub the sleep away and follow the noise out to the porch, where it's a bright, blazing day.

I can't fathom the sight at first, when I cross through the doorway. There's too much bustle, too many bodies. For a long time in my life, in this fallen city, having that many bodies in my sight lines never heralded anything good. But Sylvan's up above the sea of them, perched high on a makeshift podium at the edge of the porch.

I rush towards him, nearly falling in my haste. 'This is our home,' he's saying, and the crowd is carrying his message back, the words traveling from lips to lips through the crowd, from hands to hands. 'We will not leave it. We will not give this world up, carve it up for sale, tear it apart and suck out its marrow, like our ancestors did. We know what it's worth now, and there's nothing you can offer us in trade.' He's pointing to something I can't see, something beyond the edge of our neighbours, for I recognise the faces in the bustle now: the residents of the Garden, and the people we've known and helped and talked with all these years. The community we've made, spreading out for blocks around us all. 'If you want the Garden, you'll have to come through me.'

'And me,' Abril echoes.

'And me,' Lale signs.

'And me,' 'And me,' 'And me,' 'And me,' spreading through the body of the neighbourhood, rippling like waves until it's a cascade, a rising shout, a refrain that sounds almost, to my weary ears, like 'Amen, amen, amen.'

I push closer, to see precisely who Sylvan was indicting, though I already know. There's Maxwell, looking wan despite the protection of his indestructible lawyers, and behind them a motley crew of bruisers and demolitionists. No transport to speak of: maybe they weren't planning to give us a lift at all. Maybe they were expecting us to slog through with what we could carry.

Some of their wrecking crew have hammers in their hands, some of them mallets, some saws. They're skinny, half-starved. All he'd have to offer them to wreak destruction is a decent meal, and I almost can't blame them. I've been there myself. I know what it's like when pain has hollowed out your gut, when you'd do anything to make it go away.

I stumble forward, catching Sylvan's sleeve, careful not to touch his skin. 'Sylvan, please come down from there. It's over. We don't want a war today.'

He looks down at me, and I can tell he's pushing himself to make eye contact, to underline what he's going to say. 'This is our choice.' He gestures to himself, to Abril and Lale and all the others. 'These are our bodies, and they're not going anywhere. Didn't you say that if we were going to build a new world, a better one, we have to dedicate ourselves to it, every step of the way? No ground given. No person barred entry. Not one person left behind as the future moves forward.'

'Yes, baby, I did, but I—'

'And didn't you say if the loss of old world gave us anything, it was a chance to start anew? This is what we want, Radisha, all of us.' He spreads his arms. 'We know the risks. We're willing to give our lives, our bodies, for it. Not because they're not valuable, but precisely because they are. They're the most valuable thing in the world.'

He's a man, my Sylvan. Not a child any longer. A man, for a long time now.

I close my eyes, and try not to see the horror I fear will follow. 'All right, mon chou. All right. You're right. And this—' I look out at the teeming crowd. 'I want you to know how proud of you I am for this. I've never seen anything like it. Not for a long, long time.'

He blushes, and for a moment he's my baby. Then he cups his hands around his lips and addresses the crowd. 'Repeat after me: no going back!'

'*No going back!*'

'No one denied!'
'*No one denied!*'
'No one forgotten!'
'*No one forgotten!*'
'No one left to die.'
'*No one left to die.*'

The crowd is parting like the Red Sea as someone makes their way forward. I shiver, but as he shuffles closer, I see it's only Maxwell. No lawyers, no heavys. Just a man not much beyond Sylvan's years, looking scared as anything, but coming to stand before me, holding his ground as the crowd around him jeers.

He comes right up to the edge of the porch, not daring to put his foot on the first step, and looks from Sylvan to me. 'I didn't—' He swallows. 'I don't think I understood what this was to you. What it is to—' His eyes lock on mine, and for a moment all I can see is the darkness there. 'To have a home. But my family—they sent me here to do a job. So maybe we can reach a compromise. A way for you to stay, if we retain control—'

'No deals.' Sylvan, towering over Maxwell like a god, makes his pronouncement. 'No bribes. No compromises. Compromises with people's lives—that's what got us into this mess the last time.'

Maxwell looks back to me, and I nod. 'No deals.'

He sighs, and I see something in him crumble. 'But my family—'

'Say you don't go back,' I interrupt. 'Say you fail to return. Will they come after you, your family? Your parents, if they're living?'

'They are.' He inhales, looking away. 'In a fashion. They're mostly in stasis these days. Sedated. I was raised by AI, when I wasn't in stasis too. But there was a plan, and if the atmosphere was safe again, by today I was supposed to—'

'Forget "supposed to". Do they fear the world too much to tread in it?'

He meets my eyes. 'Yes.'

'Then they don't have the right to tell any of the rest of us what to do with it. If they're not part of it, if they're not willing to put themselves in the middle of the filth and the restoration to remake it—it isn't theirs. But if you stay, and if you think long and hard about how to make it the best it can be, and you listen and you learn from all these folks, all these folks who were making the world while you were hiding down there in the dark—it can be yours too.'

His face stills, and I wonder if I've pushed too far. The world hangs in the balance as I hold my breath. Sylvan's right. There may be other men, other oppressors, but this is not their Earth anymore. It never really was, but they had their chance at domination and we all saw where that led. No more.

No more.

'Is there any chance—' He shapes the words strangely, like he's deviating from a script. 'That is to say—if it wouldn't be an imposition—if I weren't trying to take this place, to take anything from you—'

I understand what he's saying before he's grasped the weight of it, watching him run his thumb over the scar above his eye. 'You can stay, yes. Here in this neighbourhood. Maybe even in the Garden, if everyone says yes. Either way, you can find a place.'

The crowd is restless, and Sylvan holds out his hands to quiet them. He glances down at Maxwell, and then steps off the podium, ceding the floor.

Maxwell pauses a moment, and then he steps up. His people remain on the edge of the crowd, waiting. His lawyers, improbable figments of a past I remember all too well. He could still give the order. He could bring the hammer down on all our heads.

But he doesn't. What he says instead is, 'We came here to take something from you that wasn't our right to take. We understand that now.' I can practically feel his lawyers' hackles rising, bulldogs robbed of their prize. Without Maxwell's blessing, though, they have no job to do. Unless his sun-starved progenitors want to come face us down themselves, he's the ranking authority for the people who claim to possess this place. 'We'll leave you in peace. I'm sorry if we scared you. We were wrong. And for those of us that want it—all I ask is that you let us be rebuild alongside you. Be your neighbours. Your—' His thumb traces his scar again, and I'm sure he doesn't know he's doing it. 'Your friends.'

The crowd passes on the message before falling silent. I tighten my hold on my cane, ready for trouble from all sides.

A cheer goes up from way back in the crush. 'Welcome!' shouts a voice, reedy and warm.

It sounds so very young.

'Welcome,' calls out another, and then 'welcome' from my left, from my right. 'Welcome' all around me, building until Sylvan takes the stand to amplify the message. The men with tools-that-could-be-weapons in their hands blink in confusion, like they're emerging from darkness into the sunlight. 'Welcome. Welcome.'

※

Those hungry men, the desperate ones: we've taught them to make gardens. They stretch now as far as the eye can see, on rooftops, along old avenues. Nourished by tendrils and seeds from our own, their vines climb walls and melons nest under reclaimed water towers and flowers bloom from every surface where it's possible for them to grow. The winter will be hard, as always, but for now it's early fall again, just shy of a year since Maxwell came to my porch with the intention of plundering this place. He's helping Abril with the hives now, having become her dedicated apprentice. I can hear them discussing the best strategy for dealing with one of the colonies that's struggling as Sylvan and

Kal hammer above me, constructing a new desk of bird feeders in the upper grove.

I'm rolling down the even paths, no longer able to stand, but able to move freely about the Garden as I please. I'm visiting the memorial garden, where my mother's beads still shine red and black among the azalea bushes.

No bodies are buried here yet, but I've asked Sylvan to make mine the first, when the time comes. If I want anything now, it's to nourish these plants, to feed this beauty. If I want anything now, it's to give life to the world, to my family and the family they'll have, long after I'm gone.

I look above me, and the canopy dazzles me with its greens and violets and golds, sheltering the paradise we've made, our hard-won Eden, built not from ignorance but from knowledge, from intention and learning. Someday soon, all the trouble I've known, all the fear I've felt, will be transformed and made new, under the light of this same glorious sun. Soon all my strife will be nothing but flowers in bloom.

# THE 1ST INTERSPECIES SOLIDARITY FAIR AND PARADE
BOGI TAKÁCS

## I.

Name: Rita M
Age: 16
Occupation: Farmworker

I fill out the spreadsheet pinned to one of those antiquated clip-on boards. 'Now I'll ask you a few questions that might seem unrelated,' I start, going through my usual script. 'The screening will take approximately ten minutes.'

Rita M looks at me flatly, gives me the yet-another-clueless-adult glance. 'It's pointless,' she says. 'I don't want to be recruited.'

This is the third time someone turns me down today, and it's barely afternoon. My stomach clenches. We don't have time for this. We'll never fill our recruitment quota like this.

'That's fine,' I say, and I somehow manage to keep my calm. 'I'm not going to force you. Provide a reason and I'll put it in the spreadsheet, save you the hassle next time a recruiter comes around.'

She shrugs, slowly, as if her two thick brown braids were weighing down her whole body. 'Mom and Dad need me on the farm. We're barely making do as is, and Mr Hodász no longer takes the eggs and the corn.' Another shrug. 'I'm also not really interested in the aliens.'

I believe her—all throughout our conversation, she never once glanced at the giant metallic sphere hovering next to me.

---

The two of us are taking one of the backcountry roads between farms—what used to be Győr-Moson-Sopron county back when Hungary still existed. Everything's almost entirely deserted; all the time we walk, we only meet one person going in the opposite direction, a dirt-smeared teen carrying a shovel. I stare downwards because I keep on slipping in the mud, but there's not much scenery to look at anyway. A weeping willow by the wayside, a crumbling stone cross, and once something that looks like an oversized bomb crater, somehow still not overgrown with weeds after so many years. Lukrécia floats next to me, sparing me the commentary. I'm angry and sad: angry that no one wants to be recruited for the alien communication team, sad because I see their reasons. Everyone is exhausted. After the first group of aliens destroyed everything, almost two decades ago, and the second group came to pick up the scraps, no one trusts that the third group is actually friendly. Even though they are not a singular empire or even the same species. They are of a wide variety of species and origin, and the only thing that binds them together is that their planets had been invaded like ours—by the same aliens as ours. Yet, no one believes that this time, we're all in this together. No one wants to come work with us. But we need to talk to each other, we need to find ways—we need to recruit more people...

After a while, I get frustrated enough that I start up a conversation myself.

'Do you think we'll find a candidate today? Not even an actual recruit, just someone we can take back to base for a longer evaluation?'

Lukrécia meows. She has this idea that humans will relate to her better if she pretends to be a cat from an eighties cartoon. I don't know how to tell her that this didn't work out for the second round of aliens, either. It has all been tried.

'Is that a yes or a no?' I grump at her.

'Neither,' she says, her voice level. 'It's an answer to a badly posed question.'

She's so much out of character as a cat that I can't help snorting with amusement. 'Lukrécia. You're a giant sphere, not a cartoon cat.'

'I'm not a sphere. The sphere is my containment unit.'

'I'm just telling you how you come across to people.' I poke at her containment unit and almost fall over as I slip again. I could use better boots. I could use a different life, one with well-maintained roads.

'They're remarkably uncurious about me,' Lukrécia says.

Now I'm angry with her, too. 'They're trying to stay alive, give them some credit. They'd be curious if they had a moment of respite from all that labour, just a moment, really. We're a distraction.'

We trundle in silence for a few minutes. The next time, I'm not the one who speaks up. 'Do you think we should go into the city?' Lukrécia asks. If she's already buying into the human stereotypes about farmers and rural people, I'll be tempted to throttle her non-existent neck.

I shake my head. My anger will not serve any purpose here. Not anymore. *Those* aliens are gone. 'I already made the rounds with Bubó,' I say. 'They couldn't spare anyone from the rebuilding.'

She meows. 'I don't mean Pannonhalma. I don't mean the town. I mean Győr. *The city.*'

I have approximately one hundred counter arguments. It's far. It's dangerous. The city is full of uncleared rubble and groups of militants. I will fall and injure myself, and we won't be able to get help. We won't be able to recruit among the scavengers. They'll try to hurt us. I will fall.

But we are sadly behind quota. No one from the farms or even the neighbouring town of Pannonhalma wants to be recruited for extraterrestrial communications. I feel the quotas are unfair, but I'm terrible at management—and if I complain, people will just respond with 'If you know it so well, organise it yourself'.

I take a deep breath—it comes out more like a gasp than a sigh. 'Tell you what. We do this last remaining farm today. There's an inn in Győrújbarát, they're renting out the cabins up the hillside, the old summer camp.' Lukrécia doesn't protest. I go on. 'We stay there tonight. Then we swing around and maybe we can get into the city from the west-southwest, following the river. Avoid the areas to the south.'

'That sounds good,' Lukrécia says, understanding the unspoken meaning better than some humans would: despite the anger that drives me forwards, I don't want to walk anymore today. My joints are feeling the strain. One sprain too many, one fracture too many. I'm just past thirty-five, but I also get injured more than most people. My ankles are shot for the remainder of my life, my knees hurt, and the only reason I'm out here and not back on base is that they had absolutely no one to spare, with new ships arriving daily.

'There is a paved road,' she adds. 'From Győrújbarát all the way up to Győr.'

Is she being conciliatory? It's hard to tell. Her Hungarian is smooth, with a TV anchor accent—if we still had TV. But her emotions are a puzzle to me.

When I don't respond, she goes on. 'We can walk comfortably all the way to the city outskirts, then try to cross the garden parcels to the river and head to the old freeway. Then we can just walk in. The road's wide enough to avoid an ambush.'

'You've done this before.'

'No, but that looks like the most reasonable route.'

I'm not about to argue with her. I nod at the barns in the distance with my chin. 'This one farm, and then we go to the old summer camp, get a good night's sleep.'

Name: Bálint P
Age: 22
Occupation: Farmworker, mechanic

'Will the aliens come and help me get some of the tractors in working order?'

'That's why we're trying to set up ways of collaborati–'

'Can they come tomorrow? This week, at least? Can your friend over there help me get some spare parts? No? Tell me when they can help me out, then

I'll see how I can help them out. I can't just go off to Pannonhalma on a whim, I'm needed here!'

Name: Andrea J
Age: 21
Occupation: Innkeeper

'You know what, I'd love to, but then who'll run the inn, my elderly grandmother? The cabins are up on the hillside, if you didn't come when you were a kid.' She tosses a key at me and glares at Lukrécia. At least she doesn't ignore the alien like most everyone today except the angry mechanic.

I'm not looking forward to the steps, but at least there are steps, and in reasonably good repair, too. Someone with a rake is sitting by the side, probably one of the staff taking a break: someone in her late teens, I think. We nod each other a quick greeting, then turn away. Surprisingly, the A-frame cabins look like they were renovated since my last time here—for summer camp in elementary school, just after second grade. Well before the first aliens came, when I was already a teen. But inside, the furniture is a hodgepodge, probably gathered from the village of Győrújbarát at the foot of the hills. Everything that wasn't blown to smithereens:

glazed wooden cabinets from the Socialist years, a table that was clearly built for outdoor use, school chairs and a designer sofa that must have been pricy back in the day. I resist checking for a tag.

Lukrécia barely fits through the entrance. I kick off my boots and throw myself down on the sofa. At least we're not sharing with anyone else tonight.

An eight-bed cabin and no one wants to spend a night with the alien.

---

'You've been here before, is that correct?'

'Yeah. As a little girl.' I turn on my left side. Lukrécia is hovering next to my bed. Her closeness doesn't bother me and I'm too achy to sleep yet.

'What was it like?' she asks.

'Terrible, I hated it!' I pause. 'Fine, I liked the swimming pool.'

'There is a swimming pool?'

'Down there.' I make a vague gesture. 'They might not have it anymore.' I think back. 'You know what, maybe I didn't like the swimming pool either ... I liked the water. But the kids made fun of me. Because I was too clumsy. I don't know. One of the girls stole my enamelled ring and I cried for hours.' This is not the conversation that will help me calm down and fall asleep.

'I'm sorry they made fun of you,' Lukrécia says. She's never made fun of me, ever. I wonder if she knows how. She probably does: her species is cognitively the most similar to humans, out of all the new arrivals. If all of them were like her, we wouldn't need to run around trying to recruit communications specialists.

'Thank you, Lukrécia. That's nice of you to say.'

I'm sure people make fun of her. Of me. Behind our backs. But they're also afraid. The first time aliens showed up, they bombed everything. The second time aliens showed up, they were scavengers coming in to exploit a people left vulnerable, a people whose willingness to fight they underestimated. The third time…

The third time was 'Hi, we've also been bombed by the people who bombed you. Maybe we could work together, become friends?'

A lot of humans didn't trust that. Especially as more and more aliens showed up, in scraggly beat-up spaceships; aliens of all shapes and sizes and species. Aliens who communicated by affecting the electromagnetic fields near your brain. Aliens who lived on the bodies of other aliens. Aliens who tried to convince humans that all magic was technology or all technology was magic, and then we all went down an endless rabbit hole of translation and mistranslation. A group expressed their wish of converting to Judaism. Another group asked if they could, kindly and consensually, chew on humans' hair. All of them were very enthusiastic about the fact that humans somehow managed to get rid of two waves of invaders, even though no one quite understood how. (Except maybe me and my boundless anger.)

By the time I get to the aliens who look like vintage Modernist carpets from Sweden, I finally drift off to sleep.

---

Name: Veronika B
Age: 72
Occupation: Innkeeper (retired)

'Yes, I'm interested in filling out the form,' the elderly lady says. She has to be Andrea's grandmother.

'Would you be able to get to the base? We sadly don't have much by way of transportation.' I try to sound more apologetic than combative. I did not sleep well. All that soreness.

'My dear husband has a carriage and two horses,' she says. I perk up. Wouldn't the horses be missed here? A carriage is a veritable asset. But I just nod, as if I heard a variant of this every day.

'I'll ask you a few questions then.'

She reaches out for my clip-on board. 'I know what a survey form is. Just give it to me and I'll tick the boxes for you.' She sighs. 'Before the invasion, I used to be a sociologist.'

Oh.

I hand her the board. I wonder if she also speaks foreign languages.

'Here you go.' That was fast. She blinks at me. 'How do you score this?'

I shrug. 'By this point I have it all memorised.'

'Ha! You can tell at a glance. I remember those days.' She grins.

I look down on the sheet of paper, printed on both sides. I flip it around. Openness to experience, sensation-seeking ... In these screenings, we are trying to measure who would be good at talking to the aliens. I barely have to look at her choices to know she's a solid pick.

She chuckles. 'You know, I can guess what those items measure, and I can give you any desired score.'

I grin back at her, finally more at ease. 'That in itself would probably make you a good candidate.'

Lukrécia purrs.

⁂

The retired innkeeper and her husband are not interested in driving into Győr with us in the carriage; besides, they have to pack up their entire lives. They know the way to Pannonhalma and the base is at the foot of the hill. They haven't seen the base before, but it's hard to miss, with all the landers parked around it. We say goodbye and off we go, on a cracked and occasionally caved-in—but mercifully paved—road snaking towards the north. So far so good. But we are still low on potential recruits, the base is understaffed, and everything is kind of falling apart. I'm glad I don't know what's going on back there, though I had such a weird dream last night, I can't help wondering if that in itself was a communication attempt. It involved three aliens of different species chasing each other in a circle while screaming incomprehensibly.

We get to the southern outskirts of the city in good time, and we stop to stare at the ten-storey concrete housing blocks. Someone passes us, walking in the opposite direction with brisk steps. I gaze at the buildings and try not to look like someone clearly not from here. Not any longer.

'You know, those blocks were supposed to last only for fifty years or so,' I say. 'They look in pretty good shape still.'

'Some are inhabited,' Lukrécia says. 'You can see the laundry hung to dry.'

I glare at the balconies, only open to one side. I can't quite see anything. Maybe a little movement, a flutter here and there. 'If you say so.'

'Should we go in?'

There is a veritable moat dug around the blocks of Communist-era housing. 'I don't think we can cross that.' I don't want to reproach Lukrécia, but she can float, while I can barely walk. For the umpteenth time, I fantasise about affixing a chair to the top of her sphere. Knowing my balance, I would probably fall off around the first corner. People say motor dyspraxia improves with age, but I feel like that's counterbalanced by the amount of injuries I keep acquiring over the years that never quite heal right.

Maybe it will all be different now. We'll have hospitals again. City centres clear of rubble.

Once we manage to convince all the aliens. The humans, too.

At least Lukrécia is convinced. 'Then we'll go by the original plan and skirt the city around the west side.'

More mud and treacherous terrain. At least the fences have by and large disintegrated with age, though there's always the odd chain-link that threatens to give me tetanus. I can't recall when I last had a booster shot. Before the first wave of aliens came.

'Let's go.' I nod to the left, towards the mass of small parcels of land lying fallow, gardens gone to seed, the occasional storage shed or vacation cottage. I reach into a side pocket for my fraying gloves. 'You take point.'

※

It's easier going than I'd expected, but my expectations were low. Lukrécia simply pushes over the occasional fence with the bulk of her containment unit, and then

I can tiptoe over the remains. There is a waist-high jumble of plants in places: bushes gone wild, determined perennials coming up year after year even with no one taking care of them anymore, invasives finally having free rein. But I'm used to that and mercifully not allergic to ragweed, so I just stumble across the plots in my usual way, following Lukrécia. I'll have to check for ticks when we get to a place I can undress; I don't think any part of me is exposed besides my face, but they are sneaky little things and I don't think I'm up to explaining Lyme disease or tick-borne encephalitis to Lukrécia.

I find myself wondering if her giant sphere is resistant to bullets.

## II.

We don't come across anyone until we're almost to the city, out on the freeway. I peel burrs off my camo fatigues and mentally praise the Bundeswehr for their clothing that lasts absolutely forever. I don't think Germany exists anymore, either; Austria certainly doesn't. But these camo fatigues survive. My knees are burning with pain—I sometimes feel that my pants will last longer than me.

We get to a barricade only when we're almost downtown, next to the old Science Education Society building.

'Hey, you, you there,' someone yells from the top and clambers over using handholds I can't quite see. The sun's already set, and it's getting dark.

'You're the person who's been following us,' Lukrécia notes, detached as usual.

Someone's been following us? 'You could've thought to mention that,' I groan at her. So much for alien communication. So much for me understanding Lukrécia, or her understanding me.

The person chuckles, pulls back their hat, and I realise we've met them at least three times already, always carrying a different implement. I feel that made them invisible to me, and I look away, ashamed. They laugh.

'I'm Lala,' they say, and that's a boys' name, though I'm not entirely certain about Lala's gender.

'From *Fairy Lala*?' Lukrécia asks.

'*Humans* are not named after children's shows,' I groan at the alien.

'From *Fairy Lala* indeed,' Lala grins at us. 'I wish I could watch the TV movie, the older people told me all about it. But the book was awesome.'

I want to recruit him. It's not just because he could follow us without me noticing. I'm not the most perceptive person, especially when I'm spending three-quarters of my brain resources on not falling flat on my face in the mud. It's not just because of the modern classic about the young fairy prince with the human heart. It's because he comes across as cunning. Cunning *and* cheerful. Unlike me, the angry grouch.

I mutter something about the fairy X-ray machine scene in the book, and he laughs some more. Is he stalling for time? Waiting for an armed squad of scavengers to get to us? Waiting for his backup?

'You know why we're here,' I say. I'm bluffing, but he has to know.

'Yeah, but I don't trust you,' he replies, offhand. 'I'll let you pass, and we have a place you can crash too. But I don't know who'd follow you to Pannonhalma.'

He turns back towards the barricade and opens a door—makeshift, but with a proper lock. He ushers us through, and I can feel his gaze burning at my back.

I'm suddenly not sure who's doing the observing and recruiting here.

Inside, everything is remarkably tidy. Saint Stephen Road looks carefully swept, and someone planted flowers in the divider strip, almost like before. People nod at Lala as we pass by. Many of them openly stare at Lukrécia, but they don't seem hostile.

I'm struck by how varied a bunch they are only after a few minutes, when I almost bump into a Jewish man in Chasidic garb, with side-curls. How did they get here? Chasidic Jews didn't live in Győr before the invasion, did they?

I look around more bravely. I notice that the kids playing a very intricate version of hopscotch are Romani, two elderly women sitting on a bench are talking in a Slavic language – probably Slovakian? – and a man tells his dog to back off from Lukrécia in German.

'Wow, this is how Győr must have looked before the war,' I tell Lukrécia. Or no one in particular.

'Before the invasion?' she asks.

'No, the *war*.' I pause. 'World War Two.'

Mercifully, she doesn't ask me to clarify.

We are led to the old hotel on the corner of Baross Street. I never thought I'd stay there. It looks much dingier now, but overall not in terrible shape. I feel like a visiting dignitary.

I'm sure we are being overheard, but I don't care. I want to sleep, but I also want to talk to Lukrécia.

'I think they're spreading the rumours that Győr is a devastated hellscape so that people don't come to snoop,' I tell her. I'm not sure how I feel about it. There are plenty of people in the countryside who could use a place like this, but somehow got left out when communication was disrupted. For every ethnic group I saw inside, there were people I saw outside, separate and lonely. *I* could use a place like this, and I'm an ethnic majority Hungarian. Not that Hungary is still around.

I try to refocus on what I have for now. I stretch out on the bed, nice and clean after a shower. I can't believe there's running water here, though the water pressure's terribly low.

Why did they let us in?' Lukrécia asks.

I shrug. 'For all I know, they're spying on us. Gathering intelligence.'

Before I fall asleep, I wonder yet again—why do I even bother talking to the aliens? I used to think because I was from the last generation who grew up on sci-fi. But Lala read *Fairy Lala*...

---

Lala joins us for breakfast in the dining hall.

'What is this?' I poke at the flat brown … thing in the middle of my plate, smeared with some kind of light yellowish … thing.

'Fried eggplant,' he chuckles. 'With tahini sauce.'

That's very much not a Hungarian food, though I'm sure eggplant grows here just fine. I wonder if Lala is Jewish, too—his hair is curly and dark. I feel bad about my instantaneous reaction to ethnically profile him. I'm twice his age. He's never known the country the way it was. He never had video games and social media and terrible national politics. I'm the sensible, responsible adult. If he's Jewish, so what? I'm disabled.

The eggplant tastes great, and I shovel it in with relish. I dab at my mouth with a fabric square; it's fancy if a bit faded after many washings. I blink at Lala. *Is he Jewish?*

'If you're trying to guess whether I'm trans, I'll save you the time,' he says, grinning broadly. 'I am.'

I could sink under the floor in shame. I mutter some kind of apology, which only makes Lala grin even more. I need to change the topic, fast.

'How come you never saw all this from above?' I ask Lukrécia. 'The town is clearly inhabited, and you have aircraft. You can fly.'

'It appears we have much more to learn about human habitation patterns,' she says. 'We saw, we just didn't understand.'

Lala chuckles, pokes at his own food with a slightly out-of-shape fork, something from a school dining hall rather than the formerly posh hotel. 'We're trying to hide as much as we can. Food supply is tricky. We trade a lot. One of our main procurers vanished recently and we're all starting to get concerned.'

I heard something about this in the villages. 'Mr Hodász?'

He drops the fork with a clang. 'You know him?'

'I talked to a lot of farmers lately. I haven't met him.' Lala picks up the fork. I feel like I'm a constant source of disappointment. The responsible adult! I sigh. 'The farmers miss him too.'

I steel myself and go on. 'We need to work together somehow. We came here to get some of you to work *for* us. But we'd rather work *with* you. And the villagers, too. Could you help us set up some meetings?'

I have approximately zero authority to say this, and neither does Lala, I'm certain. But if we can get people talking, something can be worked out. We can do this—

I notice with a startle that Lala looks gloomy. 'I don't know if we can work more closely with the villagers,' he says, and gestures at himself. 'I wouldn't last a day out there without disguising myself. I can only do short trips, still.' I don't understand. Because he's Jewish, trans, or from the city?

'People won't harass us with me around,' Lukrécia adds.

Lala groans. 'They're scared to death of the aliens, they just won't show it. You want to gain their trust, that's not the way to go.'

The farmers didn't look scared to me, but maybe it was their defence. *Do not show fear.* I'm honestly not sure who's right here, Lala or me; and surely Lukrécia knows even less than I do. Or maybe the villagers were just so afraid for so long that after a while, they were too burned out to fear, but they wouldn't not-fear either. I know that kind of empty feeling all too well. Maybe Lala is right after all.

'Right now we're in three different groups, all isolated, barely interacting,' I say. 'Villagers, city dwellers, and us alien contact people in Pannonhalma. If we could all work together...'

Lala wipes his mouth elaborately with a kerchief and stands. 'I'll be off. I have work to do. I'll see if I can send some people your way.'

The unspoken message is clear, even to me, even now: don't hold your breath.

˙

He'll be back shortly,' Lukrécia says, back in our room. 'Remember, they are observing us.'

I look around. There are any number of places to hide something. This was a hotel back in Communist times too. 'Are they observing us right now?'

She meows. 'I don't have the right sensors to determine that, but I wouldn't be surprised.'

My knees are less painful this morning. I chance it. 'Let's go for a walk.'

˙

The large fountain with the series of ponds is bone-dry, but both the old City Hall building and the

Communist-era County Hall across from it are still standing, neo-baroque curlicues mirrored in modernist glass. This is the centre of Győr, and maybe, maybe I can pretend the past twenty years haven't happened. But there are no skaters, no freerunners doing backflips from the stones edging the ponds, and the grass looks more like a vegetable garden than a lawn. Is this where they grow eggplant, I wonder; I know nothing about growing anything. It involves too many sharp objects and cooking them involves too many hot objects. The best I can do is yank out weeds, but even then, I tend to fall.

I found my niche with the alien contact crowd, and I don't think I'd last here very long. The patience afforded to me both among them and also here is all due to Lukrécia. But Lukrécia speaks fluent, primetime-news Hungarian so why am I even tagging along? I kick a pebble and it skitters across cracked paving stones.

I think out loud. 'How do we get people to work together? Everyone has isolated themselves, dug in. It would take something really disruptive, like a catastrophe. Back in the day, we could work together when we were facing a common threat.'

'There has already been a catastrophe,' Lukrécia notes.

'Many years ago. But the balance stabilised. Into something that will just wear us down with time. We'll finish off ourselves, finish what the invaders started.' Is it already happening? Mr Hodász vanishing, the trade slowing ... Everyone growing increasingly weary of each other, even small differences appearing larger and larger ... The city running out of food ... The villagers working themselves into utter exhaustion ... More and more aliens showing up and getting impatient, then frustrated, then angry ... Who knows when people will start dying again?

'I wish Mrs B the sociologist was around, I'm sure she'd know the technical terms for this,' I tell Lukrécia. 'We're forgetting so much.' My generation at least got to be teens before the devastation. But what about Lala and the teens his age? We were called Gen Z, but there isn't even a term for his generation.

Pacing is too hard. I sit down on the steps to the fountain.

'Our planet was destroyed,' Lukrécia says after a long silence, and I'm not sure if she's trying to one-up me or commiserate. She's my closest confidante, and I don't know her at all.

We walk to the riverside, just a few smoothly curving streets to the north and west. I can still do this. I want to see my favourite spot, from way back.

'I will not engineer a disaster,' I say to the river. 'It would bring people together. But we've all been traumatised enough already.' Lukrécia hovers next to me as I wobble down the narrow concrete steps to the water, holding on to the simple railing. The walk was short, but these steps cut into the grassy riverbank are treacherous. Yet I feel compelled to descend, to be closer to the river. I haven't been here for many years. I used to sit on these steps a long time ago, whenever I had a gap in my school schedule, and sometimes even when I didn't.

But what else could bring people together if not a disaster? Some other kind of mass event? Could we bring back something like that?

I think of how the townspeople used to march around downtown Győr every year with the relic of Saint Ladislas, singing Catholic hymns. I did it a few times with my family. I knew some of the hymns, even though I wasn't big on church. It was surprisingly uplifting: the singing crowd as it moved along the streets up the hill, down the hill, by the river—a snake made of people, undulating...

The Basilica was bombed from orbit, a pinpoint strike.

'Hey, I was looking for you,' Lala yells from behind. I turn, barely manage to grab hold of the railing by the steps in the last moment. It holds; after decades of neglect, it still holds. I don't roll down the slope and into the water.

'She hasn't been here in a long time,' Lukrécia says. 'She's reminiscing.'

'I'm thinking about how to bring the three groups together,' I say in my best complaining tone, but I'm still shaky after the near-fall. My voice wobbles just as much as I do. 'I was reminded of the march of Saint Ladislas. I liked that, but that was for Catholics.'

He hop-skips down the steps. 'What was that?' He has to be Jewish, I think, it's impossible not to know about the march of Saint Ladislas if you're Catholic, or even secular. But then he shakes his head and laughs, making a guess why I'm surprised about his ignorance. 'I'm from Komárom, originally. My parents are still there, I moved here with a caravan two years ago.' He shrugs. 'Wanted to venture forth. I have no idea what Győr was like, before.'

To venture forth? He probably wanted to live in a place where fewer people had known him before he transitioned, I think to myself, but say nothing.

Then something clicks into place and I have to hold on to the railing again. I have an idea. If I can keep myself from falling into the water before saying it.

'Hey, I'll help you up,' Lala says, 'I don't know how much punishment that rail can take.'

I stare at him. 'A Pride parade! We could do a Pride parade!'

He laughs. 'Have you seen the pictures?'

'What pictures?' I'm perplexed.

We step into the old cinema building that hadn't ever served as a cinema even in my own lifetime. Even before the invasion. I visited maybe once, back when it was used as a concert hall for the Győr Philharmonic. I barely remember how it looked, but it certainly didn't have these wheeled display boards you could pin things on, the kind that were ubiquitous when I was growing up and never seen again.

It feels like all the lost display boards of the universe have gathered in the lobby. They're mostly filled with drawings pinned to them, but there is the occasional photo, and I wonder who can still make those and how. I vaguely recall something about chemical baths and dark rooms. I step closer.

The drawings are colourful, even rainbow-y, and they run the gamut from cheery children's abstraction to more realistic portraits, all with the same bright palette. Some of them show people marching, the backdrops usually barely sketched, but I notice the more recognisable downtown buildings here and there: the Carmelite church, the Turul bird monument on that little square in front of the train station … Some are portraits of individuals, couples, smaller groups.

The labels glued under the drawings are eerily reminiscent of the sheets I have been filling out. They identify the artist, sometimes also the people in the drawing. There is no 'occupation', but there is a line or a paragraph of quotes for everyone: about love, hope, resilience. There are also some sheets entirely covered by quotes, tiny sketches, encouraging messages.

I turn back to Lala grinning at me.

'You've already had a Pride parade,' I say.

'Two,' he says, shrugging. 'We tried. It was an idea to bring people together.'

I don't think there were any Pride parades in Győr before the invasion. Maybe someone else also took inspiration from the March of St. Ladislas?

Lala doesn't quite realise how odd all of this is for me. It's like this formerly conservative city turned upside down in my lengthy absence, and I'm here for it.

'I thought I had an original idea.' I shrug back.

Lala chuckles. 'Well, *we* did not try to involve the aliens...'

Lukrécia hovers closer. 'Tell me about this idea. I want to know how to bring people together.'

This is Lala's moment, and he goes on a long-winded, rambling explanation. Lukrécia makes the occasional encouraging noise, and I keep myself busy looking at the pinboards.

'So, what better symbol of hope, uh … celebrating our differences.' Lala waves his hands, concluding. The dust we stirred up in the lobby twinkles like glitter in the sunlight. 'And besides, I know everyone on the organizing committee.'

That's great. Not the least because he doesn't seem to know anyone in the town's actual leadership. Though there are such things as formal power and informal power—again I find myself wishing for Mrs B the sociologist. Maybe we can bring her.

I remind myself that if this works out, we'll be bringing everyone.

---

It doesn't take long for Lala to gather the committee in the orchestra hall, find some tables and chairs. I expect the Pride committee members to look outrageously glamorous, but most of them look like they've been dragged away from working on their vegetable patch or hauling salvage. They're more like the crustpunks of yore than David Bowie. Lala tells me there are still a lot of collapsed buildings both further to the north, and also south of the train station. I feel bad—I assumed that just because the city hall area was preserved, surely everything else must have been, too. Even though I knew the Basilica was destroyed.

One of the committee members clears his throat. I can't remember his very ordinary Hungarian men's name. He's a grizzly old man, he looks about seventy, which probably means he's around sixty at most. People have just been aging faster with all the hardships; my mind will probably never quite recalibrate to that.

I try to pay attention. I explain haltingly that we all need to work together. They look sceptical, but when I get to the Pride bits, they seem to show more interest. This is their topic.

I get so enthused that I try to push for a march as soon as possible, but a younger woman in a headscarf waves me down. 'What you have in mind is a one-time, symbolic event, but you also need to think about the lead-up to it. The preparations are just as important, and the more people get involved, the better.'

A young person offers, 'People who are sceptical will wait just to see what would happen. They won't cause fuss in the meanwhile.'

'Either that, or they'll mobilise to attack the march,' the grizzly old man says. I think he must have been to Budapest Pride back in the day.

Lukrécia speaks up. 'They won't attack. They're afraid of us.'

I bite my tongue. Isn't that the exact impression we are trying to work against here?

People start speaking all at once, and for a moment I'm sure the meeting will devolve into disorder, but the woman in the headscarf leading the session bangs on the table and everyone falls silent.

Order is restored after that, but as the meeting goes on and on and on, my thoughts drift. I have little more to add, and what I could say, I keep to myself.

I'd rather not mention that I have been wondering if purely physical proximity to the aliens can cause humans to be more understanding. I vaguely recall pheromones from high school biology, before the world crashed on us. But would pheromones work across entirely different physiologies?

Lukrécia is entirely enclosed in a metallic globe, but there are some aliens who can live on Earth unprotected. And some who are experimenting with parasitic relationships with humans. Parasitic? That's not the right word. I search my brain, symbiotic? There was also something else in high school, about how animals eat from a common table … Commensalism? Mutualism? I'm honestly not sure. There was a chart…

Then the meeting gets to the topic of the surrounding villages, and before I manage to refocus, people have already made a decision to organise some kind of county fair instead of the parade.

Instead of?

*Combined with*, it turns out.

This will be a busy summer season, and for once I'm glad that the long-term weather has taken a cooler turn with all the dust the invaders kicked up when they bombed us.

### III.

Rita M, who turned down the screening, is now staring at me again with all the scepticism she can muster. 'A fair. And this is going to help us exactly how? Besides, you said if I put my name down, you won't come back to hassle me.'

I shift my weight from one leg to another uncomfortably. Did I walk all the way back here for this? 'We're not here to recruit you this time,' I tell her. 'We're here to help you sell your produce.' I try to keep it vague. I know very little about agriculture—I feel like I've been living an isolated life in the alien compound, even with all the recruitment trips.

'At the fair, we'll be able to connect you with wholesale buyers. And it's a one-time event,' Lukrécia says.

The girl finally looks at the sphere, tilts her head sideways. 'Are *you* interested in eggs?'

---

'You mean a tractor exhibition?' Bálint P blinks, rubs his forehead with the back of his hand.

'With a spare parts market,' Lukrécia says.

He turns rapidly to her sphere, and it's as if all the anger's gotten wiped off his face.

'All in one place,' I add meekly.

---

'People would stay here?' Andrea asks, twirling a keyring around her fingers.

I nod. 'We were thinking of using the old campground as the fairgrounds…? By the foot of the hill? And people could stay in your cabins up the hill?'

'I'm sure you'd run the inn at full capacity for the duration of the fair,' Lukrécia offers. 'And some of those visitors might be interested in coming back later, too.'

---

We stay in one of the old kids' cabins overnight—it's a big ask to use the grounds, so we might as well give the inn a bit more business in the meanwhile.

By the time I finally get to bed, I ache all over. So much walking! I wish I had enough balance to ride a bike, but the roads are in such bad shape, it might be pointless anyway. And there's no reason to go all the way back to Győr before we talk to the aliens.

I startle, and my legs twitch.

Lukrécia hovers closer. 'What happened?'

'I was just thinking about everything, while falling asleep. And I realised, when I was thinking of *we*, I was thinking of you and me…' I'm probably too sleepy to explain anything. 'I don't think we are aliens. To each other. Anymore.' I turn towards her, even though my whole body protests, and my arms get tangled in the fluffy blanket. 'I mean we've been friends. For a while. But. I just instinctively thought of you as … like me. Like here are *us*, and there are the *aliens*.'

'I assume that's good,' Lukrécia says, ever so patient. 'I do believe you should sleep, though.'

I fall asleep to her slow purring.

---

At the compound, we meet Mrs B before anyone else—she comes up to us, her face glowing with eagerness. 'The two of you gave me my life back,' she says. 'Finally, something meaningful to do!'

I'm quite sure that fixing machinery and keeping chickens is also meaningful, but I don't feel up to a debate with her. I vaguely nod, and she takes this as encouragement.

'I immediately noticed that our problem was organisation, or rather the lack thereof,' she waves towards the base. 'There are many projects, but they are not coordinated. People hide the lack of organisation with forceful demands.'

I nod, thinking of the quotas I've always felt were impossible to fill.

She goes on: 'So I designed a communication needs survey, and administered it to everyone with the aid of the nice young people here. When we could not communicate with certain individuals at all, we put that. Then we could identify areas of immediate need...'

We walk inside. She provides me with the verbal equivalent of a wall of text, and I like listening to her.

I get the impression she's neuroatypical like me, just in a different way. Is she autistic? Does she have ADHD? She probably knows all the terms for everything, but that would be a different wall of text. Maybe we can do that next time.

'How much do you know about folklore?' she asks me abruptly.

'Uh, why?' I feel like all I know about folklore, I learned from video games, back when we still had them.

'There is one group with a device that they cannot operate. It's not a translator per se, the closest we got was some kind of 'telepathy machine', but I'm questioning the use of the term. Their communications officer died in transit, and now they're looking for someone similar to use the device. They told me to find them a *witch*!' She laughs. 'So just in case this isn't *another* mistranslation, I was wondering if you could find me a witch.'

I'm not surprised by anything at this point. 'I'm sure there'll be plenty of opportunity for that at the fair,' I tell her.

'What fair?' She looks apprehensive at first, but in under ten minutes, she becomes our biggest advocate.

---

The riverside by the Carmelite church in Győr is calm and quiet. Save for Lala, Lukrécia and me.

'We convinced the city leadership,' Lala says, talking animatedly and pacing on the concrete-block fence on top of the flood bank. 'I felt the arguments were a bit on the utilitarian side, but hey, everyone likes fresh produce.' He makes a face. 'So, if your people are in, my people are in.'

I nod at him cheerfully from below—if I tried to get up there, I'd fall. 'Remember I was telling you about the elderly sociologist lady? We ran into her again and it turned out she'd made friends with literally all the aliens in just a few days. They loved her. She thought that the fair and parade would be a great idea, so all of a sudden everyone was on board.' I chuckle. 'Now we only need to find her a witch.'

Lala blinks, then bursts out in laughter and hops down. 'A witch?'

I explain, with big, sweeping gestures. I even lose track of my utter exhaustion for a while.

Lala scratches his head. 'Sanyi is handy with a dowsing rod, would that count?'

I stare at him in bafflement. He turns apologetic. 'We don't have the old utility maps. Do you have any idea how hard it is to dig downtown without hitting a pipe?'

I'm shocked: 'But that's like ... superstition. Pseudoscience?'

Lala giggles. 'He's still pretty handy with it though!'

I figure Mrs B can run a controlled research trial. My job is just to get people to talk to each other.

## IV.

I imagined something organised and tidy; something beautiful that emerges from the collaboration of thousands of different people.

What emerges from the collaboration of thousands of different people is a giant mess.

Many of the aliens grasp the concept of a parade, but clearly don't understand about floats. A giant snake slithers on top of Bálint's tractor, which has been decorated with ribbons like a maypole, then crushes the entire vehicle. Bálint starts to weep. Witchy Sanyi turns out to be one of the grizzled crustpunks from the city council and the impatient aliens have him try the machine right then and there, in the middle of the crowd, which results in him projecting his emotions over a twenty-meter radius. He is apparently very hungry. The people near him mob Rita's family stall that sells corn-on-the-cob and topple it over. A chicken brought for display escapes, until it is caught by a many-tentacled and triangular alien, who has some kind of dramatic reaction to it. Body fluids are involved, and people yelling 'Let me through, I'm a doctor', but the alien waves them away with three tentacles on three sides. I wonder if I'll ever find Mr Hodász. He could be making a killing in trade at the fair, but he doesn't seem to be here, according to every farmer I asked. I wonder if you can find people with a dowsing rod, and I make a mental note to ask Sanyi or Mrs B about this later; once they have both eaten their fill of corn.

I wasn't very closely involved with the organising in the final stages, so now I try to relax and move with the erratic, sputtering flow. I walk through the entrance, under a gorgeously elaborate sign saying 'THE 1ST INTERSPECIES SOLIDARITY FAIR AND PARADE'. It sways as people of various species bump against the entryway. Someone is carrying a bunch of signs clearly repurposed from the Pride parade and gets tangled in a clutch of kids' balloons. I haven't seen balloons in at least a decade, but someone must have been stockpiling them. I thought they wouldn't last so long, but maybe there is a way to store them ... Or were the aliens printing them on one of their ships? I can't even think of that conversation. How do you explain 'balloon' when you can barely communicate about your immediate needs?

'I thought an *apocalypse* would finally get us to give up *plastic*,' someone my age in a sparkly dress grumbles next to me. I shrug apologetically. I'm looking around for Lala. I spot him with a very tall person handing out signs. Lala gets one saying 'FAITH, HOPE, CHARITY' in rainbow letters above what looks like a very complicated version of the trans symbol.

I remember *that* slogan from somewhere—for a moment I feel something go crosswired in my brain as I dredge up the right memory from an age gone by. 'The three Catholic virtues, huh?' I nod at him, half-yelling in the noise. The unknown sign-maker must have been missing the march of St. Ladislas.

He looks at the sign in puzzlement. 'Are they?' He glances around, but the person has already been carried away by the crowd. 'You know I'm Jewish, right?' he yells back.

I shrug. 'I guessed. Here, I'll take it.' Not that I should be carrying a large sign. It looks like a recipe for injuring others.

'Are you Catholic?' he asks.

'I was baptised…'

He shrugs, too. 'I was also baptised.' He chuckles at my confusion. 'My great-grandma said you needed to have the right documents.'

'Even in an apocalypse?' I look around. A cream-coloured butterfly lands on my shoulder, then another.

'Especially in an apocalypse.'

But we don't get to think about the grim moments of Hungarian history, because a large metallic sphere rolls past, the size of Lukrécia's, but with a brass tint. It's very much not floating or doing anything that it's supposed to do. And it's being chased by a Chasid and an Austrian farmer, who are yelling at each other in what sounds like the same language, be it Lower Austrian German or Yiddish. They finally catch the sphere and steady it. They pat it and rumble at it in an oddly parental way. How do you say 'it's going to be all right' in Yiddish? I suppose exactly like that.

We stare, stunned, until Lukrécia floats calmly next to us, saying, 'I was wondering if that 'first' on the sign above the entrance was a promise or a threat.'

'I don't think anyone's going to forget this day anytime soon,' Lala nods at her. He's smiling, and he looks more relaxed than ever before, despite all the chaos and noise.

'Isn't that the kind of thing that's supposed to bring people together—shared memories…? Or commiseration?' I try to ask, but my voice is drowned out first by the collapsing gate, then by the buzzing of three flying aliens trying to keep the pieces from tumbling into the crowd. I shiver—how lucky that they were in the right place at the right time...

'If we make it through all this without anyone getting injured, that will be a miracle in itself,' I tell Lukrécia once the gate is safely dismantled.

'Fret not,' Mrs B says from behind me. 'My precognitive squad is doing double duty.'

'That didn't save Bálint's beloved tractor,' I grumble at her, because it's still easier to be grouchy than to be astonished. Even if my anger is dissipating.

'We'll get him a new one,' Mrs B says, biting into a cob; and I don't need to ask her who is *we*.

It is *us*, all of us, from now on.

# AFTERWORD

It was surreal, in the end, to find myself making a book about life after the apocalypse during a period of extreme global upheaval. And not even the global upheaval of the climate crisis that I had in mind when I conceived of this anthology.

With Defying Doomsday, Holly and I wanted to challenge the notion that only the physically fit can survive an apocalypse. With Rebuilding Tomorrow, I wanted to take that a step further and show that not only can disabled and chronically ill people survive the apocalypse, but they can help rebuild afterwards. Even better, when a new community is built from the ground up, inclusion and accessibility can be baked into the design from the start. Planning for ramps, wide doorways and sign language immediately reduces the social impact of disability, as several stories in Rebuilding Tomorrow show. Some of our stories even directly contrast the rebuilding efforts of those who've built inclusive communities with others who have a more exclusive view of how to keep surviving.

When worlds end outside of fiction, life does not immediately descend into anarchy and looting, despite what Hollywood would have us believe. In times of crisis, people help each other. Maybe imperfectly, maybe not enough, but history is filled with people trying their best, even as the world falls apart around them. After all, it takes a special kind of arsehole to murder the neighbours' baby instead of sharing some water with them. Not all the stories in Rebuilding Tomorrow are about community, but they are all about people who mean well and are doing their best.

I hope you enjoyed reading them as much as I enjoyed putting this book together.

# ABOUT THE CONTRIBUTORS

TJ BERRY grew up between Repulse Bay, Hong Kong and the Jersey shore. Her favourite pizza comes from Three Brothers in Seaside and she can be coaxed into a trap using any type of cheese. TJ has been a political blogger, a bakery owner, and she once spent a disastrous two weeks working in a razor blade factory. She currently writes science fiction, fantasy, and horror from Los Angeles with considerably fewer on-the-job injuries. TJ is the author of Space Unicorn Blues and Five Unicorn Flush from Angry Robot, as well as several short stories. Find her on Twitter @TJBerry.

ANDI C. BUCHANAN is a writer and editor based near Wellington, Aotearoa New Zealand. Their award-winning novella, From A Shadow Grave uses a historical murder as a launching point into narratives of multiple possible futures, deploying urban fantasy, historical fiction, time travel and more. Andi's short fiction is published in Fireside, Apex, Kaleidotrope, Glittership, and more - with their story 'Girls Who Do Not Drown' winning a 2019 Sir Julius Vogel Award in the Short Story category. You can find them on Twitter @andicbuchanan or at https://andicbuchanan.org.

OCTAVIA CADE is a New Zealand writer. She has a PhD in science communication and enjoys using speculative fiction to talk in new and interesting ways about science. She's sold over 50 short stories, to markets like Clarkesworld, Asimov's, and Shimmer. Several novellas, two poetry collections, a short story collection, and an essay collection on food and horror have also been published. Her cli-fi novel, The Stone Wētā, came out in 2020 from Paper Road Press. She is a three-time Sir Julius Vogel award winner and a Bram Stoker nominee and was the 2020 writer in residence at Massey University.

EMILIA CROWE is a twenty-year-old, non-binary and queer woman from Tucson, Arizona. She is autistic and has ADHD, and very much wishes the world she lives in would let those be strengths. She currently lives with her dog, three cats, and an African grey parrot who doesn't like her very much. She writes fiction and poetry, and enjoys talking at length about horror movie trivia no one but her is interested in. While butterflies are not her special interest, she still delights in finding cool new bugs and crawly things. She is very proud of her collection of yarn she swears she'll crochet someday.

S.B. DIVYA is a lover of science, math, fiction, and the Oxford comma. She enjoys subverting expectations and breaking stereotypes whenever she can. Divya is the Hugo and Nebula nominated author of Runtime and co-editor of Escape Pod, with Mur Lafferty. Her short stories have been published at various magazines including Analog, Uncanny, and Tor.com. Her collection, Contingency Plans for the Apocalypse and Other Situations, is out now from Hachette India, and her debut novel Machinehood is forthcoming from Saga Press in March, 2021. She holds degrees in Computational Neuroscience and Signal Processing. Find her on Twitter @divyastweets or at www.sbdivya.com.

TSANA DOLICHVA is an Australian astrophysicist based in Europe, for the foreseeable future. She co-edited the Ditmar Award-winning Defying Doomsday with Holly Kench, the prequel to Rebuilding Tomorrow, also published by Twelfth Planet Press. Once upon a time, she thought of herself as a writer rather than an editor and has had a smattering of short stories published in various venues. For now, she finds editing, reviewing and science-checking fiction fits better around her research into dying stars. You can find her on Twitter @Tsana_D.

KATHARINE DUCKETT is the award-winning author of Miranda in Milan, a Shakespearean fantasy novella debut that NPR calls 'intriguing, adept, inventive, and sexy.' Her short fiction has appeared in Uncanny, Apex, PseudoPod, Interzone, and Tor.com, as well as various anthologies including Disabled People Destroy

Science Fiction and Wilde Stories 2015: The Year's Best Gay Speculative Fiction. She served as the guest fiction editor for Uncanny' Disabled People Destroy Fantasy issue, and is an advisory board member for The Octavia Project, a free program that empowers girls and nonbinary youth in New York City to imagine and engineer new futures.

JANET EDWARDS is the English SF author of the Earth Girl trilogy, the Scavenger Exodus series, and related books set in the Portal Future, as well as the Hive Mind series set in the Hive Future. As a child, she read everything she could get her hands on, including a huge amount of science fiction and fantasy. She studied Maths at Oxford, and went on to suffer years of writing unbearably complicated technical documents before a long-term illness made her decide to stop work and write something that was fun for a change. She has a husband, a son, a lot of books, and an aversion to housework.

KRISTY EVANGELISTA lives in Canberra, Australia. Like her main character in 'No Shit' and 'Merry Shitmas', Kristy has Crohn's disease. Unlike Jane, Kristy didn't immediately fill a semi-trailer with toilet paper when faced with a pandemic, so it was touch and go for her during the early days of the Coronavirus. Kristy once scared away a couple of burglars by shouting 'HOY!' at them very loudly. That level of ferocity could be

## ABOUT THE CONTRIBUTORS

very handy for when the other survivors come looking for the dunny rolls, so keep that in mind when you are deciding who to invite to your doomsday bunker.

STEPHANIE GUNN is an award-winning writer of speculative fiction. Once upon a time she was a scientist, but that career path was derailed by chronic illness. She has been nominated for Ditmar, Tin Duck, Aurealis and Norma K Hemming awards. Her novella Icefall (Twelfth Planet Press) won the 2018 Aurealis Award for Best Science Fiction Novella, and her story Pinion (published in Aurum, Ticonderoga Publications) won the short form 2019 Norma K Hemming Award. She is at work on too many projects at once, including a contemporary fantasy novel and two sequels to Icefall.

E. H. MANN is an Australian living in New Zealand with their partner, a part-time puppy, and the hopeful beginnings of a veggie garden. They write fantasy and science-fiction about people who don't quite fit the mould; their stories have appeared in the award-winning anthology Mother of Invention, as well as places like Aurealis, Luna Station Quarterly, and Fabled Journey III. Proud wrangler of their very own bumblebee brain, their other passions include conservation, weird wildlife, ADHD/neurodiversity, knitting, and reminding people asexuality exists. You can find them online at ehmannwrites.com, Facebook @E.H.Mann.writes, and Twitter @ehmannwrites.

## ABOUT THE CONTRIBUTORS

TYAN PRISS is a French college student, currently majoring in Japanese studies. Despite her love for traveling, she can usually be found in her own room browsing the internet to answer her most random questions, devouring books in one sitting, and of course, writing. It never takes her long to add a new idea to her already long list of projects—which all feature a diverse cast of characters, humour, happy endings, and at least a pinch of magic or supernatural. She writes entirely in English and aims to publish a book in the future.

LAUREN RING (she/her) is a perpetually tired Jewish lesbian who lives in Seattle and writes about possible futures, for better or for worse. Her other short fiction can be found in venues such as Pseudopod, Recognize Fascism, and Glitter + Ashes. When she isn't writing speculative fiction, she is pursuing her career in UX design or attending to the many needs of her cat Moomin. Much like the protagonist of her story in Rebuilding Tomorrow, she has sensory processing difficulties and prosopagnosia, and often greets strangers like old friends.

TANSY RAYNER ROBERTS is an award-winning Australian science fiction and fantasy author who also writes crime as Livia Day. Her recent releases include Unreal Alchemy, Castle Charming and The Frost Fair Affair. Listen to Tansy on Sheep Might Fly, a podcast where she reads aloud her stories as audio serials. Keep up with her news and find out what tea she's drinking at her monthly newsletter, Tea and Links: https://tinyurl.com/tansyrr.

BOGI TAKÁCS is a Hungarian Jewish agender trans person (e/em/eir/emself or they pronouns) and an immigrant to the US. E is a winner of the Lambda award for editing Transcendent 2: The Year's Best Transgender Speculative Fiction, the Hugo award for Best Fan Writer, and a finalist for other awards. Eir debut poetry collection Algorithmic Shapeshifting and eir debut short story collection The Trans Space Octopus Congregation were both released in 2019. Bogi is neuroatypical and chronically ill in various ways, some overlapping with the story's protagonist. You can find Bogi talking about books at http://www.bogireadstheworld.com, and on various social media like Twitter, Patreon and Instagram as bogiperson.

FRAN WILDE'S novels and short stories have been finalists for six Nebula Awards, a World Fantasy Award, three Hugo Awards, three Locus Awards, and a Lodestar. They include her Nebula- and Compton-Crook-winning debut novel Updraft, and her Nebula-winning debut Middle Grade novel Riverland. Her short stories appear in Asimov's, Tor.com, Beneath Ceaseless Skies, Shimmer, Nature, Uncanny, and Jonathan Strahan's 2020 Year's Best SFF. Fran directs the Genre Fiction MFA concentration at Western Colorado

University and writes nonfiction for publications including The Washington Post, The New York Times, and Tor.com. You can find her on Twitter, Facebook, and at franwilde.net.

# ACKNOWLEDGEMENTS

More than one disaster conspired to make this book what it is. Several people helped make it possible despite those disasters.

I would like to thank my partner Lewis for all his support throughout the project. Not only did he feed me and listen to my various rants, as he usually does, he also picked up a lot of the admin work associated with this endeavour, giving me more space to focus on the creative editing side.

A big thank you goes to Alisa Krasnostein, the publisher of Twelfth Planet Press, who not only took on this project, but also stuck by me through a plethora of crises, both minor and major.

This book would not exist at all without the wonderful authors who wrote stories for it. From the authors who wrote sequels that tie Rebuilding Tomorrow to Defying Doomsday, to those who submitted stories to our open call, thank you for the time and effort you spent on making Rebuilding tomorrow what it is.

Thanks to Geneva Bowers for creating a gorgeous cover artwork for us, and Beau Parsons for the excellent cover and internal design. Thanks also to Lucinda Leyshon for her tireless proofreading and to Miriam

# ACKNOWLEDGEMENTS

Rune and Tansy Rayner Roberts for their advice and work on promotion. Thanks to Katharine Stubbs for her contributions early on in the project.

Finally, a massive thank you to everyone who spread the word and supported our fundraising — a special thank you to those backers who stuck with us from Pozible to Kickstarter. None of this would have been possible without you! To everyone who tweeted, blogged or otherwise shared news of this book, thank you! Every little bit helps.

# ABOUT TWELFTH PLANET PRESS

Twelfth Planet Press is an Australian specialty small press. Founded in 2007, we have a proven record and reputation for publishing high quality fiction. We aim to elevate minority and underrepresented voices with books that interrogate, commentate, inspire. We challenge the status quo through thought-provoking and provocative science fiction, fantasy and horror.

Visit Twelfth Planet Press at
www.twelfthplanetpress.com

Find Twelfth Planet Press on Twitter:
@12thPlanetPress

Like us on Facebook:
http://www.facebook.com/TwelfthPlanetPress

Follow us on Instagram:
instagram.com/12thplanetpress